Higher
Education

I0629625

CHRIS ELISONDO

ISBN: 979-8-9872960-0-4
Cover design by: Joyce Luk
Printed in the United States of America

DEDICATION

For Joyce and all the dreams we share.

CHAPTER 1

Back at orientation, they promised a mild, Mediterranean climate. They lied. Up in my eighth-floor dorm room, windows wide open and blinds closed, I lay there and melted. I refreshed the infernal weather app on my phone like it would do something. In the worst news yet, the app's smiley cartoon sun now wore sunglasses. Nothing to be done. My roommate's tiny desk fan sighed away, pushing the stuffy air handfuls at a time. He usually spent these afternoons prepping for club tryouts, which mainly consisted of mixing protein shakes in his undershirt while practicing combos by himself in Super Smash Bros. Instead of the usual, I rolled over in bed to find him fully dressed and picking at his hair with a long-toothed comb.

"Going out, huh."

"Yeah!" he said, lighting up. "Zelda and I are doing dinner tonight. Things are really moving, dude. Every day I just like her more and more."

Eddie, my roommate, met Zelda last week at new student orientation. "It's Zelda like Fitzgerald's wife, not the Nintendo character," she just had to say when we met. Her parents were academics of some kind, and she had all these poetical thoughts she liked to test out on us. She probably thought she would be the next Virginia Woolf or something. She said she went to a state school for college to 'find herself.' English major. Even though I thought them an odd couple, they seemed to really like each other. Besides, Zelda was always polite to me when she came over.

"Hey dude," Eddie said, "You got plans tonight?"

"Not really. I checked out this book on the Eurozone crisis, and then maybe I'll watch some anime, and that's the night."

"Wanna go out tonight? After dinner, Zelda and I are heading to Frat Row for a party. Come with us?"

"I don't know, not really my scene." I was mildly interested, but decided to myself that it wouldn't really be my crowd. All I really knew about fraternity parties came from Mom's streaming teen movies, and if a real party was anything like that, I would just find it overstimulating. Besides, I was still healing.

Eddie stepped in front of the fan and cut off my air. "Look, I get that you have your process and I totally respect you for that. But college has started! Have you joined any clubs? Have you met any new people? Everyone's getting out there, everybody's got new friends already. If you just lie in bed all day, you'll get left behind."

"Yeah, well, maybe I deserve to get left behind." As he kept up his pitch, he stayed right in front of the fan, suffocating me in the stifling heat. I groped around for my water bottle in a helpless daze, only half hearing him as phrases like 'I care about you,' 'favor,' and 'group thing' stacked higher and higher in the dead space between us. I guzzled the whole water bottle empty before his voice broke through again.

"It could be a lot of fun. Zelda said her cute roommate's coming and can get us weed."

I don't remember what else he said to convince me, but Eddie, Zelda, and I wound up at the front doors of Theta Chi frat house right on time. I felt a little self-conscious looking like their sidecar, especially since they were such beautiful people.

Eddie was tall, dark, and lithe, complete with a Superman jawline and a winning smile that lit up the homecoming court our senior year. Where Eddie's was a classic beauty, Zelda's was more ethereal. Her blonde locks of hair fell around her face in ringlets, and her green eyes flickered and flitted over everything and everyone, serving up warm smiles to match. All this taken together worried me that people at the party might ask them why they rolled up with a brown Oompa Loompa as their third wheel.

Eddie had me change my outfit three times in preparation for going out, each time citing it as 'too high school.' I finally got approval with a plaid button-down with a leather jacket and my good pair of jeans, the only ones I had that weren't too baggy on me. I remember looking in the mirror, thinking I looked like a young Mario Lopez. Well, if Mario Lopez wore glasses, and was a little on the thicker side. And was barely holding it together. So not really Mario Lopez.

"Where's your roommate?" I asked Zelda. "Is she coming later?"

"No, she's already inside. She and Dean go way back. He's a brother here, and he's our ticket in."

The frat brother working the door looked all of us up and down as we approached.

"Who do you know here?" He took out his vape and hit it before continuing. "This is a private event for pledges, brothers, and their guests."

"We're here for Dean, we're friends of his," said Zelda.

He softened at the magic word. "Oh. No doubt, no doubt. His door is gonna be upstairs, third one on the left. Alright guys, have fun, be safe, have a great night." And with that he opened the doors and let us in.

Inside was mostly like I expected, with a few key differences. Dimly lit, kind of dingy, pretty crowded, lots of white people. Check and check. What I didn't anticipate was the suffocating heat in there. As soon as the door opened, it rolled at me like a wave. It crashed down onto me, and with the first step in the door I began to sweat. Forehead, armpits, the back of my neck, and knees all started sticking to my clothes within the first moments of walking in. I should have suspected, since it had been so hot all week, but I guess I thought it would still be cool at night. Serves me right for trying not to look 'too high school.'

The three of us snaked our way through the crowd to the drinks table. They served us something called 'jungle juice,' which I later learned was a concoction comprising beer, vodka, and frozen juice concentrate whose ratios the frat social chair kept a guarded secret. I almost gagged as I took my first ever sip of alcohol, but since Eddie and Zelda kept telling each other how nice it was that they could hardly taste it, I just considered myself lucky they didn't notice me and resolved to play it low-key from there on out. Each sip stoked a tiny fire in my belly, a warmth that started at the bottom of my stomach and crept slowly outwards. I wondered if I could leave my jacket somewhere.

"Hey, the table is opening up, you guys want to play beer pong?" Eddie asked us.

Zelda beamed at him. "How fun! It can be me and you against Carlos and Julie. I'll go upstairs and bring her back." She squeezed his arm, flashed a parting smile, and floated away.

Eddie's eyes followed her out for a suspended moment before he turned to me. He wasn't listening the first two times I told him I didn't know how to play beer pong.

"Very simple," he said as he cracked open two room-temperature Keystone Lights and began pouring their contents evenly across a bowling pin formation of ten red solo cups. "In teams of two, we take turns trying to make the balls into the other team's cup. You make it, we drink, we make it, you drink. You bounce it in, and it's worth two, but we can defend and knock those away. Both of you making cups on the same turn is 'balls back,' and both of you making the same cup the same turn is worth three and balls back. Decide who goes first with 'eye-to-eye,' that's shooting at the same time without breaking eye contact. Losing side drinks the rest of the cups on the table. There's a couple more small rules, but we'll just do those as we go. Any questions?"

"Um, yeah," I said, raising one eyebrow at him. "Are you super good at this? I'm kind of getting that vibe from you."

Eddie shrugged. "The other lifeguards at the pool over summer just liked playing from time to time, I would mostly just watch." I narrowed my eyes at his response.

Just as Eddie shook out the last drops of warm can foam into the ninth and tenth cups on my side, the white streak of a ping pong ball whizzed across my vision and plopped down with a hollow knocking splash into the front cup on my side. Across the room, halfway back from the drinks table, Zelda rematerialized in a glow of self-satisfaction. She glided down to us through the party crowd in a straight-line path, cradling three drinks in the bend of her left arm.

"I don't know if Eddie's the only one you have to worry about," she teased, handing me one of the drinks.

Eddie's brain just about melted out of his head right then. "That was the hottest thing I've ever seen in my life," he said, raising the temperature of the place with his excitement. Zelda responded with an intense stare and another squeeze of his arm, and for a minute I faded out of their view. I grew impatient before she finally spoke again. "I'm so sorry I haven't introduced you! Eddie, Carlos," said Zelda, gesturing to the person behind her, "this is my roommate, Julie."

I don't usually get like this. Not that I'm some sort of smooth talker or anything, but whenever I would see someone stunningly beautiful in the past, it usually wouldn't come at the expense of all rational faculties. I don't even know how I didn't see her before. She was still standing right there before Zelda introduced her, but just this one look and I'm not even sure that I'm still standing here. Someone should make a sculpture of her. Well, not me, I don't really know how to do that. That's a really weird thought. You need a three dimensional medium to see what I'm seeing now, a photo or painting wouldn't work. You're being incredibly weird right now. Please be cool. How am I this sweaty?

I blinked and came back. From the looks on everyone's faces, I'd been swimming around in my head for more than a moment and let multiple addresses to me float by. Cool. "Nice to meet you, Julie," I said, scraping my brain off the nearest wall where I abandoned it and scooping it back into my head. "I'm Carlos, do you want to be my partner?"

I didn't so much play the game of beer pong as let it happen around me. I was trash at it anyway, and I didn't even get it on the table most of the time. Everyone else was pretty good. At least that's what it seemed like from the number of cups of beer I was drinking while trying to talk with Julie.

"Okay if you drink for me?" Julie asked. "I got an early start and I've had a few already." Yes, that was definitely okay with me. Even though the drink of choice tasted like warm wet pennies, drinking more was making me way more relaxed, and frankly, much cooler. The stress, the awkwardness, the sweaty anxiety from carrying conversation with someone I was interested in, all of that got quieter with every solo cup I drained. *Plop, plop,* balls back they said. Be nice, be cool, ask her questions about her life, listen, respond thoughtfully, and maybe try to be funny once in a while if you can do it. Focus.

Julie told me her parents were originally from Korea, but she was born and raised in Tallahassee. She loves Frank Ocean music, medical crime shows, and any news story that starts with the words 'Florida man.' And weed. Julie really knew what she was talking about, or at least I assumed she did, since I knew next to nothing. So we went at it, question-answer, my interest puzzle-piecing with her enthusiasm.

"Well, in my dorm I usually smoke out of a bong," Julie continued, shooting and near missing the nearest cup just off the back lip. She was carrying us in our game, having made three cups to my zero. On the other side, Zelda and Eddie only had two left to make, and by the looks of their PDA, they were starting to celebrate early. "Zelda doesn't like smoke in the room, so I just usually go out on the balcony. The bong is the best way to smoke, I think. Smoothest hit, most efficient use of flower, and it gets you the most high. But joints are cool too if you're on the go, and I know a lot of people that like the convenience of the pens, but that's not really not my style. Also you don't really know with those vaping diseases nowadays."

"Was it really weird or scary the first time you ever smoked?" I asked, shooting my shot and completely missing the table again.

"Oh yeah. Back in high school, my best friend brought a joint with him to one of our choir competitions, and we smoked it in the parking lot before going on stage. I was so high when we went on that I couldn't even sing, I just stood there completely spaced out making a face like this and tried not to fall over." She made the face for a second before we both started laughing at it. She was so cool. I needed another drink.

As if to answer my thought, Eddie sunk another cup with a hollow plastic knock. "One more, babe, we got this!" he said, turning to Zelda, who clasped her hands in his with interlocking fingers. She pulled him in, her chest to his stomach, wide-eyed, and they both moved in to embrace each other in a hesitant but passionate kiss.

Knock, plop! Went the ping pong ball, bouncing once before landing perfectly in one of Eddie and Zelda's cups. They broke from their embrace, only to look up and see Julie pointing finger guns. "That's two! Never let your guard down, constant vigilance!"

"Wow, nice shot," I said, going for a high five but connecting improperly with a weak hand slap.

"Wow, I came over to see if I could help, but it looks like you don't need it."

I wheeled around to see who said that, and right behind me at my eye level jutted the broad, muscular chest of someone who clearly belonged here.

"Dean!" Julie said, and ran to him and hugged him with both arms. "You saw that?"

"Hell yeah, killer," he said, tousling her hair like a television child. "It's been a minute since flip cup at choir banquet, huh. Are these your friends?"

"Yes! Well, I actually just met these guys." She pointed at me and Eddie. "But they're the ones I came with. That's my roommate Zelda over there." Zelda waved with a little toodle-oo.

"And that's her boyf—I mean, that's Eddie," she said, and Eddie managed an awkward half wave before Dean came zooming over to offer a gregarious handshake.

"So good to meet you guys," he said, seeming to grow larger and take over the group. "You two enjoying the party?"

"Yeah, it's been so cool, you guys have a really nice place!" said Eddie.

"Eddie, right? You know, if you're interested in seeing the place more and meeting the other guys, we've got rush events going on all week. I saw all those cups you've been sinking. You've got quite the arm, dude."

Eddie and Zelda looked at each other excitedly. "Yeah, I'd love to check out more of your events!" Eddie said. "Seems like a really cool place."

"You guys smoke weed?" Dean asked them.

"HI DEAN I'M CARLOS NICE TO MEET YOU," I half blurted, half yelled across the table. If I had just started to forget how hot it was, I remembered now. The nervousness and insecurity I drank away rolled back in. I felt hot again, but this time just in my face. Dean strode back over to me. I reached out to shake his hand, trying to grip him as firmly as he gripped me, but my palm was so sweaty that it nearly slipped from his grasp. He wiped his hand on his pants as he said it was nice to meet me.

"Mind if I celeb shot?" he asked, holding his palm open to me. I looked at him blankly, not understanding.

"It's his first time playing, he doesn't know what that is,
"Eddie offered from across the table.

I shot daggers back at Eddie, emoting my 'not cool, dude'
face.

Dean brushed it off. "It's all good. Once per person per
game, you can give up your shot to someone else who's not
playing in hopes they make it for you. May I?" he asked again,
moving his open palm even closer.

I didn't see a way to politely refuse him, seeing as I hadn't
made a single cup yet and he was our ticket in here tonight
besides. Of course he made it. He even took the shot from a
few extra steps back for style points, eliciting squeals from the
girls and a fist bump from Eddie when he sunk it in with the
hollowest, deepest *PLOP* of the match. Dean's entrance had
shifted the floor under my feet, and I started sweating again.
Halfway through peeling off my leather jacket, I noticed my
plaid button down was almost entirely soaked through in the
armpits and upper back, so I scrambled back into it.

Though I finally made one cup before the game ended, no
one but Dean seemed to notice, and he said nothing. Zelda sank
the game winner, nearly setting her and Eddie to jump into each
other's pants right then and there. Afterwards, Dean ushered the
four of us upstairs to his room. He led us into a cozy little dorm
space, complete with a red nylon couch, lofted bed, and stocked
mini bar. A refurbished Victrola sat on the desk under the lofted
bed, and a huge Florida state flag covered the entire back wall.
In the middle of the room stood a two-foot-tall, shiny-clean,
clear glass bong.

"It's beautiful," said Zelda, her eyes tracing the curves of glass.

"Thanks, I just picked it up today," said Dean, "Julie and I christened it earlier this evening." As he talked, Dean flipped the record resting dormant on the turntable. When he lifted and replaced the needle, the sound breathed to life, fuzzy and warm. Rubber Soul.

"Yeah, it's a real step up from the cretins we were in high school," said Julie. "Outside of the joints we rolled, the only way we had to smoke was Dean's old Gandalf pipe that he took from his grandpa's house."

"Back in high school, we probably looked more like Frodo than Gandalf."

"Was that a short joke?" Julie asked, and slapped Dean's arm playfully. Everyone else laughed, especially Zelda. Not me though.

Dean turned back to the rest of us. "Before we start, does anyone want a shot?" He held up a handle of Fireball whiskey. "Yes? Yes? Yes? Okay, that's five yeses." He pulled five shot glasses from his mini bar and lined up five shots. "To old friends and new," he said, raising his glass to us.

"Old friends and new?" asked Zelda. "That sounds like two separate shots to me."

"Oh ho, alright, I see you, respect. Old friends first then," he said, and raised his shot to Julie. Eddie came over to me and said, "Hey, dude, old friends," and clinked his shot glass to mine.

"Old friends," I said, and tipped it back.

It swished around in my mouth for a second before I gulped it down. Sweet and warm, it stoked a cinnamon fire in the bottom of my stomach, contrasting a warm inner glow against the sticky stuffiness of everything outside myself.

"One more, like Zelda says," said Eddie, clinking his empty glass on the table and grabbing the handle to fill up another.

"New friends," said Julie, venturing a timid smile over the brim of the second shot. I smiled back for a second before my cheeks got hot and I looked away. Next to us, Eddie and Zelda were already feeding their shots to each other through linked arms. The rest of us followed, draining our glasses in turn.

Fireball in my mouth, Fireball in my belly, my body betrayed me right then. Rather than opening up to let everything slide right down, my throat closed with a little cough, choking me and sending half the shot of burning cinnamon liquor down the wrong way and out again through my nose. I hacked and sputtered, breathing fire instead of air and coughing the other half of the shot back out my mouth onto my shirt and the floor.

"Woah woah, you okay?" asked Dean, rushing to hand me a cup of water while Julie grabbed some paper towels.

"I'm good," I gurgled, wiping back stinging tears while gulping down the water. But I wasn't good. Ten shots of Fireball through the nose would still feel better than the humiliation of being such a loser all the time. Here I am, sweating all over these cool and beautiful people and crying because I hurt myself trying to take a shot. I'm a joke. Worse than a joke, because all these guys are too nice to laugh.

"Hey," said Dean, reading my dismay, "You know what I know would cheer you right up? You want greens?" He grabbed the bong a third of the way down the neck and turned the bowl to face me. Inside rested a packed little mound of crushed up green flecked with orange, like freckles on a face.

"Oh, I don't know," I said, "I've never smoked before, I'm a little worried I might embarrass myself."

"Say no more," said Dean, waving me off. "We're going to walk you through all of it. Anyone else's first time as well?" Eddie nodded, Zelda shook her head. He continued, "Okay, so here's what you do. You put your mouth on the bong up here at the opening and make a seal so you can take in the smoke. Then, you hold it down at the base and light the green while simultaneously pulling air in. This is going to fill the chamber with smoke down here, and when it's as full as you want, you pull out the bowl and suck in hard in order to get all this smoke down here all the way through this and into your lungs. Julie and I can light it and pull the bowl for you since it's your first time. Cool?"

Eddie and I both nodded. I sat down on the couch to get more comfortable, bong in my lap, and Julie stood over me, one leg between the two of mine for better position to light it. With a deft and practiced *flick*, she struck up the lighter and put flame to flower. I began inhaling, and the water burbled as the smoke filled the chamber like steam from a hot bath. It grew thick and white as milk, and when Julie said, "Now," I inhaled fast and deep like I was surfacing from a dive, trying to fill my legs with air. That's when the tide came in.

I coughed and gulped down water to try to stop coughing. When I stepped back into the eye of my mind, I found my headspace familiar but strange. I felt as if someone had taken everything in the world and moved it two inches to the left as a prank I might not notice.

The feeling started in my lizard brain. I closed my eyes and felt the smoke iron out every wrinkle and chemically relax my brain stem into submission. Next was the back of my head, the muscles that might move if you were to try to wiggle your ears up and down or if you were to hear something surprising. All smoothed out and heavy, but not oppressively so. Then, pulled up by strings of their own, the muscles across the bottom half of my face spread into an irrepressible shit-eating grin I couldn't wipe off. Nothing was particularly funny, but at that moment, so was everything. I noticed my hands, feet, arms, and legs. I could feel it then, the farthest edge of me where I ended and the universe began. This awareness was like a forcefield, a perfect bubble outline stretching out no farther than the highest perched bacteria of my microbiome on the longest hair of the first knuckle of my big toe. This sage like hyperawareness of my body in space subsequently pointed me to my next observation. Throughout that whole ordeal, from flick to hit to tide to woah to reverie, Julie's leg stood not just between mine, but actually leaned so the softest flesh of her inner thigh pressed against mine with nothing between us but the denim of my one good pair of jeans. *Damn you, Levi Strauss.*

Julie finished what smoke I left in the bowl and took a second hit. Then Zelda, Eddie, and Dean each took theirs in turn.

Zelda got giggly, but mellowed out from her touchiness before. Eddie would keep insisting he didn't feel high, even when his ramblings became so incoherent we had to stop pretending to understand him. By and by, the lazy haze swallowed the whole room. It smelled good, not like the skunky, dingy weed smell you get downtown that makes you walk a little faster with an upturned nose. This smell was clean and strong, with notes of earthiness like new potted plant soil, and just the faintest trace, if you were really concentrating, of citrus. Orange?

"How are you guys feeling?" asked Dean after another round of hits.

"I'm not sure if I'm high yet," said Eddie, already half eaten by the couch.

"What strain is it?" asked Zelda from his lap.

"This one is called Cinderella 99," Dean said. "I got it from one of my friends in Santa Cruz. If you ever want to buy from me, just let me know. Only thing is we sell by the ounce."

As he talked, Dean packed another bowl about half full. He scorched the whole thing, draining its contents halfway up the glass with opaque white before snapping it all up in one breath.

"Well," he exhaled, getting up, "You guys can chill here if you want and finish whatever's left in the grinder. I'm gonna check on things downstairs." He gave us one more nod and closed the door behind him.

"You know what," I said to Julie, "that guy seems pretty cool."

"Dean has always taken care of me like a younger sister," she said.

"He nearly went feral over the phone when I called him last spring to tell him I'd be joining him at school here."

"Is it nice back in Florida?" I asked.

"Nah, it straight up sucks. Crazy hot there, all kinds of snakes and spiders and animals like that. I like college football as much as the next person, but outside of talking about it 24/7, there's not really much to do."

"Dang, I'm sorry. Well, if you wanted to go to a school where they don't talk much about college football, you came to the right place. People are saying we'll be lucky to string three wins together by the end of the season." We both laughed a little, then sighed, a little sad about it.

"Hey, do you mind if I get a picture of all of us?" I asked the room. We squeezed a little closer on the loveseat, Zelda on Eddie's lap and Julie in the middle. I snapped the photo from my phone at arm's length, and when I pulled it in to look at it I couldn't help but laugh out loud.

"What is it?" asked Eddie, sitting up. "Did it turn out okay?"

"Yeah," I said, laughing as I showed him, "but we all look high as hell." In the photo, all our eyes looked either bloodshot red or squinty faded, and we each wore a high-reflex huge grin. The bong in the picture was the cherry on top of it all.

"I don't think I'm gonna post this one," I said.

"Want to take another one?" asked Zelda.

"No, I think I'll just keep this one. Live in the moment, you know." I didn't need a post. For the first time since orientation, I finally felt like I was winning the breakup. We all sat back in our seats, and I sat especially back, listening as the Victrola's fuzzy crackle spun Paul McCartney's soothing drawl up, up, up in slow circles above the hazy room.

I left to pee around midnight. I excused myself for a quick trip, and noticing all our empty cups, I shuffled downstairs to secure refills on whatever mixed drink they were still serving, plus a little water as well. I swayed as I walked, but my feet stayed under me alright. As I neared the drinks table, I saw Dean out on the dance floor and gave him a loose-wristed flick of a wave hello. I didn't want to stare too long, but things looked like they were getting pretty serious out there. Attached to him at the waist danced a girl who I couldn't see very well through the crowd. From what I could tell, she had a full head of curly natural hair, two white Converse high tops flat on the floor, and two hands down on the floor to match. As I craned my neck to get a better view between sips of drink, I discovered these facts were the necessary preconditions for placing her whole ass on the front of Dean's pants in order to grind him down like a pencil. I blushed a bit when I caught myself staring too long and got back to filling the drinks.

As I started walking back, the music downshifted to a slow song. Stopping in their sightline, I caught them standing chest to chest, nuzzling each other's faces and necks. The music swelled, and the girl swayed with it, coming into the light like an Earth rotation seen from space. They fell into each other's kiss, tongues sliding and hands wandering, erasing the boundaries between them. As I watched them, unable to look away, my curiosity dawned to recognition then plunged into horror, shooting me down from half a room away. *I gotta get out of here.*

I butted my way gracelessly to the door, all elbows and splash. In the commotion, I dropped one drink on my shoes, a second on the floor, and a third on the vaping frat brother who worked the door earlier. Even as the path to the door seemed to elongate in front of me, I couldn't do anything else. Bodily hyper awareness and all, I didn't notice how dry my mouth was, nor how I'd stopped sweating a while ago. My eyes puffed and stung me, but my cheeks stayed dry. Still I clawed through, even as my dimly lit surroundings turned brighter and brighter, ramping now into blinding whiteness. I neared within feet of the door, close enough to feel the finally cool night air brush my face as the door opened for someone else. At that moment, my body betrayed me for the last time that night. My legs, in protest of standing up all night and in two votes for staying home with the Eurozone crisis, buckled beneath me and sent me tumbling down. My last drink and I spilled all over the doorstep as the corners of my vision faded to dark from the blinding light I saw before. The last thing I saw before it all went black were two white Converse high-top shoes, two hands down on the floor to match, and a full head of curly natural hair. *Rosa?*

CHAPTER 2

Fear once more the heat of the sun. It woke me up in the mid-morning, streaming rudely through the uncurtained window onto my face. The heat did it as much as the light. I sat up and looked around. I was on the couch in Dean's room, alone except for the wastebasket of my own vomit on the floor next to me and a half full glass of water on the coffee table. Half empty. I pulled on my jacket and glasses and struggled to remember what else Eddie had said to convince me to come here that I had pushed out of my mind. That's right. *Win the breakup, man. You got this.*

I caught my reflection in the hallway mirror as I made my way out. I noted a bruise on my forehead and a Neapolitan swirl of vomit, beer, and sweat smeared from my chin down to my shoes. I was still taking in the portrait, unable to fathom how I'd make myself invisible on the long walk home, when I saw them right in front of the door. Two white Converse high top shoes walked me back through last night, and it all came back into focus. Did I cry in front of them? Did they have sex in the room when they thought I was asleep? Did I dream that?

A moment in the shoes of last night turned my paper skin to armor. Adamantine in my indignation, I marched down the stairs and out the door, neither rushing nor looking back to vape nation doorman Bobby, who was trying to catch my attention. I took step after step, frat after frat, invulnerable.

Halfway home, I saw someone in a situation maybe like mine. She walked down the steps of neighboring TKE, closing the door on last night still wearing last night's makeup. She was beautiful, but I could see she wasn't bulletproof like I was. She was looking down, hands crossed to cover her bare arms. A full lion's mane of hair was tied up in the loosest of messy buns, threatening to give out any moment under the wobble of her walk. Her eyes looked down, down below her voluminous head of hair, below her crossed hands covering her bare arms, below the cutoff of the silky green dress she needed to keep pulling down, below her knees and shins and calves already ashy in the midmorning heat, down to where she was walking. She tried to walk fast, but didn't recede from my leisurely stride. Down below her shins, snaked inextricably around her feet, were the tallest pair of strappy stiletto heels I had ever seen.

She concentrated on each step like she was testing the surface of a frozen lake. Graceless in her inexperience, she teetered down the hill and forward into the day. I wondered how she could have gotten this far up here in the first place. *Why doesn't she take them off? Well, the sidewalk is already a little warm.* Then she turned and caught me staring. We made eye contact for less than a moment before realizing our mistake. Her face whitened with surprise and mine colored with embarrassment as she fell to, lengthening her stride and wobbling even worse than before. The exchange froze me in my tracks, and my stomach lurched, threatening to fall down and out. My very first thought was to run all the way back to Theta Chi, up the stairs, down the hall, and swipe the white Converse high tops that had run over my night; I would offer them on bended knee as a sign of my deepest apologies. My second thought, thankfully less insane, was to stop and retie both my shoes as slowly as I possibly could. I even took the extra time to loosen the laces all the way down the shoe and retighten them, snug but not too constricting. When I finished and stood up again, the girl in the heels had advanced at least beyond the range of potential eye contact and had nearly receded into the Sunday morning foot traffic. I continued my walk, slower now so I wouldn't catch up to her, and tried to speculate about her night instead of mine the rest of the way home. It didn't work, and Eddie's pitch clincher I thought I'd suppressed rattled around in my head.

"You think Rosa's not out having fun these days?"

"She is."

"I still follow her on everything and so do you! She's out there every night getting trashed and making friends and probably getting laid. I'm sorry, dude, but it's true. You want to get over her? Heal? Get drunk, meet someone cute, hit it off. Post about it." Not quite.

One walk to my building and 171 stairs later (I counted them to keep my brain quiet), I finally reached my room on the eighth floor. I turned my key, thankful that my own bed would soon swallow me up and I'd be safe again.

"AAAAAHHH!" shrieked a voice from inside.

There in his extra-long twin-sized bed, Eddie and Zelda tumbled over each other's bodies in a tangle of olive and alabaster. They'd probably been here since last night, enjoying each other in a 12x12 foot world all their own until I plopped in like a rock in still water to muck it all up. Now, their paradise lost, they knew their nakedness, and fumbled around grasping for blankets and sheets just out of reach.

"Close the door, pervert!" said Zelda.

"Shoot, sorry." I closed the door and went back out into the hallway, wiping off my glasses before they could steam up any more.

Not knowing where else to go, I paced the hallway for a few minutes before Zelda came out in the crumpled-up version of what she wore yesterday. When she saw me, a fire sparked in her green eyes, and she stormed straight toward me with the stride of someone a foot taller and the step of someone twice as heavy.

"Hey, Zelda, I'm sorry I was so weird back there I was just surpr—"

"—Stop. I don't need to hear it. You better watch yourself, Carlos Vasquez," she said, all daggers.

"Okay, loud and clear. I hear you."

She pointed a finger at me. "Be careful," she said, her voice growing deadly serious, "or you're going to end up in my novel." And with that ultimate threat, she went down and out into what I assume was her own bulletproof walk back to her own dorm.

As I turned my key and knocked this time, I took a minute to fully inhabit the body that took me all around town and drank and smoked everything I could make it. Hunger, thirst, hangover, weariness, embarrassment, and nameless longing all stuck their straws in me and drank down my vitality smoothie as every body part groaned in protest. The muscles in my legs twitched, threatening cramp. My hands tingled, buzzing loudest at my fingertips like they were still high from last night. My stomach whined, demanding I attend to its emptiness, but the lingering vomit taste in my dry mouth voiced a conflicting opinion on the subject of appetite. My skin chafed, trading salt and stickiness with my soiled clothes with every swing of my arm. But the worst was my head. I didn't even notice any of the other things until I took a minute to stand still, but since I woke up that morning, I'd felt like my head would split open down the front. My brain felt smaller than it was yesterday, and in its shrunken state it pulled on the insides of my skull so hard I ground my teeth through the pain. I felt my forehead where I fell last night. The bruise had turned into a raised bump, tender and sore except to the softest touch. Though it hurt to do it, I massaged it with my tingly hands because I remembered somewhere that's what you were supposed to do.

As I collapsed into bed, intent on never leaving again except for food and hygiene, Eddie recounted to me the missing details of my night. I was only a quarter listening.

"...we were worried about you..."

"...we needed to get condoms from the RA..."

"...I think the guys might give me a bid..."

As I drifted off, I wondered if I might have a concussion, and if it were better that I didn't sleep. I wondered what it would be like to die in one's sleep from that kind of thing. Here in this bed has pretty much been the nicest place I've been since coming to college. What would it feel like to fall deeper and deeper into the sheets, swallowed up by pillows and blankets, never to return, a kind of unbirth? I never asked to be born, you know. Yet here I am, using plastic and creating carbon and all that. Besides, I heard from somebody at orientation that if you die during the school year, your roommate gets an automatic 4.0 GPA for the semester. Pretty generous. So, it's settled then. Not that I'm going to help it along or anything, but if I die, I die.

I let it take me then, swimming down into my bed as deeply as I dared to go. As I crossed over, I thought of Rosa, Julie, and Zelda, and hoped everything went alright on their walks home.

CHAPTER 3

"In the days and weeks that followed, Zelda came over a lot more frequently. After squirming and worming about the awkwardness of timetabling their sex sessions, we settled on a 'do not disturb' system for getting the message out. Eddie would draw a little sock in marker on the corner of our dorm door's dry erase board, and that would be enough for me to know to come back later. Hardly wanting to leave my bed for class, I was naturally inconvenienced from the start by our new arrangement. Some days, I flew back to my room with my next anime already queued up on my phone and my cafeteria burrito burning a hole in my pocket, only to find the little sock drawing blocking my way. Once, I even forgot my phone and wallet inside during one of their meetups and felt myself untether from reality as I wandered through campus the rest of the afternoon. Like, yeah I'm happy for them, of course. Zelda is a pretty cool girl and I've never seen Eddie more into someone in the ten years we've been friends. And I guess I did agree to the way we're doing things. It just sucks when you don't really have your own space when you want it, you know?"

"That's crazy, bro," said Charles, probably listening from his laptop screen. We were in his room, next door to mine. It was my go-to spot nowadays when my own room was occupied. It housed three people instead of two, but in a way it was a little roomier since the other two were hardly ever home. The first roommate, Abhas, spent most of his free time at his girlfriend's on Northside. Jian, who I'd never met and who the other two barely knew, was a striving pre-med international student who studied himself into a ghost story. Charles told me that Jian slept here every night, but the only time Charles ever saw him was if he woke between 2 and 6am, since Jian got home after everyone slept and left before anyone woke up.

That said, three people meant three beds, three wastebaskets, three piles of dirty clothes, and a whirlwind of trash and foreign objects no one ever knew anything about. Today, a broken potted plant lay unbothered in the middle of the floor. Charles hadn't acknowledged it since I came in, so I thought it best to leave it alone. Leaving his door open to anyone who wanted to come in certainly didn't do him any favors in terms of the mess, but I was grateful to him for it.

He wasn't chatty, but he had said he preferred company to alone time. As a result, it became a waystation as much as a dorm room, with floormates often popping their heads in to see who was in. Today, typical of nowadays, Charles putzed around on his laptop while I did various activities requiring headphones, trying hard not to hear Zelda and Eddie's giggling and other sounds through the uninsulated thin walls and necessarily open windows.

"Hey, so don't take this the wrong way," Charles began.

"What?" I asked, knocking off my headphones and tabling my progress through a playlist of angsty teen music from the previous decade.

"I said, 'don't take this the wrong way.' You ever kick Eddie out of your room when you've got someone over?"

My face got hot. "Why? You wish Eddie spent more time on this side of the wall instead of me?"

"I said 'don't take this the wrong way,' didn't I?"

"Yeah, I guess you did. No, I haven't kicked out Eddie and Zelda in order to have sex in my room."

"Would you like to?"

I drew back in surprise.

"Jesus, dude, you know what I meant." Charles rolled his eyes. "And I'd never anyway, I only go for 6 feet and over."

"Huh," I said, "I always thought the 6 foot thing was just a girl thing."

"And that's why they made you our new Queer Studies professor?" asked Charles. "Anyway, we were talking about you and how you don't get any."

I paused for a second, but not so long that the bed-to-wall sounds would start to fill the empty space. "I'm just chilling. I like my classes, I've met a few people from the floor. I was in a pretty serious relationship until just about the end of summer, so it's kind of nice to just do my own thing for now."

"Bitch," said Charles, "lemme see your phone." I handed it over, and he only looked at it for a second. "I don't claim to be some kind of expert on straight culture, but never in the history of anything has a whole playlist of My Chemical Romance been made by anybody who was 'just chilling.'"

"What's your point?"

"My point is, there's plenty of people out there that are totally cool with spending most of their time alone without any intrigue or anything like that. But that's not you. You come in here most every day now, and when you're not talking about one girl or another from way back when, I catch you doing sad boy shit in the corner whenever it's been quiet too long. I like your company when you're around here, and I like to think we're becoming friends now. As your new friend, I just wanna be real with you. Cuffing season is right around the corner."

"What's cuffing season?"

"Bruh," said Charles, "I've heard enough of your stories to know you weren't homeschooled. Cuffing season is that time of year when everything starts to get chilly and people start walking around with lattes and beanies and all that and start shacking up. All the beds are cold now, so the theory goes, so when you get somebody to warm them up it becomes a more comfortable resting place, at least until it starts to get hot again."

"Well, it's still hot right now."

"Well I guess the people who named the phenomenon didn't think about climate change. Anyway, what I'm saying is, once it gets colder, those guys in there, their power will only grow. And if you keep up all this moping and don't take some initiative, someday soon, when you come next door, there's gonna be a little sock drawing on my whiteboard too. Then what are you gonna do?"

I deflated, imagining some time soon when I'd have no one, nothing, and nowhere, all doors closed, but to wear down the floors between the dorm hallway and the library like a pet left in the rain. Eddie and Zelda grew louder through the wall then went quiet.

"I guess you're right, I'm not really that guy. Even though I like to think of myself as wanting to be alone, I really need some sort of intimacy, whatever form that might end up taking."

"Exactly. And no one's saying that you have marry this person, or even be in a committed, exclusive relationship if that's not what you both want. As long as you've got honesty and respect, there's really no reason you can't take care of whatever this is," he gestured towards all of me in a loose wristed circle, "in a responsible, healthy way."

"Thanks, man," I said, getting up. "This has been a lot to think about, thanks for helping me put my weird angst into perspective."

"No problem, dude. You headed out?"

"Yeah, I think they finished, so I'm going to catch this window to go back in."

"Well, come back anytime between now and cuffing season!" he joked, half to himself as I was already out the door.

I reentered my room after knocking and receiving a weak 'come in' from the other side. The room was in its typical state after one of their sessions: dark and humid, with the blackout curtains fully drawn and only my little desk lamp on for light. Eddie was in pajamas playing some computer game from his bed, probably an rpg or a turn-based judging from the infrequency of button pressing. Zelda sat at my desk, using my desk lamp to light an open literature anthology, though she wasn't reading it. Instead, she leaned back in my chair, the back of which rested on my bed, musing dreamily and looking off nowhere in particular while taking up as much space as possible. Neither of them looked up when I came in.

I walked to my side of the room, trying to lazerbeam through the musk to make my presence felt. I climbed onto my bed, around Zelda, and off the other side to pull back the curtains and stream the sun right onto her to repel her occupation. It didn't have the desired effect.

"Doesn't the sunshine feel wonderful, Carlos?" she asked, turning towards the window like a flower to soak up more on her face. Someone's in a good mood.

"Yeah, it's too dark in here for daytime," I said. She had previously been all ice since I walked in on them that first time.

"That's exactly what I said to Eddie not two minutes ago!" said Zelda, turning towards me with a warm smile undimmed by my coldness. "This one over here likes to keep everything so closed up all the time, and I always tell him it's like a cave in here! I knew you and I would be of one mind on this." She got up and walked around the desks in a U shape to get to Eddie's window on his side, now inspired with enough confidence to open it. As she squeezed by me standing in the narrow space between the bed and the desk, the pink bathrobe she wore brushed against my arm. *Great, now she has a bathrobe here too.* My eyes followed her around as she wound the path to the other side. *And her own laundry hamper.* She stood on Eddie's

31

bed to reach the curtains from his side. He still hadn't looked up since I walked in. She pulled them open with a flourish, scattering dust and sunlight in every direction. Dull yellow light, streaming through the tinted windows, splashed her face and hair. She closed her eyes for a moment to bask in the warmth, charging up to be a second sun.

I caught myself staring, melting a little in the warmth of the tableau. I didn't usually find myself attracted to white people; maybe I've conditioned myself that way because none of the white people I knew were ever attracted to me. But Zelda really was beautiful. It was a vibe thing; there were intangibles. In any room, but especially in a room as small as this one, she had her own atmosphere, her own gravity. Her proximity was her power, and I was in her orbit. Or maybe I was just lonely. In any case, now that she stood here on the bed in nothing but a seashell pink bathrobe and painted toenails to match, I needed to try my best to push both the aura and the memory of the incident she was mad at me for out of my mind.

"Woah," said Eddie, pausing his game and looking up. "Hey babe, can you close my side of the blinds a little? The glare on the monitor makes it a bit hard to see."

She smiled weakly, a little put out, and closed the blinds back to about halfway.

A long silence of independent activity later, Zelda looked back up at me over her *Canterbury Tales.*

"Carlos," she asked, "have you heard from Julie at all lately?"

I looked up from my readings, surprised. "No, I kind of figured I burned that bridge after I got super weird and blacked out that night at the frat."

"Not at all!" said Zelda, closing her book. "She said she actually found you quite charming that night, and was very worried for you when your health took a turn for the worse. It was actually her that made Dean take care of you that night."

"What?" I said, and slid my readings off my lap. Breaking news.

"Yeah, I was actually just reminded because she asked about you again today."

"WHAT?"

My near-conniption caused Eddie to look up from his game. "What's going on?" he asked. A tectonic shift, that's what.

I shifted in my seat, leaving my homework where it fell. "I thought Julie was so cool, but after I woke up that next morning alone and never heard from her again, I just wrote it off like I blew it. Now it turns out she's been asking about me?"

A sly smile spread slowly across Eddie's face. "Oh ok, I see. You like Julie, huh?"

"Okay, slow down," I said, even as I felt myself getting more amped. "I just thought she was a cool person and I wanted to get to know her better."

"Yeeeeee okay," said Eddie, a pearly grin spreading wide. "But, hey, you're going to admit now that we had fun that night, right?"

"Wellllll…" I said.

"Aw come on, dude. I know you're about to be on and on about this girl now, I've seen this since we were kids. This happened at something I begged you to come to that you said you wouldn't enjoy."

"Okay, okay," I said. "You got me. Even though I thought it would end in disaster and it did end in disaster, it was only part disaster and part fun."

"And the *weed?*" asked Eddie, pointing his game controller at me like an accusing finger.

"Yeah, the weed was pretty good too," I said, and threw up my hands in defeat. "With the benefit of hindsight, it was fun. Thanks for inviting me, Eddie, and thanks for making me feel so welcome, Zelda." She flashed a generous smile before moving to open her book again.

"Also, let us know if you want us to start putting in the good word now," said Eddie. "Things are going pretty well at Theta Chi, with the rush events and all that. I've got a good feeling Dean and those boys might offer me a bid soon. Julie talks to him a lot, might be good to get the good PR rolling early, you know?"

For the first time in weeks, I recalled Dean and bristled at the memory. "Thanks, but it's a little early for that. I haven't even talked to her since that night."

"Also, maybe Zelda could put in a word for you too. Right babe?"

Zelda creaked open the pristine pages of her anthology and tipped back again in my desk chair. "Well, darling, Carlos has been so kind and welcoming during my visits here, I don't think

I'd have anything but kind things to say about him should the subject come up." I couldn't tell if she was being nice or if she was playing me; I'd always been bad at knowing that. Anyway, if I'm supposed to read between the lines and this is supposed to be transactional, that wouldn't be the worst thing.

"Zelda," I began again before she could restart her readings, "what do you think I should do now?"

"Well, I'm no Troilus, but the next thing I'd do is follow her on all relevant social media and send her a message."

Losing no more time on readings, I left them on the floor for the rest of the night and picked up my phone. Not too many Julie Kims down the search list, I found the right one with the right mutual connections and geography.

"All of her accounts are set to private." Here goes nothing.

"Real ones only," said Zelda. "That's what she says all the time."

"Oh my God." I looked up as I said it, almost dropping my phone. "She accepted immediately."

CHAPTER 4

After the Accept, the rest of my afternoon fell away as I redirected my full attention to the art of the opening message. No music or distractions aside from Eddie's wrist-rocking mouse clicks and Zelda's lilting Middle English decryption murmur, I pored over Julie's tweets, timelines, posts, pictures, and updates. I scrolled back and back, going all the way out to the obligatory middle school Scene phase that got us all back then. I even found a lurker account wholly dedicated to encounters with smashed-face dogs. I swiped through school dances, topical Halloween costumes, and a brief stint on the trombone. And a lot of Dean. They really did go way back. Every twist and turn, a broken arm, a choir performance, Universal Studios, he got a picture in there. Maybe a good word would do me some good after all. I kept up the research until I felt too creepy to keep going as the afternoon grew long.

"How did people do it in the old days?" I said aloud. "Hours at this and I'm not any closer to any kind of opening."

"Well, back in the 19th century," said Zelda, "gentlemen suitors called on young ladies at home and courted each other by chatting about current events and topics relevant to both of their lives under the supervision of her parents or some other authority figure, and if it was deemed a suitable match after a while things were all arranged."

I thought for a moment. "That's actually really helpful. It gives me an idea."

"Really?" asked Zelda. "I was just trying to mess with you. I guess I'll have to try harder."

"Well, this time you helped. Topics relevant to both our lives. What I end up saying should definitely be related to her interests and what we were talking about last time we saw each other."

With my new direction and fresh inspiration, I set out to craft my message. A simple image search for 'man behind taco bell security footage' and a news headline generator yielded good results. After that, it only took a few minutes to create, refine, and send the link to my fake headline news story, 'Florida Man Finds Dead Body, Takes it Home for *CSI: Miami* Roleplay.' I sent it off and waited for a response, laughing to myself as I reread it a couple of times. She got back to me a couple minutes later.

    Florida Man Finds Dead Body, Takes it Home for CSI: Miami Roleplay. FLN-NEWS.US

...
LMAO
Haven't seen that one, my news alerts have failed me

    Oh, it's not a real one, I just made it up

Thought it would be good for a laugh

No kidding, pretty scary how anyone can just make fake news these days

Oof, I was thinking that too

Anyway, pretty spooky since I was JUST watching CSI: Miami right now

Oh wow that's crazy

Do you want to come over? Watch it together?

I almost fell out of my chair then. "Guys, she just invited me over."

Eddie looked up from his desktop. "Yeeee boi, let's get it."

"Say hi to my room for me when you go," said Zelda, "it's been a bit since I've been back, but I guess you already knew that."

"What should I say?"

"What the heck?! Say yes, you weirdo!" said Eddie.

"Ask her if she wants you to bring anything," offered Zelda. I went back to my phone.

Yeah, let's do it. You want me to bring anything over?

Hmmm
You live on Southside? Can you bring over some Blondie's Pizza?

Sure

And some for yourself too
I don't like to eat alone

The walk up to Julie's dorm proved as steep as it was long. Nestled in the city's eastern foothills, up past the football stadium, I climbed uphill all the way. I had heard people say they saw wild turkeys and even an occasional mountain lion up there, but I didn't really see how until I went for myself. Panting as I crossed leg over leg, I saw now that Zelda had at least one good reason for going home so infrequently. Still, I pushed through undaunted. Excited with the promise of a nice evening, I could have floated up to the foothill dormitory if I were just a few pounds lighter.

I knocked on Julie's door at the end of all the stairs. The door opened just a crack, half a face poked out of it, and one long-lashed eye peered out at me.

"Password?" the voice behind asked playfully.

"Blondie's?" I said, holding the pizza box up to the crack in the door.

"YES." The door swung open and Julie jumped out from behind it, as excited to see the pizza as I was to see her. "Come on," she said, and signed me to come in. "I've got the next episode all queued up."

The foothill dormitories had a different layout from my building down on southside. Whereas mine was a long hallway with rooms on each side going all the way down, these were instead self-contained mini apartments, with a common area shared between three bedrooms and a front door that faced the hills. There in the living room, like she said, the title screen of *CSI: Miami* awaited us from a small television on the coffee table. The screen, scarcely bigger than a desktop monitor, faced the couch. All over the couch, the floor, and the other chairs, draped plush throw pillows, duvets, and blankets that transformed the apartment into a cushiony den of softness.

"I love what you've done with the place," I said, moving to sit down.

"Not me," said Julie, flopping down on the couch next to me. "I don't have one-tenth this soft-girl energy. One more guess, but you already know who it is."

"Zelda." Of course. "At first I thought this might be over the top even for her, but I totally see it now." I thought of the seashell-pink bathrobe and the prospect of Zelda at full power.

"Yeah, when I moved in here at the start of the semester, I wasn't halfway to a full set of bed sheets. An hour after I got my two suitcases in here, she came in with all these helpers and box after box like six people were moving in. Half those boxes, when you opened them up, were all this bed and blanket stuff. Everything she couldn't fit in her room ended up out here. I didn't like it at first, but it's grown on me."

"So what do you think of Zelda?" I asked.

"That conversation," Julie said, "is something that'll go a lot smoother once we get a little high and a little pizza."

I took the box off my lap and set it on the coffee table between us. "I should tell you, I haven't smoked since that one night with you and Dean.

Her face changed. "Oh, I'm sorry, did you not want to? I didn't mean to pressure you. We don't have to if you're not feeling it."

I waved her off. "No, I'm down for sure, but that last time was the only time I've ever smoked before. It was a lot of fun, but it kind of ended in a bad way."

"Oh, I see. Worry no more," she said, and rubbed her hands together like a cartoon villain as she put on a silly voice. "Come under my wing, my young apprentice. I will be your guide to these higher mysteries. Together we shall see wonders great and small."

"I already feel a whole lot better. Let's get started."

Julie left for a minute and came back with her own bong and a drawstring bag of smoking paraphernalia. The piece was short and stout, about half the length that Dean's had been, and was brown and ashy on the inside. She took out the bowl and the downstem and handed it to me by the neck.

"Can you dump this and refill it with fresh water? Right to this line here. Also please be careful, Chanandler is my baby."

"Chanandler?"

"Yeah, his name is Chanandler Bong."

I cracked a smile. "*Miss* Chanandler Bong?"

"YES! A man of culture as well, I see. Usually people have to look that one up when I tell them it's a *Friends* reference."

I got up to fill Chanandler, and when I brought him back, I saw the contents of her bag lain ceremoniously on the table. I noticed a ceramic ashtray with an unfolded paper clip inside, a spare bottle of water I guessed was for drinking, a sleek and heavy metal lighter, the bowl and downstem, the grinder, and in the very middle, a sealed black plastic canister with stickers all over it. I noticed fandom stickers, political stickers, special interest stickers, and joke stickers all over, combining in a mosaic of Julie's likes and interests as an intimate friend might know her. She reached for the canister and held it open to me.

"Smell this, and take out a nug and look at it."

I put the canister up to my nose and breathed in. Piney, mellow, with a little bit of something herbal. I pulled out a piece of weed and turned it in my fingers to examine it. It looked knotty and green at first glance, but when I looked closer I saw little orange veins winding all over the surface. The last thing I noticed, only when I held it up to the light, was a snowy dusting, like frost, around the edges and tips. "It's beautiful."

"This," she said, giving her jar a shake, "is your first foray into the world of indica. Stop me if you've heard this already. People who grow and sell typically divide strains into two broad classifications: indica and sativa. As far as I understand, it's not exactly scientific, but there are some differences. Traditionally, sativa, the type you tried last time, is supposed to make you energized, uplifted, creative. It's the one that stereotypically gives people all those wild 'high thoughts' about starting a band or how the Berenstain Bears used to be spelled 'Berenstein' when we were kids."

"Wait," I said, "I'm pretty sure it's always been 'Berenstein.'"

"You're not even high yet," she said, "I've lost many a good sesh on that one, I'll leave you to work it out on your own time. Anyway, the other strain type, the one we're trying today, is indica, my favorite. This one makes couches comfier, TV more entertaining, and food more delicious."

"So you're saying it's the perfect thing for what we're doing right now?"

A slow smile crept across her face as she rubbed her hands together like a deviant. "Plans within plans. One warning though. This strain is pretty strong, and if you oversmoke you can get some serious couchlock. So don't go too hard and slump out."

"Got it."

With artisanal care, she selected a nugget from her jar and placed it in the grinder. Next, she ground it down and opened the middle section of the grinder, plucking out the product pinch by pinch and packing the bowl compactly but without crushing.

"You have really steady hands," I said.

"Thanks, they've pretty much always been at work helping my parents in their restaurant. You want greens?"

She pushed the glass toward me but I shook my head. She went first, taking her hit deep and slow. I could see how the change washed over her immediately. Just like me, she had been playing it cool, but now the nervous energy began to slide away. A steady calm clicked into place, and from the first exhale she settled more snugly into the couch, grounded. For the rest of the night, I would continue noticing how her eyes would blink slowly, almost lazily like a cat's, and how her smile, which before had a purposeful timing about it, now came and went easily, like the sun from behind clouds.

"What kind of restaurant is it?" I asked.

She passed the bong to me and helped me take a hit. "Just standard American barbecue fare. I think we do it pretty well, but it's the kind of thing you'd find anywhere in The Panhandle. We cook mainly Korean at home though. I could make you something sometime if you want."

Already feeling my mouth water at the thought, I knew the first hit was taking effect. "That's cool that you know how to cook, and probably really well, too. I don't think I've ever cooked anything in my life outside of quesadillas and instant noodles."

"Really?" asked Julie through a cough of smoke. "Food is one of the most magical and wonderful things in the entire world! And even more than that, no matter where we are, it helps us keep in touch with our people."

"What do you mean?"

She emptied the charred remains of the bowl into the ashtray, scraped it clean with the paperclip, and packed another as she spoke. "Can I be real with you for a sec?" As she asked me, I felt my nervousness return.

"Yeah, always."

"Back in Tallahassee, there aren't very many other Koreans. We speak Korean at home, and we drive all the way into the city for church, but other than that it's always been easy to feel kind of disconnected from the kind of community my parents had always known and talked about before they came over here. I never really had anybody in my classes who looked like me or had my kind of experience, at least not until this year. People look around and kind of assume you're not like them, and to some extent that's true. But I also wasn't sure who I was like, if that makes sense. And that's one of the reasons I came all the way out here and pay this ridiculous out-of-state tuition. To find my fit." Her voice broke a bit at the end, and her gaze unfocused. She reached for the lighter again, hands less steady now, and gulped down another hit.

"That's beautiful," I said, grabbing the bong she handed to me and setting it on the table. My hand grazed hers with a spark during the exchange. "And sad." I was surprised at how quickly this turned into real talk, but I wouldn't be caught off guard. I caught her wandering gaze right then and held it with mine. I peered through the lashes, down into the wellspring eyes whose fathoms had been previously closed to me until just that moment. *Honest and kind.* "Obviously I could never fully relate to your unique experience," I said, "but I really have felt adrift in my identity for most of my life as well. Being American-born too, I don't really feel like one thing or the other, and hell, I don't even really speak Spanish at home. I just took it in high school. So having a tether, like good hands for authentic food, that ties you to your roots, that's something special. Really, I'm jealous."

She didn't break eye contact. "Well dang, Carlos Vasquez, I think my hunch was right about you."

"What do you mean?"

"Real ones only." She laughed as she said it, and from there we pivoted to lighter things.

CHAPTER 5

I hadn't seen it before, but *CSI: Miami* had me instantly hooked. Julie had seen the episode before, but she had a lot of fun listening to my theories on the whodunit. No hints, of course. Waist-deep in our high, she finally let us open our pizza boxes when we plumbed the deepest point of our munchies midway through the episode.

"Mindfulness is key," she said. "The last thing you want to do is scarf it down. Really taste it." I opened up the box, a welcome treasure chest below the surface of our sunny-day sea. I picked up my slice as Julie grabbed hers. I looked at it, smelled it, felt it in my hands, then took a bite, eyes closed and mind full. Love at first bite. We bit down, crunch, crunch, crunch, until we were satisfied, and leaned back into the couch again.

Julie kicked her bare feet onto the couch as we continued talking about the episode. Short, square, and very cold, her feet approached inch by inch until they rested with the lightest touch on my outstretched forearm.

"So who do you think it is?" she asked.

"Not sure yet." She prodded me with her feet. "Aww come on, it's almost over, you have to guess."

"Okay, okay. In real life, I'm pretty sure it's the spouse most of the time who did it, and the husband seems pretty shady, so I'm going to go with that."

"Final answer?"

As the reveal and denouement began to play out, my heightened single-mindedness that first trained on pizza and then on show now zeroed in on the subtle skinship playing out here in our seats. To feel it in the moment, it seemed to me that we both kept as still as possible. At least I knew I was. When her feet came to rest, they were so cold at first that I nearly shivered and shrank away. I resisted, and slowly I felt her skin temperature tick up until we reached a thermal equilibrium about half a minute later.

I've always found a sense of peace and connection in human touch, though I didn't experience it often. I always loved having my hair cut. Near the end, the person cutting my hair tilts my head this way then that, taking their electric razor carefully to the back and sides of my neck in order to get the lines just perfectly straight. The interaction always felt so intimate to me, and my monthly haircut marked at least once on the calendar when my touch-starved brain could rest, all for the low price of $25 plus tip. I felt myself feeding again today, supercharged with heightened touch and taste from the indica.

"Damn, it was the pool boy?" I said, knocked out of my reverie by the show's reveal.

"Crazy, I know," said Julie. "Never who you expect."

"I guess murder mystery wouldn't be very good if it was always the husband who did it."

Julie smacked her lips ponderously, tasting the air. "Bold idea. Wanna go get boba?"

I smacked my own lips, ghost-tasting her proposition with my superpowered munchies. Now that she mentioned it, I felt over-parched and under-caffcinated, and a little excursion sounded fun. "I think the indica commands it."

"Sorry, I should have warned you. With this strain, the munchies get pretty loud. But let's do it! Southside adventures."

We put on our shoes in the doorway, and Julie swiped a sweater, a joint she had rolled earlier, the lighter, and two sets of keys on her way out. We could already taste the milk tea as we waited for the elevator.

"So, as I was saying earlier, after getting to know Zelda a little better, I think she means w—" Julie cut off as the elevator opened. "Oh my goodness, hi!" She ran into the elevator and gave out a generous hug. "How have you been? I didn't know you lived here! How is Dean doing? I heard you guys were dating now, that's wild! This is my friend, Carlos, by the way. We met the same I met you, actually, at Dean's frat."

Not like this. The East Wind rolled out of the elevator then. My fists clenched, and I felt my body go into a stress response. I planted my feet apart in the elevator threshold like I was bracing to hold it closed, and I double-checked my facial expression to make sure I was doling out a countermeasure of lethal venom.

"Actually, we already know each other," said Rosa, meeting my gaze with a glittering eye. "Things are good, I'm just back for a quiet night in. See you guys around!"

Rosa strode directly out of the elevator I was de-facto blocking, and would have shoulder checked me if I hadn't balked at the last minute and moved aside. The scent of her shampoo whooshed across my face as she went by. Mulled apple spice, autumnal. I could have thrown something down that hallway after her if only my fists would unclench.

A long walk of sullen silence, charmless deflection, and tarnished rapport later, it took a boba straw to the mouth for me to finally relax my jaw.

"I'm sorry, Julie," I said, sliding back the tapioca, "I didn't expect to see Rosa tonight. I was caught off guard and kind of flew off the handle."

"So what's the deal with you guys?"

I set my drink on the table. *I don't really want to get into it.* "Well, I'm still not super ready to go through it all… and besides, I don't really want to drag anybody's name through the mud…" Julie seemed to grow farther away for a moment. "But," I continued, "since I was so weird just now, you deserve some kind of explanation. Basically, Rosa and I used to date in high school. We were together a couple years pretty seriously, codependently maybe, if we're being ungenerous."

In the short time I was talking, Julie had crushed down half her drink. "When did you guys break up? What happened? Why didn't she seem upset to see you?" Her eyes widened, and she drew back for a second. "Do you still like her?" She floated that last question softly, cautiously where she had been chipmunking before, and it hung over us like fog until I broke the suspense to fan it away.

"No, I definitely don't," I said. "I know that much. I've got lots of anger and no closure, but no. I definitely don't."

"Well, is there anything else you'd like to share with me that might help? I'd still like to have a fun evening, if you're interested."

Yeah, everything. Sitting across from Julie there, a part of me wanted to unload every piece of baggage and get instantly real. Prom, the summer, orientation. Not yet. I haven't even unpacked it myself yet. "Thanks, Julie, I really appreciate it. I've got my healing process, and I'm going through it. I'm just trying to figure out how to belong here at this school right now."

"Where else were you trying to belong?"

"Well, I had gotten into Stanford and was thinking—"

Julie startled me then, cutting me off by blowing a raspberry with her hand and mouth. "Nah, fuck Stanfurd, dude." Somehow her drink was empty now. "Is that what you're sad about? What do they have that we don't? Wait no, don't answer that. You know what we have here that they don't? You. And me. And it's okay so far, right?" She clinked her empty cup with my half-empty one. *Half full?* "Not that I don't respect your struggle. I do. In my life too, I know that if we go back and change one thing, it all goes differently. Sometimes I wish it was all different. But I suspect, based on the story so far, that life from here on out is gonna be about walking through some doors and closing others. But wishing you did something else isn't really how you get anywhere. At least it's not how I got here."

I didn't really like what she said, but I didn't really want to argue against it either, since it seemed like she was trying to be kind. So I just looked back at her and didn't say anything. I tried to set my facial expression like I was thinking about her words and not like I was upset by them. Finally, after an extended silence, feeling my high wearing off and my boba running low, I knew I had to say something.

"I want to be grateful, I think." I couldn't look her in the eyes as I said it, but I tried to make myself make eye contact again as I jumped back into it. "Well, I want to be happy anyway, and I think the way to do that is by practicing gratitude for what I have and where I am, and by letting go of the negativity and leaving it in the past. I don't want to be entitled, and I don't want to sound entitled. I know there are plenty of things for me to be thankful for, and there's plenty that could be worse. But the way things have been going, at least since I started here... I just don't really feel thankful."

"For anything?"

"Well..." I thought for a second, then blushed a little, hesitating for a moment to say the first thing that came to mind. "I'm absolutely, positively, unequivocally thankful I met you. The two evenings I've spent with you have been the two highlights of college so far, so thank you."

Julie leaned over the table like an interrogator on *CSI: Miami*. "Yeah?"

Though I could feel my face heating up, I forced myself not to look away. "Yeah."

Julie leaned back in her chair and relished my pinkness for a moment before responding. "I can tell you mean that. I like that I can tell." She pretend-swirled her empty boba cup thoughtfully. "I think you'd at least make my top five highlights for sure." She got up and tossed her empty cup into the nearby trash can with beer pong finesse. "And who knows, the night's still young." With one more flourish, she gestured me out of the shop, pushed my chair in as I pushed hers, and started us on a night walk through campus.

Over and around hills on hills, campus crawled by as we hoofed past building after building of neoclassical architecture, only interrupted here and there by a couple bricky ones and one brutalist behemoth I would always think looked like the Death Star. "Reason number three hundred and five you can be thankful to go here," Julie said, "everybody who graduates here comes out with a great degree and a toned ass that won't quit. Leg day, leg life." I laughed out loud at this, and couldn't help but check hers out kind of reflexively. I think she caught me, because she paused her ascent to bump me playfully, hip to hip.

"Where are we heading?" I asked.

"Almost there." It was a quiet night on campus. We only saw a few people near the beginning of our walk, probably heading to or from the library, but all human sounds faded as we reached the treeline. The creek that ran through campus babbled softly on our right. It wasn't too imposing, just a little thing with walking paths crisscrossing over it. I felt glad I brought my jacket; it finally felt like fall out here. I might even have been cold if not for the exercise. A few more steps and we found ourselves in the middle of campus, out on the esplanade under the university bell tower. Julie stopped at the base of the tower and looked up. "You ever come this way?" she asked.

"Yeah, I have lecture right in there Tuesday Thursday." I pointed across at the squat, unimposing building on the north side of the quad.

"What do you think of it?"

"Well, it's American History, so mostly so far it's just been review of what we learned back in AP—"

"—Not the class," she said, pointing at the tower.

"Hm." I looked at it up and down for a minute. "As far as dicks go, I'd say it's one of the nicer ones."

"As far as *dicks* go?"

"Well," I said, "I'm no expert in architectural history, but you don't really need to be in order to know that there's a whole category of buildings that are just dicks. Towers? Dicks. Skyscrapers? Also dicks. Pretty much anything where they want you to ask how tall it is, is a dick in the minds of the people who designed it. Kind of a Freudian thing I guess."

"Hm." Julie thought for a moment before answering. "And do you know how tall it is?"

"307 feet. A few different people told me during orientation."

"No kidding, like five people told me how tall it was on orientation day too. I guess it really must be just a dick then. Patriarchy." We went quiet for a moment, consumed with thoughts of the patriarchy. "You want to see it from the top?"

My eyes went back and forth from the observation deck to Julie. "You serious? YES. But how?"

She pulled a set of keys from her pocket and jingled them like treats. "Swiped these from my third roommate. Well, not swiped, borrowed. She's one of the carillon players, the bells in the tower—and anyway I'll put them right back before anybody sees."

We rode up the small, dark elevator close together, shoulders touching in the dim lighting. It might have been a gloomy ride if Julie hadn't started us riffing on more dick and shaft-related jokes until I got too embarrassed to keep it going.

"When I visited Stanford, I went to Hoover Tower too," I said as we neared the top. "Our tour guides told me it was 285 feet tall."

"Oh, gross."

"Yeah, so squat and tiny."

"Give me 300 feet at least or don't bother."

"Downright chode-y."

We both broke down into nonsense as the doors opened onto the observation deck. In the center, encased in windows on all sides, stood the hub that controlled the carillon bells. I thought it looked like a piano, but with wooden hand pedals instead of keys. All around it, looking out into the open air on four sides, we could see everything else.

My eyes went out and around in wide circles, out into the glittering night landscape in all directions. Down, onto the campus grounds and north to the sleepy, leafy northside houses and graduate apartments. To my right loomed the rugged eastern foothills and the state park beyond, a dark, rustly, unquiet tangle of shrub and eucalyptus, mammals and birds. Its foothold began just past the highest edge of the football stadium and rolled far out of view. As we circled around, Julie lit another joint and started playing Frank Ocean music from her phone.

We walked together to the south-facing side as she passed me the joint. I let my eyes wander as I exhaled, following the line of Telegraph Avenue from the drunk and munchy student sidewalk Saturday night Southside bustle out to the quiet streets and glittery skyline of greater Oakland beyond.

"So," said Julie, breaking the silence at the end of another long drag, "other than the previously established, sexy, and virile extra 22 feet, how's this stack up to Hoover Tower?"

I smiled a bit at this, but the atmosphere had changed up here. My frivolity blew away with the smoke, and I felt my mind go out as far as my gaze. "It's beautiful, thank you for bringing me."

"Well don't thank me yet," she said, drinking deep pulls from the joint like she drank her boba, "you haven't seen the best side yet." She handed me the last nubbin of joint, pulled away from me, and drifted over to the west-facing, and final side. Maybe I was just that high now, or it had felt so natural to me that I didn't register, but not until she broke away did I realize we had walked the last two sides arm-in-arm.

I followed her to the bars of the observation window and looked out on the twinkling night landscape, perfect as a screensaver. Close to us, on campus and beyond, everything sloped down, bending gently into the San Francisco Bay.

Though its dark waters stirred choppily, they still reflected the full moon against the starless sky. I would find out later, in an astronomy course I would take in a subsequent semester, that this phase on this night was called the 'Harvest Moon.' In place of stars, the city lights from here to San Francisco twinkled against a diffuse fog. They glittered along every building of every shape from here to the TransAmerica Pyramid, culminating in the string of lights, straight ahead across the bay, marking the Golden Gate Bridge, the dividing line between home and the Great Beyond out on the dark water. I brought my gaze back into Julie and to where we stood together.

We huddled together and braced against gusts here on the windward side. My cheeks chapped with cold and my eyes watered behind my glasses. In a moment of calm, the moon broke from below a fog bank and fell on our faces in a streaming silver beam. She gave me another playful bump, hip to hip.

"Thanks, Julie, I do belong here."

"I know, I just wanted to hear you say it."

Overwhelmed with an outpouring of emotion, I turned to face her head on, half-closed my eyes, and leaned in about 90% of the way to a kiss. Julie smiled and turned her face away, and then broke into a full throated laugh.

As cold as my cheeks felt up there in the wind, they had no problem heating right up again. I wanted to slam my face into my hand.

Julie was still laughing. "Hey, hey, it's okay. I had a good feeling about you, and so far, my instincts have been right." She took my hand in hers, interlocking fingers, and leaned her head into the bend of my neck. "But how many nights have we been hanging out? Let's string a few more of these together first, okay?"

Her fingers felt ice-cold in mine, which almost set me to shivering when I wasn't before. But still, they felt nice, comforting, and my low acclimation to human touch flooded my brain with good feelings only multiplied by the weed. I breathed in the smell of her hair with the tower's chill and the dissipating weed smell and settled into a comfortable snuggle. Just then, I remembered Charles's voice in my head and laughed to myself. "Cuffing season."

"What'd you say?" asked Julie.

"Nothing."

Looking out over our home, our school, it seemed in that moment that there stood a whole world of promise available, doors open to us every way we could look. Frank Ocean sang out from Julie's pocket, projecting in a lofi croon just to blow away on the wind.

Julie snuggled me for another minute before looking up. "Hey, I almost forgot. I'm planning on buying some psychedelics soon, hoping to do a trip one of these days. Would you want to do it with me?"

"Oh wow. I've always wanted to do a psychedelic trip, actually. *Magical Mystery Tour* and all that. I'm interested in learning some more information first, but, yeah, pencil me in as a yes!"

Julie squeezed my hand tighter when she registered my enthusiasm. Then she pulled off, rubbed her hands together as much for warmth as for dramatic effect, and said, "Oh the places we'll go."

She embraced me again and we went back to our view. Fall was finally here.

CHAPTER 6

Over the next three weeks, the new autumn seemed to come down all around us. There were still hot days, here and there, but as we got more into the swing of things, I found myself zipping up more layers and crunching more leaves on my now daily hikes up to Julie's place. I wouldn't be heading over today, though. Along with the leaves, the real work of college started to come down hard, culminating in this week from hell for pretty much everybody I knew.

Midterms, papers, problem sets, lab reports, and exams swamped us until we were each completely inundated: clearly we weren't in high school anymore. I had a twelve page research paper on colonial-American religious denominations of the late 17th century. It was for my history class, the one I stopped attending weeks ago when I decided I'd rather hang out with Julie instead. Due tomorrow, hadn't started. So it felt like a pretty easy decision to take a big pile of library books, a smaller pile of canned espresso drinks, and chain myself to my desk until I finished. Well, not my desk.

"You mind if I have one of those double shots?" asked Charles, looking up from his laptop. "I can pay you for it, it's just a whole thing to go out for coffee."

"Don't worry about it." I pulled an espresso can from the top of my pile and tossed it to him. The fact that I could be here in his room and sprawl my stuff out in probably the last empty desk at this university was thanks enough.

"Dang, they're really going at it today," said Charles, taking off his headphones and glancing over at the opposite wall.

"Yeah." I tried really hard not to think about it. I had forgotten my headphones when I left the room, but on my life I couldn't go back in there and get them. So I just sat there, leafing through book after book collecting quotes for my outline, pretending to not hear the noises I was hearing.

"... Jesus Christ, Eddie..."

"... I can't believe you right now..."

"...that's a goddamn lie!"

I wasn't exactly sure when it started, but over the past weeks, Eddie and Zelda had been blasting each other with bad vibes. It would start out innocuously enough, usually with some look or some comment, or some difference of opinion one could find between any two people. They only escalated from there, though, and the tension would usually ratchet up until I grew uncomfortable enough to excuse myself from the room, no sock drawing required. I felt pushed off to Julie's about as often as I felt pulled, but today of all days was not the time.

"Dang," I said, and turned to Charles. "Does it usually go on this long?"

"Nah, this is rare form today, bro." He leaned back to stretch in his chair. "Usually, about ten minutes after you leave, it's either make-up sex, angry sex, or somebody's outta there."

"Can you tell the difference?"

"Dude, listen to that wall. It's basically a window."

"Wow, I'm glad I'm gone then."

Charles swiveled in his chair. "Oh yeah, how's it been going with that girl? You took my advice then?"

I felt myself smile. "Really good, actually. We've been spending a lot of time together since we started hanging out, and I think I really like her."

"That's really cool, dude. You guys made it official yet?"

"Well, no. But that's not a super big deal. We're just kind of hanging out right now, seeing where it goes."

"Right." Charles began to go back to his work, looking sorry he asked.

"But we are planning to do psychedelics together and have a trip," I added.

"WHAT?" Charles swiveled back in his chair to fully face me. "Are you serious, dude?"

I felt alarmed by the concern in his voice. "Well, yeah, just planning right now, we've been so busy—"

"—And you say it's not that serious. Sounds serious to me, man."

"How do you figure?"

Charles cracked open his espresso can and took a swig. During his pause, a bang came from the other side of the wall, then quiet. Charles continued, "I have this cousin, a few years older, that was into this kind of stuff a few years ago when he was in college." I sat up straighter to listen to him. "Anyway, one Thanksgiving we go to see their family… and he's a little bit weird now."

I took a drink of my own coffee, bewildered. "Weird like how?"

"Like quiet, skittish, wouldn't really look at anybody. And he was pretty different from before. After a couple drinks, my aunt said that he'd been going to therapy because he had some sort of 'psychotic break.' When it was just the two of us, my cousin told me that he had a bad acid trip and it got him *messed up*."

"Jesus." I sat back. "What happened to him?"

"Well," Charles said, "he wouldn't say a lot. But what I got from him was that the trip just hit him sideways that time. He started getting really stressed and really paranoid. Then he started hearing things… and seeing things. Horror movie and worst nightmare kind of stuff, looking real, real as I do sitting here. Long story short, he was some kind of traumatized, and to this day he's never really been the same."

"Wow," I said after a short pause. "How long ago was this?" Eddie and Zelda's voices picked up again.

"That Thanksgiving I'm talking about was almost five years ago. He's still like that today."

"Dang, that's really scary."

"Yeah man, do whatever you want. Plenty of people do acid or shrooms and then feel how they feel about it, good or bad. I just say it's not really for me, with the family history and whatnot."

"So why are you telling me this?"

Charles sat up defensively. "Well, shit, man, you asked me why I feel the way I feel. All I'm saying is that doing psychedelics isn't just like pouring a drink or lighting up a joint, it's kind of a big deal."

At that moment, the door to my room swung open hard, and Eddie came out steaming mad. "I'm out of here, I can't deal with this," he yelled back through the closing door. A bang came from the other side, where it sounded like Zelda had thrown something.

Charles and I both craned our necks all the way out without any subtlety. Eddie turned around and caught our gaze as he waited for the elevator. He didn't say anything, but acknowledged us with a grimace and raised eyebrows as he stepped through the open elevator and left the hallway.

"Well," I said, "I'm getting my headphones. I'll probably be back in a minute. Hopefully."

"Cool." Charles turned back to his laptop. "By the way," he said as I was getting up, "my roommates and I are done with midterms tomorrow night, so we're throwing a little get-together in here for the whole floor. You should come. Bring shrooms girl."

I thought about it for a second. Julie's last midterm was tomorrow during the day. I'd be free too, if I got this paper done. "Thanks for the invite, we'll let you know."

"Invite Zelda and Eddie too. Well," he added, as I was halfway out the door, "invite them if it looks like they're handling this better."

"Will do," I said, and ducked into the hallway.

I tapped on the closed door; a voice shot at me from inside. "Forgot your keys, asshole?"

"Zelda, it's me, I'm coming in." I peered around the door as I unlocked it, worried she might throw something, but nothing came. I stepped in to see Zelda lying on her back, looking up at the ceiling from Eddie's bed in the dark. I switched on the lights.

I could only look at Zelda's face for a moment before I felt bad enough to turn the lights off again. Her eyes looked puffed and swollen, and her cheeks flushed out in streaks where the tears hadn't dried. I crossed my side of the room in the dark and switched on my little desk lamp in order to look for my headphones. Other than her sniffling and my rustling, we went quiet for a minute.

"I can't do this, Carlos," she said to the ceiling.

"Sorry, what?" Still no headphones. *Shit.*

"Everything is so hard now," she said, trying to not cry again. "Even when Eddie and I are together, I still have times when I feel alone."

"Hm," I said, turning things over faster now in search of my headphones. *Come on, where are they?* I still had all of this paper still to do and I wasn't the person to handle this. Finally, on the verge of fully tearing through my side of the room, I found the headphones stuck in the crack between my bed and the wall. I picked them up and headed toward the door.

"Carlos, please. I feel like I have so much to do and I have no help and I just *feel alone.* I can't deal with this alone on top of everything else."

I stopped short of opening the door. "Zelda, I'm sorry, I really am. I see that it's pretty hard right now for you. Do you have anybody you can call? Your roommates?"

Zelda almost laughed me out of the room. "Roommates? You know the last time I was back there? I don't. They're probably your roommates by now."

Well, shit. I walked back over and sat down on Eddie's bed. "Look," I said, "It seems like we've both got a lot going on right now, but I do think you're a nice person and I want you to be okay." Zelda sat up and nodded her head. "So, I assume you've got some huge thing due tomorrow just like everybody else. I don't really know the context of your relationship stuff, and I don't think either of us really has the time to get into it right now, but if you don't want to be alone, we can both be in here and work on our stuff at the same time. Okay?"

Zelda showed a small smile. I smiled back, satisfied with how I handled the situation. It seemed to me that she got a few of her bubbles back that had flattened since I last heard her through the wall. Then, Zelda closed her eyes slightly and leaned her face in towards mine.

"What the hell?" I said, jumping off the bed. "Did you just try to kiss me?"

"No, I—" she stammered, "—I'm sorry, that was dumb, I feel silly. I'm just so... *mad* at him."

"Okay," I said, relaxing out of my flinching stance. "Well, don't do that again please."

"Yeah, of course. Sorry. Will you still stay in here though?"

"Well, this is my room, so I'd like to work here, but you're going to have to stay on your side."

"I don't know what came over me," she said, rubbing her forehead. "I mean, I don't really find you attractive at all, like, *at all* at all—"

"Okay, ouch. Let's just forget about it. I'm going to go next door and grab all my stuff, be right back." I opened the door to leave.

"Carlos," she added, "You won't tell anybody about this?"

I thought for a second, standing in the open doorway. "Only if none of this ends up in your novel." I laughed at my own joke as I stepped out of the room. Out of the corner of my eye, I saw Charles duck his head back down to look at his laptop.

CHAPTER 7

The coffee stopped working sometime after midnight. I had been at it all evening; I guess I stopped processing the caffeine. I skimmed over what I had written so far. Okay but not great, I still had about half to write. Maybe I wouldn't sleep tonight.

I looked up at Zelda over the glow of our screens. She kept buzzing along, wired to the point of muttering to herself. I could only assume from the keystrokes that she was better off than I was. I probably shouldn't have passed on the Adderall.

She had offered it to me a few hours earlier when we had finally settled into our work. "I only take one in the longest sessions," she said, pulling the clear pill bag from somewhere in her dress. I had politely declined, not wanting to try anything new last minute, and later I messaged Julie about it.

Zelda's spiking pretty hard on ADHD meds right now

Wild, I didn't think she was the type but tbh I see it

Yeah, she offered me some too, I passed though

Probably for the best, I hear for a lot of people it doesn't affect them the way they expect. How's she looking?

Pretty wound up, but it looks like she's getting work done. How are you?

Pretty bad. I don't really feel prepared at all for the midterm. Should get back to studying.

Alright. I miss you. Can I see you tomorrow?

Meet at my place after my test?

See you then

My heart fluttered a bit as I read Julie's last message. I really felt like melting into a puddle whenever she got cute with me. I might have let myself right then, if I didn't have all this school in my way. I silenced my phone, and right as I set it down I heard the notification chime. I checked, but it was actually Zelda's phone, and she hadn't noticed. It dinged again.

"Zelda. Hey." She snapped out of her intensity to look at me and then her phone. I realized too late that I shouldn't have said anything.

"What the hell is this?" She showed me her phone screen.

"I have no idea." We both looked at a blurry, dark photo taken from what looked like the inside of a kitchen pantry with a bunch of different people's body parts all crammed together. I could make out different people's hands, arms, chests, and a couple of heads sticking into the photo, all at too close proximity to tell what was going on. The phone dinged again, a message of incomprehensible gibberish. Both texts were from Eddie.

"Who does he think he is? What's all this even about?"

"Maybe he's drunk."

"He shouldn't be, he has more work to do than I do tonight. You know what, he probably blew it off."

"Yeah, don't worry about it, we should probably just get back to work and have him explain later."

I ended up getting back to work, but Zelda didn't. An hour passed, then two, and she spent that whole time sucked into her phone. She hunted for Eddie's activity with the same intensity that she had been writing her paper, all the while getting more and more wound up. I watched her saucer eyes narrow and widen again as she flicked, scrolled and clicked. The blue light of the phone screen glowed coldly on her face, washing her out in waifish white. I made a comment every once in a while about getting back to work, but it was no use. I couldn't pull her back.

By two in the morning, I felt completely exhausted and ready to stop writing. My eyes burned and closed by themselves as I tried to reread my work. Terribly rushed, hastily researched, and barely coherent. At least I had made progress and stayed on topic. I could probably still pass if they were feeling generous. I had given up on Zelda an hour before, who had gotten so wound up by now that she started to make strange sounds. She still scrolled feeds on her phone, but had now curled up in bed and pulled her knees to her chest. She had been spiraling for two hours and seemed on the verge of some kind of meltdown. At least she had switched her mug of coffee to water. All this negative energy made me all the more ready to give up as the clock turned 4am and I hit my minimum page count. I crawled into bed, pulled up the covers, and collapsed in a heap. I felt too tired to wonder what she saw on that phone.

Just as I dozed off, a crash against the door made me sit up in a panic. It sounded like someone lowered their shoulder and slammed into it. Zelda bolted up too and let out a yelp of surprise. I waited for the person to try the doorknob, knock, or slam again, but nothing happened. Zelda and I both pointed at the door like the other would answer it, then I got out of bed and went. I peered out the eyehole. Someone was covering it up. I turned the knob cautiously. Without warning, the door swung open with Eddie's full weight behind it, and we both went tumbling to the ground.

"What the hell?!" I sprang up, ready to yell or fight or both. I looked down at Eddie, demanding an explanation, but as seconds passed, he didn't move. He just lay there in a crumpled heap, motionless. He had been leaning against the door, barely conscious. "Help me get him up."

With considerable effort, Zelda and I together got Eddie into a sitting position on the bed. As we put our arms under him, we noticed the smell first. It was a rancid blend. He smelled like expired food, vomit, pee, mixed bodily odors, alcohol, but most of all, cinnamon. He felt sticky to the touch, leading us to believe he had either dumped on himself or drank and sweated out at least a fifth of Fireball whiskey. As soon as we sat him up, Zelda started yelling.

"What the hell have you been up to? Have you lost your mind? I've been following your posts and stories, what kind of depraved weird shit have you been up to today? Did the frat put you up to this? Is this a pledge event? Are you being hazed? I assume you didn't finish any of your midterm studying." As she went on, Eddie gave no indication that he heard her nor even that he knew where he was. He just sat there with eyes unaffixed in a long, glassy stare and breaths fixed in short, shallow gulps. His usually olive skin had turned gray-green, growing more discolored by the moment.

"Zelda, stop," I said. "He's going to throw up." I ran to the corner of the room and grabbed the wastebasket, trying to empty it out and replace the bag as fast as I could. Too late. In one fluid motion, Eddie tilted his head forward, leaned down, opened his mouth, and vomited onto the floor in front of him. At least it was on his side of the room.

"What is that?" asked Zelda, pointing to the vomit. Alarmed, I ran over to the vomit spot. Something moved and flipped around in the soup. "Is that a *goldfish?!*"

Zelda gasped. She looked around for a moment, and then to my amazement, she sprang into action. She reached into the puddle, took the goldfish into her bare hands, and plopped it down into her mug of water sitting on the desk. Eddie didn't seem fazed or even aware of his fishy issue. He grew faint and went limp, sliding off the bed and nearly landing in the vomit spot on the floor. Zelda and I caught him and laid him on his side in bed. In the quick reaction, Zelda touched my arm with her goldfish hands, and I lost it right then. Last straw.

All the inconveniences of the night, all my grievances with my roommates and frustrations with my situation all pointed one way right then. I grew quiet, centered, completely calm with my words and actions. Eye of the storm.

"Sorry," said Zelda, pulling her hand away and wiping it with a napkin. Too late. Neither fast nor slow, I finished rebagging the wastebasket and placed it on the floor next to Eddie's head. I took my water cup, refilled it halfway, and placed it on the desk next to his head. I moved the goldfish mug out of the way so he wouldn't drink it by accident. Then I grabbed up my pillow and blanket in a careful bundle, slipped my phone and keys in my pocket and headed for the door.

I opened the door and said, "You can sleep on my bed, but watch him. Make sure he sleeps on his side. If he turns blue or cold to the touch, call the RA on duty or 911."

"Wait, what about—" but I walked out before she could ask. I went down the hall, found the other doors all closed, and settled for the 8th floor laundry room. *At least it's warm in here.* I ducked in and plopped my pillow down on the piano bench by the dryer. Somebody left the dryer running. I pressed stop, not bothering to check if their clothes had dried. No more today. I flipped the lights off, settled in, and shut my eyes hard. *Next.*

CHAPTER 8

I woke with the sun a few hours later. I cracked my back where it had stiffened from the hard sleep and tiptoed back into my room. Without bothering to change out of my pajamas, I quietly gathered my backpack, sweater, and wallet. Zelda slept in my bed, above the blankets but sprawled out in every direction. Eddie, on his own bed, still slept on his side. I checked the trash can, no vomit. I checked the water cup. Still half full. I slipped on my shoes and grabbed my last canned coffee as I went out the door, chugging the whole thing on the elevator ride down.

I went step after step over the hills of campus, only half awake through the architectural transition of neoclassical to brick to brutalist. Just between brick and brutalist, I ducked into the library for a minute to print my midterm paper. I looked it over once on fresh ink as I climbed past the babbling creek.

...Therefore, it can be reasonably concluded that in the early American colonies, the presence of organized religion played a varying role in formation and structure of colonial society depending on denomination, geography, and terms of respective colonial charters...

Hm. Not likely to win any awards, but looking over again, everything might actually turn out alright. I perked up a bit as I passed under the shadow of the university bell tower and made my way across the quad to my classroom in the squat building on the north end. Up the stairs, into the lecture hall, down some more stairs to the front of the room, I found the professor's graduate student assistant presiding over the stack of midterm papers. He looked down at my pajama pants through tortoiseshell eyeglasses, but didn't say anything as I placed my paper on top. Sorry, graduate student Miles, but I'm not really feeling this class today. Intent on going back to bed, I crossed the room again and made my way toward the door. Maybe I just hadn't been to class in a while, but I didn't remember the previous lectures quite so full. Students crowded elbow-to-elbow in every row I passed. I almost made it through the door when Miles looked up and called out to me across the room, "Excuse me, where are you going?"

I wheeled around to check to see if he was talking to me. He was, and now he looked over his tortoiseshell rims instead of through them. "Oh, I was just feeling kind of sick," I said.

"You'll fail this class though if you don't take the in-person portion of the midterm."

"There's an in-person midterm?!" I couldn't stop myself from yelling. At that moment, most of the class burst out in different reactions, laughing, guffawing, murmuring to each other, texting their friends. "Bro, this guy's fucked," I heard someone say to his seat neighbor. I immediately started sweating.

"Yes," said Miles, "that's why everyone is here and has test materials out. We've been discussing and preparing for this midterm for the last three weeks of class lectures. Let me know if you need to borrow any testing materials."

Three weeks? Kill me. If I had been to this class even once in that time... Defeated, but too embarrassed to react with all the eyes still on me, I walked back to the front of the room to borrow a test booklet. Despite the almost full classroom, I still tried to sit as far as possible from anyone. When time started, I had no clue how to answer the first essay question. I skipped over it, and luckily the second question was something we went over in one of the first weeks of class. I started making my outline, rubbing my tears away so I could still see my writing, and didn't even look up when someone burst in late through the door.

"Sorry I'm late," she said panting, putting her paper on the top of the stack.

"It's ok," said Miles, "did *you* know that there's an in-person midterm today?" Someone I couldn't see snickered under their breath at this.

"Yeah," the girl said, "I'll get right on it." She grabbed a test booklet and sat down next to me in the last empty seat in the room. I wiped away some more tears and sniffled, but as I did so, I caught a familiar scent. Mulled apple spice. *No fucking way.*

I looked up and saw Rosa next to me, looking just as surprised to see me as I felt to see her. "Carlos?" she whispered. "What are you doing here? You look terrible."

I felt my eyes dry instantly. I almost got dizzy at the speed with which all the blood left my head and went down into my clenched fists. "What are *you* doing here?" I hissed back.

"Are you kidding me?" She kept her voice low as Miles had started to notice us. "I come to this class every week. I'm a history major. *You're* the one I've never seen here."

"Excuse me," said Miles, who had walked up behind us while our eyes were off him. "I don't know what this is, but there's no talking allowed during the midterm. If I have to come back here, you'll both be kicked out of the exam and receive a zero score."

"We're so sorry, it won't happen again." Rosa batted her eyes before turning her whole body to face away from me.

"Sorry," I said, and went back to my test. Twenty minutes in, and I finished all the questions I knew how to answer and stared at the rest. Three weeks of blank space stared back.

I looked at Rosa's test, then at Rosa. I remembered her loopy cursive and that pretentious fountain pen from all our time together in AP Everything. The sight of it made me so mad I couldn't bother cheating. Other than her slow dancing in the dark at Dean's frat, I hadn't taken a long look at her in months. Her curly mane of hair rolled up in a tight bun behind her head, and she dressed in full business attire and full-face makeup. Her white button down shirt creased stiffly with fresh starch, and below that she wore a gray pencil skirt, nylon stockings, and matte black flats. She draped her old debate team captain's blazer behind her chair. For good luck, she always said.

Back in high school, Rosa always had anxiety on test days. Nothing really helped her get it under control until she started dressing up for tests like job interviews. I swung the opposite way with my test day clothes, going as baggy and casual as possible for maximum comfort. She would laugh and say we looked like such an odd couple. Once, she kissed me in front of our whole AP Gov class after I said that she put the 'model' in 'Model UN.'

I snapped out of my daydream and scolded myself for smiling at the memory. *She threw you away. She doesn't care at all what happens to you.* I forced my fist to unclench, only to feel my palm ignite with the fireball I couldn't push down anymore. "Why won't you leave me alone?" I whispered, loud enough for her to hear me. She looked up for a moment to scowl at me and went back to writing. I continued, "I haven't even gotten an explanation, and now you're following me around now making sure I can't rebuild my life."

"Carlos," she whispered, "we can't be talking right now."

"Classic." I crossed my arms.

"We're in the mid—"

"—Excuse me," said Miles, who had walked up behind us. "I'll take your tests. You had been warned."

"Please," said Rosa, "I was just telling him not to talk to me."

"I'm sorry," said Miles, "but I caught you both talking, you could have been cheating."

"We weren't talking about anything!" Rosa's eyes started to mist, and she looked to me for help. Miles turned too and searched my face. The rest of the class mostly stopped writing to listen in.

I looked around the class before I responded, calibrating my launch angle for maximum damage. "I know Rosa pretty well," I said, flames in my hands, "and she's mainly interested in a different kind of cheating."

My answer stunned Miles for a moment, leaving him at a loss for words. Rosa started to cry. Other students started chattering again and pulling out their phones in response to my grandstanding, and it took a few moments and threats for Miles to win the room back.

"You two are out of here," Miles said as he turned back to us, clearly flustered. "Consider yourself lucky that I'm not opening an investigation with the Office of Student Conduct." He spoke the last bit to the whole room.

I grabbed my bag and stood up. "I was just about to leave anyway." I walked out without looking back.

Rosa caught up to me under the shadow of the university bell tower. "What the hell is the matter with you?!" Foot traffic scurried around us, but a couple people stopped to stare. I still felt high off what just happened in class, and in the eyes of the passerby I felt another glorious spotlight start to shine on us.

"Oh, so now she wants to talk," I said, putting on my best sneer.

"You're a rat bastard, you know that?"

"You know I just failed that too, right?"

"Are you kidding me? That was all your fault! Four years of your victim narrative bullshit and it still hasn't peaked yet."

I felt my hands shake like lightning might come out. "Oh, so we're getting into it? Because if you're not going to run away with no explanation this time, I have some things to say."

"Fine, but I'm going first," she said. "I'm not going to get shit on by you twice in a day before I have my say."

"Go ahead then."

"It's obvious that you don't want to be here. It was obvious today, it was obvious when you followed me to come to school here even though you didn't want to, and it should have been obvious when I decided I didn't want to start this new chapter of my life chained to a self-hating piece of shit like you."

I screamed so loudly in my head that my stomach started hurting. I felt like my brain was going to split in half. At the same time, the sleep and caffeine debt came back to collect. I felt weak and unsteady, and the morning brightness layered on top of my white-hot rage to make me light sensitive and dizzy. The only thing keeping me standing? A full-body stress response cranked all the way to fight mode. Rosa and I still knew how to push each other's buttons. Despite everything, right then there was nowhere I would have rather been.

Rosa continued, "From the moment you registered here, you treated me and everybody else like we were beneath you, and you *still* do. Just because you could have gone to *Stanfuuuurd,* I should be indebted to you for choosing me and worship the ground you walk on? And if I don't, you gaslight me about how ungrateful and bitchy I am? You're vile."

I waited a moment before responding. "Are you done? My turn? Ok. First of all, I disavow and disagree with everything you said. Alright, debate captain? I would go into detail, but I'm afraid the second I get into it, you'll up and leave *again* without listening to anything. So I'll keep it short. I'm not gonna indict you, like you just did to me. We've got no judge except us anyway, so no point. I'm just gonna ask you three questions, and if you're real in your answers, I'll be satisfied."

"What the hell is this, Jeopardy? Suck on it, Trebek."

"In Jeopardy, Trebek gives statements, and the answers are questions, idiot. Just listen."

Rosa rolled her eyes and crossed her arms, but stayed where she was. I continued, "Question one: If you didn't want to be together, and you didn't want me 'chained to you,' why did you ask me so many times to come here to school so we could 'be together?'" Rosa scowled at me but didn't say anything. "No, nothing? Alright, question two. All this stuff you're saying, all these things you're mad about, it's news to me. Why have you never said any of it before right now? We were together for *years*. We couldn't have a conversation about this even once during that time?"

Rosa looked away, furious. I thought she would hit me right then. I would have preferred that. Instead, she lowered her eyes, turned her back to me, and started walking away.

I couldn't restrain myself. "Really? Gonna do this again?" The other students in the morning foot traffic walked widely around us, and a small group standing close by talked amongst themselves about whether they should intervene. "Question three!" I yelled after her. "Why'd you cheat on me before you ended it? How many times? How many people?" Rosa receded into the sunlight, picking up her pace without looking back. "Rosa! ROSAAAAAAA!!!!"

Just then, Dean and two Theta Chi frat brothers came fast-walking up to me. "Hey, you harassing my girl, bro?" Dean said, peacocking into my personal space. He pushed his chest out, tabletop-wide, within inches of my face.

"Get your filthy hands off me, you goon," I said, and tried to push away his raised arm with mine. Instead, Dean grabbed me hard by the wrist and twisted my arm behind my back so that I spun around to face away from him. He put his right leg in between mine and swept my ankle, bringing me down to the ground hard but controlled. I strained against his weight on top of me, but he was too strong.

"I'm not trying to hurt you," Dean said, as much to the lingering crowd as to me, "but I am going to stop you from trying to hurt anyone else!"

"What the hell are you talking about?" I wheezed through the knee pressing my chest.

"Calm down," Dean said, loudly again. Then he whispered softly to just me. "Stay down until we've gone away if you know what's good for you." I kept trying to struggle against him, but it was no use. He continued, "Rosa's told me all about you. Maybe I should tell Julie what a problematic woman-hating piece of shit she's hanging out with."

He got off me then and started walking away with his posse. Blind with rage, I leapt up and charged him at full speed, aiming to punch him in the back of his head. Instead, he spun around at the last second, grabbed my wrist again, and brought me down just like last time, except harder and all at once. As he slammed me down on my back, I hit my tailbone on the asphalt and felt a sharp pain shoot up my spine. Blocking with his body so no one could see, he dug his elbow in hard underneath my ribs, knocking the wind out of me and leaving me unable to talk or even cry out.

"Stop attacking me, leave me alone!" he said for everyone to hear. Then he bent down and whispered to me, "Julie can make up her own mind, but I'm going to tell her the truth about you. If you ever do anything to hurt her, *I'll kill you.*" He got up and left me where I was, gasping for air on the ground. "Stay away from Rosa, she wants nothing to do with you!" he said in a parting shot. One or two bystanders cheered, but almost everyone else turned about-face and went about their business. The other two Theta Chi brothers lingered for a moment, but walked away when they saw I couldn't get up again.

My body, faint and exhausted, gave out on me right there in the heart of campus. For the next half minute, I couldn't do anything but lie on my back, stare up at the old bell tower, and try not to cry or pee myself in public.

CHAPTER 9

I was supposed to meet Julie after my midterm, but I put it off. I couldn't bring myself to go right away, so I made some excuse and rescheduled for the afternoon. I didn't remember the walk home; after I got there I took a long shower and cried the whole time, only forcing myself to stop when someone walked into the communal bathroom and might have heard me. I shut myself in my room for the rest of the morning, alone but unable to sleep despite my weakness.

From the moment I got off the ground until I walked up to Julie's door hours later, I could only spare half a brain on myself and my surroundings. The other half thought about Rosa and the things we said to each other. I never got any closure since the day we broke up, so I had closed a door in my mind to some of the things that caused me pain. I still wasn't ready to open it again, but Rosa's words today made me want to look back through the keyhole. As I dusted myself off from Dean's aggravated battery, I thought about the last time Rosa and I were happy together. The last time she asked me to come to school here together.

We went to senior prom together last spring. I had asked Rosa during debate team practice. It wasn't the most grandiloquent proposal of that season, the way I did it was actually kind of nerdy, but I felt like we made it something special and our own. During practice, one of my teammates posed the debate question: "Should Rosa go to prom with Carlos?" I took the affirmative argument. After presenting for a short amount of time about all the reasons we'd have so much fun together, I went off script with my closing arguments. "Lastly, we should go to prom together because I love you."

At the end of my spiel, another one of our teammates rolled a whiteboard from the back of the room and flipped it around, revealing "Prom?" spelled out on the back in judge's scoresheets. Rosa, not usually the sap, cried and hugged my neck when she said yes.

"So, are you excited for tonight?"

I looked around, snapping out of my flashback. I came back to my building on the eighth floor wearing only a towel and holding my shower caddy. "What?" I asked, still trying to reorient myself in time and space after leaving my brain in the sun.

"I said, are you excited for tonight?" It was Charles, who had caught me between my room and the bathroom as I made my way to the shower. "Come on, bro, you didn't forget, right? Our party in our room tonight? You and shrooms girl still coming?"

"Right, yeah," I said, and remembered. "Yeah, it's been a hell of a week, we'll come over and unwind. Is it going to be a lot of people?"

"Pretty much just people from the floor and their S/O's. Might get a little crowded for one room, but if that happens, we'll just ask somebody else to open up theirs."

"Alright, cool." I fiddled with my shower caddy and realized I forgot my shampoo. "Need us to bring anything?"

Charles thought for a second. "Could you bring some weed? If it's not too much trouble. Jian has us covered for the alcohol."

"Jian, really?" From everything I heard, Jian was a sheltered workaholic that had never even been to an American party before. "Is he gonna know what to buy?"

"Dunno." Charles shrugged his shoulders. "He seemed pretty excited about it, even said he'd pay for it himself. So I said why not? Worst case, we'd pretty much drink anything anyway."

"Alright, see you tonight then." I left him and my shampoo, retreating into the shower and back into my memories.

*   *   *

As I had remembered it, prom last year succeeded in every way it needed to. They held it in the lobby of the California Science Center. Pictures turned out really well. The music and food flopped, but didn't matter. Rosa and I laughed together as we danced, mostly ironically, to what she called 'bar mitzvah turn-up music.' Later I always remembered her as cynical, but back then you couldn't be cool without being too cool for something. Personally, I'd rather be happy than cool, but I still don't know how to do both. Eventually, a slow song came on and all the couples came out to dance. As Rosa wrinkled her nose and laughed us off the dance floor, I pretended I wasn't sad about it. "What's wrong?" she asked.

"Nothing," I lied. "We heading to where all the cool kids are or what?"

She searched my face for a moment. Though we stood way off the dance floor by now, she squared her shoulders parallel to mine and put her arms around me like we would two-step. I put my hands on her hips in response. I felt the curves of her waist under her silver sparkly sequined dress. I smiled at her.

"What is it?" she asked.

I pulled Rosa a little closer and swayed to the music. I looked her deep in the eyes and tried to think of something that would make her smile. "You look like a sexy disco ball."

She pulled away and slapped my arm, but laughed the while doing it. I had her.

"You know what, you're right, let's go where the cool kids are," she said. With a sparkly pirouette, party lights glinting off her dress, she twirled around and beckoned me to follow her. Following the click of her heels on the hard ground, we walked away from the dance floor, up the escalator, past the table of cafeteria-quality food, and around behind the prop photo booth. The crowds started to dwindle as we reached the farthest back corner of our designated event space.

"Where are we going?" I wondered aloud.

"You'll see," she smiled. "I scouted it out right after we got here. Will you follow me?" Rosa gestured under and past a velvet rope that marked the end of our supervision and blocked off the entrance to the rest of the museum.

I fidgeted with my tuxedo for a moment, straightening my bow tie and pulling down my shirt sleeves underneath my jacket as I looked to the exhibits beyond. I felt a sweat coming on, and I couldn't tell if I was too nervous to be excited or too excited to be nervous. "I'll follow you anywhere," I finally said.

Rosa smiled wickedly, her eyes matching the hunger that she must have seen in mine. I knew immediately that I gave the right answer. "Then come on, cool kid," she teased. She bent low at the waist in order to clear underneath the velvet rope, making a point to rub up against me in the process. If she asked me right then, I'd have done a front handspring over that rope.

* * *

Out of the shower, out of my own head, and back in my room up on eighth floor, I was finally too tired to keep crying. I was alone, thank goodness, and finally had a free moment for the first time in a day and a half to take stock of myself. I felt a lot better after showering, but still nowhere near okay. Down to my bones, I felt about ten years older today than yesterday, and all I wanted to do was sleep forever. But not yet.

I'd have to drop that history class. I doubt that with a zero on the midterm there'd be any way to make up a halfway decent grade by the end of the semester. I could just take it in the spring. As long as that's not exactly what Rosa was doing as well. I need to get high.

It took a few minutes of rummaging around my room for me to find the remnants of a half finished joint Julie and I had shared a few days ago, and a few more minutes to find the lighter that fell underneath my bed at that time. During the search, I noticed a new fixture on top of Eddie's desk. I went over and examined it carefully as I flicked the lighter and took my first drag.

"Goddamn," I said to the walls through the joint in my mouth, "That was fast." Sitting on Eddie's desk was the goldfish from last night. It was inside a large fish bowl, complete with decorative pink rocks, a ceramic skull, a plastic treasure chest, and a fun little scroll that read, "DEAD MEN TELL NO TALES". *Three guesses who pulled this one off.*

Zelda's goldfish kept me company for the rest of my smoke session. It was an easy silence. We would stare at each other for a few seconds, then he would turn back to guarding his treasure and I would go back to getting comfortably numb. I could tell he was going to make a great roommate.

Once the joint was finished and I was sufficiently spaced out, I crawled into bed and finished reliving my memory of my time with Rosa at prom. Though I was too high to finish it off, I touched myself while I thought about the rest of that night those months ago. I didn't even remember to feel guilty this time.

*   *   *

Rosa and I zipped all around the museum, excited by our rebellious streak. We kissed passionately in the Transportation exhibit as we hid from a school chaperone making his rounds. Our hands wandered more than we did in Air and Space, and we tried and failed to get into each other's clothes in the IMAX theater (it was locked up for the night, unfortunately). Each time, as we neared the moment where we'd become fully enmeshed, Rosa would break it off, tell me she was looking for a place more exciting, more romantic, more perfect, and flit away. She led me around by the belt buckle, and I was happy to follow.

Finally, we made it to the place where our dreams were real: the ecosystems exhibit. We laughed and skipped around, but then we came to a room that stopped us dead in our tracks. It was a large tunnel all encased in clear glass. Through it, in the murky blue-green semi-darkness, was a whole kelp forest, a lush tangle of plants and animals. I grabbed Rosa's hand as we surveyed the exhibit all around us. Small sharks swam in lazy circles overhead, spiny lobsters crawled slowly across the seafloor, and pancake-flat rays slid their way up and over the glass as the kelp swayed back and forth in the churning water.

I turned squarely to face Rosa. With her high heels, we were about the same height, and from that vantage she looked straight into me with starbright eyes. She smiled at me then, not slyly or mischievously like she had been all night, but timidly, almost blushing. Seeing her like that made me timid as well, and I smiled back. We leaned forward to kiss, differently from all the other times that night. We were slow, bashful, like it was our first time. As we touched, the undersea forest swirled around us, our little bubble outside of time and words.

"Are you glad you followed me?" Rosa asked, still embracing me after our lips parted.

"Like I said, I'd follow you anywhere," I said, love in my eyes.

Rosa's sly smile returned. "That's good to know. Actually, on the subject of following me, I have something to talk to you about."

"What is it?"

"Oh, we can get into it later. Time and place."

"I love you." As I said so, my hands wandered around her waist and hips, tugging over and around the fabric of her dress.

Keeping that smile, Rosa didn't respond at first as she searched for something in my eyes. I could feel her weighing and measuring, and I prayed she would find what she was looking for. After a suspended moment, she softened. "I love you too." She flashed her teeth as she pulled her hair tie off her wrist and wound her hair into a loose bun. There in the kelp forest, we didn't stop ourselves anymore from doing everything we wanted to make each other feel good.

We were both nervous, but we laughed each other through every clumsy unzipping and fumbled unbuckling as we tried to navigate the edge of the world together. Through the whole experience, I only fell out of the moment once, when a largemouth bass swam up to the glass to investigate what was going on. I freaked out a little when he made eye contact with me, but after a few seconds, unable to make heads or tails of what he was looking at, he turned and drifted away.

CHAPTER 10

I used the walk to Julie's dorm to compose myself and put thoughts of the spring and summer out of my mind. *This morning too. Or has she already heard?* I had already done a lot of reflecting and crying myself out today. Julie and I had spent weeks together by now, but at this point we were still unofficial. Bursting my emotional baggage all over her was the last thing that would help the situation. Besides, I missed her a lot this week while we were so busy. A happy reunion would be best.

I took a breath, put on a smile, and knocked. No response. I texted Julie that I was at the door and waited a moment. No response. So I knocked again.

"Who is it? What do you want?" yelled a voice from inside the door. I stood up straighter in surprise. It was a woman's voice, but not Julie's. Also, whoever it was wasn't standing right inside the door, but sounded like they were yelling across the length of the apartment.

"It's Carlos, I'm here to see Julie."

The voice changed to yelling in Korean, and wasn't directed towards the door anymore. There was more yelling, then more knocking from the inside. It seemed like she wasn't getting responses either.

My hands started sweating. "If it's too much trouble, I c—"

The door swung open right then. The girl who opened it eyed me warily, holding the door only halfway open. I regarded her for a moment before realizing who I was talking to.

"Oh, you must be Carolyn, the third roommate! Nice to finally meet you."

Carolyn didn't respond, but continued to inspect me with her gaze. I couldn't help but do the same.

Carolyn was a head taller than Julie but rail-thin, and had straight black hair with stark bangs. I only met her eyes for a moment. They were dark brown, almost black, piercing, and narrow. When we locked eyes, hers narrowed even further in unreserved suspicion, sharpening until I felt I was staring down the tip of a spear. I yielded and looked down at the ground. I don't know how long it was, but once our mutual circumspection started getting awkward, Carolyn turned away. She abandoned her post at the threshold, walked straight back to her room, and closed the door to her room behind her, all without speaking or looking back.

I shook out my jitters as I stepped inside and closed the door behind me. The place looked a little more lived-in since I last saw it, but that seemed only natural with all the studying we'd all been doing this week. Dishes and papers covered every flat surface above ground level, and the chemistry textbook sitting on the coffee table was left open to a section called 'ion chromatography.' I crossed the room to Julie's door and knocked. No response.

"Julie?" I creaked open the door. There on the bed, one square foot stuck out from under a heap of linens. I crept to the front of the bed about where her head was. I couldn't see her face under a bird's nest of hair. "Julie," I repeated, sitting down beside her.

Suddenly, one naked eye flashed open and Julie let out a shriek of surprise.

"It's okay, it's me!" I said quickly, getting up.

Julie sat up, but pulled the blanket over her head and body so I couldn't see her. "What are you doing here?"

I tried not to sound hurt by her question. "We were going to meet up here when we were both done with midterms. I texted you that I was here, but I guess you were asleep. Carolyn let me in."

"Hm." The mound shifted underneath the blanket. One arm shot out from under the blanket to grab her phone before retreating back in. "You scared me. Is it time for that party on your floor already?"

"Well no," I said, "but I thought it would also be nice if I met up with you here and we hung out a bit before getting ready."

"Oh no, can't do that." The mound shook gravely underneath the blanket. "You're going to have to wait outside."

My heart rose in my throat like it might choke me. "I'm sorry I snuck in here and startled you, I didn't mean to—"

"–No, it's not that." One hand came back out again, this time to hold mine. My anxiety quickened. Was she really upset with me? Are we not working well together? Is she tired of this? Did Dean tell her about today? About whatever Rosa told him? Or did she independently come to the same conclusion about me as Rosa did? *I didn't want to start this new chapter of my life chained to a self-hating piece of shit like you.*

"It's just that…" Julie continued, "I don't want you to see me without makeup yet."

"Whaaaaaa…" I didn't understand. "But the first night I came over here, we were just watching movies on the couch, you weren't wearing any makeup then."

Julie's mound shook with laughter and changed to her Sith lord voice. "My sweet boy, your innocence is so cute. But yeah, I was wearing makeup then, and eyelashes. And those pajamas were planned too, I usually just sleep in my underwear." To illustrate her last point, she swung one leg out from under the blanket, exposing herself out to her mid thigh before sliding it back under.

"Well, okay," I said, reaching to pull off the covers, "I don't really care how you look without makeup, I'm sure you're bea—"

When I tugged at the blanket, Julie let out another screech and clamped herself in tighter.

"Okay, I'm sorry, won't do that again. It's just been a really long week, and I miss being with you a lot."

"No, I'm sorry," said Julie, "you must think it's really stupid."

"No, not at all. It's okay." I hugged the mound right about where her shoulders were. "I'll work hard and build our trust and earn the Julie no-makeup edition. And when I do, I'm sure I'll find that Julie just as beautiful and special as all the other versions 'I've seen." The hand that retracted before came back out to squeeze mine. I thought for a moment. "Actually, I have an idea. Don't move, I'll be back in ten seconds."

I left Julie's room and crossed the common area to the farthest door. On it was 'Z E L D A' spelled out in pink foam letters. I knocked lightly to make sure she wasn't in there and let myself in. *Let's see, I've seen her wear it before, but not recently, meaning it must be here.* I spotted it on her desk, an anatomically-correct ceramic skull wearing my prize: a glittery pink sleeping eye mask. I picked it up. Across the front of the mask I read, 'perchance to dream' in white embroidery. *English majors.* "Now get thee to my lady's chambers," I joked to myself as I slipped it on over my eyes.

I felt my way back to Julie's room without peeking. "Julie?" I called out. "You can come out now, I promise I can't see you." A few seconds passed under the blindfold, then I heard the blanket rustle off. "Can I sit with you?"

"Come to bed, but leave that on. Hold me." I scrambled under the blanket and pressed against her seated frame, chest to back. She was mostly warm under the blanket, but I still had to hold back a shudder when she grazed me with her cold hands. "So," she asked, "how was your week?"

"Straight madness. Unbridled insanity."

"Unmitigated malarkey?" she asked. I laughed at this. We continued riffing until we scraped rock bottom six or seven later with 'big bad sad mad,' then I continued on.

"Eddie and Zelda are fighting all the time, Zelda got a goldfish, Eddie might be getting hazed, I drank about twelve cans of espresso last night—"

"—Eddie might be getting hazed? At Theta Chi?" she interrupted. "That's pretty problematic, I should talk to Dean about it." Uh oh.

"No, don't talk to Dean," I said too hastily.

"Why not?" I was still blindfolded, but I could feel her eyes on me.

"No need," I lied. "'Hazed' is a bit of a strong word, I don't want to get anybody in trouble over what might be an exaggeration."

"Are you exaggerating?"

"Well, no, but I think Eddie sees it more generously than I do and I don't want to rock the boat."

"Okay…"

I changed the subject. "How was your midterm today?"

Julie let out a heavy sigh. "I studied so hard all week for this chem midterm, and I didn't even finish. I'm so mad at myself. I think I could have figured out everything, but I ran out of time."

"I'm sorry," I said, squeezing her hand. "What can I do to help you feel better?"

"I'm sure I'll think of something." She leaned back to rest her head in the crook of my neck. In response, I lifted my arm and wrapped it around her shoulders. "For now, I think I need to just get really trashed and forget all about this week."

"You said it," I agreed. "I just need to party it out too."

"Oh yeah? How did your paper turn out?"

"Alright, mainly just tired from staying up all night finishing it." *Time and place.*

"Happy for you. If it sounds good to you, we're okay to chill here until we're ready to head over."

It did sound good to me, so I leaned back until I flopped down in bed. Finally at rest, I felt my brain and body start to shut down in waves. The sleeping eye mask certainly didn't help.

I was nearly unconscious, I don't know how many minutes later, when Julie rolled over and asked me if Carolyn could come to the party. I was incredulous.

"Are you sure it's really her kind of scene? Think she'd have fun?"

"Oh yeah, Carolyn is really shy and stays home a lot, she definitely needs this."

"Hold on." I sat up. "I've been here every day for the last three weeks and this is the first time I've seen her."

"Well, she's been here every time, she just stays in her room."

"WHAT?" I exclaimed, whipping off my eye mask. In response, Julie let out a yelp and ducked under the covers. I thought about the thin walls back at my own dorm. "So she knows when I'm here? She can hear us when we—when we're in here?"

"It's okay," she said, slipping my mask back on with her hands and coming out. "Carolyn looks out for me, gives me good advice, makes sure I don't get up to too much trouble. She's like the *unnie* I never had growing up." Julie ran one hand over the top of my shirt and pants, and swung one leg over my two. "And besides," she continued, starting to rub the flat of my back, "I don't know that many people at this party, I want more friends to talk to. Is that okay?"

I caved easily with her hands on me. "Yeah, I'll talk to Charles." Julie squealed and gave me three kisses on the eye mask, cheek, and lips. As she did so, she rolled fully on top of me, chest to chest under the blanket. At that moment I had the urge to strip off my clothes to match Julie's 'pajamas,' but I let it pass, not sure yet where this was going.

Julie and I rolled around playfully for a few moments, but my complete exhaustion overtook me once again and I was powerless to stop it this time. The last thing I heard as I fell asleep was Julie remembering aloud, "By the way, Dean messaged me earlier today. He said the acid tabs are ready and he wants you to pick them up.

CHAPTER 11

A blustery wind whipped us as Julie, Carolyn, and I set out that night from the foothill dorm. I was thankful Julie and I had decided to dress warmly when we were getting ready. Already, the leaves of fall started to blow through the air. I watched one as it glanced off my windbreaker and lodged itself in Carolyn's long black hair. She uncrossed her arms for a moment to pluck it out, and then continued on, bent double against the wind.

The sight of her made me want to zip my jacket higher; Carolyn had dressed for indoors. It was probably going to be warm in the tiny dorm room crammed with all those people, so she only dressed in shorts and a shirt before coming out with us. I could hear her teeth chattering behind me as we went.

"Here," I said, scrambling out of my jacket, "put it on."

Carolyn didn't speak, but instead looked at me, looked back down at the ground, set her teeth to stop them chattering, and walked on. "Alright," I said, and put my arms back in the sleeves. I kept walking, but Julie took one arm from her long overcoat and fit Carolyn inside with her, shoulder to shoulder. I bristled a little but tried not to show it. Carolyn had sequestered herself in the bathroom with Julie back when they were getting ready, and now this jacket thing made me third wheel twice in one hour. I could see Julie all made-up and long-lashed again, but how was still a secret.

"So when and where am I picking up the tabs from Dean?" I was asking for the third time that evening, hoping she'd give me some new information that she hadn't shared already.

"Again, he said sometime this weekend, at Theta Chi." Her voice sounded matter of fact, but I wondered if she was just hiding her questions better than I was. *Stop asking.*

"Why me?" I asked, unable to stop.

Julie thought for a moment as she braced against the wind. "Didn't say. He probably just wants to catch up with you, know how you're doing. He asks about you all the time."

I started to shiver, but not from the cold. The idea of going to see Dean alone under this pretext filled me with dread. Was he going to assault me again? Set his guys on me? Haze me like he was doing to Eddie? I thought about not going. One thing was clear: he hadn't told Julie about what happened today. Clearly the worst way to come clean with Julie would be for him to expose me, and he'd probably dig up Rosa on top of that. Besides, I had already given Julie an enthusiastic 'yes' when she asked to trip together. There was no way to go back on that without inviting more questions.

"Tell Dean that I'll see him soon," I said, and set my teeth closed against the wind.

When we finally came up to my building, we found a guy and a girl huddled together close to the building entrance. They looked up from their phones and moved out of our way when I got my keys out.

"Hey, I'm really sorry, but would you mind letting us in?" The guy asked me.

"Sure, you live here?"

"Sort of. My roommate is hosting this kickback on our floor right now, and I guess he hasn't checked his messages to know we're down here."

"Is Charles your roommate?"

"Yes!" he said, lighting up. "You know him?"

"Yeah, I live next door. You're Abhas, then?"

"Yeah, that's me," said Abhas. He was on the taller side, but to my eyes, that was about all he had going for him. His bony hand skewed out and grabbed mine awkwardly, wriggling at the wrist. After an appropriately long moment, I extracted my hand back. "Also," he gestured to his right as he said it, "this is my girlfriend, Priyanka."

Before I had the chance to put my hand back down at my side, Priyanka cut in and grabbed it with surprising strength. "My friends call me Priya," she said, smiling broadly, "I'm so excited to finally get to know our floormates. What did you say your name was again?"

Our floormates? "Carlos." I tried to break the handshake too early, resulting in an awkward exchange where I tugged for a moment before she let go. "And this is my—this is Julie." I lost all momentum as I said it and tried to fade away. The rest of our group of five all exchanged names and greetings, except

Carolyn, who only forced a small smile and nodded to each of them.

Once inside, we all squeezed into the tiny elevator. "Anybody want some gum?" asked Priyanka. Everyone accepted, and soon the air filled with the smell of sugar–free spearmint.

"Abhas," I asked, trying not to smack my gum, "if you live here, why don't you have a key?"

"Right, that." Abhas gave a nervous tic, making me sorry I asked. "I lost it just about the first day I moved in. I didn't want to buy a new one, since I'm staying at Priya's most of the time anyway, so Charles just lets me in whenever I need clothes for something."

I nodded and turned to face the door, and gum chewing filled the silence for the rest of the ride up. Finally, we spilled out onto eighth floor and found a lively bunch of people overflowing from Charles's room.

The first thing I noticed upon stepping in, besides the crowd, was the cleanliness. On a typical day, this room that I had spent so much time in was full of trash all over the floor and dirty even in the smallest ways. Not only was the floor clean *(did they rent a vacuum?)*, but the layout of the room was completely changed too. One desk in the middle had solo cups and a lone bottle of half-empty fireball whiskey on it, but the other two were moved out into the hallway to make more space. I panned out and examined the obvious: the room was bursting with people. They were all crammed together in the 12x12 foot space, sitting in the desk chairs, standing, even sitting up in the lofted beds.

Good turnout. I searched around for Charles until I spotted him sitting up in his loft bed and looking at his phone worriedly. I started moving my way over to him, but Eddie caught my attention first.

"What's up, dude?" he said, gathering me up in a bear hug and squeezing until he lifted me off the ground.

"Hhhhhh," was all I could get out. He put me down after a moment. I caught my breath. "I'm good. How're you feeling?"

"Oh man. I have had the hangover *of my life* all day. I'm just living on water and ibuprofen. I was only able to force down some food at dinner a couple hours ago."

I nodded gravely. "I believe it. You remember much about last night?"

"I don't remember much after leaving Theta Chi. Zelda told me today that you helped take care of me when I got back." He stooped down to my level and stared into my eyes, grabbing both my hands in his. "Thank you so much, man. You're a true friend."

"It's nothing." I blushed and pulled my hands away. And it really was nothing. Eddie had always been affectionate and touchy with me since we were kids, and I didn't particularly mind, but it felt a little weird in front of everybody.

Julie cut out from behind me and went straight for Eddie. "Hey, guy, how are things over at Theta Chi?" She put on a friendly face, but I could feel she was probing.

"Julie!" He put out a hand to shake, but Julie went in for the hug. They embraced and he grinned with satisfaction. "Things are good, yeah. Dean is such a cool guy, I'm really happy to have him as our frat president. He talks about you all the time, all the wild stuff you used to get up to in high school. Not like *this* guy." He pointed at me and laughed as he said it.

"Yeah," said Julie, looking nostalgic. I started to steam up over the Dean love party playing out in front of me. I was still crafting a way to cut back into the conversation when Priyanka beat me to it.

"Hi," Priyanka said to Eddie, flashing two rows of perfectly straight white teeth. I hadn't noticed in the darkness of the outside or the dimness of the elevator, but Priyanka's far-and-away best feature was a winning smile that looked like something out of a toothpaste commercial. Set against her brown face, it was dazzling, bordering on ridiculous. *Maybe her parents are dentists or something.* Still smiling and chewing her gum, she continued, "Do you know where the bathroom is?"

"Yeah, about halfway down the hall on the right, going away from the elevator." Eddie flashed his own smile right back, almost as perfect, and between the two of them I thought I was watching the homecoming court parade. "I'm Eddie, by the way."

"My friends call me Priya." Priyanka beamed again. As she did so, she ran her eyes conspicuously across the length of his arms and chest. She went in for a hug as well, but Eddie held her to a handshake. She continued, "We're so excited to see you all in our room, I'm dying to make some new friends." Finally, she walked away. *Our room?* I remembered and looked over at Abhas, who was still barely inside the door. He fidgeted and looked at the ground; he hadn't even talked to anyone yet.

Even Carolyn was doing better, at least she was all the way inside and looking for alcohol.

"Know where I can get a drink?" I asked Eddie.

"Yeah, that's the thing," he said, scratching his head. "Looks like our guy hasn't shown up yet. Charles said his other roommate was supposed to take care of it, but nobody's heard from him."

"Dang." I looked around again. "Without alcohol, most of these people will probably just go to bed."

"Yeah, Charles is really stressed about it." He pointed to the lone liquor bottle on the desk. "I put the rest of my Fireball up for grabs, but I don't have many takers yet."

"I guess people don't want to just shoot straight whiskey and nothing else," I said. "Still, it was really nice of you to pitch in."

Eddie made a sour face. "Not really. After last night's whole thing, I can hardly even look at a bottle of Fireball ever again."

I picked up the bottle and a solo cup and poured in a splash. When I put it to my face, my body reacted on its own. I gagged on the smell so hard I accidentally swallowed my gum. The cinnamon odor flooded my memories. For a split second, I was back on the couch in Dean's room, on hands and knees over the wastebasket, wringing my stomach inside-out. All the smells were mixing and swirling around my face, but especially cinnamon. I put the cup down.

"Yeah, me too." I looked around the party. By now, the people I walked in the door with were intermingling, and Eddie and I were alone in the crowd. "Hey, before I miss the chance,

I wanted to ask you. What happened last night at the frat? What happened to you?"

A shade passed over Eddie's face. He caught the slip in an instant, though, and put the breezy smirk back on. "You mean, why did I come home with a live goldfish in me? Alright, I guess I owe you an explanation. But later. I've been at it with Zelda about it for half the day already, and I'm just trying to have some fun right now."

"Well, okay, I guess I am too then. Catch up soon." I turned to leave, but Eddie caught me by the shoulder.

"By the way, I've got some good stuff to try later, once the party gets more underway. Come find me if you want some." He tapped his nose with his finger as he said it. I didn't know what he meant, but I still nodded before turning away.

I started getting sweaty from the stuffiness, so I went to find Julie and store our jackets in my room. Carolyn followed us in, not knowing anybody else. I opened the door expecting an empty room. I should have known.

She never told her love,
But let concealment, like a worm i' the bud,
Feed on her damask cheek: she pined in thought,
And with a green and yellow melancholy
She sat, like patience on a monument,
Smiling at grief. Was not this love indeed?

Without looking up out of her bed, Zelda started her soliloquy the moment I opened the door. She was slurring her words and holding back tears, but it was clear she had practiced for this.

"Is she serious right now?" I looked around incredulously. I quickly wiped the smile off my face when it was clear that Julie and Carolyn weren't amused. I turned back to Zelda. "Everything alright?" Just then, Zelda stopped holding back and burst into dramatic sobs. I couldn't hide my grimace. "Nope, alright, I'm out of here." I tossed my jacket onto my bed from across the room and turned to leave. Julie blocked my way.

"We can't just leave her like this," she said, looking at me seriously. "She told me the other day that you guys were becoming friends. Let's see it, then." I held back a grumble as I walked over. I poured Zelda a glass of water and took a seat at Eddie's desk chair as the other two joined her in bed.

It was a few minutes before she was ready to talk. During that time, Carolyn sat with Zelda's head in her lap and stroked her hair while Julie soft-spoke positive affirmations. I was mostly on my phone. Finally, Zelda's sobs got short enough and breaths got long enough to talk with us.

"What's wrong, babe?" asked Julie, curling up in bed next to her.

Zelda sniffled. "It's E-e-eddie. W-w-we talked, and I-I-I don't know what we're gonna do."

I straightened up and put my phone away. "Did you guys break up?" I asked.

Zelda immediately started crying again. Julie went back to trying to soothe her, and Carolyn shot me a venomous look. "No, but I dun-n-no what's g-g-gonna happen," Zelda gurgled. I didn't notice from far away, but now that I was up close, it was easy to tell that she was incredibly drunk. Fireball too, from the smell of it.

Carolyn spoke up. "No matter what happens, you have a place in our dorm and friends to lean on as well." I listened carefully. It was the first time I heard Carolyn's voice other than the yelling through the door. It was deep for a girl's voice, and breathy. It worked on Zelda though, who embraced more hair stroking and snuggled her head deeper into Carolyn's lap.

"Here, girly, drink some water," said Julie, handing her my cup. Zelda drank up greedily, finishing the full glass.

"Thank you guys so m-m-much," said Zelda, trying not to cry again. "I was worried that if I made any more of a mess of things, I wouldn't have anyone but Ishmael here to take care of me." She gestured toward the fish bowl on the desk.

"Well, we're here now, so don't worry," I said, trying not to sound cold. "What did you and Eddie talk about?"

"Hold on," said Julie, pulling out a joint and lighter from her pocket and holding it out to Zelda. "If you want. It's indica, calm you down. Carlos, is it alright if we smoke in here?"

"Go ahead."

"It's okay," said Zelda, wiping a puffy eye, "I brought my own." She sat up in bed and pulled a loose cigarette from somewhere in her clothes.

"What the heck?" I said, straightening. "You smoke cigarettes? Isn't that really bad for you?"

Zelda lit her cigarette with Julie's lighter. "Only when I get writer's block. Helps me focus." She inhaled and let the smoke unwind her a notch. "And isn't everything bad for you? I'm pretty sure drinking until you throw up a goldfish is bad for you. Want some?"

Cigarettes for writer's block, Adderall for midterm papers. I sighed. I saw that the hand with the cigarette stopped shaking after she lit it. I don't know why I took her up on it at the time, but I did know we all needed to chill out. I took the cigarette from her hand and tried it, long and deep. I was pretty used to smoking joints by now, so I was careful not to embarrass myself by coughing.

The effects hit almost immediately. I felt my blood quicken. I felt my body buzz and my head swirl, not as strongly as with weed but not as foggy either. My head was calm, but from the neck down, I felt like I chugged a whole cup of coffee. The smoke tasted kind of gross to me, but it felt good. *A little too good. Best not make a habit of it.*

I took a hit of Julie's indica as a palette cleanser and to smooth out the jitters. By the time our substances passed around once, Zelda was still swaying in place, but ready to talk.

"I didn't sleep last night," she began. "I dozed off a few times, but I couldn't stop worrying about Eddie. I ended up waking up the RA, but after we went back and forth about calling an ambulance and I said no, she went back to sleep, saying there was nothing more that she could do. Thank goodness I had Ishmael with me." Zelda looked at me as she said the next part. "I really felt like he was sticking it out with me, despite probably having the worst day of his life. I knew then he was a true friend."

I crossed my arms, looking for her reproach. "And that's when you decided to buy him all this stuff?"

"This morning," said Zelda, gaining back some effervescence. "I decided I was going to give this fish a good life, so I went to the pet store when it opened and picked up everything I thought he might need."

"And when, between then and now, did you start rehearsing that Shakespeare monologue?" I teased, trying to make her smile.

Zelda wrinkled her nose at me in response. *Almost.*

"Hey, Zel," asked Julie in between puffs, "Did you and Eddie talk about what happened while he was out last night? Was he getting hazed?"

Zelda grew quiet and steadied her swaying. In the silence, she burned down the last third of the cigarette in one long drag. I started to stress as I watched the ash part grow longer and longer and threaten to fall on the bed, but it didn't. She exhaled long and let the butt slip through her fingers into the empty water cup in her other hand. "Of course he is," she said, "But he didn't want to talk about that. I've been completely devoted ever since we got together, and I even top it off with saving his life last night. But I just ask for a little bit of honesty," she slowed down her speech to keep her voice from cracking, "and he turns around and tells me he doesn't feel the same way about me anymore? Who is she, Carlos? Do you know?!" Zelda startled me by grabbing me by the shirt collar as she asked, green fires burning off the water in her eyes.

I shrank away. "I'm sorry, I don't know anything."

Zelda softened and started to sway again. "Probably not. He's just been so different since he started going to those pledge events. I don't know what I'm going to do." She turned to Julie and Carolyn. "I'm sorry guys, but you may be seeing me a lot more around our dorm really soon. I'm sorry for intruding."

Carolyn threw her arms around Zelda's neck in a flush of tenderness. I would never have guessed her piercing gaze could soften so quickly. "We've missed you so much!" Carolyn gushed. "We'll be so happy to have you back. Come on, let's go home." Carolyn started getting up and gathering her things.

"Hold on a minute," said Julie. "The party hasn't even started yet. Why don't we stay a little? Zel, I know you've had a hard week, and I know *he's* going to be there, but we can just have a lot of fun together, and we'll back you up if you need. Carolyn, you're so sweet and good to us, but I can feel that stress coming from you when we're in the apartment all day. Come out tonight? And you." She paused for a moment to put her hand on my knee. "We didn't really talk about it, but you've been just about to burst all day! Me too, let's have some fun.. What do you say, guys?" She looked up at each of us through long eyelashes, entreating.

Zelda finally smiled. "Alright, but I have a considerable head start on drinking, so you'll need to work hard to catch up." Carolyn smiled too and gave a small nod.

I climbed out of the chair onto my feet. "Let's do it. Charles's roommate should be back with the alcohol by now, but let me pop over and check." *I hope he didn't buy a bunch of sodas by mistake.* "Be right back."

I left the room in good spirits. Julie really was so cool, and at that moment I knew I wanted to do anything I could to show her a good time tonight.

"Hey! Carlos, right? Really nice to meet you!"

My eyes zipped around past the guy talking to me and widened to take in the three-foot stack heaped up on the desk behind him. "What the heck is this?!"

CHAPTER 12

I kept looking past Jian as he said something I wasn't listening to. There, on the desk amidst the previously lone bottle of Fireball towered a cornucopia of beer, wine, and spirits piling halfway up to the top bunk. Green bottles, and red, pink, and blue glistened back at me. A few dripped with condensation, promising to be ice cold. I didn't know any of the brands; the labels were all in Chinese.

"Sorry, are you not Carlos?" he asked for probably the third time.

"Yes," I said, hardly taking my eyes off the alcohol, "great to meet you. Did you have any trouble getting all of it?" Jian shook my hand in both of his and bowed a couple times as he did so. He wasn't taller than me, but his good posture made me feel like he was when he straightened back up.

"Yes, I just told Charles all about it and told him sorry for my lateness. I needed to go all the way to Oakland to find the alcohol I like. Try some?" I felt myself smile.

"I'd love to, I'm excited. But I'll be right back."

I brought the girls back and everybody promptly started drinking. As I had suspected, the delay in start time led a lot of people to clear out, but they weren't missed.

"To be honest, this is about max capacity right now anyway," said Charles when I asked him. "More drinks for us, and maybe even a chair if we feel like it."

I started with what Jian told me was the plum wine. It was strong, sweet, and drinkable. I drained one glass then another, and felt a knot relax in my shoulders.

"So, do you have a fake ID, or how'd you buy it?" I asked Jian.

"No, I'm actually 22 years old," he said. "I always told my parents I wanted to attend an American university, but I needed to take extra years to become qualified."

"Well, your English is very good," I immediately regretted saying, not sure if I was being offensive or not.

He smiled, making me think I was okay. "Thank you. In China, many parents enroll children in English lessons from a young age. I'm excited for tonight, I always wondered if college would be like I saw in the movies."

I smiled back. "Me too. And thanks so much again for the alcohol, it's amazing." I walked on.

Everybody seemed to loosen up as we all got more drinks in us. Julie and Carolyn were smiling and chatting freely, though Carolyn's face started to flush red after the second drink. Even Eddie and Zelda seemed to be getting on alright. From where I was, it looked like they were talking and drinking normally, occasionally turning to chat up the other partygoers. Until Priyanka stepped up.

I couldn't really hear them from across the room, but I could see it clearly. Priyanka was being too forward. Nothing came of it since Abhas and Zelda both stood right there, so it just served to make everyone uncomfortable. I decided to walk up and try to diffuse the situation. Eddie thanked me with his eyes as I joined the circle. "Anybody need another drink?" I asked around.

No one responded for an extended moment; I almost thought they hadn't heard me. Priyanka didn't even look over at me, and Zelda looked so steamed up that she was almost huffing. Abhas didn't look at me either, but answered by tipping his cup all the way back and finishing his drink. I was feeling a buzz from the alcohol by now, but Abhas was in a league of his own. Clearly he was drinking heavily tonight.

"I could go for another drink," Eddie said finally. "And a fun way to drink it too. King's cup?" He looked at me as he asked.

I waited for an explainer. I didn't know what that was, but I could safely assume it was some kind of drinking game. I turned to Charles, who was standing close to me in the small room but faced toward his own group circle. "King's cup?" I asked him once I caught his eye. He looked at me and then Eddie.

"King's cup," he agreed before raising his voice for all to hear. "King's Cup?!"

Everyone who wanted to play sat in a circle for King's cup, and everyone who didn't started to spill out into the hallway and the other rooms. I sat cross-legged between Abhas and Julie on the floor, my knee resting snugly against hers.

Most of us didn't know how to play, but Charles and Eddie were nice enough to give us the short version. Setup consisted of all players gathering in a circle, drinks in hand, around a ring of standard playing cards, leaving a spot in the center for the eponymous 'King's Cup.'

Charles stood above us and we all quieted down. "So, pretty much all you need to know is you draw a card and do what it says. Almost every card makes somebody drink for some reason, you'll find out as you go."

"Can we get an example?" asked Zelda.

"I gotchu babe," said Eddie, and he stood up. He pulled a card for demonstration and turned it over. "So 4 is 'whores,' so all the girls—"

"—What in the *Handmaid's Tale* did you just say?!" interrupted Charles. "4 is whores the way you play it?"

Eddie looked around, embarrassed. Zelda had visibly winced both times they said 'whores.'

"Right, so we're not doing that," continued Charles. "4 is floor usually, so when someone pulls it, everyone has to touch the floor and the last person to do that drinks. Same goes for 7, but it's 'heaven' so you point up." We all nodded in agreement. "Those are the only ones you have to do for speed, the rest we can explain as they come up."

My first draw, I pulled a 3, which Charles said meant 'me' and that I had to drink. Julie went next, and drew a 10.

"Categories," informed Charles. "So you pick a category, and then we go in a circle giving examples from that category, and when someone can't or messes up, they drink."

"Okay," said Julie, tapping her face with the card, thinking. "How about... State capitals? I go first? Tallahassee."

"Sacramento," said Carolyn softly.

"Austin," said Charles.

"Seattle," said Priyanka.

Jian stayed quiet for a few seconds, looking puzzled.

"Well, there it is," said Charles, "if you don't know dude, you gotta drink."

"No," said Jian. "Seattle is not a state capital."

"Then what is it?" asked Priyanka. Her voice went up, trying not to sound annoyed.

"Olympia," he answered. We all looked at each other, surprised. Charles pulled out his phone to double-check.

"Well look at that. You're right, our bad," said Charles, and turned over to Priyanka. "It's your drink then." Priyanka took a small sip of the drink she was holding, and for almost the first time that night, closed her lips to sheathe her intense smile.

From there we went around and around, and I was only half-focused on the game. Once in a while, someone would tell me I had to drink. I would, and then go back to talking.

"Carlos, what card did you pull last?" Priyanka asked me at one point.

"Uh, let me check," I ruffled through the growing pile in front of me.

"Ha! Drink! I'm the question master." She showed me her card, a Queen. I obliged, and it was all too easy to internalize the lesson that I would ignore her next time.

"Two," Charles said, reading his card. "You. Shrooms girl." He pointed at Julie.

Julie made a sour face at the name he called her. "You told him about that?" she asked me in a low voice.

I drew back. "I'm sorry, I didn't know it was supposed to be a secret."

"It's not." Julie receded, and drank her assigned sip.

"Sorry," Charles continued, "but you wouldn't happen to be selling, would you?"

I shot him a look. "No, I'm not," she said curtly. She shifted in her seat, ending up about six inches farther from me than where she started.

A few draws later, Eddie pulled a King, so he emptied the remaining drink from his hand into the large cup in the middle.

"When the fourth King gets pulled," Charles clarified, "that person finishes the whole thing." We kept going around, and eventually the second King got pulled and the third. Carolyn and Zelda each poured generously into the middle when they pulled kings. The cup swelled with every kind of alcohol that Jian brought, but didn't look like a bad mixture thanks to the quality of the individual drinks. It was his turn to pull a card.

"Eight?" Jian asked.

"Eight is mate," said Charles. "Pick a partner and you'll be linked up for the rest of the game. Whenever one of you drinks, you both do." Jian scanned the circle for a moment until his eyes fixed on Carolyn. Her sharp eyes flicked immediately up to meet his, but softened once she registered a shy smile from him. They each drank their own drink through linked arms to seal the bond, leaning forward into the circle to do so. As they leaned almost cheek to cheek, I thought to myself that their faces were flushed the same shade of red.

We went around the circle once more, starting to get tired of the game. All through the dig for the fourth King, Priyanka made the most of her 'Queen' status.

"Whose turn was it again?" she asked.

"What did you say your major was?"

"Sorry, what did you say?"

She tried especially hard with Eddie, much to his discomfort and Zelda's. She asked him outright to choose her as his mate when he drew an eight, but he went with Charles instead. "What do you think of these shorts on me?" She got him to look, though he didn't respond, on the second try. Abhas nearly ripped his card in half as he drew it.

"Ace," he said. "That's a waterfall." He tipped up the full drink he had just opened and started chugging it without hesitation. I followed, sitting directly to his left. Waterfall, as we knew by this point in the game, made the person who drew the card start drinking, and then one by one for each person to their left would start drinking after them. Only after the person to your right stops can you stop as well. Abhas, clearly deranged by this point in the night, kept going until his bottle was empty, so I was able to put everyone out of their misery only once I finished my beer and pulled the empty bottle from my lips.

"Right," continued Zelda, pulling the next card. "Jack is make a rule, yes? My rule is that the question card doesn't count, and we retire the Queens from this game."

"But w—" Priyanka began to protest.

"—House rules, we'll allow it," interrupted Charles, and that was that. Zelda stole a sideways glance, pleased with herself.

It didn't much matter, as Priyanka pulled the fourth and final King on her next draw. She made a face as she tried to drink it all, but gave up about a quarter way through, sputtering and coughing.

"Did you need any help?" Eddie asked, reaching. Zelda frowned.

"I'll finish it for you, baby," slurred Abhas, reaching for the cup with bony hands and tipping it back to consume it all in six long gulps. I watched his face lose all color and turn gray as he put the cup down. "Be right back." He burped as he said it.

"Sweetu," Priyanka said, grabbing his sleeve before he could leave, "could you please fill this up with some ice from downstairs? Thank you so much!" She kissed him on the cheek as she slipped the large cup back into his hands. He nodded and wobbled away.

Game over, the circle started to break up as we each stood to get more drinks. Priyanka grabbed up an empty bottle and played with it in her hands as she started talking to Eddie again. It had been a Chinese liqueur, strong as Fireball but clean and mild tasting where the whiskey had been sweet and sticky. It was oddly shaped and ornamental. She tapped the glass with her nails, and the sound carried with her voice as she made her proposition. She spoke to Eddie, but loud enough that it seemed meant for everyone.

"Did anyone want to play Spin the Bottle?"

Zelda laughed aloud. "As if! What is this, your seventh-grade boy-girl party?" She looked around to the rest of us for support. I cringed at the sight. Her words had landed flatly. Zelda was drunk and angry, but she was no good at being mean. Still, we told her we'd back her up if she needed it, and I really didn't want to play spin the bottle anyway. Thankfully, Julie spoke before the silence got too long.

"Yeah, Spin the Bottle kind of seems like a whole thing," she said.

"I'd be down," said Eddie. Priyanka smiled, wider than I had seen her smile all night, and squeezed in between him and Zelda. That was enough for Priyanka. And for Zelda.

The change caught fire in Zelda immediately. I had only seen her this mad once before, after I saw her naked. You could always feel her aura, even in normal times, a little glow in her smile, her voice, or the way she moved. But now she was incandescent with rage. At that moment, I could have singed myself on her blonde locks and blazing eyes, usually only flickers of gold and green. I turned to check in with Julie, but she couldn't see me. Her eyes were watching Zelda.

Priyanka had stopped smiling when she saw, but Zelda didn't notice. She was only looking at Eddie.

"You'd be down?" asked Zelda. Fire roiled under the surface of her every word. "Fine. Me too then. Let's play."

Eddie's eyes stayed locked on Zelda, but the rest of us all looked at each other, not sure what to make of it.

Julie spoke up again. "Zel, it's okay, we don't—"

Zelda turned to face Julie, and that alone stopped the words. Zelda became still, statuary from head to toe except for her eyes. She wasn't looking at me, but even I had to look away from them. I saw them, long past the point of drunk and upset. She was unhinged. Finally, she moved again and spoke.

"You said you'd back me up. Do this with me?" Her eyes moved from Julie to Carolyn to me, not moving on until we each met her eyes. We didn't say anything, but didn't have to. We were in.

Charles spoke up. "I don't know, it seems not that fun that I might be the only queer person in the game. Doesn't really appeal to me."

No one spoke for a moment. He seemed immune to Zelda's atmosphere. Then Eddie spoke up, "It's not like it's romance or anything. Anyone can kiss anyone, it's just a bit of fun."

Charles regarded Eddie for a moment. They exchanged a look. Then Charles said, "okay," and opened another drink.

Only a fraction of the party was still in the room by the time we were ready to start. As Spin the Bottle's greatest advocate, Priyanka declared a 'no spectators' rule for the duration of the game.

"Join or leave," she said to each person who was still standing by the drinks or lingering in the doorway. She cleared the desk and set us up around it, taking care to put herself next to Eddie. Priyanka hefted the empty liqueur bottle in one hand, loosening her wrist for the first spin. Before she could, Zelda wrested it from her and took it for herself.

"You should wait until your boyfriend comes back," said Zelda. Priyanka looked for a moment like she might respond but closed her mouth. Zelda placed the bottle on the surface of the desk and spun. The bottle rotated judiciously, making three or four full revolutions before stopping to point at me.

I looked at Zelda. It took me a moment to read her facial expression. She wasn't excited or disappointed. Her face was set. She was determined, and that scared me. Zelda leaned across the circle, and I looked over at Julie. She just shrugged. Zelda kissed me firmly on the lips.

I knew it was coming, so I didn't startle. She smelled nice, so I didn't pull away. I felt her tongue in my mouth, and the taste of it reminded me of the cigarettes and alcohol. I was thankful that I had chewed gum earlier in the night. I knew she was making this kiss count, but not for my sake. She pulled away after a moment and looked at Eddie. He met her gaze, not with jealousy, but with something vaguely sad. It was good enough for Zelda. Her anger ebbed a little as a smug smile came on.

Priyanka went next. During Zelda's turn, Abhas had come back with ice and sat down on Priyanka's other side. She snatched the bottle out of his hand, effectively skipping him, and spun it without looking back. It wobbled once after she let it go. If she had her own designs on the bottle, then she was a quarter turn too short. The bottle slowed to a stop on Abhas. He grinned stupidly; maybe he thought he was being cute. She returned the smile and leaned in to kiss him. At the last moment, she moved to plant the kiss on his cheek instead. I wasn't surprised; he probably just came back from vomiting outside. Zelda relished the whole exchange.

Eddie went next. He gave the bottle a steady spin, sending it around and around. It seemed to follow his eyes instead of the other way around, and his eyes stopped on Charles. He looked from the bottle to Eddie, amused.

"Yeah, alright," he said, and shrugged. He leaned forward to kiss Eddie, but was surprised by how Eddie kissed him. I wasn't surprised, though. Eddie didn't really talk about that side of him, and that was his choice, but we've known each other since we were kids. Zelda didn't look surprised either.

After their lips parted, Charles eyed Eddie warily, saying nothing. Jian broke the silence by taking his turn next. He put his wrist into it, an honest spin but full of expectation. His eyes widened when he saw it stop on Carolyn. A smile blossomed across his face, but wilted on the vine as soon as he met her eyes.

Carolyn's face, which had been flushed red since she started drinking, drained of its color when she saw the bottle stop on her. Then, when she looked up at Jian's face, she startled him with a look of horror. She got up to leave. "Wait," said Jian, but that only made her quicker. She was gone.

"I'll talk to her," said Julie, starting to get up, but Jian was already standing.

"No, I should," he said. "It's my fault, I need to apologize." Julie took him at his word and sat back down. No one spoke for a minute.

"Well, that's about it for this one," said Julie, picking up the bottle. She felt its weight in her hand before tossing it into the nearest wastebasket to clatter against discarded solo cups. Then she pulled out another joint from her pocket. "Anybody want to smoke?"

CHAPTER 13

We were all glad for the scene change, and shuffled out to crowd our eighth floor fire escape. It was no bell tower, but still a nice view. Against the whipping wind, only Julie's steady hand could have lit that joint on the first try. I checked myself and unwound a notch further as I took my hit.

Half of our group didn't stay around past their first puff. Eddie pulled out a sandwich bag closed off with a twist tie and held it out to us.

"Anybody want some coke?"

"Thanks, I'm good here," said Julie, holding up the joint that just came back around to her.

Zelda didn't say anything, but merely glowered.

Abhas made a noise, but likely unrelated to Eddie's question. He was down on his hands and knees with his head through the bars of the railing, holding on tight like he was at sea.

Eddie looked at me. I shook my head and said, "Thanks man, but I'm going to stick with Julie for a bit. Catch you next time." He nodded.

Priyanka and Charles both took him up on the offer, and the three of them went inside. When they were gone, Zelda pulled out another cigarette from somewhere in her dress and lit it with Julie's help.

"Oh man, another one?" I asked. The glow of the end lit Zelda's face in the semi-darkness as she inhaled.

"I don't need this energy from you right now," she said.

"I'm sorry, Zel," said Julie. "This whole night's been a mess. I'm sorry for dragging you out here to hang out."

"No, it's fine," said Zelda. "I think I got some clarity tonight. I'm going to end it with Eddie. Probably tomorrow."

"I'm sorry," said Julie. "We'll be here for you, whatever you need."

Zelda took a moment to breathe in another long drag. She breathed it out slowly, and looked me in my eyes. "You'll be getting your room back, you probably won't be seeing much of me around here anymore. I know you guys are close, but I hope we can still be friends."

I didn't know the right thing to say or do at that moment. Maybe I was just drunk and high, but right then the feeling just washed over me and I went in to hug her. I felt relieved when I felt her hug me back.

I said, "Yeah, he's my friend, but he's been acting pretty messed up toward you, and I'm gonna tell him that." Zelda gave me one more squeeze before we broke apart. "And besides, you're my friend too."

Zelda and I smiled at each other for one more moment before she went back to smoking.

"And you!" Zelda said, turning on Abhas. "What the hell is going on with that girlfriend of yours? Doesn't it bother you?"

Abhas made another noise, but kept his head between the bars. He was still conscious, but not cognizant.

"Yeah, I think it does bother him a bit," Julie spoke for him.

Just then, the door to the inside swung open and Priyanka stormed in. She went straight to Abhas and pulled him to his feet with surprising strength.

"Come on, we're going now," she told him.

The rest of us all exchanged glances. "Heading out?" asked Julie.

"Yeah, it looks like we did everything we're going to do tonight," said Priyanka, hardly looking at anyone. "It was nice meeting you all." She had Abhas wrap his arm over her shoulders, and looked like she was supporting half his weight without any trouble. "Good luck with that boyfriend of yours," she said to Zelda as she walked through the door.

"Yeah, you too," Zelda said half under her breath. Then we watched them go through the door, down the hallway, into the elevator, and they were gone.

"Wow, what is the deal with those two?" I asked after a long silence.

"Unimportant, I doubt I'll be seeing much of them anymore," said Zelda.

"Do you need anything? Is there anything we can help you with?" asked Julie.

"No, I feel strangely alright. I'm going to go find Carolyn so we can catch the night shuttle together. You two deserve some alone time. I'll see you guys in the morning, or whenever."

I smiled at Julie, but she returned an expression I didn't quite understand. Zelda finished her cigarette, gave each of us a hug once more, and was gone.

Finally, Julie and I were alone and settling into the quiet of the night. I started to notice how chilly it was. "Pretty wild night, huh?" I said.

Julie looked at me again, and I finally realized the expression I couldn't place at first was something between hurt and anger. "Why did Charles call me shrooms girl?"

"What?"

"When we were playing King's Cup, he said, 'you, shrooms girl,' and then tried to buy drugs from me. Why would he do that?"

"I don't know, I guess that was pretty rude of him—"

"—Alright," Julie interrupted, "I don't think you're hearing what I'm asking." She turned to fully face me. "Are you too high to have this conversation with me right now? Or are you good?"

I was startled by the force of her words. I scanned her face carefully before answering. "I'm good," I said. In reality, I was swimming in mental fog, but the look in her eyes made me aspire to sobriety.

"Okay then, what would lead this guy to call me 'shrooms girl' and try to buy drugs from me?"

I thought carefully about my words before answering. "Alright, I did talk to him about you, but not in that way. I told him a little about you so I could invite you to his party tonight. I did mention we planned to do an acid trip, but that was it, I swear. The rest of the assumptions and name calling was all him."

Julie shook her head. "All him then? So when he makes everybody think I'm some shady dealer, and you nod along, that's all him?"

I started to feel defensive. "Well no, but should I have corrected him right there? Should I have fought him over your honor or something? What did you want out of that? What's going on here?"

"You don't have to fight anybody to be on my side."

"Why do you even care what people think? What's this really about? Why are you upset?" I probably shouldn't have said that. Julie's expression, which was hard to read before, was unmistakably angry.

"I just... I didn't like it, and I was uncomfortable, and I wanted you to say something and you didn't." I looked Julie in her eyes. Below her long lashes, they were filled with tears that hadn't yet fallen. I felt like I might cry myself.

"I'm sorry," I said. "I'm sorry for what I said about you and for what I didn't say for you."

Julie wiped her eyes. "Thanks." She turned to leave.

"Wait, hold on. What's happening here?"

"I'm tired, I'm going to catch up with Zelda and go home."

"Can I walk you to the shuttle stop at least?"

"No, I'm going alone."

"But I don't know if it's safe—"

"—Well you could have made me feel safe earlier but you didn't okay?" Her response stunned me into silence, and it took her opening the fire escape to go inside for me to try and speak again.

"What does this mean for us? Can I talk to you tomorrow?"

Julie smiled at me through the tears, and I held onto that smile in my mind for a long time afterwards. "Yeah, talk tomorrow," she said. She crushed out her joint and let me walk her to the elevator at least. As we walked, piano music played her out from somewhere down the hall. I didn't know it at the time, but back in the laundry room, Jian was accompanying Carolyn on the piano.

I was still thinking about Julie's crying smile when I went back to my room. I unlocked the door without noticing the sock drawing on our whiteboard. Eddie was so startled when I swung open the door that he fell bare-ass out of bed. I was just as shocked. "What the hell is going on here?!" I yelled. *"Charles?"*

CHAPTER 14

At that moment, I didn't know what to say or how to feel. Do I storm out? Do I yell at him? Ask about it? Do I tell him I understand? How drunk was I, and how high? Each new crisis, minute to minute, over the past two days had exhausted me, and this was the last breaking wave that was going to push me under. I needed a saving throw. I watched from outside my body as I walked to my bed and flopped myself down. I saw myself pull my knees to my chest and looked into my own wide open eyes, seeing nothing. I didn't see Charles leave, and I didn't hear Eddie try to talk to me. All I could do was watch my motionless body and try not to think too hard about anything in particular.

"Hey, man, can we talk?" asked Eddie.

"..."

"Hello? As you can see, I've got a lot going on right now, and I want to talk to my best friend about it."

"..."

"HEY ASSHOLE. I know it's probably easier to play the hollowed-out shell after performing all week for people you don't really like, but I'm gonna need our decade of friendship to mean something to you today."

That got my attention. I dragged my body into a sitting position against the power of my dissociative fugue state. I forced myself to look him in the eyes. His face was haggard, and his eyes betrayed a hunted look. His normally statuary posture sagged like a snowman left in the sun. He was jittery too. Maybe it was the drugs, maybe it was everything else. He looked back at me, and I suspected I looked even worse.

"We look like shit," I said, and we both started laughing. Eddie's laughter was always contagious, but as we kept laughing together, our sorrows, fears, pains, and tiredness started to well up to the surface as well. Eddie was usually even-tempered, but as he laughed, tears began to stream down his face and his laughter turned to half-sobs. I cried too.

This went on for a few minutes, each of us crying from our own bed, not quite able to look at each other but not caring to hide our faces and noises either. I let myself feel everything that I usually repressed, and as I did so I acknowledged that I was crying for me and mine, not for my oldest friend. I couldn't know it for sure, so I just hoped that Eddie was just crying for himself as well. We had always led such different lives, experienced different struggles, even as kids. We supported each other, but usually each went our own way on our own terms when the time came. Maybe that's what made us a little more distant than what best friends ought to be.

After a few minutes of this, we both calmed down enough to talk again.

"Dude, it sucks here."

"Yeah, college really isn't anything like I thought it was going to be."

"How'd you think it was going to be?" I asked.

"I don't know, I didn't really think too hard about it. I guess that was the problem."

I finally looked at him again. He was still pantsless from when I walked in earlier, so I threw him his shorts that had inexplicably ended up on my side of the room. I needed a best friend performance. Of course I would mean what I said, but caring enough is still hard. I pushed through the physical and emotional exhaustion anyway. "I'm sorry that I'm not always in the best state to be there and hear you out. I know we don't say this kind of stuff to each other often, but I really am concerned about you and the things I hear are going on in your life these days."

"Thanks," he said, "I appreciate that."

"Do you still want to talk about what's going on with you?"

"I did, but now I feel like it's so much that I don't know where to start."

"Why don't you start with what I just walked in on tonight, if you're okay to talk about it."

Eddie was silent for a minute. It seemed to me like he was thinking hard about it, so I waited in silence too. "Well, last time you saw me, Charles, Priyanka, and I went back inside to do a little coke. It got us feeling pretty amped, and we started talking about how the party was going and the drinking games and how spin the bottle went. Both Charles and I started getting pretty excited when we talked about that kiss, and I guess Priyanka ended up getting weirded out and left. One thing kind of led to another in there until you came back in."

"How did you feel about what went down between you guys?"

Eddie twisted in his seat. "Pretty bad *now*," he said. "I mean, I cheated on my girlfriend, and that's pretty messed up. Things are probably gonna be awkward as hell with Charles now, so that's not fun."

"What about at the time?"

Eddie waited so long to answer that I almost thought he didn't hear me. I was about to repeat myself when he started again. "It was nice. Yeah, we were pretty high, but I was there for it and knew what I wanted to do." Eddie sighed. "Things are hard, man. With Zelda, I mean. When we're hanging out together, everything just feels *forced*, like it's hard to do. And I don't know, tonight… you know how Charles is. He's easy to hang out with, and I guess at the time it was just easy to do what felt good."

"Is that all you feel about Charles? Do you like—"

"—Hey, I don't know man," he interrupted. "This stuff is hard, and honestly I'm still coked up right now. I've obviously got a lot of stuff to work through, and I appreciate that you're here to listen."

"Alright, but you know your story is important to me right?" I swayed as I said it, feeling probably just as bad as I looked.

"Thanks for being a friend. And thanks for listening to what I wanted to say in the way I needed. There's definitely more stuff I need to talk out, but now that I'm here I need to take a little more time to figure out how I feel."

"Talk more tomorrow?" I asked, starting to lie down.

"Yeah, how about you take a nap for a couple hours while I think more about this, then we'll go downstairs to the dining hall when it opens and talk more at breakfast?"

"Sounds nice," I said, closing my eyes.

I awoke in a few hours to a shaft of light streaming through the partly open curtain that caught me directly on my face. As I gathered consciousness, I registered the sound of Eddie clacking away at his mechanical keyboard. He was in the middle of some game, but he wasn't completely absorbed, for when he noticed me stirring, he let his hands fall away and peered at me over the top of his monitor. I tried to speak, but my mouth was so parched that I could only make dry sounds. Eddie helped me out.

"Dining hall?" he asked. I nodded and sat up.

Though it was only 7am, our university's largest dining hall was already too bright, too loud, and too crowded for what I'd put myself through last night. Eddie put his hoodie down at a table to claim it, but I kept mine on. I put my hood up and drew the strings so tightly closed as to leave only my mouth, nose, and one eye exposed to the morning. We separated to hunt our breakfast and meet back at Eddie's table.

I went straight for the smoothie bar. They only ever offered smoothies during breakfast hours, and with the way I was feeling this morning, a wholesome fruit drink was just about the only thing that could have gotten me out of bed. I felt the condensation on my hands as I closed my fingers around three cold cups of smoothies on the counter. I had already turned around to walk away with them when the employee at the smoothie station spoke up.

"Excuse me, sir? Sir?"

I turned around and looked at her through my hoodie eye hole. "Yes?"

"We have a limit of one smoothie at a time."

I looked at her again across the kiosk and then down at my cups. She looked about the same age as me, probably a student here as well. For a second I considered ignoring her and walking away. She was smiling at me, but not in a friendly way. I thought of Priyanka and her perfect teeth.

"This is an all-you-can-eat dining hall," I said. "I'm going to drink all of these."

"Yes, I understand sir, but we need to make sure we have enough cups for everyone before giving out seconds." I looked down at the counter. Full smoothie cups squished together across the entire surface. Some were already melting in the back and separating into an unappetizing mixture of pulp and liquid.

"Look," I said, starting to back away, "I'm definitely going to drink all of these and put them right back."

"Sir, if you take all those cups with you, I will have to report you and you may be ejected from the dining hall."

I sighed and put the cups back on the counter. "So I have to drink one and put it back before I have another one, yes?"

"Yes."

"That's the policy?"

"Yes."

"Well ok then." I picked a smoothie cup off the counter and started chugging down the contents while trying my best to keep uncomfortable eye contact with her. When I finished the cup, I picked up a second smoothie cup and chugged that one as well. This time, I started to get an uncomfortable brain freeze and my stomach started to get bloated, but I kept it down. Near the end of the third cup, I coughed and nearly spit up half a smoothie again, spilling some of it down the front of my hoodie. I picked up a fourth cup and brought it with me as I walked away, leaving the three empties on the counter. Her facial expression never changed.

When I got back, Eddie was already seated in front of a large waffle, an omelet, pancakes, bacon, eggs, and a bowl of cereal. I set the smoothie down in front of him. "Do you want this?"

"Sure," he said through a mouthful of food. He looked up and down again. "Not hungry?"

"No, I'm ok."

We sat mostly in silence as Eddie ate down four plates of food and went back for more.

"Looks like they ran out of smoothies," he said as he came back from getting second servings.

I sat as still as possible, trying to settle my upset stomach. Finally, after a considerable time, Eddie cleared his last plate and set them all on top of each other in an imposing stack. He reclined in his chair and patted his stomach. "So," he began, "Zelda said she wants to have a talk with me today."

"Yeah," I said. "What about?"

"She didn't say." We were both quiet for a little bit. "She's probably gonna end things, isn't she?"

"Probably."

"You think I should tell her about what happened after she left? Or do you think that would hurt her more?"

I thought for a minute. "Yeah, I think so. It probably will hurt more, yeah, but I think you've gotta own your actions. Both for her sake and for what you're dealing with yourself."

"Dang, this is gonna suck then."

"Yeah, it probably will. Proud of you for doing the right thing though."

"Hey, we've been friends a long time right?"

"Yeah, I'd say so."

"Was there ever anything when we were kids that made you think I was gay or bi or whatever?"

I squirmed in my chair, but for the sake of our friendship forced myself to think back. "I don't know, do you think it's right for me to say?"

"Well, I guess I have all this sexuality stuff I'm questioning right now, but a lot of the things I'm working through feel kind of new to me. I always kind of thought you were just born gay or bi or straight or however, so I wondered if you could ever tell any of that from how we were growing up."

"Hm, I don't know man, I'm not really sure what I'm supposed to remember as a sign. I mean, I remember when we were in eighth grade and you held my hand at Halloween Horror nights because you were scared. I remember when we shared a sleeping bag at my ninth birthday sleepover, but I never took that in any kind of way. I never thought you were anything other than what you told me you were. Tell me differently and I'll believe you, but it's not like I would know first."

Eddie smiled, not his homecoming mask smile, but the real one. I could tell the difference because when I saw the real smile, it made me smile as well.

"I've always liked girls too, you know," he said. "And thinking back on it, really all the girls I've ever liked have also liked me, and when I've looked around, everybody has always nodded me on and been really supportive of it, so I guess relationships with girls have just been way easier to do."

"You don't think people would have been as supportive if you dated guys in high school?" I asked.

Eddie laughed. "First of all, no. Second, what guys? There were like two out gay guys in our whole school, and I'm pretty sure they ended up getting together."

"Well there you go," I said. "I guess that means you shouldn't feel bad for starting this journey now and not earlier."

"Thanks, dude. I think my head would have exploded already from this if I didn't have such great support. You, as well as the guys from Theta Chi, have been such good friends."

My stomach lurched so hard that my smoothies almost came back up when he said it. "Wait, you told the frat guys all about this?" I felt my pride sting, supposing I was the one on the inside track. I also immediately felt guilty for feeling like that. *Feeling bad while feeling bad for feeling bad. Nice.*

"Yeah, I've been working through all this stuff for a while. They've all been really supportive."

"Really?"

"Yeah, Dean especially. Last time we talked about it, he was probably my biggest supporter."

"Dean?!" I said, unable to hide my incredulity.

"Yeah, man, he's a really all-around great guy."

I was standing now. From a distance, I might have almost looked like I wasn't massively hungover.

"You might not remember this, and that honestly might be the problem, but Dean made you black out and eat a live goldfish the other day."

"Right, yeah, our talk was before that," he said, unfazed.

I struggled to keep my emotions in check. "Look, dude, it's nice that they're supportive and that you've found a nice community and all that. In terms of your personal journey, I think you're going to be just fine and have nothing to worry about. This other thing though has me pretty worried. I might call it hazing, you might not, but as your best friend of ten years who took care of you that night, I think I deserve to know what's going on."

Eddie fidgeted with his plate stack. It was obvious he didn't want to tell me, probably because he knew how bad their practices must sound, but I wouldn't be denied this time.

"Alright," he said, "I guess I do owe you an explanation, for that night at least. Like I said, at Theta Chi they're all really nice guys, and it's been a really great community for me. That being said, the new guys all have to pay our dues, you know. Nothing too crazy, usually they just make us drink a lot or do some light humiliation."

"Uh huh."

"So that night the pledges were doing a group bonding exercise. We all had to strip to our underwear and then the twelve of us all piled into a coat closet together, and couldn't come out until we finished a handle of Fireball. We almost did, but a couple of guys ended up yakking so they called it off early."

"What about the goldfish?" I asked.

"Right, so I don't really remember anything after the closet, but a couple of other guys filled me in afterwards. Basically, there was this Fear Factor kind of thing where—they didn't force us, you know—but they make a bunch of gross stuff and we can get various amounts of points for eating it depending on how gross it is. I don't really remember it, but they told me later that I won that."

I sat back for a minute and let his words float around the table. "I'm not gonna lie, dude, that sounds really bad, and somebody should probably report that."

"Well, it kind of sounds a little bad when you say it like I said it."

"Right…" We were both quiet again for a minute, and I reached down to check my phone in the gathering awkwardness. I had a message from Julie.

Meet at my place after you pick up the stuff from Dean?

My hands started sweating so badly when I read it that I almost fumbled my phone.

No problem, be there in about an hour.

Eddie immediately picked up on my change of mood. "What's going on?" he asked.

"I have to go, I need to pick up my acid trip stuff from Dean. Then Julie and I are going to have our own talk as well."

"Do you want me to come with you?" he asked.

I thought for a minute. I didn't really know how things were going to go. If Eddie was there, it wouldn't be very likely that Dean would sic his guys on me or try to hurt me again. On the other hand, Dean would probably put up his nice guy act and I wouldn't be able to get to the bottom of what was going on over there. Besides, I bet that Eddie was probably mostly concerned with making sure I didn't say anything about the hazing.

"No, it's ok," I said. "Zelda's coming over to talk, right? You should probably just chill out and prep for that until she gets there. I'm heading straight to Julie's after as well, but thanks anyway." And with that, we gathered up our dishes and each went our own way into the blinding midmorning.

CHAPTER 15

I reached the driveway of Theta Chi more quickly than I wanted to. I'd been dreading this moment since yesterday, and the anticipation had long since turned the walk to frat row into a bouldering feat in my mind. Despite these misgivings, my feet still knew the way and went on almost without me. My hungover husk of a body seemed destined to learn this path both backwards and forwards. I thought back to the girl in the green dress I shared this sidewalk with weeks ago; I even looked around like I might see her again. Instead, I caught the eye of someone else.

"Carlos, is that you? Good morning!" said Rosa, too nicely for my liking. She'd probably just spent the night with Dean, but here I was the one doing the walk of shame. I averted my eyes and cut across the lawn in a wide circle, but it was no use. She stood there, feet planted, directly obstructing the front door.

"Hey," I said finally, not daring to look up at her.

"Are you feeling any better? You're still not looking so good these days," she said, as cheery as if I hadn't embarrassed her in front of our whole class and failed us both on the midterm yesterday.

I glowered at the ground, but said nothing. I was still wearing my hoodie in a completely stupid way, with the hood strings pulled into an eyehole. I instinctively reached up my hand to loosen it, but stopped. It didn't matter. We knew each other well enough by now. Rosa was probably just putting on this fakery to get under my skin. I wouldn't give her the satisfaction. I knew what I signed up for when I came back to Theta Chi alone, and I knew I was going to have to armor up. Besides, Dean and his lackeys would probably love an excuse to step out onto their front porch and kick my ass again if this went badly. *I hate this place.*

Rosa continued, "How are things going with that girl you're hanging out with? Jennie, right? Are you guys official yet?" She still wouldn't move. Now that she was bringing Julie into it, I pushed myself to raise my eyes to hers and shoot a look back at her. I tried the meanest, angriest scowl I could muster, as angry as I felt. To Rosa, I probably just looked cornered. I kept my silence.

"Well, anyway, I'm gonna head out. Got a makeup midterm today, don't want to be late." She saw the flash of recognition register in my eyes and jumped at it. "Oh, yeah, I talked to our TA after he saw us in the courtyard and explained the situation. He agreed that it was all your fault, so we were able to work something out."

She stepped out onto the driveway, leaving me frozen amidst the lingering fragrance of her apple spice shampoo. She strutted down the street like an action movie star walking away from an explosion, her stylish-but-sensible debate team matte black flats clicking under her every step. Now that she was far enough away and I wasn't hiding my eyes anymore, I finally saw her black pencil skirt pressed for success, her debate team blazer that fit tightly around her waist but square at the shoulders. I saw her usually flowing, curly mane of hair curled all the way up into a tight bun, and I knew. *She's gonna ace that midterm.*

"Oh, I almost forgot," she said, and turned back to face me from the bottom of the driveway. She raised her voice loud enough to carry through the whole block in the quiet of the midmorning. "Good luck on that *acid trip*, sounds fun!" Without another glance, she was gone.

I quickly opened the door and went inside, not so much because I was ready as to flee from Rosa before she could witness my anxiety attack. I closed the door behind me, and once inside, I slumped to the floor and sat there quietly for a minute or two trying to recover my breath control. Did Miles the TA really see everything that happened yesterday and side with her? They agreed that it was all my fault? I let out a long slow breath. I definitely had to drop that class now.

After a minute or two, I got up, started walking, and started thinking about Rosa's parting words to me. Good luck on your acid trip? Maybe she was just trying to embarrass me in front of the neighbors by yelling about it like that. But could it be more than that? She and Dean clearly both hate my guts, and I'm buying drugs from them. *They wouldn't lace it with something, would they?*

I was still swimming in this thought when I took too many wrong turns and ended up in the Theta Chi kitchen. There were half a dozen frat brothers in there, each either making breakfast, eating it, or getting a head start on the day's drinking and drugs. I must have startled them when I walked in, because Vape Nation Bobby immediately went back into doorman mode. "Hey, whoa, wait a second," said Bobby as I tried to retreat back the way I came. I froze, and he put down the can of beer he was having with his morning Cheerios and stood up. "Are you here to see somebody, can I help you with something?"

"Dean," I responded, the word getting stuck in my throat. "Here to see Dean."

Bobby frowned. "Alright, well, you can't just walk in when you don't live here. Make sure to check in with somebody when you come in."

"Sorry," I said, looking at the ground. As he looked me up and down, he pulled his vape pen out of his pocket and hit it. I heard it crackle once as he inhaled.

"Hey, do I know you from somewhere?" he asked through a breathy, mango-menthol flavored exhale. I shook my head. "Alright, so why do you need to see Dean?"

"Personal reasons."

"Personal reasons, or buying product reasons?" he asked.

"Why does that mean—m-matter for anything?" I stammered out.

"Alright, answers my question. I'm also the finance chair, gotta keep the accounts." I imagined Bobby wearing one of those green accountant visors, hitting his vape while presiding over a lamplit record book filled with Dean's drug deals. "Anyway," he continued, starting to point, "Dean's gonna be up over—"

"—Wait a sec, I know where this guy's from!" another frat brother shouted out. Everybody looked up from what they're doing to get a better look at me. "This is the dude who passed out on the dance floor at the August invite!"

I saw the light of recognition dawn in their eyes before Bobby split into laughter.

"Yoooooooooo," he said laughing, reaching back for his beer. "I knew I knew you from somewhere! Can I get you some water, little man?" I felt my face get hot and started to back out of the room. "Yo, this guy went down HARD after a couple drinks, completely out cold," he said to the last frat brother present who still hadn't recognized me. "Man, we were legit scared for you, all blue and shit. You guys remember Dean's girl that night? Man, she said we should just call an Uber to the hospital and throw you in."

"Damn, that's cold," somebody chimed in.

"Yeah, man," said Bobby. "But Dean wouldn't have any of that, and went and took care of this guy himself. Dean's got that heart of gold, man."

"What a good guy," somebody said. By now, I had backed almost fully out of the room.

"Alright, you can find your way around then?" Bobby asked me. "Ok, take it easy, little dude, don't pass out on us again, aight?" he said, and laughed some more as he started to pour his beer into his bowl of Cheerios. As I backed my way to the stairs, I thought to myself that in fact, it would have been nice to get a glass of water if they really were offering. *I hate this place.*

Finally finally, I made it to the top of the stairs and barged my way into what I remembered was Dean's room. I thought I'd gain the initiative by bursting in without knocking, but of course he was expecting me. He was holding a lit joint in his hand and swiveled in his chair to face me. It was so silly I almost laughed. He could have been going for some sort of pulpy hardboiled noir performance, but he couldn't have pulled that off even if we were living in black and white. He hit his joint.

"I'm here for the drugs," I said. The stagey unreality of my put-on airs clattered painfully against his, and we both repelled each other for a moment, feeling stupid.

Dean finally spoke. "In a minute. Julie messaged me last night." I got scared for a second; my stomach nearly fell out the bottom of my body. It lurched so badly I felt my smoothies unsettle again. "She said you were being pretty rude. Is that true?"

"That's none of your business," I piped up, determined to remain strong.

"You see, that's where you're wrong." He stood slowly, rising and rising until he was over a head taller than me. "Julie's my best girl and my oldest friend, and she's always counted on me to watch out for her. That means watching out for biting insects like you." He took a slow step toward me and I immediately tensed up.

"You don't even know me," I said, summoning my lower register.

"Don't I? With my own eyes, I've watched you make problems every time I've ever seen you. You drank everything you could get your hands on and passed out in my home. I cleaned up your vomit myself, nursed you through the night myself. Knowing what I know now, I probably shouldn't have. But hey, Julie appreciates a good guy."

"Well I don't th—"

"—I'm not finished," he cut me off, now towering over me. "You went out of your way to try and sabotage your ex-girlfriend's midterm, and you got belligerent when it didn't go your way. And that's just what I've seen. Rosa told me all about the gaslighting, the emotional abuse, the threats of self harm that you put her through just so she could get out of her toxic relationship with you. I know exactly who you are, and I'll be damned before I ever let you do anything like that to Julie."

"Well what about you?" I asked. "Everyone thinks you're this great guy, but you're—you're hazing people and hurting them! I know about how you forced people to drink in a closet, somebody should report that."

Dean sighed; he was so close now I could smell his weed and mouthwash. "I'd ask who told you that, but we both already know. No big deal, I'll just take the punishment out on him later. Try to report us if you want, but things have always been like this and they always will. Admin won't do a thing."

"The drugs then," I said, scrambling. "I'll report all of you for drug selling, and you'll be in big trouble."

"Drugs? You mean the drugs you're here to buy today?" I was grasping, and we both knew it. I might have been able to hold my own if I hadn't just been tilted twice before walking in, but I sounded afraid.

He continued, "Again, go ahead, but I wouldn't do that either if I were you. You see, we've got a bright young pledge that's become something of a star around here. We're really happy Eddie decided to join up with us. So happy, in fact, that I recently promoted him to be Bobby's co-finance chair. That spot's usually a one man job, but between us, Bobby's an idiot. Eddie actually sells more of these drugs than I do nowadays, so make sure you report that too." Shit.

"What if I just tell Julie about your hazing?"

When Dean's affected pouty face turned into a real scowl, I knew I got under his skin.

"I'm bored of this, you're wasting my time now," he said. "I shouldn't have had to remind you, but Rosa reminds *me* every day that she lives just down the hall from Julie. Every day, she wants to go knock on her door and tell her every truth about you, every trauma that you ever inflicted on her, and every reason to steer clear of you. It's only because of me that she hasn't already; I think Julie's smart enough to see what you are all on her own. But as soon as you're in a sharing mood, let me know. We'll both say what we know and see what happens."

He looked at me hard for a few seconds after saying this, just long enough to confirm he had me beaten. I let my shoulders slouch and I went quiet.

"Alright," he said finally, "let's get you those drugs." He walked over to his wooden desk and put on some latex gloves. He used one of the keys on his keychain to open up cabinet storage in the bottom. He pulled out what looked like a mini poster and unrolled it onto the desk. On the front swirled designs of red, blue, yellow, green, purple, and black. I thought at first it was paisley print, but looking at it closer, faces and eyes started peering out at me from the paper. The colors blended in Grateful Dead style, swirly and cartoonish. If Zelda were here, she might have called it 'Dantesque.' Once he was done unrolling it, Dean flipped it over to reveal a grid of squares like graph paper against a white background. Each square was no more than a quarter inch across. He took scissors to it next, carefully cutting eight tiny squares out of the graph paper pattern. I noticed that even before he started, there was already some missing. Gloves still on, he wrapped the eight little pieces in a sheet of aluminum foil, which he then put in a sandwich size Ziploc bag.

"There you go," he said, holding it out to me. "Julie should know this, but one tab each should be plenty for your first time."

I hesitated to reach out for it. "You didn't lace it with anything, did you?"

For the first time in that conversation, I saw Dean get genuinely mad. He jerked his hand back and I instinctively flinched; for a second I thought he would hit me.

"Who the *hell* do you think I am?" he asked, fuming now. "Maybe you would consider doing something like that, but that's seriously fucked up." He reached his hand back into the bag, and for a second I thought the sale was off. Instead, he pulled out one of the squares and popped it in his mouth as easily as if it were echinacea.

He continued, "When Julie asks why there's one missing, tell her you had to test it to make sure I didn't poison you. No, man, this is nothing but real shit. As bad as I know you are, I don't need to do anything to you. I know you're going to do it to yourself. You see," he continued, shaking the sandwich bag, "this stuff right here–if you do it right, and I think Julie's going to do it right–should give you what I call a 'moment of clarity.' You get to see things how they really are. No spin, no bullshit, just real. And I'm betting that if she hasn't already, once she gets a little 'higher education,' she'll ask herself why she ever wasted her time on the likes of you."

Dean looked down and watched my hand close into a fist. His eyes glittered, daring me to try and hit him. Instead, I took a breath, opened my hand again, and held it out to take the bag from him. "You're wrong," I said, though I feared he wasn't.

"Good man," he said smiling, "settle up with Bobby downstairs." Then he turned around and sat down. "One more thing," he said as I turned to leave. "If I ever hear that you've hurt Julie or inflicted trauma on her while you're high on this stuff, I'll kill you." He was calm, and deadly serious.

I didn't settle up with Bobby. I went down the stairs, straight out the front door, and up the street at almost a run. Bobby would have overcharged me anyway. *I fucking hate this place.*

CHAPTER 16

I didn't slow to a walk until I was completely winded a quarter mile later. I caught my breath and tried to calm down. The walk to Julie's would be uphill the rest of the way, and once inside, the conversation wouldn't be any easier. I closed my eyes and tried to breathe as I turned to face the sun. I tried to focus on the feeling of the warmth on my skin, hoping the distraction would pull the anvil off my chest.

The sun was high by now, and morning was over. I reckoned it was almost noon. Even though it was clear and sunny, the air was cool with a breeze, autumnal. Seasons change, I can change too. *I never apologized for that summer.* I breathed out and started to walk again. I wanted to focus on what I'd say to Julie, but my thoughts kept going back to the Ziploc bag in my pocket and what Dean said about it. 'A moment of clarity.' If everything really goes like it should when we take our trip, Julie should see the truth: that I'm a really great guy and I really like her and there would be nothing to worry about. Then why was I worried?

My thoughts outpaced me as I climbed up the hill, floating up until they settled on a flock of wild turkeys tramping through the undergrowth in the middle distance. The last turkey must have noticed, because he turned his head to look at me and gave a strong head nod before turning and disappearing into the brush. I was still scanning for turkeys when I collided headfirst into Jian.

"Aiya!" he exclaimed as we both tumbled to the ground. As I fell, I bumped my elbow hard on the concrete and it started tingling all over.

"Sorry man," I said as I scrambled to my feet and tried to help him up. He looked flustered. He must not have seen me either.

He recognized me after a moment. "Carlos? What are you doing here?"

"I'm here to visit Julie," I said, dusting myself off. "What are you doing here?"

"I, uh, I…" he trailed off, not finishing his answer despite my waiting for it. He closed his mouth and his cheeks started to flush, and that was answer enough.

"Well, if you're here to visit somebody, we could walk up together." We were standing at the bottom of the stairs to the foothill dorm, just a short walk left to Julie and Carolyn's place. Instead of answering me, Jian checked his phone and started pacing back and forth.

"Hey, man," I continued, "I'm going up now, want to come?"

"Uh, no," he said, shaking his head without looking up from his pacing. "I'm going to wait down here." I raised one eyebrow at him.

"Okay then, stay safe and all that, and sorry for bumping into you." With a parting wave, I turned and made my way up the stairs. Leg over leg about ten flights, I started to break a steady sweat by the time I reached the top. Before knocking, I opened my phone camera and checked how I looked.

I smiled into my likeness and tried my best not to look haggard. I wiped my camera lens on my shirt twice before realizing my smudgy glasses were the problem. I took them off and wiped them on the bottom of my hoodie and put them on to look at myself again. My eyes looked tired, a bit sunken. After a few seconds of examination, my gaze started to get bleary and glaze over with tiredness. I shook my head and snapped back to focus. I'd had dark circles under my eyes since middle school, but it looked like things were lately getting worse. Also, I wasn't sure if it was my camera or the lighting, but I wondered then if I was paler now than I was before. It could have just been the lighting, but it looked like my skin had a slightly yellow tinge to it. *Probably nothing.*

I shook my hair and ran my fingers through to style it after it had been inside my hood all morning. I hadn't gotten a haircut since the summer, and now it was in that middle stage where it was consistently shaggy but not yet long enough to be able to say I was growing it out. I swept my hair back one more time and smiled into the camera. It would have to do.

I knocked twice at the door, and was startled to see it swing immediately open. Carolyn must have been waiting right behind it, and she beamed out expectantly. She was dressed nicer than yesterday, wearing a modest checkered dress, headband, and even a purse that hung from her shoulder. Her smile gradually slid down and off her face as she looked behind me, past me, and down the hall to discover that I was in fact alone at the door. I smiled back glibly and even threw in a little hand flourish to punctuate my entrance. Her eyes sharpened back into the spear tips I remembered.

She said something in Korean over her shoulder, then without any address to me, walked past me and down the stairs, leaving the front door open behind her. I stepped inside and closed it behind me.

Upon entering, my glasses immediately steamed up on me, and I needed to pause to wipe them down again. When I did, I saw Julie standing by the kitchenette, chopping away. She was cutting zucchini to add to a multicolored pile of vegetables. She didn't look up, but kept her focus on her knife and vegetables. The knife flashed in her right hand as she fed the zucchini to it with her left, chopping it into bite size pieces with commercial speed and precision before adding it to the pile. Behind her, a pot and pan bubbled away on the stove. The pot was just boiling water, but the pan was simmering with a thick black sauce that filled the tiny dorm with its fragrance. Taking a deep breath in, I smelled sugar, sesame, soybean, and something else I couldn't place. I breathed it in and felt my stomach groan with hunger. My three smoothies had run their course.

"Hey," I said, taking off my shoes and stepping further inside. Julie didn't look up, but emptied the chopped vegetables into the black sauce and began to stir. "What are you making?"

"*Jajangmyeon*," she said. She worked fast, adding noodles to the boiling water while stirring the pan with a wooden spoon and tasting the mixture at the same time.

"What's that?" I asked.

She didn't look up. "Black bean noodles. In Korea, people eat it on Black Day to commiserate over being single."

I felt my pulse quicken. I had made a few weak attempts in the past weeks at defining the relationship, and I didn't need a traditional Korean dish to remind me that I hadn't succeeded. "I told Zelda I'd make it for her," she added, as if she'd heard my thoughts.

"Well, it smells really good." I waited, to no response. "I got the stuff from Dean." I even held it up to her and felt silly for it.

"Cool, put it wherever."

"I want to talk while we're here alone. I want to apologize."

After a suspended moment, Julie finally put down her knife and wooden spoon. "Sure," she said, "let's go to the room."

Julie drained the noodles, set the sauce to simmer, and left to join me in her room. I made a spot for her next to me by the headboard, fluffing a pillow for her backrest. Instead, she perched at the foot of the bed, the full length of the mattress between us. Both her legs dangled off the foot of the bed like she might hop off. I started to move closer to her, but stopped short when she started to edge away.

"Hey, so thanks for letting me come over to talk to you," I began. Julie didn't respond, but stole a glance before returning her gaze to the noodles through the doorway. "First, I wanted to apologize for my behavior yesterday. I've been thinking a lot about it, and I realized too late that yeah, I should have said something right there, right then to Charles to correct him. And I should have done a better job of listening when you got upset." Julie shifted slightly towards me, putting one leg on the bed and turning forty-five degrees. I did my best to catch her gaze and hold it.

I continued, "We've been seeing each other like this for a few weeks now, and I can honestly say that the time I spent with you has been my favorite so far since I came to this place, and I hope you feel the same. That's why I've been thinking a lot about how we can make things official between us, and if you'd like to—wait, hold on!"

Julie had started turning away and was getting up to leave. "Please, let me finish," I said. "What I was going to say was that I wanted to be the person that you could feel like you could rely on, and I'm disappointed in myself that I didn't reach that yesterday. You've done so much for me, and I want it to go both ways, and—"

Julie cut me off with her embrace, enveloping me in both arms and both legs. She buried her face in the length of my neck until I could feel its roundness, its coolness against my own bodily warmth. She hadn't been getting up to leave, as I'd guessed. She had gotten up to hug me. I let out a sigh, releasing with it a full body tension that I hadn't realized I was carrying before. All my muscles started to relax, and over the next half minute we sat there in silence holding each other, settling into bed together like stones sinking to the bottom of a pond. I wanted to cry, but all I could manage with my tiredness were long exhales with my eyes closed.

After a few minutes of stillness, Julie finally spoke. "I'm sorry too."

"For what?"

"I don't know, I guess I don't really know how to say it. Or I don't feel comfortable saying. In my life, I don't know if there's anyone I can say these things to. It never felt like it anyway. I was kinda hoping you could be that person." We were sitting up back-to-front now, with me on the outside in the big spoon position. My arms were wrapped around her in a loose embrace, but I moved them down underneath her shirt and put my palms flat against the small of her waist on both sides.

"You can trust me," I said into the back of her head, pressing her sides twice with my palms for emphasis. I felt a little silly saying it, even stagey. Still, I meant it and I wanted it to be true. The side squeezes seemed to do the trick. She giggled, ticklish, and squirmed for a minute, but didn't pull away. Instead, she reclined her head to rest on my shoulder.

Over the last few weeks we had shared, I learned a couple things about how to talk with Julie so she'd open up. Though I had my intimacy issues from not getting enough affection as a child, Julie from the first was a physical being. Hugs, arm touches, skinship, even a brush past while squeezing by communicated more from her than the entirety of the surface conversation that accompanied it. I didn't do too well with it at first. I was cagey, ticklish everywhere, and hurt her feelings with nothing more than my physical distance more than once. I wasn't much better now, but at least I knew what to look for and what language I was supposed to be speaking.

"What was Florida like?" I asked. I squeezed again, just once and softer this time.

She responded immediately. "Hell. Dean loved it, but I mean, look at him, of course he would." She was quiet for a moment. "Elementary school was probably the worst. I remember one day when I wanted to play handball, but the other kids wouldn't let me because that day was 'blue-eyes only.' I never told anyone, but after that I went to the bathroom and washed my eyes with blue Gatorade, hoping it would do something. I was sent home with an eye infection, but I never told my parents why I did that."

"That's horrible," I said, wandering with my hands until I reached her midriff.

"Yeah, it was. Middle school came, then high school, and once there were a couple more Asian kids around, everything was only bad in the normal ways. Until I got busted for drugs."

"Oh my God," I said. I started to pull my hands away so I could lean forward and look her in the face, but she caught me by the wrist and held my hands where they were.

"Yeah, it was the day of our choir field trip too. We were all going to Disney. Our show that year was Lion King, and even though we weren't any good, our director somehow got us a performance spot at Animal Kingdom in exchange for free admission. Anyway, the choir kids got high all the time, so it wasn't weird or anything when Dean asked me to hold all their vapes and edibles. Like an idiot, I stored them in my locker the day before the trip and got busted by one of those random searches. They had drug dogs and everything."

"That's terrible," I said. I rested my chin on her shoulder in a conciliatory gesture. I was all wrapped around her now, backpack style, for maximum surface area.

"It wasn't so bad, at least at first. My parents got called in, and they seemed even more upset than the school was. I think that's why admin let me off easy with just a couple days suspension. I told my parents I wouldn't do it again, and I had to go to a lot more church after that, but that was about it. At least until I got back to school. The news had become such a big thing that anybody who had ever heard of me started asking me if I could sell to them or if I could point them to somebody who could. I never once said yes, but the talk kind of snowballed and I got stuck with a stupid nickname the rest of high school. Now I've moved almost 3,000 miles away and it seems like this is one thing that's staying the same."

I rested my cheek in the crook of her neck. "What's the nickname?"

She reached up to touch my hair with her hand. "So stupid, I don't even want to say it."

"Come on, I won't laugh."

"You will. Kids are idiots."

I untangled myself from her and came around to look her in the face. I needed to know. "Come on, please? I swear on all the weed I'll never smoke again if I laugh."

This got her attention. "Alright, but I should tell you if I can't smoke with my boyfriend anymore, we can't be together." More than her threat, the word 'boyfriend' made me grow instantly serious. "The nickname," she said, "was Juul Weed."

It was almost too much for me. Almost. I felt the laugh mount in my belly and bit my tongue hard to keep it down. "*Juul Weed Kim?*" I repeated, unable to keep from cracking a smile.

"Don't you dare."

"I'm not, kids are stupid. I can see why you're mad."

"Are you making fun of me?"

"Not at all."

She studied my face for a minute. "Oh, God, worse than making fun of me. You like the nickname."

"Hey, Shady Shake, Flying J, could you hook me up with some of that sweet kush? Oh, man, out of business? Looks like I gotta hit up Juul Weed Kim, baddest bitch in all of show choir." We both broke down into laughter, and in our play I grabbed her up in my arms and suplexed us down onto the bed. We giggled and played around for a few minutes before growing pensive again.

"But really," I said, "I am sorry for the shit time you had. Things will be better now we're together, I promise."

"Thanks," I could feel her face growing warmer next to mine.

I sat up and untangled myself from her. "So, you know already that I really like you and I want us to be official at some point soon," I said. "I'm not asking for today, but I have been a good sport, haven't I?"

"Hm," she said, narrowing her eyes. I couldn't hide the eagerness in my voice, and she caught it immediately. "Yeah, I guess you have. You want something. What is it?"

"Something only you can give me." To my surprise, Julie burst into a fit of giggling. I tried to hug her again, but she squirmed away from me and started laughing harder, as if I was tickling her.

"No!" she said through her giggles, almost squealing.

"What?"

Julie was already pink in the face from laughing. "From all the time we've spent together, I had you pegged as pretty vanilla. You're not coming out now to rope me into some secret kink are you?"

"What, no!" I said, blushing now. "It wasn't a sexual thing."

"Oh," she said, sitting up again. "You're missing out, then. I was down to try something new today." She waited for my expression to turn before bursting out in another fit of laughter. "Something only you can give me," she barely managed to say between laughs. She was trying to imitate me, but without her composure, all she could manage was a low rasp that might have passed for Batman.

"Okay, okay," I said, shaking my head. "Anyway, no it's not a sexy thing, but it is something new I wanted to try if you'd trust me with it."

Julie shook out her wiggles and sat up in bed. "Alright, well, now that you've got me in a mood, let's try this new thing. Yes, I trust you, go ahead."

"Close your eyes and don't peek. I'll be right back."

"Can't wait," she said, making a silly face with her eyes closed.

I stepped out of the room and into the apartment's bathroom, rummaging around for about half a minute before finding what I was looking for. I grabbed it and ducked back into the room. "All done?" Julie asked.

"No, keep 'em closed," I said. I sat cross legged on the bed with her, face to face. I took a minute to admire her. She had her hair tied up in a yellow bandana. She was also wearing a big t-shirt that extended all the way down to her upper thighs, so that when she stood up, it just barely covered her athletic shorts underneath, lampshade style. I shifted in my seat and moved my face close to hers.

"Whatcha doin'?'" she asked.

"Just a sec, and thanks for being a good sport too. Do you trust me?"

"You're making me nervous," she said, still trying to sound playful with her eyes closed. She was wearing less makeup compared to yesterday, and I leaned in to admire her work. I pored over the details, the faintest pigments of peach, honey, and rose. I saw the evenness of her color, the slightest blush in the cheeks, the clean lines extending into the smallest wings across the edge of her eyelids. All of it was done in her rocksteady, surgical hand, and the art was in the subtlety. I leaned over to kiss her on the cheek before reaching up with my hand to get started.

Possibly by instinct, she opened her eyes and caught my hand at the wrist, no longer in a laughing mood. She looked down at the makeup removing wipes and then back up at me. I didn't back down. "Still trust me?" I asked.

She looked into my face for a long moment with the same attention to detail that I had just been looking into hers, as if she might make a topographical map from it. Then she sat back and shook out her hair, removing her bandana and tying it back up with a hair tie from around her wrist. "Let's do this lying down."

I worked slowly, lovingly, like an archaeologist dusting off his find. I started under her chin and worked my way up, wiping her face with gentle strokes until she was as clean and clear as the day she was born. Her lips were thinner now, though almost imperceptibly so, and nearly the same color. I kissed them once before moving on. Her nose, chin, and forehead were almost the same as well, though here a little lighter and there a little darker than the color that came off onto my cloth. Her eyebrows lightened by a few shades and the clean lines blurred as I wiped them off, leaving behind the faintness of a simple arch. As I removed the contouring from her cheeks, they became rounder and rounder until her face became an almost perfect circle. I laughed to myself at the cuteness of this discovery, but had to stifle it when Julie started to become so embarrassed that she almost called the whole thing off.

The biggest difference of all was in the eyes. I didn't dare say it, but the change in her eyes made her look almost like a different person. I needed her help to remove the false eyelashes. Only after she took them off did I realize I had never seen her without them before. The lashes that were left were wispy and unassuming, almost bald. Next, I wiped a conspicuously heavy layer from her under eyes, revealing the same deep gray-purple half-circles of sleep deprivation I had. My heart went out to them for each of the long sleepless nights they signified, all of the late studying hours, all of the midnight worrying. I kissed each of them before moving on. Finally, I rounded the corners of her uncreased monolids with my wipe, and there she was, bare and beautiful.

She peeked through one eye then the other in an attempt at comedy. "Well?" she asked. "What's the damage?"

"It's just as I thought..." I said, shaking my head gravely. I waited for her to react before letting myself crack a smile. "Still beautiful."

"Liar," she said bashfully, but I could see she was pleased. She held one hand to her cheek to obscure it from my view.

"I don't know what you were so worried about," I continued, trying to pull her hand down, "you're cute like this. Hey, what do you say we go to the dining hall right now?"

"AHHH," she said, yanking the sheets up from the bed and hiding herself under them.

"Hey, hey, I'm just kidding," I said, embracing the blob of sheets. "One step at a time."

She peeked back at me from under the sheet. "You really don't think I look like a third world little boy then?"

"What? Of course not. And that's so weirdly specific. Has someone said that to you before?"

"I don't want to talk about it."

"Well, thank you so much for opening up to me like this, it really means a lot," I said, leaning forward to kiss her.

"And thank you for being the kind of person that I can trust and rely on," she said, kissing me back. As she did so, I remembered what Dean said to me at the frat, and I felt the tabs of acid crinkle in my pocket as I shifted in my seat. *A moment of clarity.* I pulled back after a quick peck.

"What's wrong? Is something the matter?"

"No," I lied, but I could feel the floor tilting underneath me. *As bad as I know you are, I don't need to do anything to you.*

"Do I have something on my face?" she asked, attempting humor.

"No, I uh—" I stopped short, drawing a blank. *Good luck on that acid trip, sounds fun!*

"Oh, I know what it is," she said, sitting up. "I'm sorry I'm putting you through all this and we haven't made it official yet. I just have a lot of barriers I need help taking down. You know. But you've helped me so much already, and I feel like I can trust you a lot. I just need a little time… and maybe… something special?" She batted her eyelashes entreatingly, but admittedly they didn't have the same effect with only a few hairs on each eye.

Something special. *Once she gets a little 'higher education,' she'll ask herself why she ever wasted her time on the likes of you.* "Something special," I repeated, more to myself. "I am. Something special."

"Really?!" asked Julie, so emphatically that she snapped me out of Dean's psychological chokehold. "Oh, how romantic!

Babe!" She threw her arms around me. I liked how it felt. She had never called me babe before. After she broke away, I sat there for a few seconds until I realized she was expecting my response.

"Yeah, you got me," I lied, "I am planning something."

Her eyes glinted greedily, as if she might eat me up right then. "Oh man, don't tell me. You're planning something special for when we do our acid trip, huh?"

My anxiety crested a peak at this suggestion, and I instinctively gripped the side of the bed like I was gonna be sick. "Can't tell you, it's a secret."

Julie started to get so excited that she stopped noticing my behavior. "You're right, you're right, don't give anything more away. When you can, just say when it is and what to pack. So exciting!" She proceeded to kiss me on both cheeks, the nose, and forehead.

I took a few breaths to calm down. "It'll be fun, it'll be good," I said, more to myself than to her. *It has to be good.*

"Wow," she said, slowing down to run a hand through my hair. "I've never had anybody plan a trip for me before. Who knows what'll happen, and what's going to come out of it. I'm lucky I've got someone so kind and thoughtful to come all the way here and share this bed with me." She wrapped one arm around me and we both reclined in bed again. The idea of an acid trip vacation had turned her giddy, girlish, and it was clear I would have to jump on this moving train before it left me behind.

"It's nothing. Thank me later."

"Thank you later?" she repeated, coyly. "Is it okay if I thank you in advance?" And with that, she proceeded to slide her body down along mine and shimmy her way down the bed, leaving me alone above the blankets. She pulled the sheets over her head, all the way this time. I tried to speak, but forgot the words. She did her very best to thank me in advance.

CHAPTER 17

I spent most of the next week worrying about what I would do. I constantly scolded myself for fretting too much, and told myself that things in fact were going about as well as they possibly could. Julie and I had made up, she was excited to spend more time with me, and the ball was completely in my court for how our acid trip would go. After Eddie and Zelda's breakup, things were even peaceful at my dorm. Still, I worried myself sick over my lack of plan, and though at first I resolved not to, I ended up soliciting advice from everyone I could.

"Hm," said Zelda thoughtfully when I asked her. She closed the book on her assigned reading, Ovid's *Metamorphoses*, with a snap. "If it were me, I would want to make a day of it." Her eyes grew wide and hungry as she mused over the possibilities. "Ooh, I'm thinking you guys take the train to SFMOMA in the morning, become absolutely *inspired* by their exhibitions, then have some tea and sandwiches for lunch in the city. Next, walk around and take in all the sights and sounds of modernity, and then in the evening, go see a show. I heard the SF Opera is doing Wagner, it's supposed to be quite the production."

I considered this for a moment. Going into the city for the day was certainly worthy of a special occasion, and I liked modern art well enough. It was the opera that made me a bit uneasy. Tripping hard in the opera house might be stressful, and there would be no seatbelts flying with Wotan on the skyways of Valhalla.

"Something more modern then," she said, reading my face, "I think they're doing *The Lion King* at the Orpheum." That wouldn't do at all, but I didn't say so. Zelda really was excited for us, and was trying her best to be helpful, but she didn't understand my sense of fear, my nervousness about the activity. She seemed to think the whole affair would be wonderfully aesthetic, that we might contemplate Wagner and Braque as our eyes got as wide and hungry as hers. I was just trying to figure out how not to freak out and ruin everything.

"Here," she said, handing me the book, "I'm pretty much done with this week's reading. Give it back next class."

The previous week, I had managed to drop the American history class Rosa and I shared. The drop deadline was dangerously near, and after casting about unsuccessfully in the dregs of the history department for something to fill minimum course requirements, Zelda let me know that her Intro to Classics course had a last opening. It didn't conflict with any of my other classes, and since I couldn't get a history class on short notice, Classics seemed the next best thing. I also thought it would be nice to have Zelda in there with me, though I didn't tell her that. She made an impressive show of staying up with her readings despite taking four literature courses this semester, and as much as I didn't want to admit it, I would need some help catching up if I joined almost six weeks into term. Also, there was the biggest plus of taking a literature course with Zelda: I felt its crisp, pristine hardcover in my hands when she handed it to me. She bought them new. At this point in the semester, I didn't have hundreds of dollars for even more books.

At the beginning of the year, I told myself I would budget carefully. I took out a small student loan to cover my day-to-day expenses for the semester, thinking it would be more than sufficient for everything through December. Long story short, books cost more than I expected, as did alcohol, as did my new weed habit I hadn't anticipated in the budget. Add to that a few dates a week with Julie and a daily coffee or boba, and just like that I had used up more than half of my loan by the first week of October. At this rate, I'd either be working part time or selling drugs for Dean by Thanksgiving, so I was grateful to Zelda for lending me her books.

Money stayed on my mind as I continued asking around for advice.

"I don't know man, I still don't see why you can't do it here," said Eddie when I asked him that same week.

"Here?" I repeated, hardly believing what he was saying.

"Yeah, it's chill here, you don't have to worry about much, and I'll be in and out probably during the day in case you guys need anything."

I nearly laughed aloud at the thought of us completely wacked out as he sat there on the other side of our dusty bedroom, clacking away at his mechanical keyboard. Maybe he'd even go to Theta Chi and come back alcohol poisoned again. "I already told you man, it's gotta be *special.*"

"Alright, how about you guys get a motel? There's plenty of places within distance of public transit, and you guys could get a place with a pool or something. That could be really nice."

"Yeah, maybe."

Charles painted a different picture when I asked him what to do.

"You're probably going to feel like shit," he said, looking up from his laptop screen. "You're not gonna want to walk around anywhere. That's why I don't think walking the city is a very good idea. If I were you, I'd get a quiet hotel room, draw all the blinds, and put on some music that calms you down, sink into the floor, and try not to piss yourself for about 12 hours."

I tried not to let the bleak picture upset me. "That bad, huh."

"I don't know man, like it might be fine but also it might not, so if I were you I'd just be as prepared as possible for whatever might happen." It was enough to scare me, and his fear was exactly the worst case scenario that I was trying not to speak aloud.

"Hey, have you talked to Eddie recently?" I asked.

"No, why would I?" said Charles, trying to reabsorb himself in his laptop.

"Well, I don't know, just wondering where things stand."

"Who's just wondering?" he snapped. His charade was slipping.

"Hey man, I just want to be real with you because I consider you a friend." I waited and watched his expression oscillate between affected scorn and reluctant curiosity. I looked at him seriously and waited for him to settle before continuing. "If I'm being honest, I'm the one wondering. Eddie hasn't talked to you at all?"

Charles's expression curdled on his face. "No, not once. But what did I expect? It's whatever to me."

"Well, I was wondering because I talked with Eddie the morning after, and he said he wasn't sure if he was straight or not."

Charles swiped his hand through the air to brush me off. "Yeah, whatever man. I wish him the best, and I hope he figures his shit out, but I'm not waiting around for that. You know *he* came onto *me* that night, right?"

"I wasn't there, but I heard he was pretty drunk."

"Bullshit, dude. You've seen him too drunk before, but not that night. If anything, I was the one that was kind of gone. You know those blue bottles Eddie kept drinking from Jian's stack? Those were sodas. I took one sip from one at the beginning of the night and put it down because I was trying to get trashed. Eddie had about four of those."

"But I don't understand," I said. "Why would he do that?"

"I don't know," said Charles, "but he hard rejected that one Indian girl and came onto me right in front of her. I was pretty flattered at the time. Eddie's a good-looking guy, and he seemed so sure, so I was down."

"But he had a girlfriend."

"Yeah, and you saw how that was working out for him. I knew it was over right when they did, right through that wall."

He pointed behind me. "You're kidding yourself if you think I had anything to do with breaking them up."

I considered him for a moment. "So you were down for everything and didn't regret any of it. So why are you mad then?"

Charles put his laptop to the side. "At the time, I was a bit surprised since I didn't know he swung that way, but in the moment, he seemed comfortable with everything that was going on so I was too. But now I know he's not sure or questioning or experimenting or whatever and I don't want to be a part of that."

"What's the problem?" I asked. "Sexuality is a complicated thing. You know, some people experiment and take a while to figure out—"

"—HEY." As he said it, he slammed his laptop closed so hard it startled me. "Look at me." He leaned in close, so close that for a second I thought he might bite me. I had clearly set him off, and as he came closer I saw the violence in his eyes. Face to face, a few inches apart, he said to me in a low voice, "nobody *experiments* on me." After a moment the shade passed over his face and he withdrew, looking tired. "Get out of my room please," he said, "and never straightsplain queerness to me ever again." I gathered up my things and hurried out.

"Hey," he called after me. I hesitated to turn around but I did. "I didn't say so before, but shrooms girl seems nice. Don't do any experiments on her, ok?"

'Don't call her shrooms girl' stuck in my throat and I didn't say it, so I merely nodded and walked out.

A few days of asking and too many opinions later, I was right where I started. I couldn't go out and I couldn't stay in. That Friday, I went out to meet Julie on Faculty Hill just overlooking the bell tower. On Fridays, the bell tower had carillon concerts, and Carolyn asked Julie to come and hear her play. Julie had asked me to join. It was almost start time, and though I looked around the busy hill among all the picnicking students and faculty with their blankets, I didn't see Julie anywhere. I was nearly about to pull out my phone and message her when I saw a familiar face smiling and waving to me from the middle distance.

"Hey, Carlos, over here!" he shouted.

I walked up to him. His impeccable posture always made me instinctively want to stand up straighter when I saw him. "Hey, Jian, what are you doing here?"

"I'm here for Carolyn's concert," he said. "Isn't that what you're here for as well?"

"Yeah, I guess it is. Can I join you?" We took a seat together on the grass while Jian pulled out a bag of chips. On the other side of him, I spotted a bouquet of grocery store flowers wrapped in cellophane.

"How've you been? Good?" I asked, looking conspicuously from the flowers to him as I said so.

"Yes," he said, beaming and without hesitation. "Very good."

"That's nice."

We sat back as the first bells of noon started clanging above us. Obviously, we couldn't see the performers from almost 300 feet below, but Jian told me that Carolyn was slotted third to perform. I had never heard a tower bells concert before, and at first I didn't know what I was listening for in a good performance. I had seen the instrument before, thanks to my excursion up there with Julie.

We sat through the first two songs without comment. I didn't recognize what the songs were, and for the most part couldn't tell them apart. If I were just passing by, I might have thought it was just extra chimes to note the hour. I looked around. Most of the picnickers were chatting and eating through it, and aside from a few scattered claps, no one noticed when the players switched out. I looked down at my phone and messaged Julie.

I'm here on Faculty Glade, where you?

...

I watched the 'typing' bubbles briefly pop up and then disappear. I waited for her reply, but none came.

Finally, it was Carolyn's turn, third up. Jian told me when she started, but he didn't have to. Her playing struck me as immediately different. The first thing I noticed was the crispness. I could see in my mind's eye not only each key she pressed, but how hard and with what expression she did so. Her touch was delicate, but deliberate. Here a low bell, the base of a chord, rang out strongly and died away slowly, and there a high one tapped just so, blending in a balance that added up to more than the sum of its parts. By comparison, the first two players sounded garbled, like they cycled their bells in an electric dryer. Carolyn played them like a pianist.

Jian told me her song was some Bach chorale. I looked around again at the audience on the hill. The chatter subsided into stillness with the invocation of the muse. Jian closed his eyes and reclined his head skyward, leaving his chip bag and flowers beside him in the grass. I didn't understand why they didn't give her pride of place at this concert; she was a class above the other amateurs up there. Each strike of the bell resonated down to something deep in the bottom of my stomach, harmonizing with the frequency of my own inner bell and soothing me to stillness. I laid back. I felt the grass beneath me and the breeze on my face. It was a beautiful day.

After the concert, Carolyn came down to meet us. She wore a black dress that was long everywhere but tight in the waist. Along with her black hair and eyes, the only color on her came when Jian handed her the bouquet of roses and her cheeks reddened to match.

"That was incredible," he gushed, going in for a hug but hesitating. They both navigated the dance for a few seconds before embracing in a side hug with one arm each.

"Thanks for practicing with me," she said. "And thanks for dressing up. It would feel so weird to dress up alone." As she said so, I noticed for the first time that Jian had dressed nicely, not concert formal like Carolyn, but his business casual slacks and dress shirt hung well on him. I was still staring at them when they turned to me. Suddenly, I became aware of my depression sweatpants and sauce stain on my high school hoodie.

"You sounded really good," I managed to say before the pause got awkward. "You were the best one by far."

"Thanks," said Carolyn, fidgeting with her bouquet.

"Do you know where Julie is? She was supposed to come to this with me, but I haven't heard from her."

"Oh yeah," said Carolyn, "she messaged me a little bit before the show. She had to catch her professor's office hours to make up for a bad exam score."

"Huh." I didn't ask aloud why Julie didn't bother telling me.

"We're going to get boba now to celebrate, do you want to come with us?" asked Jian.

"Um, I'm not sure, I have to see about Julie." I checked my phone again. I had double texted since the first message, and still no response. I looked up at Carolyn, who for once looked at me like a fellow human being and not like a piece of spoiled food.

"You know what? Sure, I'll come."

At the boba shop, I got regular instead of a large, and over ice instead of blended like usual. *Time to start cutting back.* Playing third wheel wasn't so hard with these two. Jian acted like we were just three friends, and Carolyn went as far as to treat me with polite indifference. I was content with letting them talk as I drained my cup and refreshed my phone.

Jian turned the conversation to me. "So, Carlos, Carolyn said you and Julie have big plans coming up, are you excited?"

"Yeah," I replied, hardly sounding like it.

"What are your plans, if you don't mind my asking?"

"Well, you see, that's the thing. I really want it to be special, but I don't really know what to do. I don't really have my plan finished yet."

Carolyn, who had so far avoided engaging with me, suddenly wheeled on me and flashed a leer that might have curdled my milk tea. She seemed for a second like she would start yelling at me, but checked herself in a moment and recomposed.

She turned to Jian. "Babe, I'm feeling a bit hungry, would it be possible to order some popcorn chicken to-go? I can pay you back later."

"No need," he said, "Please let me treat you, we discussed it before. If you let me pay, it's a date, yes? I'll be right back." She kept her smile on him until he turned his back.

As soon as he was out of earshot, Carolyn stepped in and took a swing at me with a closed fist, punching me so hard in the shoulder that I dropped my empty cup.

"Ah—" I gasped, trying to stifle a yell. I knelt to pick up the cup, but Carolyn kicked it clear away from me. "What the—"

"—What the hell is the matter with you?!" asked Carolyn in a raspy scream-whisper so Jian couldn't hear her. "Do you have any idea what you've done? What you're doing to her?"

"Yeah, I said I—"

"—I know what you said, and it was stupid. What are you planning?"

"I'm not really sure—wait wait!" I put up my hands, thinking she might punch me again.

Carolyn put down her hands but kept her stance. "You're worse than I thought. All week, this trip has been all she's talked about, and I told her, I told her not to get her hopes up because it would probably be shitty, but I didn't think you had no plan. You're supposed to do this tomorrow!"

"I know," I said, hearing a crack in my voice, "I really want this to go well, and I want it to be special, but I just don't know what to do. I've never done *that kind* of trip before, and I don't know what would be good for it."

"Well, think of something now, because as much as I want you to fall flat on your face, I don't want Julie to get hurt. So think of something and make it good. What does she like?"

"Hmmm… Well, she likes *CSI Miami*."

"So what, you're going to take her to a crime scene? Try again."

"She likes singing, cooking… California. Better than Florida at least."

"Unbelievable."

"We can go out in nature, to the beach, rent a beach house—"

"—Wrong. They have beaches in Florida. She doesn't like the beach."

"Okay, we can go into the city, see an art museum, have lunch."

"And have to walk all day when you'll probably want to sit down?"

"Yeah, I guess not. Well I guess we could stay h—"

"–Don't even think of finishing that sentence," she interrupted. Her anger seemed to soften now, not to pity, but to a certain kind of sadness as her needlepoint gaze changed from piercing to prodding. "You really are lost on this, aren't you? Don't you know her? Won't you fight for her?"

I didn't respond, but let my shoulders sag, depleted of all inspiration and resigned to my failure.

"Order number 30, popcorn chicken!" yelled the cashier.

Carolyn sighed, out of time. "Take her to the California Redwoods, rent a cabin, have your trip there. She'll love that."

"Thank you," I said, and made a move to hug her but she backed away.

"Don't thank me, it's not for you. Get good or leave her alone." As she turned from me back to Jian's approach, her countenance changed back to soft and smiling.

"Here you go," he said, smiling. "Extra spicy, just the way you like, right?"

Carolyn smiled back. "You remembered. My place?"

CHAPTER 18

Such a frenzy overtook me then that I don't remember the trip back to my dorm. I must have taken the stairs, for my hands and face were completely slick with sweat as I opened my computer and started pulling up tab after tab on my internet browser. I worked feverishly, trawling site after site for routes, itineraries, points of interest, and lodging for my new plan. Finding a place to stay on a day's notice was the hardest part, and the most ideal bookings on all the major sites were completely filled up. I found one in a good location, a moderate distance away, with all the amenities that I was looking for on a third-rate vacation rental website, but seeing the price made me hesitate long enough to check my bank account for sufficient funds. This proved a mistake, as the cart didn't reserve my place, and by the time I went to check again, the place had been booked. I got so frustrated at this that I slammed the lid closed on my laptop and flung my body to the bed, determined to cry until I stopped feeling. Before I was able to achieve the dissociative state that would tranquilize me, I remembered Carolyn's words. *Don't you know her? Won't you fight for her?*

Maybe I didn't know Julie as well as I needed to, as well as I wanted to. I could work on that though, tomorrow and the next day and the next as long as she'd have me. But fighting for her, for her happiness and our mutual benefit that made being together worth it to her, that was something I could do right now as well as any other day. I got back up and stoked my fever again, going past the tenth search engine results page until I finally found something to fit all my needs. This time, I didn't even register the price until after I paid up for the reservation. It was outside of my budget, but so was anything beyond boba here in my room. I figured I would just have to make it worth it. Looking closer after I confirmed my reservation, it seemed almost perfect to me. It was cozy, picturesque, and the listing photos stirred feelings of magical mystery within me. I was surprised that I had to scroll through so many pages to find such an ideal listing, at least until I started planning my route. It was perfect in every way but one: Orick, California, a 6 hour drive. A little out of the range of the rideshare apps I was counting on.

Someone I knew had to have a car I could borrow for the weekend. I thought about it for a while. Eddie certainly didn't, and he complained endlessly about it through all of high school. Julie wouldn't have a car either, or else I would have seen it by now. *Maybe Zelda?* She was definitely rich enough, and she had enough stuff in her dorm to need multiple cars to transport it all. I messaged her.

Hi Zelda, do you by chance have a car I could borrow?

I waited an agonizing three minutes for her response.

Who is this?

Unbelievable.

It's Carlos. I got your contact from Eddie, I hope that's ok

Yes that's fine

Do you drive? Do you have a car I can borrow?

I sat on my hands for yet another four minutes awaiting her response.

Sorry, I don't. I don't even have my license, people are usually around to drive me where I want to go lol

I tossed my phone onto the bed after reading that. What was I going to do? I couldn't very well just walk down the halls of eighth floor asking anyone within earshot if they would lend me their car for the weekend, and I couldn't get my money back for the booking. *Dean probably has a car.* He'd probably lend it to me too, if I said it was a special thing for Julie. He definitely would, great guy Dean. And then the whole way up the coast, Julie would probably talk about how nice the car was and how it had Bluetooth and how cool it was that Dean bought it himself after earning money for three summers working at a Tallahassee ice cream parlor. And I'd know he bought it with drug money, and couldn't say anything, and get too tilted on acid and freak out. She'd probably thank him three times for making the trip so special with his car and it will become Dean's car's road trip and I'd get so upset that I'd crash it into Theta Chi when I brought it back and then I'd die. *No thanks, Dean, I'd rather walk to the Oregon border.* Nice try, I'm not falling for it.

I went to look up car rentals and guffawed at the prices. I'd probably have to take out another loan to cover it, and I told myself I wouldn't do that. Even if I was considering abandoning myself to financial ruin, you have to be 25 to rent a car. Right as I was about to throw my plans in the trash, I noticed a blue bottle in Eddie's wastepaper basket and remembered. *I needed to go all the way to Oakland to find the alcohol I like.* There was no way he took that cornucopia of a beer haul back on the bus.

Hey, Zelda, is Jian there with you guys?

Five minutes passed before she answered, and I was about to go out looking when I felt the message vibrate in my pocket.

So sorry, just saw this.

[...]

He was here with Carolyn, but they left a minute ago before I saw your message. They didn't say where they were going.

Also, Julie is here, and is asking me why you haven't messaged her back yet. Is something wrong?

Shit and shit. I checked my other messages; Julie had sent a few. First, she told me she was done with her business and asked if I wanted to meet up. Two hours ago. After my long silence, she asked me what was wrong and if everything was okay with me. That was an hour ago, and nothing since. First things first, I had to message her back.

Sorry for the late response, everything's fine

I'm finalizing some stuff for tomorrow's trip, so can't talk, but get excited!

Pack an overnight bag and a swimsuit, in the morning we're going to the Redwoods!

I couldn't take any time to look at what she might say, so I pocketed my phone and ran out the door.

I ran the incline up to the foothill dorm in case I caught Jian walking back down to me. I had no luck, and was panting from exertion by the time I got to the top of the hill. Where would they go? Not back to his dorm, I would have seen them on the way, Besides, Jian was never there anyway. Not to dinner, because they got an order of popcorn chicken to-go. Most likely they were studying; he was always studying. I ran through four floors of our main library and got yelled at for doing so, but didn't see them. I went to the pre-med library in the Life Sciences building, but no sign of them there either. I checked the faculty club, the physics reading room, and even the music library by the bell tower, but I didn't see them anywhere. They could just be in some random classroom, or studying outside, or at a cafe, or in a friend's room, or could have even taken Jian's car off campus anywhere ever.

I was out of guesses, and it was dark. On the verge of giving up, I slowed to a walk and resolved to take the gentlest sloping, most well-lighted path back to my dorm. That path took me through campus instead of down the foothill, and by chance as I passed by the engineering library. I saw a student walk in, eating from a big bento box. *Are you allowed to eat in the engineering library?* On that hunch, I followed her in, and right by the door, found whom I was looking for.

"Hey, guys," I said to Carolyn and Jian as they ate their chicken with bamboo skewers. Jian gave a polite head nod and covered his mouth, but Carolyn gave a startled cough and almost choked on her food when she saw me.

She swallowed hard before she spoke. "What are you doing here?"

"Looking for you guys," I said. "I checked just about every library on campus before finding you here."

"I told Julie where we were going when we left. If you asked her, she would have told you."

"Oh, okay, I'll be sure to ask next time," I said. "Why are you here anyway? I thought this library was for engineering majors?"

"I am an engineering major," said Carolyn, brandishing her bamboo skewer at me. "Did you just assume I don't belong here?"

"No no, it's not like that," I said, backing off a bit. "I guess I just don't know you that well."

Carolyn seemed to be on the verge of saying more, but Jian reached across the table and took her hand in his. Instead, she just skewered another chicken piece and chewed it more aggressively than necessary.

"What's the matter?" Jian asked, turning to me.

"Well, as you know, I'm taking Julie on a trip to the Redwoods tomorrow, and I was wondering if I could borrow your car for that trip."

Jian looked at me confusedly, and then at Carolyn, but didn't answer.

"Is something wrong?" I asked. "Would that be okay?"

"I'm sorry, I don't understand," he said.

"That day you brought all that alcohol back to our dorm for the party, did you ride the bus or the train with it or did you take it back in a car? Can I borrow the car from you?"

"Oh, okay, I'm sorry," said Jian. He put his hand to his head and laughed a little. "I'm sorry you had to spend so much time looking for me. Yes, when I bought drinks for the party, I drove them back here, but it was in Charles's car, so you need to ask him. He may say yes, but he was so nervous to lend it to me that I needed to say a lot to convince him."

"Charles," I said, and smacked my hand to my forehead. *Of course.* Carolyn just shook her head and ate more chicken. "Thanks guys," I said, and ran out into the night.

I didn't have any trouble at all finding Charles; he was where he always was. As I ran back to eighth floor, I thought about how to ask him for his car. He said he liked Julie, and he seemed pretty invested in the success of my relationship up until now. He was pretty wary about the drug aspect of it though, and I'd be using his car for the plan. And then there was where we left things. I probably had to do more to smooth things over before I came out and asked him. As I arrived out of the elevator, I was greeted by the sound of wrist-rocking mouse clicks and keyboard clacks. At first, I thought it was Eddie as usual, but as I came out into the hallway I saw Charles's door propped open and realized he was playing. I could hear him say some incomprehensible tactical jargon through his headset and decided to take a shower first and wait until he had finished.

By the time I had showered and changed, I checked back in on him. He was in the post-game screen queuing up another match, and I knew from my experience with Eddie that this window was the best time to cut in.

"Hey, man," I said, knocking at his door and sticking my head through the crack.

"Oh, hey," he said, and took off his headset reluctantly.

"I didn't know you played that game. Eddie has been trying to get me into it for years."

"Yeah, I just started. He actually got me into it this week."

"Oh really?" I asked, sitting down in a chair. "How'd that happen?"

"Yeah, it'd been a wild time. Basically, this week Eddie came to me and talked about how things ended with Zelda, and he said that while he still wasn't sure about how he felt about everything going on with him, he wanted to spend time together with me in some way." I was surprised to hear this, and I felt a little sad that Eddie hadn't told me any of it himself.

Charles continued, "Well, you know me. I don't really like going out much, and Eddie still clearly has a lot of stuff to work out, so I didn't want to do anything too crazy. He suggested gaming, and while I don't play many video games, it was free to download and I didn't have to leave my room so I was down to try. We've been playing together and talking over voice comms, and it's been fun."

"Were you guys playing together today?"

"Yeah, a little, but I've also been playing solo too. I'm playing by myself right now since he left for his frat a couple hours ago. Turns out I'm kind of good at it." He smiled and pointed to his post-game stats page, and while I didn't really understand the numbers, I took him at his word.

"Wow, seems fun. Maybe I should download it too and play with you guys."

"If you do, be careful," said Charles. "I basically blacked out today. I've been playing non-stop since this morning."

"Dang, well, glad you're having fun," I said. "Listen, I wanted to talk to you about something."

"Right, about our talk before right? Look, before you apologize, I wanted to say I'm sorry too. That issue we were talking about was pretty personal to me, but you were just talking and I kind of went zero to a hundred on you pretty fast."

I had actually almost forgotten to lead with the apology and was going to jump straight into asking him for his car, so I was grateful for the reminder. "Hey, man, you're good. I'm the one who came here wanting to apologize. I should have approached the whole thing with more sensitivity and tried to see your perspective from the beginning. I don't really have any claim to judge anybody about this. I told Eddie a similar thing when we had our talk, but even though I don't have any special qualification to give you any advice on anything, if you want a friend to talk to, I'm here for that. Just let me know and we can get into it whenever."

"Thanks man, I appreciate that. I don't really feel like I want to dig all that up just now, but I appreciate the offer. All I want to say for now is that dating in high school was incredibly wack. If I were looking for something with somebody, I would want it to be pretty no-nonsense, you know?"

"Yeah, I kind of got that vibe from you," I said. "Well, I'm happy I could talk to you. We cool?"

"Yeah, no worries," he said. There was a stretch of silence between us, as if Charles expected me to leave then, but I didn't move. "And what about you?" he asked finally. "What's up with you these days? Finally got those trip plans all worked out?"

"Yeah, almost." I took a seat next to him to indicate I was sticking around. "We're renting a cabin in the redwoods."

"No kidding!" he said, my words pulling him back from the blue glow of his computer screen. "How far is it?"

"Not far," I lied. "But that's kind of the thing though. Transit wouldn't get us where we're trying to go, so I was wondering if I could possibly borrow your car…"

Charles was giving me his full attention now, and his old shrewdness began to return as he examined me with scrutiny. "You said it's tomorrow, right? Why are you only asking me today?"

"My other car fell through," I lied again. "Dean was going to let us borrow his, but he changed his mind to spite me."

"That bastard," said Charles, shaking his head. "Still I don't know. Melvin's a bit finicky, and I usually don't like other people to drive him."

"Melvin?"

"Yeah, that's the car's name. He's my baby boy, not the greatest car in the world, but he's mine."

"Alright, well, I know it's a big ask, but you know how much Julie means to me, I really really need this to go well. I'm trying to make things official with her and this weekend is supposed to be the big moment. You said you liked her, right? You're the one who told me that I should go for it and make this happen? I promise I will, I just need this bit of help."

Charles eyed me for a long moment, appraising me and considering in his mind. "You know I like shrooms girl, don't you?"

"Yeah."

"And you understand that car means the world to me? I nearly shit a brick when Jian brought it back late on the night of the party."

"Yeah."

"How long do you need it for?"

"Just the weekend, back on Monday," I said.

"Hmmmmmm... Well alright. But on one condition."

"Anything," I said, clasping my hands together in thanks and relief.

"How many tabs of acid you got?" Charles asked.

I was taken aback by his question. "Uh, eight," I said. At the time, Dean's stunt where he ate one slipped my mind.

"I want four then."

"What?!" I said. "Why?"

"Why else?" he asked. "I got my reasons."

"Isn't four a lot?" I asked. "And I thought you were the one person who was so against this to begin with and with all that stuff you said about your cousin besides."

"Yeah, I know. But I think I'll keep safe, and like I said, I have my own reasons. And yeah, four is a lot, but borrowing my car for the weekend is a lot too right?"

I squirmed under this question. Charles really was shrewd. I didn't like it, but there was nothing else to do. As I took out my baggie then and there, I only realized when I was counting them out that I was only left with three. Still enough for the trip at least, and one extra. Maybe I could even buy more later.

"Good man," Charles said, pulling out the keys. "Don't rev the engine too much, and take hills slowly. Also, Melvin's a convertible but not anymore. Don't put the top down, he doesn't like it." Charles was about to hand me the keys but pulled them back at the last minute. "And no driving under the influence, got it?

CHAPTER 19

I picked Julie up the next morning in Charles's car. He had told me to find it in a dingy little garage a few blocks from campus; I had wheeled it out and up the foothill without giving it much of a look. It wasn't until I parked it at the foot of Julie's building and waited about fifteen minutes for her to come out that I began to look closely at what I was driving.

The green convertible was more sturdy than sporty, older than me for sure but not 'classic' or 'vintage' in a cool way. It showed all the typical signs of a car that had been driven a long time: cloudy headlights, worn upholstery, saggy seats, and a weak air conditioner that didn't get cold. However, along with the signs of wear, there were signs of care too. The gas tank was full, and the interior of the car, for all its shabbiness, was clean and bright without a crumb out of place. After all the time I had spent in his room, I could hardly believe the same Charles inhabited both spaces. There was even a pack of car interior wipes on the passenger seat and car freshener inside that made everything smell like orange. Julie had messaged me that she wasn't ready yet, so I took the extra few minutes to check around the outside and make sure everything was road trip ready. I checked the oil and the tire pressure using a gauge I found in the glove compartment; I couldn't afford anything going wrong. Everything looked ship-shape, with the exception of a conspicuous San Francisco Giants license plate holder. *Boo.* Even the tires were new. I guess he really did love this car.

Julie finally came out and waved to me from all the way at the top of the stairs. I had been leaning on the hood of the car trying to look cool, but after a few minutes of waiting began to feel silly, so when she came, I was just standing there with my hands in my pockets.

"Morning!" she said, beaming. I took her duffel bag from her and tossed it into the back seat, after which she hugged me with both arms and legs. Her smile was infectious, I couldn't help but beam back. After a quick drive thru coffee and breakfast, we were out on the road. Julie claimed the aux, and a steady intravenous drip of 70's lite hits played us out as we traded in the Bay Area fog for the wide-open skies of Sonoma County.

"Did they say, 'alligator lizards?'" I asked. The song in question was "Ventura Highway" by America.

"What was that?" asked Julie, adjusting her sunglasses and ducking back inside the rolled-down window. Outside, the land flattened before us, dividing into cross hatches of yellow, brown, and green beneath the blue sky.

"Alligator lizards," I repeated, "the lyric. What's that supposed to mean?"

"Oh yeah, isn't it great?"

"Mmmmm, I don't know," I said, "seems a little silly to me. The song is pretty catchy overall, but I think that lyric kind of pulled me out of it."

"Really?" she asked. "I think it's great. If anything, I'd say that's my favorite part." As she said so, she reached her hand into the car's ashtray, which Charles had repurposed into a change drawer, and raked out all the coins in one big fistful. Without losing a single one, she let them slip through her fingers a few at a time into the cupholder. Then, in a single motion, she pulled out a joint from her jacket zipper pocket and pointed it through the windshield up at the sky in front of us. "What's that look like to you?"

I leaned over the steering wheel to have a better look. "Cumulus, maybe cumulonimbus." She laughed. "You're messing with me. Come on, what shape does it look like?"

"Hmmm… Maybe a mushroom?"

"Yeah, maybe. Then again, most of them look like mushrooms." She put the joint in her mouth, made a wind tunnel with one hand, and lit it with the other. I thought of saying something to stop her, but let it pass. "You know what it looks like to me? Ankylosaurus."

Ankylosaurus. I thought it was a bit of a stretch, but feeling in generally good spirits this morning, I took another look at the cloud and tried to be more generous. It was bumpy like Ankylosaurus. *Like a cloud.* It had a long tail like one, and a short head like one. In all honesty, it looked about as much like Ankylosaurus as it looked like anything.

"Need help seeing it?" asked Julie, holding out her joint to me.

"No, I see it now," I said, waving it off. We were quiet for a while, and Julie tapped off her ash to the rhythm of the acoustic folk guitar.

I broke the silence first. "You know, when I was a kid, Ankylosaurus was my favorite dinosaur."

"No kidding?" said Julie, perking up. "How come?"

I thought for a minute. "Well, it's tough and strong but still an herbivore. And it has enough armor that it doesn't have to take crap from anybody."

Julie laughed while taking her drag such that she started coughing. "What?" I asked. "What's so funny?"

"Nothing," she said, still smiling.

"Come on," I said, "I'm feeling embarrassed now. You think it's a loser pick or something?"

"No, not at all. It's just so you is all."

"What's that supposed to mean?"

"I can just think of little Carlos wanting to be a big bad armor boy and 'not wanting to take crap from anybody.'"

"And what about you?" I asked. "What's your favorite dinosaur?"

"Guess."

"Pterosaurs."

"Nope."

"Velociraptor."

"Nope."

"Hadrosaurs."

"What's that?

"The ones with the duck bill."

"That's nobody's favorite."

"Alright, the big ones that swim in the ocean?"

"Nope."

"The long neck ones."

"No."

I soured. "Alright, it's not some crazy obscure one I've never heard before is it?"

"No. Give up?"

"Alright, what is it?"

"T. Rex."

I blew a raspberry. "Boo. Basic pick. Thumbs down. Let me get a hit of that joint."

"T. Rex is the coolest one," she said, holding it for me to inhale.

"But that's everybody's favorite," I responded.

"You'd be surprised," said Julie, shrugging. "I don't think so. I don't think anybody older than ten years old picks it because of what you just said."

"Because it's basic? It is."

"Well, I didn't pick it because of what anybody said or didn't say about it. I picked it because it's badass, a true classic, and like you said, doesn't take anybody's crap. And by the way, in my opinion, I think that's the problem with our modern times more generally." As she said this, she sat back in the seat and moved her face into a shaft of sunlight to warm it. At the same moment, I started to feel the smoke in me and tore my eyes from her to safely watch the road.

"What, too many haters?" I asked, looking forward now.

"No, not people hating or being critical specifically, but I guess that's part of it." She took a deep drag before continuing, filling herself to the eyes with smoke. "It's people not admitting how they really feel and feeling it deeply. Like, yeah, I like the T. Rex, but I like it because I like it, not because of anybody's list or judgment or because it's everybody's favorite."

"I don't know, it's kind of hard not to feel like other people's opinions matter."

"Yeah it's hard, and that's why it's rare. So that's why I've got to keep looking for it."

"Looking for what? Realness? Authenticity?"

"Hmmm… it's kind of hard to describe. I kind of hoped the trip would help me figure it out. I guess there's a kind of purity of feeling I'm looking for. An earnestness. I just want to scrape off all the glosses, all the winking and smirking and secret meanings and references off everything and just feel how I really feel. Does that make sense?"

No. "Um, I guess. But how do you do that?"

"I'm not sure, but I think I'll know it when I feel it. I think this kind of music comes close for me."

"Alligator lizards huh?" I said jokingly. Julie wasn't laughing now, but tapped off her joint again in the ashtray and took another hit.

"Yeah, exactly," she said. "The kind of stuff that people call sappy or silly, I think is nice, though it's not quite there yet where I'm trying to go. It's still too hippyish, still baked into some specific time in the past. I'm still looking for a flavor I can't quite find, but I'm hoping to get some clarity."

"Clarity," I said after a pause. "Well, thanks for letting me know, let's make it happen. I think the spot I picked out will be a great environment for that kind of thing, and I'm really excited to go to those places with you."

"Thanks," she said. "And thanks for not making me feel crazy."

"Well, don't thank me yet," I said, "Because I think you're crazy if you think T. Rex is more badass than Ankylosaurus. My dinosaur could kick your dinosaur's ass."

Julie gave me a playful slap on the arm and laughed again. "Yeah, in your raving acid delusions maybe."

"What's he going to do? Bite my armor? *Not* get clubbed in the leg?"

"Alright, get comfortable," Julie said, "and listen to my twelve-point presentation on why you're wrong."

We went back and forth, slamming each other with facts and figures that would have made our ten-year-old selves proud, alligator lizards in the air.

The fog started to come back as we spotted the first redwoods of Mendocino County. A gas station here, a rest stop bathroom there, and even an exotic jerky shack in the middle of nowhere kept the wheels turning over lengthwise California. The weather, the car, and the chain smoking of joints all conspired to settle us into the stillness of seventy miles per hour. Out on the open road, I nearly forgot where we were going; I wouldn't have really minded if we kept on like this until we ran out of either road or mind–altering substances, whichever came first.

"Holy shit, stop the car," Julie said. Her words startled me out of my head swimming, and I immediately looked left, right, and backwards to see if I was about to crash us.

"What, what's wrong?"

"Next exit, there's a Redwood you can drive through. Let's do that."

"Oh, thank God," I said, "I thought we were in danger."

"We're in danger of missing it, pull over right now!"

Startled all over again, I yanked the steering wheel a hard forty-five degrees, the most I would dare at this speed, and cut all the way from the leftmost lane, leaving skid marks and an angry truck driver on the road right behind me. He honked his big boy truck horn and flipped me off, and I would have responded in kind if my reactions weren't slowed so much by the weed. I was still deciding between the classic middle finger, the sarcastic clap, and the timid one-hand wave when the exit lane forced me off and he was gone. Asshole.

"Nice moves," said Julie.

My hands felt shaky, and my stomach roiled with the stress of what I just did. "Can you pass me some jerky?" I asked.

"Yeah, elk or buffalo?"

I finished my elk jerky as we slowed up near the tree. Although my foot was on the brake, it almost felt to me like the car rolled to a stop on its own, arrested by the towering growth rising over us. It was beautiful.

"Wow," said Julie. "Look at this. Imagine what this tree must have seen."

It really was striking. I hadn't taken any particular interest in trees before, but this one was magnificent. From our view at its foot, it reached up, straight and sturdy past the edge of our vision, ancient and knowing. Just ahead, as advertised, was a rough-hewn rounded hole large enough to drive through. I looked over at Julie, who didn't see me anymore but only looked at the tree. Her eyes grew bigger now, drinking it in. If she only could stare long enough, her hungry eyes might bud out from brown to green with treeish meaning. I stopped inside it.

"Check this out," I said, and flipped the switch that pulled the top down of the convertible. It sputtered with mechanical strain, but after a few seconds, folded in and down just like it was supposed to. Above, we traded black roof for brown, and maybe in another thousand years we might trade it for green as well. I put the car in park, and we gazed up into the ledger of recorded time. We spent a while like this, poring over every crag and ring, every blade mark and knife etching made by visitors, lovers, vandals, and roadside tourists. After a while, other cars came up behind us, so we circled the lot and came back to the entrance to start over. Julie grew quiet during this time; what she was thinking I couldn't know. I thought of the acid tabs and wondered if they'd help me feel higher than the trees, if I could overleap them with the secrets they took thousands of years to learn, or if in my pride they might throw me down in ruin.

We spent the last hour or so of our drive winding along the coast, here and there peeking out between the tree line over the rocky cliffs, the crashing waves churning the blue black water below. The shadows grew long in the afternoon, and I slowed down as the road got more and more winding. We had been in the car for hours by now, and Julie began to grow languid from either the weed, the drive, or both.

We passed this last hour in a kind of doldrums, becalmed in every sense but literal on account of the breeze through the open top. Finally, off a highway exit so nondescript we almost missed it, the road changed from asphalt to gravel to dirt and curved into the woods. There, along a gully between two forested hills at the end of the road, we found what would become our own slice of time and space.

CHAPTER 20

Late afternoon shafts of light refracted their way through the tree canopy when we were finally unpacked and ready to start our trip. The cabin was only one room, a little studio in the woods complete with a shiny tin roof and a pair of French doors that opened wide onto a deck extending lengthwise above the forest floor to the gravelly driveway. We both changed into our bathing suits and turned on the hot tub before I got the tabs out.

"One last thing," she said, grabbing the bathroom towels and draping them over the mirror.

"What's that for?"

"Sometimes mirrors freak people out when they're tripping. Some people don't mind it, but no need to risk it if we don't have to."

We moved back to the hot tub. The tabs were small in my hand. One had a face on it and was red while the other had a cut-off piece of a swirl on it and was green, but I flipped them over to their white undersides when we took them, so I didn't know which one I grabbed. As Julie instructed, we put them under our tongues for half a minute, then swallowed them.

"Any more advice before we get started?" I asked.

"Yeah," said Julie. "I know it sounds kind of obvious, but try to be chill. Your attitude determines your altitude."

"What if I start getting scared?"

"Well, that's why we're here together," she said. "If you need anything, I'll be there for you, and if I need anything you'll be there for me, right?"

"Right." With that, we walked out onto the deck, slid into opposite ends of the hot tub, and sat there waiting for something to happen.

As we soaked ourselves, I took in the sights, sounds, and smells of our little patch of spacetime and let myself fold in among them. Above our heads hung rows of string lights over the deck, a runway for our liftoff and a porch light to guide us home again. And above that were the old gods. The tree that we had driven through on the way here had been impressive, but it was just one. Now we were on their land, and our tiny cabin, tiny deck, and tiny bodies were just a foothold of human civilization in a place that clearly didn't belong to us. They were primeval giants, and we were merely small things scurrying beneath their gaze. The smell of earth, bark, and clean water swirled around me, pointing me in a direction I could follow but couldn't indicate in three-dimensional space.

"You feel anything yet?" asked Julie.

"No, I don't think so," I said. "Just looking around."

"Oh yeah, it's so beautiful," she said, leaning back into the water, "downright primordial."

"How long has it been?"

"Hm." Julie checked her phone. "About 20 minutes, shouldn't be long now."

"It's been really nice to get away," I said. "Campus feels like such a bubble sometimes, I forget that there's anything or anyone outside it. Thanks for coming out with me."

"Thanks for inviting me," she said. "And I know what you mean about the campus bubble. The most I've seen of California since I got here has been from the plane. Before I came here, I thought I'd be taking trips across the Golden State every weekend."

"Yeah, I'm lucky if I can get from my bed to class to lunch and back again."

"It's so beautiful here, and I've always wanted to go. How did you know?"

"I'm just a considerate guy, I guess," I said, and used the moment to touch her foot with mine under the water.

"Oh, wait, I think I feel something!" Julie said, starting up.

"Ha ha, very funny."

"No, I'm serious," Julie said, sitting up now. "It's kind of tingly, kind of buzzy, in my arms and legs." As she said so, she leaned back in the hot tub, submerging everything but her face in the water and looking up at the patch of sky between treetops.

I started to feel the same as she described within a few minutes. I had felt tingly in my limbs before, whether it was when I did edibles or when I slept on my arm wrong. This was different. I might have been completely in my head. It was a reminder of a connection, or rather a disconnection, that I was separately a consciousness and a body.

In addition to the tingles, I felt a bit of a stomachache. It wasn't debilitating, so I resolved not to say anything and be a downer. I followed Julie's lead and lay back in the hot tub. To my surprise, I found that when I closed my eyes, I was unable to keep them closed for any length of time. After a few moments closed, they would fall open again on their own.

I sat up. "I think I'm feeling something too. The same stuff you said you were feeling earlier."

"Nice, right on schedule then," she said, checking her phone again. She reached into her bag, which was sitting next to us on the ground, and pulled out another joint and lighter. "Here, you'll want to smoke some now."

"Why?"

"Chill you out. The ride we're on keeps going up for a while before it comes back down again. Also, it'll probably help with that stomach too."

"How did you—"

"—I took the same stuff as you, didn't I?"

"Yeah."

"Now here, I want to make sure we're on the same wavelength and both sufficiently chilled out. That's really important for what comes next."

"What comes next?"

"I think the technical term for it is ego loss."

*　　　*　　　*

"What's that?" he asked, and startled himself doing so because he immediately felt different.

"Try to stay calm," she said again. "Remember, it's you and me, we're two." He tried to hold onto this idea as the snow began falling in his mind. It made sense to him logically, but it was slippery. He could feel a part of himself rising up; his personal 'I' was high above him now, looking down on a scene in miniature.

"We're having fun, right?" he asked, trying to stay calm. He tried to smile, and to his relief, the smile became real when he touched her foot with his under the water. *Heaven contains multitudes, but Earth is only Julie.*

"Yeah we are," she said, maneuvering in the hot tub so they were sitting on the same side now. It was only logical that they were two. She takes up that space over there and doesn't always say what he's thinking. Two made sense, though it somehow seemed beside the point. He looked at these hands, the closest ones. The fingers were pruning now, wrinkling raisins in the tub water. He had learned somewhere that the central nervous system sends a message to the blood vessels in the extremities to contract after a prolonged exposure to water, cold, or both. The leading theory said those wrinkles improved grip and footing in wet environments, but he didn't feel grippier. *Flesh is a prison.*

"These trees are blowing my mind," she said, mostly to them. He looked around again, and they seemed to look back without eyes.

The redwoods surrounding them took on a different air than they had before. In daylight and sobriety, they had seemed like monuments, awe-inspiring and impersonal. But he wasn't really tuning in then. They stood sentinel now, looking at him with a mixture of authority and judgment like chaperones at the school dance. Julie got up. "Let's go exploring."

He followed; they both wanted to go. Together they left the tub and receded from the glow of the porch lights. He wasn't scared, but he was wary; somebody could trip, or they could get separated and lose each other. Julie walked ahead, touching each tree as she went. He fixed his eyes on her ombre hair and thought about how he wanted to comb it. She picked up pace, walking then streaming then flying ahead. He wanted to cry out, but forgot what he might say. All he could do was fly after her, at a full run now, watching her bare limbs streaking through the wind as she leaves. The wet footprints of her reaching strides grew fainter as she started drip-drying. Then she turned a corner and was gone.

He ran and ran, taking turn upon turn. The artificial light had dimmed into the distance by now, so he only had the moonrise through the trees. He asked after Julie, but each one he questioned only frowned without a mouth and shrugged without shoulders. None of them were her. Then he heard running water not far off, and some splashing of feet, and crossed over the Acheron to where he heard she was. Then he saw her.

She was planted in place, like the others. She looked different from when she had left him, but he knew it was still her. Her limbs were now hard and heavy, her smooth skin was enclosed in delicate red bark, her hair was leaves, her arms were branches, and her square feet rooted and held, and her head became a treetop. Everything was gone but everything was still here. She was beautiful, and he loved her still. He wrapped his arms around her middle and held her for a while, not knowing how much time passed.

"Hey, are you okay?" she asked.

He wheeled around and saw Julie, the real Julie, a human in a bathing suit, and hugged her instead. Tears fell, but he wiped them soon after they embraced. "Sorry for running off," she said, "I thought you were a tree. Let's go back."

He felt the fatigue catch up to him on the walk back. He had let his mind get ahead of his body, as he usually did. He took her hand, and together they ambled back toward the faint glimmer of porch light in the distance. It felt farther than the trip out, and his body was tired. He was mad at it for that. The drug was for sure doing something, addling his insides or sapping his grip strength or changing his point of rest to flat on his back, but that wasn't the whole story. From his psychic vantage, his personal 'I' hovering 200 feet in the air, he could see that he was always this way. An otherwise young and healthy person who was lucky not to have any preexisting conditions ought not to feel like this. He looked down from his place high in the trees and saw how he got here. It was the espresso-only dinners in college, the nocturnal-by-choice benders in high school, the vegetable-free boyhood. He stood up a little taller, rolled his shoulders back, and felt his vertebrae pop uncertainly in and out of place like an advanced-stage Jenga tower. His body was run-down, and he had done it to himself.

"We should eat something," he said aloud. Of course, he had thought all of this before; vegetables are good for you and all-nighters are bad. Everyone knows that. This time was different. He could feel his "I" as an entity separate from him. He could pick up the pieces of self in his hands like toys in a sandbox and see them, judge them. Change them? It was all so clear, and all the ways he was wasting his body seemed so stupid now.

He looked at the other body now, not his. It was small but strong, with defined muscles in the legs and a healthy plumpness in the arms. He admired her neck, which held straight up where his bent forward. He couldn't know how that neck got so straight, how Julie's mother had placed a knee between the girl's shoulder blades and pulled back as Julie sat at her living room piano bench and practiced Yiruma for the church recital. He never saw her neck bend forward when she asked her mother if she could quit.

"Are you okay?" Julie asked. "You look tired." The dirt and moss underfoot had changed back to wood planks. They were back.

"I'm tired," he said. "And weak. But I want to be strong." He touched her shoulder and felt the muscle to show her what he meant, and she touched him back.

"We can go to the gym together if you want," she said. "I would love to get strong again. I used to go all the time in high school, but I haven't had anyone to go with recently."

"You used to go with Dean?" he asked, not hiding his tone like he knew he should have.

"Yeah."

"I know you guys are friends and all that, but I'm pretty sure he likes you or something."

"Yeah?"

"Yeah."

Julie paused for a moment, which felt to Carlos about a minute and a half in acid time. "I'm pretty sure you're right," she said finally. "We used to date, after all."

The response was unexpected, but for some reason he felt rooted enough not to blow over this time.

"What happened?"

"Well, Dean and I dated in high school, and it was nice. He was the popular, lacrosse-playing valedictorian who could sing, and I was his girlfriend. He was a year older, so when he went off to college, he wanted to do long distance and I said no. Then he said he'd wait for me, and I said no."

"Why did you end it?"

Julie scrunched up her nose before answering. "Dean was always so nice to me and cared about me a lot, but I just never felt like I fit into his life. His friends, his parents, his politics, all that made me feel like I was from another planet, and I just wanted to be me. So I took senior year to be me, and it was nice too."

"Did he want to get back together when you told him you were coming to school here?"

"Yeah at first, but I told him I needed him to be a friend to me out here in this new place. I wanted to find out who I was alone, and I think I did that. I now want to find out who I am in a relationship, and I think I'm doing that now, but I couldn't really do that with Dean."

"So do you guys still have feelings for each other?"

Julie exhaled fully and breathed in again before responding. "I wanted him to be my friend and look out for me, and I want to do the same for him. As for Dean, I can't really say I know, we haven't really discussed it since we tried to be just friends, but he's in a relationship now and I don't think he'd be unfaithful to her. I know you and Dean have been weird with each other and neither of you will really talk about it with me, but I care a lot about you both and I know you care about me too, so please try to get along?"

Julie pleaded with her eyes and hands as well as her words, and Carlos felt moved. He saw a kind, beautiful person who was vulnerable, and he fell in love while trying to help her. He suspected Dean must've felt something similar.

"You know," Carlos said, "Dean doesn't think I'm good enough to be with you."

"And what do you think?"

He thought about Rosa, and a door appeared in his mind that he didn't want to open. "I want to be, I'm trying to be."

"I want you to be too! And I want to be good enough too! So let's do it then. Let's be the best at support and emotions and all that shit and be the best selves and partners we can be. Then either you win him over or his opinion doesn't matter because we know we're the best. Now let's eat."

Mealtime proved more of a challenge than expected. They had started with a cup of tea, which proved simple enough. The cute little ceramic mug was lumpy and hot to the touch, and though the tea bag string fell in almost immediately, it didn't really matter. The mint flavor was hot and clean-smelling, and Carlos was grateful for something to counteract the gathering chill of the evening. The food was another thing.

It was sandwiches, and while he couldn't find any part of it particularly bad, they still repelled him. He had only suggested they eat in a moment of self-care related clarity, and in fact, he wasn't a bit hungry. The acid had acted to suppress his appetite and the stomachache from hours ago was still there. He took a bite. As he tried to taste it mindfully, every sense was too loud, creating a clamor in his mouth. He could feel and hear the dry graininess of the bread as it chafed the roof of his mouth. He could taste and smell the condensation of the lettuce from when it sweated in the bag. All at once, it was too dry and too moist, too meaty and too veggie, too textured and too smooth. Yet, to the neurotypical on a typical day, it could have been just a sandwich. It certainly looked the part.

As Carlos forced down another bite, he found that as long as he focused on some other thought, he couldn't taste anything at all. Julie put her sandwich down after the first bite and it disappeared for a while.

Two cups of tea later, she picked it up again. "I guess I'd better eat this," she said. Examining it intently, she pinched the end of crust and peeled it all the way around until it came off in one piece.

*   *   *

"Cheers," I said, clinking my sandwich with hers, and as I did so, the interoception of mind and body anchored me back to my fleshy burden. I waited for my esophagus to roll, squeeze, and push the bread out of my way before talking to Julie again.

"How are you feeling?" I asked.

"Tired as heck, but not quite sleepy."

"Yeah, same… Did you end up feeling the ego loss thing we were talking about before?"

"Hmmm, hard to tell for me," she said. "The thoughts are pretty hard to follow, but when we're quiet for a long time, I definitely feel something. Like I'm watching us instead of just being here. That might be something."

"Dang, I feel the same way. For me, it's like part of me kept floating up and up and then looked down on us from the tops of the trees while the rest of me was down here. I've been watching the trees too."

"You know, some of the oldest ones around here are probably 2,000 years old. And I get the feeling that those trees are watching us right back."

"Pretty spooky." As I said so, our little studio felt smaller than before, and I felt that the branches and bark and leaves were leaning over a little more to reach back for what was theirs.

"Whether they watch us or not, there's definitely a consciousness here, and that's what the acid has helped us key into. Maybe it's the ego loss, but maybe everything really is all connected somehow, and we're all part of some kind of oneness. I don't know, do you feel any of that?"

"Yeah, I definitely feel that," I said. "With the other stuff I've tried, weed and alcohol and coffee and cigarettes, there was always the feeling that I was somehow filtering my perception when I consumed them, bending or stretching senses in a way that felt fun or good. I definitely feel different now, but not in the same kind of way. I feel like the filtered perception was what I was walking around every day with, and this is some kind of... not clearer perspective maybe, but different point of view."

"So what do you want to do with it?"

In response to her question, about a hundred different ideas surged through my head at once. "I don't know, but I feel kind of unlimited. I feel like with world enough, tabs enough, and time, I could get to the bottom of anything. I could find a great piece of art or music or literature and sit with it until I know it better than I know myself. I could talk to the trees until they tell me what they know. Or I could change what's in my mind, improve myself, and become the best version of who I could be. I could know what it means to be. I could stop being everything that's holding me back, not just one time, but forever because I could change the fundamental building blocks of how my mind works."

I felt my brain heating up and my mouth falling behind as it tried to take dictation. I continued, punching the air, "I could soar through the infinite until I come up against the boundary of whatever this is and then break through to the blank space and start creating a world all my own! I almost feel like existence itself is a kind of limitation and the really unlimited exists in the possibility of where nothing is but something could be, you know. I could make something. My soul feels like a paintbrush through which I can conduct an act of creation. I could write a novel, and in the novel they would do acid and they could push the limits of their existence until they found out they were in a novel. I should tell Zelda that, she'd write it well. I could—"

I stopped then, as I had noticed that Julie had stopped looking at me a while ago. Though she was still next to me, she seemed impossibly far away, and it only could have been because of what I've been saying. Since I started this trip, my brain felt like it was speeding through a nickel tour of all creation, and somewhere along the way I had gotten untethered from Julie. Even in the same room and same conversation, one well-met tangent could trampoline somebody out of all known creation. Did I need to be master of the universe, the best version of myself, knower of mysteries? Why was I here, and how did I want to spend this time?

I unstuck myself from the grand designs and looked at Julie for a while. She didn't seem to notice that I had stopped talking, and I let her be while I tried to imagine what she was thinking. Was this her moment of clarity, that even in a room the size of my dorm I could go trapezing, worlds away? It had been a while since I asked about Dean, but why did I do that? Because I wanted to uncover her past, or because I wanted to secure something for myself? Am I a good partner, or at least on track to being one? The trees might be better company.

"Hey, Julie," I said, waving my hands. I watched her eyes refocus in stages: beyond me, through me, at me, on me, and finally with me. "Hey, I could do all that, but why would I? Your story, our story, is right here in front of me, and it's not over until I get to the bottom of what's in that look in your eyes." She smiled without looking away. "Why do you never look away when you look at me like that?" I asked.

"Like what?"

"Like in that telescoping way. Sometimes you look at me like I'm really far away even when I'm close to you and sometimes it's different. Where do you go and what are you thinking?"

"Well, well, well," she said, leaning back in her chair and kicking her feet up into my lap. She dipped every word and gesture in syrupy smugness. "Wouldn't you like to know?"

"Aww come on," I said, trying to keep it light so she wouldn't tip into being angry with me, "I find you fascinating, and I'd like to get to the bottom of it. The whole reason for coming all the way out here was so we could really connect with each other, right?" As I said so, I reached for her hand with mine, extending a tether and hoping to tie it fast. As I did so, she leaned back in her chair and put both hands behind her head.

"If only we had tabs enough and time," she said, aiming that same look, almost a leer now, right at me.

"That's it," I said, and in one motion swooped one arm under her legs and the other behind her shoulders and picked her up in my arms. Far off, it started to rain.

"What are you doing?" she asked, playing the damsel.

"What I should have done a long time ago," I said, and tossed her onto the bed.

"What are you going to do to me?" she asked, scrambling back to upright.

"Well, I'm going to take your hand…"

"Yeah." She leaned forward a bit.

"And I'm going to look into your eyes…"

"Ooh okay, bold." She leaned even more, until our noses were touching.

"And I'm going to stare at you until I figure out what the heck your deal is." She laughed, almost squealing, and fell back into the bed. She took a moment to get her giggles out before coming back up to me.

"I'm sorry," she said.

"For what?"

She looked down and away for a while, and for a moment I worried that I lost my tether. "I want attention. And wanting attention on acid feels like falling through the vacuum of space."

I took her face in my hands. "Hey, you don't have to apologize. I'm sorry. I came here because I wanted to spend time together and do this trip together. I just didn't realize what that really meant until now."

"Well, you figured it out without me saying anything, so that's points to you."

"Were you waiting long?"

Her eyes telescoped away from me then.

"Julie, were you waiting long?" I repeated.

"Yeah," she said, looking back at me. "I've been waiting since before these trees were even thought of."

I watched her grow distant again and telescope away from me. I couldn't lose her now, not now and, as I was starting to hope, not ever. I reached back and grabbed hold of what I could.

"Hey, teach me to roll a joint."

"What?"

"You always show up with these perfect joints that look factory pre-rolled, and I actually thought they were until Zelda told me you do them all yourself. I want to learn. Show me."

Just as I hoped, once I saw the spark come back to her eyes, I knew I had her.

"Okay, but I want you to know I don't do this for just anyone. You're watching a master at work."

We relocated to the kitchen counter and rejoined our previously abandoned tea and sandwiches. Though Julie had brought plenty of pre-rolled joints, she forgot her papers, so we had to make do with leaves from the Gideon's Bible left by our rental host.

"Leviticus, always Leviticus," she said, flipping to it and tearing out half a page to share between us.

"Why?"

"Nobody reads that one, so no one will miss it. We don't want to ruin the experience of someone looking for guidance in here."

"Are you a Christian?" I asked.

"Hm… I think I still am, yeah." She tore the half page into strips and folded each into a trough before giving one to me. "I've been going to church with my family since I was a kid, though I considered stopping. I haven't been to church since coming to school here, but I think I might try and find one. What about you?"

I took a sliver of Leviticus 15 and read a bit of it as Julie took out her grinder. "My mom was raised Catholic, but we only ever went to mass on Easter. I spent a lot of time in middle school on Atheist YouTube, but I haven't given the question much thought since then. On this trip though, I felt something new, a kind of universal one-ness that I need to think more about. I just don't know."

"Consider. I believe that God gave us this," she said, holding up the Bible, "and this," she continued, holding up a nug of weed. "God is good."

She ground down the nug and opened her grinder to get us going. She started by sprinkling the grounds into the fold of paper while leaving the last centimeter empty. I did the same, careful to put in an ample amount like she did without overfilling.

"And now for the great 'filter vs no filter' debate. Some people add a filter to their joint like the ones on cigarettes, which is usually a rolled-up piece of card stock that goes right here on the end. The advantage to this is that you can hold the joint easily all the way until you finish it, but the drawback is that your last hit will probably burn the cardboard and leave a bad taste in your mouth. Now, on the other side of it, you can just leave a little space and have no filter, and what should happen if you do it right is that it causes a resin buildup on this side and creates something called a 'roach,' which should be a natural place to hold it and a natural stop that keeps weed from falling into your mouth. Do you remember which one I always do?"

I struggled to recall every joint we ever smoked together. I closed my eyes and imagined my lips closing around it as I inhaled. *Resin or cardboard?*

"No filter," I finally said.

"Awww, he does care," she said teasingly. "Very good. In my opinion, every drawback to the roach method isn't really a drawback if you roll and smoke it right. So let's do it. Pick up your paper and roll the sides back and forth between your fingers until the weed packs into a tight cylinder. Good. Now the tricky part. You're going to take one side of the paper and fold it over until it tucks in between the other side of the paper and the weed. Folding it straight across is okay, but I like to make the mouthpiece in a bit of a cone shape so it's tighter and you don't lose any on the mouth side." In one smooth motion, she bent both thumbs over the paper and tucked it into a tight cone, then licked the edge to seal it off.

"Wait, I didn't see that," I said, almost dropping my paper.

"It's okay, just try it."

The acid made the endeavor about ten times harder, and it felt like my fingers lost all memory of their own, demanding a conscious effort for every micromotion. The result was a sad, lumpy, crumpled stick of a thing, though I told myself I'd practice more and get better later.

"Okay, we can work with this," she said. "Now just close and twist off the end, pinch the mouth side, and you've got it. She did both these things simultaneously, one with each hand, and held up a picture-perfect movie prop of a joint. I did the same with my own and came out with something I wasn't even sure would light. I would find out momentarily.

"Okay, now to learn how to light it."

"I already know how to light it," I said.

"Yeah, I gotta confess something. You actually don't know how to light it. I've let you start one a couple times, and it's always burned weird, so I stopped letting you but never said anything. Sorry about that."

"You never told me? What was I doing wrong?"

Julie held up the unlit end as she explained. "When you light it, imagine the flame going up in a perfect line. The line needs to cover the entire end all the way up so it burns evenly. When you light it, you miss either the top or one side and the joint ends up 'boating,' or burning down quickly only on the top half while leaving an unburnt bottom that needs to be fixed by constantly rotating and relighting. It's a whole thing."

"But wait," I said, fiddling with my joint in my confusion. "I've never had to rotate or relight one that I've started.

"Oh, sweet boy. Poor boy. No, you haven't. I'm the one that does it, and I've never had the heart to point it out to you. It's okay though, you're learning now, so don't sweat it."

I felt a little put out by the revelation, but I resolved to take it positively as a sign that Julie cared enough about my feelings to spare me the confrontation. I lit it as she showed me, and we sat across the table and smoked our own until my weed fell out the bottom halfway through. Julie laughed, gave me some constructive criticism, kissed me, and then laughed again when she tasted the grains of weed I'd sucked into my mouth but felt too embarrassed to spit out in front of her. As the acid began to wind down, our sense of time sped up to get closer to normal. We played cards, rolled and smoked more joints, and started mixing our hot tea with whiskey we'd brought. All through the evening, the rain pattered on the tin roof, giving me ASMR tingles whenever I cared to listen. We tried to have sex too, but the acid thoughts had me too distracted and I couldn't stay focused.

Instead, I taught her how to shuffle cards while she taught me how to unhook a bra with one hand, and we practiced over and over until I pinched her one too many times and she called it off. We stayed up together until the acid hit a certain number of half-lives and grew weak enough for the weed and whiskey put us to sleep.

CHAPTER 21

I listened to the rain nearly all night, dozing off and coming to as Julie slept heavily beside me. I spent the waking time thinking about rain and what it all really meant, and sometime in the early hours of the morning I figured it out and jumped out of bed with a yell.

"THE CAR!"

I ran out the door, over the deck, and down the driveway to find Charles's car in total ruin. I had been a complete idiot and left the top down, and the driving rain had turned the inside into almost a second hot tub.

"Shit shit shit," I muttered as I opened the doors to let some of the water out. The cloth seats were completely soaked through, there were a few inches of water covering the floorboards, and I was pretty sure the stereo was broken. I cried as I worked, only stopping for a moment to tip my hat to God for the well-aimed shit he took in my dinner.

Julie came out to check on me within a few minutes, standing there barefoot in my college hoodie and a borrowed umbrella. She was calm where I wasn't, and had the smart idea of checking to see if the car would still start. I kissed her when the engine sputtered to life, but my relief was short-lived. When I pressed the button to roll up the convertible top, the mechanism clicked and whirred for just a second before going dead.

I groaned and pressed my head against the steering wheel horn. "I've killed us. I'm sorry."

"Hey, it's alright," said Julie, smoothing my forehead wrinkles with her palm. Her touch made me feel secure again, and already I felt the wheels spinning inside me slow back down to normal. "We've got this, we can take care of it."

"But Charles—"

"—Won't see the worst of it, when we're done it'll be almost fine. First thing we have to do is get it out of the rain."

Nothing we tried could force the top closed, so we resolved to cover the car however we could. I reparked it where the tree canopy was thickest, and for extra coverage stripped the cover from the hot tub and draped it between the windshield and the front seat headrests. Julie found a bucket and mop in the closet, and after we got as much water as we could out of the floorboards we took every towel, rug, blanket, and sheet from inside and padded the entire car with them. Once there was nothing more to do but wait, we went back inside and stripped off our wet clothes. Julie pat dried her hair with the last piece of linen in the place, and as I watched I couldn't help but love her more.

"How are you always so calm when everything goes wild?" I asked.

She gave me a smirk and looked around with stagey incredulity. "This is wild? Out here your rain is baby shit. Back in high school, Tropical Storm Debbie flooded my parents' restaurant two days before we were supposed to host choir banquet and they refused to cancel it."

"What did you do?"

"Same thing as we did just now, it just took more than a mop and a couple of towels."

"Did the banquet go okay?"

"Yeah, the only thing was that we couldn't get that damp mildew smell out in time. My parents didn't love it, but I had the idea of just burning a ton of incense and passing it off as an Asian thing. Nobody could even tell."

"Oh so you're just a little scrappy scrapper, huh?" I asked, poking her in the ribs.

"Ya girl had to survive. After two days of round the clock de-flooding, you *know* I got high as hell for that choir banquet."

Julie turned out to be right about the mildew smell. We got back on the road once we packed the place up and left an apology note for the wet towels, but all the wetness inside quickly started to dampen our spirits.

"Ugh, I think the water activated something in here," Julie said as she wrinkled her nose, "smells like dead cat or something." We were happy to keep the top down the whole way back on account of the fresh air, but every time we slowed down enough that the wind died out, the mildew smell came rising back up. An hour into the drive, our pants were fully soaked through from the seats.

"Alright, I can't take this," I said, pulling off the freeway. We changed into our last clean shorts and piled the rest of our clothes under our butts on the seats. We stopped once for air freshener, again for food, and a third time for a desiccant dehumidifier (Julie's idea). She even smoked in the car to mask the smell, and I had some too.

I wasn't sure if it was a residual effect from the acid, but we were both pretty spaced out for most of the way back. The sun got high pretty soon after Julie did, and though it wasn't a hot day, the directness of the rays raisined her into a balled-up nap in the seat next to me. All alone, I watched the road unroll like a big tongue in front of me as I contemplated the facts of my existence to the sweet stylings of Julie's '90's Frat BBQ' playlist.

I wasn't tripping anymore, or at least I didn't think I was, but I couldn't shake the feeling that something was different now. I had felt tired before this. I'd had mornings where I hadn't slept for three nights before some school function and felt like a reanimated corpse in my own body. I had been so hungover just this year that I felt my brain shrink to two-thirds its size in my head, tearing at its fixture in my skull until I felt like screaming out. Nothing was like this though. I felt so tired, not physically, but existentially, like I had somehow artificially existed all this time by a conscious act of creation that was itself expiring now. I've heard the word 'God' thrown around a lot at times like this, and I certainly wouldn't go as far as to discount the faithful experiences of any other person who subscribes to that kind of thing. After all, how could I ever know something like that with any certainty? I was always agnostic about the whole God question, and generally just considered it none of my business. But the acid had put something uncomfortable into my view that made me reexamine something within me. During my trip, I felt myself go up, up, up, and then look down at myself. Now, or at least since, I have gone up, up, up, and instead continued to look out at what could possibly be beyond the realm of my own personal experience. I've since begun to feel a disturbance from that.

When one looks out at the vast expanse of the universe bounding ceaselessly outward before them, my expectation is that person would feel something like awe or sublimity in the literary senses of those words. The Vikings at Niagara Falls. Wordsworth crossing the Alps. Space, the final frontier. But as I looked up and out and into the face of God (I use this expression in a literary, not literal sense), I came to feel precisely the opposite. I felt too big for the space I inhabited, not cosmically important but kind of penned in, like the great universe was not only not infinite but in fact not even large enough for me at all. I imagined running my hands up and down the shiny glass terrarium of life, the universe, and everything, and finding it bounding my experience got me to questioning. If this feeling represents or even comes close to the true nature of what my existence really is, there are some follow up questions that I must ask of myself or of my creator, if they in fact can hear me or care to. Who else knows these limitations? Does my knowledge make me universally important? Is there anything outside of here, and if so, does it have any effect on this place? What is the nature of my creator, and what, if any, is my purpose or anyone else's? Is what happens, who I am, and the contents of my being, determined or do I have a will of my own?

I sat smoking for a while and felt like I was in a painting; a lacquered highway brushed under my wheels as an acrylic coastline shone pacifically on my right-hand side. I shook my head as I turned the facts and feelings over again. Doubtless I'd never get to the bottom of it, at least not without some deus ex machina, so I at last concluded that neither the mechanics of my created environment nor the mind of my creator were any of my business. As for my own individual purpose in this existence, I couldn't think of a better pastime standing on the edge of creation than to take it for a canvas upon which I could do some creation of my own. My creator, if in fact I have one, has some kind of craftsmanship I can respect, but I can see from here they left some blank spaces. To make something where there was previously nothing, even if it's just a good story about me and a good girl, is to know the mind of God.

As I sat there, capillary action of the clothes drinking the wetness from the seats, speeding toward the place I had decided to make my new home these next few years, I began to take stock of what kind of story I really was. How different was I now from the person I was half a year ago? What do I want to be different now, and how do all these new relationships reflect that? Was I a bad person back then, and if so, how much change makes a bad person a good one? The acid wasn't active anymore, but there in the car with thoughts enough to fill up the half-length of California, I flipped my perspective outside in and took another look at the questions that really mattered.

*　　*　　*

Mr. Carlos Vazquez,

Congratulations! We are pleased to offer you admission to Stanford University Class of 20—!

Mom and I didn't usually hug, but we did that day. That last year, she had always wanted to fight me over every little thing. Dishes or laundry or curfew or friends or Rosa; I was fine fighting back until I wasn't. The senior year class-rank race, debate team, model UN, and the SAT's all wore me down until she noticed we weren't fighting anymore. That spring, whenever she would engage attack mode, I wouldn't do anything but throw up my hands, drop whatever I was doing, and start working on whatever she was mad about. I think it stopped being fun for her after that, and when she asked me what was wrong, I could only respond, "I just have to get through it. Nothing you can do." I think she was even happier than I was when I got that letter. I could still be a burnout failure-to-launch if I wanted, but now it wouldn't happen on her watch. Any way you could see it from the outside, she raised a son all by herself and did a damn good job.

Even Don, Mom's boyfriend-for-now, told me congrats, "even though the universities have been captured by the liberal agenda." Not that I cared, but that was the best I could have expected. I was pretty lukewarm about the whole thing for the most part, but that all changed when we made that spring break visit up to Palo Alto.

Wide open spaces. That was the first, best impression I got when I set foot after foot after foot on The Farm. Over 8,000 acres of runway for a big mistake or two. Mom had questions enough for the tour guides, but I let my feet do the wondering as I turned stone over stone in what seemed no less than a garden of earthly delights. Following the vibe of the orientation, I splashed my way into no less than three different fountains, almost bought a bicycle on the spot, and even attended the last act of a student production of The Taming of the Shrew where they reversed the genders because feminism. There in the NorCal not-too-hot spring sunshine, I imagined myself all in cardinal, bantering with a lively group of attractive genius friends on our way to Stanford stadium to cheer on the team to yet another Big Game win, all while the ghost of the too-soon departed Leland Stanford Jr. smiled down at us onto the red adobe roofs like the Teletubbies sun baby. I looked back at Mom and shared a smile with her. Our kiddie dreams of Steinbeck and Silicon Valley weren't so silly anymore.

"–And they said that the campus is the size of 96 Disneylands, isn't that crazy?" I asked. Fast forward a week, and I was still going on about it to anybody who would listen. At this point, 'anybody' was only Rosa.

"Shhh, it's starting," she said with one finger to her lips. It was a rare Friday without any debate team or Model UN anything, so Rosa and I had decided to go to the movies. We settled on some teen tearjerker flick, one where the main girl almost dies near the beginning of the movie and most of it was some kind of out-of-body experience where she determined for herself whether her boyfriend loved her enough to merit staying alive or not. I didn't really get it, and looking around the mostly empty theater at the other teen couples in there, it seemed to me like the whole movie was just an excuse to make out in a dark theater.

"You think she'll die?" I whispered to Rosa. As she brought her hand into a yet more aggressive zipping motion across her mouth, a theater employee with an orange light-up usher wand made his way up the stairs in search of all the noise. I sat back, sipped my blue slushie, and let the intro credits roll on.

The movie was slow and uninteresting, but that seemed to be the preference of all the wandering hands and mouths in that dark theater. I sat next to Rosa and wanted her, and it really seemed at a certain point like we were the only two people in there not doing something. I thought she was mad at me, maybe for all the Stanford stuff. I reached my hand to hers and grabbed hold with interlocking fingers; she reciprocated and with the other picked up my blue drink to sip. With my free hand I played with the material of her skirt, feeling it between my first two fingers and thumb. It was leopard print, and while I hated the look of it, the material always felt nice in my hands whenever I had the chance to touch it. She always called it her 'easy access skirt,' so while I never really liked the article of clothing itself, I was always excited about what came from her wearing it. Feeling my way along the outside of the material up her thigh, I looked for the next green light on the road that every other teen in that theater was driving. Through the skirt, just the faintest outline around the ring of Rosa's upper thigh, I grazed the bumpy intertwine of her lace underwear, an article I knew very well that confirmed her expectations for how this night was going to go.

"AHHH—" I tried to choke back the yell. In one swift motion, she had grabbed my hand between the thumb and forefinger and pinched the skin so hard it hurt me. "What are you doing?"

"What are you doing?" she hissed back. "You're insufferable."

"I have no idea what you're talking about."

"I highly doubt that." Before the teen ushers could be put on alert about the disturbance, Rosa was already getting up and walking out.

"Rosa," I whispered as loudly as I could. "PSSSST," but she was gone.

In protest, I stayed and finished the movie. We went in Rosa's car anyway, so she could have driven herself home for all I knew. It was a few miles for me to walk, but I didn't care. I got it in my head that it would somehow completely burn her if I got super into the movie while she wasn't there and that the best revenge was to thoroughly enjoy myself in her absence. I tried, but it was still hard since the movie wasn't very good. I even tried getting up to sneak into another theater showing something else, but nothing was quite right, and I came back without having missed much. The most fun I had was with a weird sense of voyeurism I got from watching the other people in the theater, but I couldn't really enjoy myself without feeling creepy, so I gave it up after a few minutes. I wondered what Rosa would think of me if she were a post–car crash disembodied ghost deciding whether I was worth her waking up from her coma or not. *She'd probably let herself die.* Would she tell me that I had a bright future ahead of me and to move on without her? Or would she wake up, so long as we could stay together? Any case that involved her not dying made me feel like I was somehow heroic, somehow worth it for her. Was that all that love was? Making enough sacrifices for someone so they don't die, so that what you gain by being with them outweighs what you give up for it*? Either way, I'd better apologize for being an ass.*

Out of my reverie and back on the 101 freeway with Julie, I looked around and wondered about what I had really sacrificed to be where I was now. There was certainly no Teletubbies sun baby here, but the sun I had was perfectly nice albeit a little strong.

Even though my 'sacrifice' didn't end up going as planned, the story playing out for me was still a good one. Maybe relationships weren't so transactional as I once supposed. After all, I never really knew what I gave up and never could have imagined what I would get on the other side.

CHAPTER 22

Finally that evening, backs stiff and clothes wet again, we rumbled back down University Avenue into all the old smells of eucalyptus, bad weed, and pee that you only notice when you've been gone a while. As I filled my nose and throat with it, long and deep, I got a strange mix of feelings such that I couldn't determine whether these smells were miasma or ambrosia to me. If I made a candle out of the smell, I'd probably give it a bad review online but still keep it on hand and use it every time I forgot what it smelled like, just to remind myself that I didn't in fact like it.

"It's good to be back," I said.

"Is it?" Julie asked, looking at me incredulously.

"I don't know, I feel like I'm just supposed to say that." I dropped her off first at her dorm and kissed her goodbye, telling her I'd call tomorrow and good luck on another hard week of classes. The car rumbled and sagged its way back to the garage, and when I parked it I took one last look at the state of it.

The seats, while not fully dry, weren't sops anymore either after six hours in the uncovered sunlight. The tire pressure seemed low now, but after examining the wheels all around, I couldn't find any nails or punctures and so thought it was fine to give them back as is. Bugs and grime speckled the whole front grill for seasoning on the shit sandwich, and I felt bad that I hadn't remembered to gas up before bringing it back.

Biggest issue of all was still the roof. Carjackings and burglaries happened all the time in this town, so it wouldn't do at all to leave it with the top down. I tried the button again. Dead. I didn't like it, and I wasn't very confident, but the only thing to do was to put a little force on it. I found a tire iron in the trunk and stuck it in somewhere that seemed like it would force the issue without doing too much damage. I started off easy, but slowly worked my way up to pulling quite hard until I heard a *click click pop* come from the affected area and the roof came free. I was thankful for it coming up, but was too afraid to look and see if I had damaged anything so I resolved not to take too much notice. I pulled the thing closed as best I could until it flopped on top of everything and did my best to make it all look like it worked. The mildew smell came quickly back in the enclosed space, but I decided there wasn't much more to do than leave the desiccant dehumidifier in the back and hope the issue resolved itself within a couple of days. I looked back one last time at Charles's car as I walked away, and the last thing I remember noting was that his San Francisco Giants license plate holder was still as shiny and nice as it ever was. *Boo.*

I spent most of the 40–second elevator ride back up to eighth floor reliving private victories and past sleights from random insignificant parts of my past, when somewhere around fifth floor, my internal litigation was interrupted by an inhuman animal scream coming from somewhere in the building. *Not my floor, please.* Even worse.

I took the last three floors and 15 seconds of the ride to think about the sound I had just heard. It had started off long and low, and when it first became audible, I thought it had to do with the mechanics of the elevator. However, its rise in both volume and tone to its eventual fever pitch soon put those ideas out of my mind. After cresting its apex, the long drone settled into a low moan, human now, dying away with any peace I might have found on my long weekend.

When the elevator opened, there was already a small crowd gathering in the hallway, and those who hadn't come all the way out were peeking out from behind their dorm doors to see the source of the ado. All quiet but the murmuring crowd, when suddenly that primal yell crescendoed again, followed by a crunching crash and a fluttering of papers. *Charles's room.* I put out my lead shoulder and wedged through the crowd into the room next to mine to find Eddie stunned and Charles manic.

"What the hell is going on here?" I asked Eddie in a low voice, removing the door stop and letting the room close off.

"Uhhh... I... uhh..." he barely articulated, and one look into his boba-sized pupils and powdery complexion told me all I needed to know.

I shook my head and said, "My god, man, wipe that shit off your face please, this isn't a bakery." Eddie looked like he might start foaming at the mouth, but at least he seemed lucid. Only a little bit of questioning led Eddie to reveal to me not only that they took all the acid I gave them, but also heaped on top of it all of Eddie's available supply of coke, an eighth of weed each, and a fifth of Apple Jack Daniels to share. "You could have killed Mick Jagger on less than this, dude," I said.

Charles, for his part, actually looked like he had been dragged away by wild horses. Eddie wouldn't, or maybe couldn't, tell me why Charles looked like he did. His hair, usually easily combed to one side, was wisping out by the left and right temples like he had been pulling at it, and while it was hard to tell, I suspected him of tearing some out. His skin was a jaundiced yellow color, and what I at first thought was water soaking through his shirt was actually pouring sweat that had already dried at his arms and neck in a salty dust, but still persisted to dampen his clothes with a smell like pee, fear, and vinegar. Closer inspection determined there was pee mixed in as well.

Charles looked like he succeeded in bringing everything but the beds down around his ears. The crashing sound I heard when I entered the scene turned out to be a whole bookshelf, and it was only by luck that no one got hurt from it. The room, which no one ever charged with being too clean, looked like it had been burglarized, and a closer look at the broken potted plant in its usual spot on the floor revealed a smattering of blood across one of the ceramic shards.

All through my observation and subsequent attempts at shaking and rousing him, Charles persisted in that low animal moan I first heard in the elevator but couldn't now get him to stop making. "What's wrong with him, why is he doing this?" I asked.

"Uhhh, I dunno," said Eddie shrugging.

"Jesus, dude, work with me here," I said. "I see you're trashed as hell but give me a timeline. It's like 8pm now. When did you take everything?"

Eddie's stare turned placid like he was remembering an old war story. "Well, we've been working on the fifth pretty much all afternoon, and same for the rest of the snow I wasn't able to sell. We, uh... fooled around a bit, and afterwards Charles wanted to smoke too, but we didn't have any on hand and had to go out and buy. The tabs we took about an hour ago."

"An hour ago? Oh my god, Eddie, this shit lasts like 12 hours! When did he start acting like this?"

"Uhhh, I don't know, but not very long, I can't really tell the time," he said. I couldn't be sure if it was in response to either of us or to some nameless phantom only he could see, but just then Charles wailed louder than ever, so loud I had to cover my ears and Eddie pinned him to the ground to try to knock the wind out of him.

"We gotta calm him down, he can't keep screaming like this," I said. Just then there was a knock at the door.

We knew from just the knock that it was our floor RA, Rebecca. She'd introduced herself as Rebecca at the first-ever eighth floor meeting, but had since regretted it and tried to rebrand herself as Becca, Becky, and Bec. None of them really ever stuck, either because she tried too many names or, as I thought, because she was at the heart of it all a 'Rebecca' through and through.

The first thing she had told us in her introduction was that she was from San Diego. If you ever get the chance to meet anyone from San Diego, the first thing they always tell you is that they're from San Diego. The second thing is how much they like being from San Diego. I don't know, I guess it's nice there. Poor Rebecca. Only in her second year at college and she thought she'd have a chill time getting free rent in the dorms for just the small price of keeping the floor's supply of condoms and reminding everybody of quiet hours from 10pm-6am, but of course it didn't go that way. In response to noise complaints on our floor this year, she had already at this point walked in on three alcohol poisonings, a nasty case of norovirus, people doing coke off other people's butts, and one notable fight between roommates that both started and ended with one pooping in the other's bed. To me, Rebecca seemed worn down by knocking and entering when she didn't want to, fearing someone might die on her watch when all she really wanted to do was enjoy her favorite $6 extra-sweet hazelnut iced coffee and struggle through her lower division poli-sci homework in peace.

Since she wanted to be a good RA, she could never successfully stay in her room and ignore the noise nor the subsequent noise complaints when they came up. The only thing she could do to defend against seeing what she didn't want to see was to develop a signature knock that would tell everyone to knock off what they were doing so she could poke her head in, give a stern look, and go away having fixed everything and earned her room and board. It was a good knock, solid and authoritative but polite and even a little bit fun; she picked for her knock rhythm the immortal cadence of late night hosts, Looney Toons, car horns, and Vietnam POWs: the classic 'dah-di–di–dah–di, di–dit' (or [-..-. ..] in morse). She didn't like me much, I think because I once caught her practicing on her own door when she thought no one was around and I finished the cadence in call-and-response fashion, and she didn't like that unsolicited intimacy. I smiled to myself and thought about knocking back for a moment, almost forgetting where I was.

"Is everyone okay in there?" Rebecca asked through the doorway. "RA, open up."

"Coming!" I called, and signaled Eddie to handle Charles as I opened the door. "Hey, Re–Becky, what's up?"

Rebecca stuck her face in the crack and tried to look past me. "What's going on here?"

I opened the door a bit wider to show Charles and Eddie on the floor. "Oh, you know, Charles is pretty upset about some personal stuff, so we're just trying to cheer him up." Eddie was sitting behind Charles on the floor and wrapping his arms around his shoulders in a bear hug and coo-cooing him like a baby; thankfully it was working.

"Okay, well it's quiet hours so we can't be crying too loud. If you need anything, feel free to use the anonymous comment box or schedule with my office hours." She took one last look at Charles before turning to walk away and made the mistake of making eye contact with him. I watched in horror as he held her with his glittering eye, unhinged his jaw like a snake's, and through the open portals to his soul squeezed through the bitterest sights and sounds of mortal anguish I've ever witnessed in another living being.

Charles transfixed us both in his beam, and we watched his eyes well with tears and stream down his face as his voice grew louder with the sound of psychic death. Up close, we couldn't cover our ears this time nor look away. The tears couldn't hide his eyes, nor could all the water in San Francisco Bay have been able to obscure the window into what his mental health professionals would later refer to as his 'psychotic break.' Helpless against his gaping eyes and mouth, we looked deep inside him and didn't see Charles, nor did he see us. All we could see was his experience of seeing something, something too horrible and unspeakable to even name. Fresh off my own acid trip yesterday, I knew where he went. He went up, up, up, and out, out beyond the clouds and beyond space and beyond the leviathans of the deep. He reached the glass terrarium at the edge of all creation just like me, but unlike me he didn't like what he saw and took a second tab. Mistake. What we saw of him now was all that was left of his shattered psyche, after Charles felt the full force of ego death and subsequently smashed himself through the glass to demand an audience with the lizard gods at the end of all things. I could see in his eyes that he not only found them, but he was still with them. I could never, would never, go where Charles went that day, off to see the wizard to ask for a brain. It looked like a pretty one-sided conversation, but then again I would never know what he got out of it. All I could hear were the screams.

Poor Rebecca. I was looking at Charles, but Charles was looking at her; she got the full blast of it. All she had ever wanted was to get through college at the school she was proud to attend, add bit by bit to her wardrobe of expensive athleisure, and come out the other side ready to pursue a career as a mid-level employee at some socially responsible corporation with a San Diego office that didn't burn the planet with the same gusto as the other guys. Here in the shadow of Charles's Eldritch eye, all of that seemed kind of silly now. She started crying too; I don't think she knew why.

I couldn't tell how long the four of us were trapped in the amber of that moment, but in acid time it was long enough for all of us to forget how we got there. If everything stayed exactly like that, we all might have held serve right there in the antechamber of eternity, peeping through the keyhole of Charles's self-destruction until each and all of us collapsed from physical fatigue within hours or even days. Mercifully, it didn't come to that, and at long last it was Charles who broke the tableau for himself, tossing a fat rock into the glassy pond to break up the illusion. In one motion, he wrenched himself out of Eddie's embrace and slammed his hand down upon the ceramic pottery shards covering the ground, cutting himself and drawing blood afresh.

The blood came out slowly at first, and for a few seconds it seemed like he hadn't cut himself at all. We were all disabused of this thought when at last the broken skin filled its opening with one large, blooming red drop that started flowing off his hand, along his wrist, and down his arm. It took nothing less than these sights and sounds of human frailty to recall Rebecca to life with us.

"Oh, hell no," she said finally, starting to back out of the room, "No, no, no, he needs emergency services." She turned and ran off right then, phone in hand, back down the hallway and out to her room at the end of the hall. I tried to stop her, but by that time Charles had already done more than enough talking for the both of us and she couldn't see me anymore through her wet eyes. Upon my return to the room, I went immediately to Eddie.

"Dude, this is really bad, EMT's are probably going to be here soon, we can't let them take him. We've got to get him right."

This new urgency served to sober Eddie up a bit. "Hold on a minute," he said. "Do you think if Charles spends the night in the hospital, they'll investigate where he got all these drugs from?" We looked at each other for a second and both knew the answer.

Eddie took charge of the first aid, having been a summer lifeguard. He took Charles to the bathroom to wash out the cut before wrapping it with gauze and taping it all up within just a few minutes. All the while, I tried to find him there within himself.

"Hey Charles," I said, "We're here for you man, you're safe here." No acknowledgement, no response.

"Charles, the EMT's will be here soon, and all of us are here for you whatever you need, but I just wanted to let you know that it's in everybody's best interests for you to play it cool, okay? If not, all of us might be in a lot of trouble. Charles?" No response but the same glassy stare.

"Goddammit, Charles, they're going to kick us out of school! Me, Eddie, we gave you illegal drugs and if we're not arrested or something, at the very least the Office of Student Conduct is going to investigate us and kick us out once the report reaches them of you getting transported from the dorms by ambulance, please don't let that happen. Be a trooper, Charles, be a team player, save our lives and yours, and be cool and everything will be okay! Please man, it's all you." He might not even have heard me that time. Almost ten minutes of this, and the only response to my devolving groveling was a distant sound of sirens growing steadily closer. Whatever else I was thinking, I had to acknowledge that on-campus emergency response times were impressive.

I was just on the verge of giving myself up, imagining what I'd say to Mom and Don when I called them for bus fare back to SoCal after my dishonorable discharge, when Eddie took it into his own hands. He squared his shoulders to face Charles, took both hands in his, and looked deep into his eyes until he found something to grab onto. The same instant he felt Charles catch the line of his personal attention, Eddie yelled directly into his face, "Hey, bitch!" before subsequently kissing him and then slapping him in the face with medium firmness. Charles was with us.

"$1000, man," Eddie began, "That's what we're playing for here. Cost of this ambulance coming to get you is $1000 for a trip of only a mile and a half, and that's before you get seen by anybody inside that hospital. Is that what you want?" Charles mutely shook his head. "Good," Eddie continued, "Me neither. Now, those EMT guys are coming up the elevator right now, so all you have to do to secure that bag for yourself is to tell them that everything's fine and you don't need to go with them. Easy, right?" Charles nodded, and Eddie touched him on the nape of his neck. "Good. We get through this, and every date from now on is on me until we get up to that $1000, deal?" Charles nodded. Eddie looked at him and then at me again. "Let's fucking go, then."

The EMT's arrived in short order along with Rebecca, who led them in from the street level. Technically, I think they turned out to be firefighters, and one of them even carried a fire ax, but I guess it makes sense that firefighters are just EMT's who also fight fires.

"Here he is," said Rebecca, opening the door to his room.

"Good evening," said Charles, with an affected coolness that chilled me with its contrast.

"We got reports of injury and excessive use of controlled substances," said the one with the ax.

"Yes, that was me," said Charles, smiling and holding up his bandaged hand. "My apologies, I had a bit too much to drink and got a bit rowdy, but I'm okay now thanks to my friends here." Charles looked from us to the firewoman to Rebecca, but Rebecca, still puffy-eyed, wouldn't meet his gaze. I sat there nervously, afraid to say anything. Charles sounded weird to me, kind of stagey, like he was pretending to be who he was.

"Are you telling us that you don't need or want emergency medical transport?" asked the EMT.

"Yes, but thanks for thinking of me," he said. *Weird thing to say.* The EMT scribbled something on her clipboard.

"Alright, but we'll need to do a medical examination and ask you some questions for the report."

As I watched, I could hardly believe that Charles in his state of complete physical, psychological, and emotional breakdown could wear a mask as convincing as this one. After his stilted introductions, he answered every medical question and submitted himself to every field test with a coy magnanimity that was almost charming, pooh-poohing himself for his 'messiness' and seeming deeply sorry for the inconvenience he caused all parties involved. Of course, he still had alcohol, weed, cocaine, and acid coursing through him, and whenever he looked at someone too long, his yawning black pupils nearly gave away the dark secret that he had imparted to Rebecca and me not fifteen minutes earlier. The examiners weren't exactly satisfied, but at the bottom of all their bags of medical tools and at the end of the long clipboard onto which they wrote his responses, they couldn't justify a reason why they should stay nor why he should leave with them.

Of all the reasons that I could think of for Charles's collectedness, Eddie's special connection to Charles, Charles's concern for our eligibility for this school, Charles's worry about the financial strain hospitalization would put on him, none fit as well as this single self-evident, universal truth that any substance user of any persuasion will know: nothing sobers you up faster than the arrival of first responders.

"Alright, that's everything then," the EMT finally said. "This report will be forwarded to the Residential Office, so they will likely have you take an alcohol safety online training course as a result of tonight's events, but don't worry, if there's nothing else you need to tell us, we'll be leaving now."

"Alright," said Charles, wobbling to his feet to show them out of his tiny room, "Thank you and have a great night, we will be safe!" He smiled his paper smile, dying in the eyes, as the firefighters filed out and down and onto their next assignment. Rebecca was the last to leave, lingering to see if any trace of mania remained in him.

"Good night, Becky," I said, waving her off.

"Just call me Rebecca, thanks. And be safe," she said that last part to all of us and retired to her room.

Charles was still smiling after everyone left, and when he finally caught his reflection in the full-length wardrobe mirror, he smiled and smiled even bigger, turning his petrifying gaze in on itself and contorting his face into a maniac leer, never breaking eye contact.

"Well, damn dude, I think I just about lost my buzz from all that excitement," Eddie said to me. Meanwhile, Charles trained his demoniac grin onto his reflection and added a gentle, back and forth rocking sway.

"Hey, dude," I said, trying to get Eddie's attention.

"—I mean, I'm still high as hell right now, but like, kind of unbalanced now, you know? Should I smoke more or drink more or what?" Eddie continued. Without breaking from his reflection, Charles ramped up his swaying, adding unnatural contortions of his arms and neck like some kind of primitivist interpretive dance.

"Hey, you ok?" I asked Charles now, but he stopped hearing me. His swaying and contortions escalated even further, and he began spinning around and gnashing his teeth without making any other sounds, always coming back to face the mirror.

Eddie continued, unheeding, "like damn, bruh, I really thought they had us for a minute there, I was super scared, I didn't know what we were going to do if they—" Just then, Charles in his hysterical contortions smacked against Eddie with his wrist, and that drove him over the edge. Eddie finally noticed him, but too late. Charles locked in with his reflection, set his feet like a track star, and jumped at the sound of a gun only he could hear. I saw everything in the mirror, which for some reason seemed more real than the real Charles. He coursed across the tiny room in only a second, the whole way continuing to pretzel his limbs like he was trying to take flight to join a legion of demons. The last thing I saw in the mirror was his twisted smile, mangling his face into a dough of anguish and ecstasy, spreading wider than ever. The next moment his head went fully through the mirror and he went still.

CHAPTER 23

Compared to what preceded it, the ride to the hospital was uneventful. Though we roundly succeeded at avoiding the $1,000 ambulance ride, Charles's split forehead now made skipping the emergency room out of the question. Fresh off my road trip, I took the three of us in his car. Charles sat in the back and Eddie joined him, if only to stop him from putting his head through more glass. As I drove, the soft top roof rattled, and the wind whistled in. I kept glancing at Charles in the rear-view mirror; he hadn't seemed to notice anything but kept pressing the bloody towels to his head.

"Ugh, something stinks back here," said Eddie from the back.

"No it doesn't," I answered, then corrected myself, "I don't smell anything."

We arrived at the emergency room to find the place clamoring. Usually in this town, at this time of night, at the end of a weekend, the emergency room might have a few alcohol transports but was otherwise slow. When we arrived, we couldn't even find seats in the waiting room; we had to take spots on the floor against the wall. Luckily, Charles impressed us with his executive functioning, accurately filling out a whole clipboard of medical questions and even producing his insurance information for the hospital administrator despite his bleeding head and deranged mind.

We waited more than an hour before he was admitted. During that time, EMT's kept showing up in a steady stream, wheeling gurneys occupied by hard-breathing, vomit-covered patients from the street and disappearing into the inner wings of the hospital. The other wait room occupants seemed to know the patients, and every time a new gurney showed up, the chatter would die down and about half the room would stand to see if the rolling bed contained the face they were looking for. A little while after Charles was shown in, Eddie and I heard a familiar voice from among the wait room crowd.

"Oh honey, my sweetu, I'm so sorry!" said Priyanka, going up to the newest gurney to arrive. "Although you should have come with me, and it is really your fault, but no, I can't say that now… Will he be alright?" she asked, turning to an EMT and clutching the gurney so firmly that she hampered its movement.

"Miss, step aside, we need to treat him," said the EMT with short shrift. Abhas, strapped down with his face congealed with blood and vomit, inclined his head to smile weakly at Priyanka but said nothing as they wheeled him away and out of sight. Priyanka sighed a little and turned away, but in an instant caught us staring, the light of recognition registering in her eyes. As she returned our gazes, her great-white-sharky grin flashed into high relief like lightning across a night landscape.

When she was only halfway across the room she cried, "My floormates! So nice to see you. What brings you here this evening?" as if we were running into each other at the mall and not in an ER waiting room.

"Charles is in a bad way," Eddie answered for the both of us.

"Oh, I'm sorry to hear that, he is such a sweet boy," said Priyanka, pushing out her lower lip as she said so. "You know, he is always so good to my sweetu when he goes to visit, he always tells me so. Yes, I am here for my Abhas. He's gotten himself into trouble again."

"What kind of trouble?" I asked. "Do you know what's going on here?"

"Yes, unfortunately, I do." She slid down between me and Eddie on the floor, and I had to move away to not graze her shoulder. "Most of these people, including my Abhas and myself, all came from the same party." I turned my body to face Priyanka. She sat between us cross-legged, with a straight back, and hands resting on her knees. Despite whatever other feelings I had about her, she seemed to have a certain magnetism. Usually repelled by her, both Eddie and I drew closer to hear her speak.

"The evening started off normal enough," she began. "Tonight, we attended a party hosted by the Desi Student Association at the Pi Kappa Phi fraternity. We were celebrating the 21st birthday of our friend, fraternity brother, and DSA social chair, Sahil Khumar. Do you know him?" I shook my head; Eddie nodded.

"Sahil the Thrill?" Eddie asked. "Yo, that guy's wild."

"Yes, he was a delight this evening," said Priyanka, retreating into reminiscence for a moment. "But anyway, the party went as expected for a while, with drinking, games, and even a Bollywood dance contest in which my Abhas received an honorable mention! He is really quite talented, my sweetu. Unfortunately for me, that witch, Preetha Pichai thought so as well. She claimed runner-up in the dance competition, which, yes yes, was impressive, but after that she was all over him, and he didn't deny her either. He had much too much to drink, as usual, so I was sure he would end up with her tonight. I told him my displeasure and said he could walk home tonight for all I cared. I left in my car and made a plan to lock the doors at home."

Eddie and I waited a few moments for her to continue her story, but she merely looked at us. "So how did all these people end up in the hospital?" I asked finally.

"Oh yes yes, that. On my way home I was passed by no less than seven emergency vehicles going the other way, and after the seventh I just had to turn around and make sure that it wasn't the house I thought. Unfortunately, it was. I arrived back just before the police closed it off, so I was able to reenter the party. It was horrible. There was enough vomit to cover the whole floor of the place, and those who could talk to the medics said they were burning on the inside and had trouble breathing. From what the police were saying at the time, they believe the drinks at the party were poisoned."

"Poisoned?" exclaimed Eddie, wide-eyed.

"Oh my God, that's demented," I said, taken aback.

"Yes, it's horrible," she said. "It seemed to the medical staff that someone spiked the jungle juice with some kind of household chemicals. Luckily, I didn't drink tonight because I planned to drive. I looked around for my sweetu at the house, but someone told me that they already took him to the hospital. I put whoever wanted to come with me in my car and came down here, but I still have no idea how my Abhas left before me in an ambulance and didn't arrive until after I did."

"Does anybody know who could have done that to the drinks?" Eddie asked.

"Not yet, but police are investigating who might have wanted to hurt Sahil, the DSA, Pi Kapp, or all three. Here's what I do know: the event was invite-only, so whoever did it must have been a guest." Eddie and I each looked away from Priyanka with a shudder, and she stared back ominously. "The police might be treating it as a hate crime because all the victims were Desi students. For my part, I hope whoever did it rots in jail, an unmarked grave, and Hell one after the other."

"Man, that is *deeply* fucked that somebody would do that," said Eddie after a silence. I nodded in agreement, unsure of what else to say.

"So what about Charles, what happened to him tonight?" asked Priyanka.

I answered for both Eddie and myself, sticking to our official story and keeping it short so as not to incriminate ourselves. "He just had too much to drink and hit his head," I said. Priyanka looked from me to Eddie, maybe hoping to get some more information, but when she saw he had nothing to add she began to stand up.

"I'm sorry to hear that. Well, I'm going to go out to smoke. Join me?" she asked, facing entirely toward Eddie as she made her proposition.

"Uh, I'm okay thanks," he said nervously. "I'm actually gonna wait here until one of these chairs opens up."

"I'll go," I said, surprising even myself. Priyanka looked a little put out by Eddie's raincheck, and I wondered if my presence was any consolation at all. For my part, I wasn't really sure why I accepted at the time. Maybe I was finally getting nicotine addicted and that made it easy to accept free tobacco from someone I usually didn't like. Maybe it was my fatigue from lily-padding from one crisis to another for weeks now that made certain substance buzzes feel like quality repose. Maybe it was the cosmic horror and human evil of this dark night of the soul that made me want to gather round in fellowship with anyone who claimed to be opposed to those things. Maybe I was just tired of sitting on the floor. Either way, I didn't think any more about it as I stood next to Priyanka under the lights of the carport, the recommended 25 feet from the hospital entrance, just like the sign said.

"It's chilly out here," I said, rubbing my bare arms. "You don't have a jacket either, huh?"

"I just came from a frat party," Priyanka said matter-of-factly.

"So what, what does that mean?"

"You're not supposed to wear a jacket to a frat party, everyone knows that," she said laughing. I didn't say anything, but reflected on my own first frat experience at Dean's August invite where I didn't know that and had to find out.

"Do you need a lighter?" I asked, digging around and finding one in my pocket.

Priyanka unsheathed a magnanimous smile, saying, "No thank you, but I appreciate it." As she said so, she pulled out a cassette-sized gadget from her purse with a snub-nosed spigot protruding from one corner.

"Ohhhhh, I was thinking cigarettes," I said, sliding my lighter back into my pocket.

"Cigarettes? Interesting. So... Bohemian." She took her first hit as I puzzled over whether to feel insulted or not. The device whirred and crackled under her suction, and as she exhaled, a cloud of smoke big enough to consume a whole cigarette escaped her with a fruity bittersweetness that I couldn't quite place.

"What flavor is that?" I asked.

"Peach green tea," she said, "one of my favorites." She handed me the vape, and as I breathed in, a torrent of dense flavor came rushing at me with a strength that almost knocked me over. I coughed and sputtered and handed it back to her, and within moments I felt a buzz like I had shotgunned three cigarettes at once.

"How long have you been vaping?" I asked after I finished coughing.

"Too long," she said, sighing, "I've been meaning to quit for years now but somehow I just keep buying more cartridges."

"Well dang, that's not good," I said, and had to clench my teeth to keep them from chattering from the effects of either the cold or the nicotine jitters or both. I felt my hands and arms buzzing and goosebumps forming as Priyanka hit her vape again.

I began, "Priyanka, I have to ask you—"

"—Uh uh uh," she interrupted, wagging the spigot of the vape pen at me like a disapproving finger, "my friends call me Priya, I thought I told you?"

"Right, okay," I said, not going as far as to call her my friend. "Do you think Abhas will be alright?"

"Of course!" she replied instantly. "He's much stronger than he looks, my Abhas, and besides, he wouldn't dare die on me. I'm sure he'll be fine by tomorrow."

"Alright then." Unable to keep still from the jitters, I started to fidget. "Don't take this the wrong way, but why are you guys together?" A different sort of smile came across her lips then. Always elsewhere flashing her brilliant, perfect teeth even to the point of aggression, she smiled this time with closed lips and a smug expression.

"Thank you for flattering me with your interest," she said slowly, "but I'm sorry that I don't feel the same way about you."

"What?" I almost shouted, feeling my cheeks heat up. "You don't understand, I'm not propositioning you."

"Don't be embarrassed," she said, winking at me. "I'll keep it between us. Floormates need to stick together, after all."

"But you're not even—" I said, becoming flustered, "alright, forget it then. But here's what I really want to know. When I first met you, you were all over *Eddie*, not Abhas, and while he was watching you do that, *your Abhas* drank nearly to the point of passing out. Now tonight, you're at this party, and Abhas now seems to be the one who's all over somebody. Clearly you sounded upset about it, but at the end of it all you left him with her."

"Yes," she replied.

"He would have spent the night with her if everybody wasn't hospitalized."

"Perhaps."

"So there."

"I don't understand, what's your question?"

"My question is what is the deal with you guys?! You say you love each other and all that, yet you both act like you can't wait to get with somebody else."

Priyanka didn't respond right away, but leaned back against the wall of the carport and took another hit of her vape. She seemed to drink from it like she was trying to fill her legs with smoke. When she exhaled, she disappeared for a moment behind a peach tea fog, and I didn't see her again for more than a moment.

"Here," she said, handing me the vape, "I see you're becoming agitated, probably because of your friend, and I don't want to cause you more stress." Despite my rapid heartbeat and trembling hands, I hit it again. "Better?" she asked. No. But I kept quiet.

Priyanka began again. "Now, I haven't known you very long, but I gather that you've never been in a relationship before?"

"What?" I said, taken aback. "What makes you say that?"

"Oh well the way you insert yourself, of course," she said. "The last time we saw each other, you were coming right in the middle of your roommate and his girlfriend, not to mention between me and my Abhas as well. As I had just met you, I decided not to say anything, but at the time you struck me as very lonely."

"Insert myself?" I exclaimed, growing even hotter now. "I think, Priyanka, if anybody was doing that, it was *you*. And besides, you're wrong. I am in a relationship. With Julie."

"Julie?" She thought to herself for a moment. "Oh, that short girl with the wavy hair? That is interesting. I thought she was annoyed with you when I met you both, but I must've been wrong. It seems I don't know you very well, Carlos, but at the same time I think you don't know me very well either. My Abhas and I have a… special arrangement."

"What, so you're just cool with everything each other does with other people?" I asked.

"Well, I don't think it's that simple. My Abhas and I first told each other 'I love you' when we were eleven years old. We've been together ever since. Now, you can love someone with all your heart, but when you devote yourself so young to someone else who is so young also, there is no way that you can experience all of human feeling with just one person. Now, neither of us loves this fact, but my true self loves experiences, people, and pleasures, and Abhas does too."

"So like polyamory? An open relationship?"

"We don't really like either of these words. They just come with so many… preconceptions," said Priyanka. "I guess if I had to define it, I would say we just both love love."

"How do you not feel jealous when you see them with somebody else?"

"I still feel it; we both do. But at the end of the day, I have chosen to love him, and he me, in the way that we can, and it will always be this way."

I reflected on this for a while, so much so that I obliged myself to take another vape hit. "My last relationship lasted for a while," I finally said through a smoky exhale. "We didn't meet at eleven years old, but we were young too. She was also looking for different experiences with other people, as you say, and when I didn't like it we ended up splitting up. Are you saying that if I let her be with whoever she wanted and just dealt with it, it would have made all the difference?"

"Of course not. The difference is you, stupid boy," Priyanka said, shaking her head. "I can't say anything to you if you won't listen, so listen to me now. I've been in love with the same person for eight years now, and I'm saying to you that love is a choice. Not for one day of it have things been easy for us, and they're not easy today. To stay together, every day you have to choose to advance the health, happiness, and well-being of another person as well as yourself, and if those things are ever in conflict between the two of you, you have to solve it. Abhas and I love life as much as we love each other, so we're trying every day to make that work. People who stay together try every day no matter what their feelings are. People who break up decide, for better or worse, that they are choosing not to try anymore."

It took me a while to process what Priyanka said, unexpected as it was. "And how do you know when someone isn't choosing you anymore?" I asked.

She thought for a minute before answering. "Well, hopefully they tell you, but if they don't, they'll leave and never come back. That's how you know." I shivered as she said so, and not from the cold. For me, it felt like Priyanka was throwing a new light on an old story.

"Well, shoot," she said, tapping on the cartridge of her device with the flat of her palm, "Dead." Just then, a sleek little Hyundai, clean and compact, drove up from the street and caught us in its headlights. I was blinded for a moment, but as the car pulled closer and the lights lowered out of eye level, I recognized more of my friends.

"Hey, guys," I said, "What are you doing here?"

"Eddie messaged. We came as soon as we heard," said Jian, stepping out of the passenger seat.

"I'm sure Charles will be really happy to see you," I said to Jian as I went in to hug him. He was surprised, but he let me do it and even hugged back a little. "Hi, Carolyn," I said, stooping down to see her through the open window. She didn't reply, but made a little salute as if she were tipping an invisible cap.

"Wait a minute," I said, "why didn't you tell me you had a car when I was looking to borrow one?"

"You didn't ask," she said, shrugging. She then rummaged through the center console and found a book. "Here, Zelda said to lend you the week's reading for your class." I took the book from her and scanned the cover: Virgil's *Aeneid*. Other than all the colorful sticky tabs poking out from the pages, it looked brand new.

"You gonna park and come in?" I asked.

"No, I need to get back to Julie."

"Oh, is she alright?"

"Yes," she said, "but she's been struggling in our Chem class and I'm helping her." With that, she seemed ready to drive away, but Jian came around to the other side. Without saying a word, he opened the driver's door, palmed her cheek in his hand, and kissed her like we weren't there. Feeling herself perceived by us, Carolyn flushed pink from chest to forehead but didn't pull away. When Jian finally pulled back, Carolyn looked almost too flustered to drive, and I wouldn't have been surprised if I saw her straight, black hair curl itself up like shavings from a pencil sharpener. She lingered a moment looking at Jian, almost spoke but didn't, and drove off. Priyanka, Jian, and I then turned and headed back inside.

"So how are things between the two of you?" I asked Jian when we had made it inside. The hospital crowd had thinned out a little by now, and Eddie had secured seats for all of us in the corner.

"Amazing, it's been like a dream," he said as we all sat down together. "We couldn't be happier."

"Well, that's nice," said Eddie, chiming in.

"How long have you guys been together?" asked Priyanka.

"One-two months," Jian said, "Carolyn can tell you exactly, but I somehow have this feeling like we've always known each other." He smiled to himself as he said it.

"That's really cool, man, I'm super happy for you guys," I said.

Jian looked around at all of us seriously before he continued. "I know we're all here to support Charles tonight, and I don't want to take away from that. But I have something important to tell everyone, and I don't know the next time I'll see you all at the same time."

"Well, of course you can tell us anything. We as your friends will of course support you," said Priyanka, grabbing Jian's hand with hers. I couldn't hold back a deep sigh and an eyeroll, and was about to say something exclusionary when Jian squeezed her hand back and thanked her. I just nodded and kept quiet.

"Okay," Jian continued, "the start of this year has been one of the most special of my life, and I'm so grateful to all of you for everything you've done to make it that way. As my closest friends at school here, I wanted you guys to be the first to know. I'm planning to ask Carolyn to marry me."

All eyes whirled around our little chair circle as we traded looks of surprise, bewilderment, confusion, reflection, and genuine joy.

"Wow, dude, that's incredible," said Eddie, speaking first. "You really think you found the one, huh?" Jian couldn't contain his excitement anymore and didn't even speak, but just nodded emphatically.

"Yeah, man, pretty cool," I said, searching for my response. "You don't think you guys are kind of... young? Like, it's pretty cool and all if you're sure, but wouldn't you want to get a bit more life experience?" I couldn't help but meet Priyanka's gaze as I asked the question.

My question seemed to return Jian to his collected self, and I could almost hear his perfect posture click into consideration before he answered me. "Well," he said, "in terms of age, I'm a little older than you guys. I'm 22, which is the legal age to get married in my country and normal if you have a good job. I'm still a student, and would like to attend medical school after graduation, but my family will be able to support us until I can become a doctor."

"Wait a sec, you're not... crazy rich, are you?" asked Eddie, looking at Jian as if he were waiting for a big reveal.

Jian laughed heartily. "Unfortunately, no. My parents are both country doctors. They'll take care of us, but nothing glamorous. As for 'life experience,' I've spent all my life watching your American movies and shows, especially about love. It seems to me a very American concept to be in a relationship for practice or experience; I don't think I need that. When I came here for school, my first goal was to get an education, but my second was to find a wife from the beautiful nation whose culture I have loved from afar all my life. I think I have all the experience I need."

I looked at him as he spoke. He needed neither advice, opinions, nor convincing. I just smiled at him. *Maybe it's a cultural thing.*

"And what does your girlfriend think of getting married so soon?" asked Priyanka.

Before he spoke, Jian smiled a broad, mischievous smile. As I looked on, he reminded me of Julie when she wanted to propose a scheme. "What better way to find out than to ask her?"

After that bombshell, the rest of the evening was uneventful. After a few hours, Charles was released back to us all stitched up, no questions asked. Abhas ended up having to stay overnight for monitoring, but just as Priyanka had said, he ended up being fine eventually. I ended up not being able to sleep at all, so I passed the rest of that night in bed, buzzing away from the nicotine, and wondering what it would look like for me to be together forever with someone.

CHAPTER 24

"Hey."

"Hey, wake up, time for school."

"HELLO? ZELDA?"

For the third day this week, Zelda was napping in my bed. I thought it had ended when she and Eddie broke up, but she still had our room key and they were apparently on good terms again.

"Why can't you just take a nap at your place?" I had asked back on Monday, the first day I found her here.

"Becauuuuuuse," she had said, poking my nose like I was a silly goose, "I live all the way in Foothill and all the English classes are right here across the street. It's a perfect two-hour gap. You can always wake me up before our Classics course."

"Why can't you nap in Eddie's bed?" I had asked back on Wednesday, the second time I found her here.

"Over there?" she had asked, touching her collarbone and pointing as if I had asked her to sleep on a mound of dead fish. "We may be alright now, but he's still my ex. What would it say about us if we were always in each other's beds?"

Today, Friday, the fifth day since Charles's trip to the hospital, Zelda wasn't saying much of anything. She was completely sprawled out and twisted up in my sheets and blankets, hours-old drool dried on her mouth. Talking, yelling, and even poking hadn't done anything to rouse her, so I picked up one of my pillows that she had cast to the floor and prepared to hit her with it, just hard enough to wake her. I examined it up close as I decided how hard to go.

Zelda had shed her golden hair all over it, just like the rest of my bedding. I could hardly believe how much there was. I definitely had to wash it all this weekend; the sheets had even started to smell like her. Vanilla, almond, lotion, and that baby-sweet musk one's sweat gets from a comfy childhood with lots of love from Mom and Dad. Not that the smell was gross to me or anything. My bigger concern was that I liked it when I shouldn't have.

I brought the pillow down medium-hard on her face. No sooner had I done so than Zelda opened her eyes, bolted upright in bed, grabbed my arm with surprising strength, and said, "the death of the soul!" loud enough for Charles to hear next door.

"What the hell?" I exclaimed, retreating from her. She didn't let me get far; she kept her grip on my arm.

"You, you!" she said, still wild-eyed.

"Yeah, it's my room," I said. "You ok?"

"I just had the strangest dream," she said.

"About what?"

"Hmmm... funny, I can't remember. Time for school?"

We walked together from my dorm straight to our class in the English department building. It wasn't so far: our side of campus, right past the front gate and before you even reach the quad with the bell tower. It was the neoclassical one with more columns than windows, just before everything turned to brick. Even though it was close, Zelda always talked quickly and walked slowly beneath the main plaza's pollarded, knobby trees.

"I still can't believe Jian is going to propose to Carolyn, isn't that wild?" she asked. Class had just let out at the top of the hour, and the entrance to campus swelled with students squeezing through all kinds of fundraisers, activists, and solicitors.

"Excuse me sir, may I ask you a question?" some guy with a flier asked me while trying to push one into my hands.

"No thanks, I'm good," I said without looking at him. I never broke my stride as I turned back to face Zelda. "Yeah, I can't really get my head around it either, they just seem so young, you know?"

"I don't know, I think it's kind of sweet. I kind of believe in them, you know?" She broke from me to go around a little table helmed by a smug Republican wielding a sign saying, "Communism has failed everywhere it's been tried. Change my mind."

"Bible study?" asked a middle-aged Asian man, holding out a little book to me. I didn't even respond this time, but just ducked away without making eye contact. "Look," I said to Zelda, "even if it's nothing out of the ordinary to him, do you think Carolyn would really want to marry at 18? I don't even know if she's had a boyfriend before, do you?"

"I'm not sure. Wait, one moment," she said, and broke ranks even farther from me this time to fully circumnavigate a vegan protest taking up most of the walkway. The activists were squeezing themselves into kennels and pouring red dye all over each other. They had just started playing animal death noises through their speakers. I didn't even try to talk or hear again until we had passed under the green gate marking our departure from the main plaza. "You never know," she said after we finally reconvened where the crowd was thinner. "It could be all she's ever wanted. With those two, I kind of just see it."

"Do you think you could ever see Julie and me getting married?" I asked as we reached the stairs to our building. Zelda just threw her head back and laughed; I hadn't meant to be funny. "What, you don't think so? What happened to 'you never know?'"

"Oh, come on," said Zelda as we began ascending the faux marble steps to the third floor, "You're not going to get offended, are you? They would get married like this; you and Julie wouldn't. Neither of you. Are you even officially together by now? How long's it been?"

"Well, I guess we had planned to talk about it when we went on that road trip last weekend," I admitted. "But that doesn't mean anything. We had a really special time and just didn't get around to it. We're seeing where it goes."

"Exactly," she said as she flipped her backpack in front of her and started rummaging through it. "That's what you always say, both of you. That's fine if it works for you, but you guys are non committal and they aren't and that's why I think the proposal will work. Ah, here it is."

"What are you doing with blackboard chalk?" I asked as we reached the door of our classroom. She didn't tell me, but just put one finger to her lips and smiled wickedly. We walked in and sat exactly front row middle–middle, Zelda's usual spot. Zelda arranged her stationary, readings, and chalk at her desk while I just sat there with my arms crossed, enjoying my headspace before we had to get underway. I didn't have anything else to say to Zelda; she seemed giddier than usual.

As I waited, I thought about what Zelda had said and decided to be offended. What did Jian and Carolyn have that we didn't? Yeah he was proposing and I wasn't, but I could if I wanted to. We were just enjoying each other nowadays; nothing wrong with that. As I considered, I thought about how I hadn't seen Julie all week, pretty much not at all since our trip. She had said she was really busy with schoolwork and studying.

"Hey, after class, let's go to your place," I said to Zelda, but she wasn't listening. Class had started. Our graduate student instructor was here.

"Hello class, and welcome to another Friday Intro to Classics discussion section! I'm excited, I hope you're excited, so let's just jump into it! Today, we'll be discussing what Professor Garvin went over this week, so let's pull out your *Aeneid* and turn to Book IV."

Alix was our GSI, a postgrad on loan this semester from the English department. They always started class with that same little refrain, and while I admired the enthusiasm from my seat, I never quite found it contagious.

They always wore a patterned button-front shirt to class, sometimes checkers, sometimes stripes. Today, it was plaid, paired with the usual high-waisted pants and combat boots. I thought they caught me staring and turned my eyes down, but when I looked up I realized Zelda was the one caught and she didn't care. This was her favorite class.

Before looking away from Zelda, Alix smiled back awkwardly and brushed back a tuft of frizzy hair; it might have reached shoulder-length if it wasn't always pinned back.

I couldn't tell if Zelda's was just an intellectual crush or something more. I had gone with her to Alix's office hours once, hosted weekly at the de-facto liberal arts study cafe a block from campus (the two chief factors that made it a liberal arts hotspot were the italian-style macchiatos and the absence of outlets). We went in with the intention of discussing my catch-up plan after my last minute transfer in. After two hours and no clarity, I was just sitting there scrolling on my almost-dead phone, a third wheel at my own appointment. In that time, Alix and Zelda got to the bottom of Alix's PhD thesis proposal on Yeats and the Irish national narrative, plus two macchiatos each.

I never went back to office hours, but Zelda did the very next week, armed with a self-composed love poem based loosely off "The Song of Wandering Aengus." Alix's best and only response was to correct the prosody in green ballpoint ink.

"They don't like to grade papers in red because it's too confrontational," Zelda had told me afterwards, hugging the scraps. *English majors.*

"Alright, class," began Alix, "today I want to discuss one of the most famous tragic romances in all of literature. In terms of notoriety, you probably have Romeo & Juliet, Antony & Cleopatra, and today we'll be discussing my personal favorite, Dido & Aeneas." As they said so, Alix scratched 'dido & Aeneas' on the blackboard with a nubbin of chalk. Then they started pacing.

"In a minute, I'll be having you discuss with your seat partners, but first I want to lead you off with some questions. First, the narrator often speaks of love as an affliction, like a wound from an arrow or a consuming fire inflicted by the gods. So I wanted to ask you guys, both in this text and in your experience in general: how much of love is our own free choice? Was Aeneas really fated to fall in love and out again because the gods put their fingers on the scale, and could he have even stayed with Dido if he wanted to, given his destiny to found Rome? Then of course, the next implied question would be if it's just fate, who's to blame for how things end between them? As you guys know from the reading, Dido curses Aeneas before her death with one of the most scathing reproaches in literature. Does he deserve it if he can't change it?"

As Alix talked, they paced wall-to-wall with a nervous energy that splashed onto me in my middle front seat. Stimming as they spoke, they gestured at every turn of phrase with lobster-claw hands, woven-unwoven fingertips, wheel-turning wrists, and collarbone-piano fingers, breaking the chalk piece ever smaller until their hands and clothes were covered in white dust. I stopped following once I started getting dizzy, but next to me, Zelda looked like she was about to tag into a tennis match.

"Pst," she whispered to me once the class started chattering, "ask Alix to write the questions on the board."

"Why?" I asked. "Why don't you do it?"

"Pleaaaase?" she asked, trying to make her eyes look as big as possible.

I grumbled and acquiesced. I don't think I refused Zelda even once in all the time I knew her. "Excuse me, Alix?" I asked, raising my hand. "Would you mind writing the questions on the board? I have a hard time remembering."

"Sure," they said, and started writing. They only got through the word 'love' before the last crumb of chalk shrank onto the blackboard and disappeared. "Shoot, where is—" they mumbled to themselves, and started pacing up and down the blackboard in double time.

As she watched, Zelda opened her box and pulled out a brand-new finger-long cylinder of chalk and held it out at arm's length. Pacing faster and faster, Alix almost bumped into Zelda's white arm before they saw it. "Perfect, thanks," they said and reached out a hand. Zelda didn't make it easy, but slid the piece all the way down into her palm so that they practically had to hold hands to hand it off. During the exchange, Zelda tried to tell her feelings with only her eyes; Alix's eyes widened and looked around the room before turning away to face the blackboard again.

"Oh my God," I mouthed soundlessly to Zelda once Alix's back was turned. She shot me a cheeky wink.

"I think," Zelda began once we were finally back to the assignment, "love is a choice. Both for Aeneas and for all of us. Maybe Cupid can make you feel things you didn't decide, maybe Juno can make it rain so you end up in a cave alone together, and maybe Mercury can show up and remind you how important you are, but Dido always chose love. Aeneas backed out, and that's the bottom line. Rome or no Rome, he broke promises and the curses he got were deserved."

I didn't usually say much in discussion. I usually preferred to keep under the radar. Get in, get out. But today, Zelda's antics were too much for me. She was still sleeping in my bed. She had called my relationship 'non committal.' Now she was using me as a pawn in her weird student–teacher fantasy. No more. She wanted to play this class like she's so smart, fine. I did the reading too, and I wouldn't let my boy Aeneas get disrespected like I felt disrespected. I would take the negative.

"Well, actually," I said, pushing up my glasses and shifting my voice into *that* tone, "Aeneas had said himself that the two of them were never technically married, and they didn't have kids or anything, and he did have that commitment to found Rome still. It was always supposed to be a temporary stopover. I don't see anything wrong with two rulers just enjoying each other's company. It seemed to me like Dido just got the wrong idea."

Zelda straightened in her seat. She paused for a moment, long enough to check in and see if I wanted her to bring it. I didn't look away. "Not technically married?" she asked, raising one eyebrow and thumbing through the book to the correct color-coded sticky note, "Is that what you call it when the Roman goddess of marriage literally bears witness to your lovemaking and you go back to the capital to live openly as lovers all winter? She could have killed him, you know, and all the Trojans when they first arrived in their broken ships. Instead, she sacrifices everything for him, honor, reputation, kingdom, and even her life just so he could curve her with the 'we weren't official' and leave before the winter storms calm down? Please." She shrugged and flicked her hair as she finished speaking, pleased with herself.

"Well, maybe she sacrificed more than she should have," I replied, squaring to face her full on. "Mind if I look for a page number?" She handed me her paperback and I quickly found what I was looking for. "Dido had responsibilities as a ruler. She shouldn't have stopped all her construction projects, shouldn't have neglected diplomacy with the African warlords, and shouldn't have let Carthage fall apart on her watch. Aeneas had responsibilities too. To his father, his country, and his gods. Seems to me like he never lost sight of that and she did." I handed the book back open so she could follow my argument, but she shut it immediately and pulled out a separate note taking system she had in reserve.

As she shot back her response, I could see the incandescence start to burn in her eyes again, and I could feel myself getting more animated too. I had started off annoyed, trying to knock Zelda down a peg, but now having the argument felt weirdly good, like I was getting something inside me unstuck. Zelda looked up from her notes. "I suppose it wasn't Aeneas's fault either that he tried to sail away in secret in the dead of night? Or that he was half of the relationship that angered the African chieftains? Maybe Dido *did* sacrifice too much for a guy like that."

"So they're only together a few months, and they have to be married or it isn't real?"

"Well, it's more real if you're really married, you can't dispute that."

"The gods made him leave, they didn't make her fall apart."

"Having 'responsibilities' only when they benefit you is called excuses. He abandoned her." Neither of us were looking at notes anymore.

Now I was standing. "She killed herself on a big pile of her ex's stuff before the ships were out of sight. That's toxic behavior and that's on her."

Zelda stood up too. "He sailed into Carthage and took liberties with everything that she had, everything that she was, made her think he'd be there, and wasn't."

"She's a melodramatic cry baby and a bad queen for not looking out for herself," I said.

"Well, he's an inconstant fuckboi and the reason she died," Zelda responded.

"Alright, class, let's settle down," said Alix, coming between us to break our eye contact. I slowed my breathing and looked around. Zelda and I had both been yelling, and the rest of the class had gone quiet a while ago.

"I love what I've been hearing," Alix continued, "the passion, the insight, this is what discussion section is all about. Good job, you two. Why don't you sit down and let's bring it back together?" We sat. "I think you both made some excellent points there. Carlos, I liked when you said that rulers have responsibilities. We're not all destined to found the future Roman Empire, but sometimes we just have jobs, roles, and responsibilities that get in the way of things, no matter what our true feelings may be." They looked at Zelda as they said it.

"And Zelda," Alix continued, "I like what you said about pointing out some of the unfairness here. Duty or no, lying to Dido and trying to sneak away were free choices. When he left, Aeneas made sure all his ships and men were okay, but didn't do the same for his lover, married or not."

Alix smiled sadly and put the chalk back in Zelda's hand. "And this is what I love so much about literature. It gets us going at it, makes us ask the hard questions, makes us all use our empathy. Maybe the Western literary canon is a bit Eurocentric and male-dominated, I'd agree with you if you said that about Virgil or even most authors. But to me, it's still a good place to start in your higher education. These discussions we're having, they've been going on for hundreds, if not thousands of years. The conversation can change as the faces in the discussion change. I'm sure you're all very bright young people, going to a school like this one, and I'd encourage you to remember not just the things you've said, but the things you've felt here today.

We're not just here to learn reading lists. We're here to learn how to be more discerning, empathetic human beings. As you go forward, make sure to look around once in a while with a literary eye. After all, life imitates art more often than you'd think."

As Alix replaced Zelda's chalk, all the nervous energy seemed to go into it and dissipate. They smiled, and inflected with a gesture once in a while, but body and mind seemed to grow roots and hold as our attention held up front. Finally, Alix noticed the clock.

"Shoot, well I guess that's all for today. Good work everyone, and I'll see you all in lecture on Monday." The class began emptying and the hallways started to swell again, but I waited behind for Zelda as she dallied at the front of the room. Alix was still there, erasing the chalkboard.

"Sorry, I was wondering if I could talk to you alone later," she asked.

Alix finished erasing and turned toward her. "Is this about *The Aeneid?*"

"Ummm, no," said Zelda, siphoning the nervous energy from the chalk piece and fidgeting with it herself.

Alix touched her shoulder for a moment before pulling away. "If you want to talk about literature, you can come to my office hours next week like the other students. Otherwise, I'll see you in lecture on Monday." Then, they picked up their teaching materials in their arms and walked away, the clog of their combat boots fading away into the traffic.

"Hey, are you okay?" I asked her when we had started walking back to Foothill dorm.

"Oh yeah," she said, though she sounded dreamy and far away. "Great job in discussion by the way, we really got it going in there."

I smiled then and forgot why I got mad at Zelda in the first place. That's what I always appreciated about her: literature was her life, but her life wasn't literature. I perked up then. I was on my way to see Julie for the first time this week, and Zelda and I were walking together in comfortable silence under the bell tower, alone in our own daydreams.

The dream broke off as somebody called to me across the esplanade. "Hey, Carlos! Hey, wait a minute!" *Oh shit.*

I broke from Zelda without saying a word and started running, but it was no use. My backpack was too heavy and my legs were too short, and Dean had caught up in ten strides.

"Woah, hold up, hold up, I come in peace," he said, throwing up his hands dramatically. Zelda had caught up to me by then, and was looking back and forth between us to gauge the situation.

I summoned my best venom. "What do you want?"

"Hey, man, it's alright, I'm sorry for coming off so confrontational with you the last few times we talked," said Dean. "You got a minute?"

"Just tell me what you want," I said, and turned to start walking.

"Hey, nothing on you man, I just wanted to check in. How's Julie doing? Is she okay? She hasn't responded to my messages this past week."

"I actually haven't seen her," I admitted. "She's been busy with schoolwork and studying, she says she's pretty swamped, but I'm sure she's fine."

"And the trip? Can I ask how it went? Everything ok with her?"

A week ago I wouldn't have said anything about it. The old me, the one before the acid, would have told him to go to Hell. But as I looked at him, I saw pleading in his eyes. Desperation, even. A little acid, diffused in my spinal fluid, came loose when I cracked my back and gave me a mini flashback to my moment of clarity. *He cares about her. He's trying to be nice.* I even looked at Zelda; no help. Her stupidly big green eyes looked between us; she wanted to know too. I sighed and acquiesced.

"The trip was… good. Really good, actually. That moment of clarity you talked about, I had one. It made me want to be a better person, a better partner. It was a special time. We both had fun."

I felt stupid at first for telling him the truth, but I felt a little better when I looked in his eyes and saw that I hurt him. He tried not to show it, tried to smile through it, but I could tell.

"Well, I'm really happy for you man," said Dean, putting a hand on my shoulder. It took all my restraint not to squirm and swat it away. *Liar.* "For both of you. Let me know if you ever need to stock up on more, or anything else."

"Alright, if that's all then," I said, starting to turn away.

"Wait, one more thing," he said. "Theta Chi is having a Halloween party last Saturday of the month. You and Julie should come through. You too," he said, looking at Zelda.

"Oh, Eddie and I aren't together anymore," she said, waving him off.

"That's okay, even better. You're a cool girl from what I remember, and you help our guy-girl ratio besides. See you guys there?"

"Thanks, we'll think about it," I said.

"Alright, if you come, wear a costume. It's your ticket in. See ya," he said, and with a little two-fingered salute he turned on his heel and walked the other way.

"What a nice boy," said Zelda when we were alone again.

"Don't start with that please," I said, and we walked the rest of the way in silence again.

CHAPTER 25

Zelda turned her key and we were inside. I was eager to see Julie; throughout the walk I had imagined her in the kitchen with sleeves rolled up and brown apron on, cooking something that smelled delicious. She would give me her old smile, then we'd get high and eat together and cuddle and watch *CSI: Miami* until we let the couch eat us. I was surprised when I came in and couldn't find her anywhere.

"Julie? We're home," I called. No answer. I walked into her room and started turning over the pillows and sheets in the unmade bed, thinking I'd find her tucked inside. No Julie. I followed Zelda to her room, but she just shook her head at me and closed the door behind her so she could change out of her clothes and back into her pink bathrobe. No Julie. I tried Carolyn's room, but the door was locked when I tried the handle. Julie wouldn't be in there anyway. The nicest way to say it was that Carolyn was particular about her space, and usually locked the door when she went out. I moved back to the living room.

Julie must've been here recently. The countertops were filled with days-old dishes: bowls of empty this-and-that, dirty chopsticks, and cups. So many cups. If they weren't hosting a cocktail hour, then the sensible explanation would be that Julie got a new cup of something every time she stood up for the last five days. I leaned on the counter and bumped a cup with my elbow. I picked it up and smelled its remaining contents. Barley tea.

Then there was the couch. It looked like everything Julie owned was piled up on it. I recognized her chemistry, math, and physics textbooks, all open and all crowding each other on the couch arm, threatening to knock each other off. Loose leaves of class notes in Julie's scrunchy scrawl lay strewn all over the couch like a bulletin board without any thumb tacks. Even her backpack was there, tipped upside down with its contents spilled on the floor next to it.

I didn't know what to make of any of this, or where she could be. Probably at some library, out for lunch, or a walk. I checked the message I had sent her a while ago. Still no response, still unread. I was done with class for the day, so I resolved to sit there and wait for her. I started to clear a seat for myself: I moved the open textbooks to the coffee table, pulled about ten leaves of paper into one stack, and folded three different sweaters into a neat pile. That made just enough room for me to squeeze on at the far end of the couch.

I had only settled in for about five seconds when I felt the couch move. A few leaves of paper on the other side fluttered off their pile and onto the ground, and the next moment I felt a chill touch the skin of my thigh and send me up with a start.

"Agggghhh!"

Standing over the couch now, I saw the whole pile rumble and move, and after a few shakes, the debris parted and Julie hatched out of it. As I watched her return to life, the days when she wouldn't let me see her without eyelashes felt like a long time ago.

Over the last few days of hard studying, Julie had been eaten by the couch, and in turn had morphed into a kind of couch-human hybrid. What I originally took for some blonde-brown stuffing hanging out of the couch's armpit I now recognized as Julie's hair, matted and folded into an ombre bird's nest just barely visible beneath some more papers and trash. Her small frame had balled up almost imperceptibly into the cushion under some jackets and more notes, and now I recognized her feet as the cold touch on my leg.

"Hey there," I said, watching her eyes blink into recognition.

"Oh hi."

"Working hard? Everything okay with you?"

"Yeah, just studying. Must've fallen asleep out here," she said, rubbing her eyes.

"How long's it been?"

Julie sat up fully now, letting most of the papers fall to the floor. She looked around for her phone, and not seeing it, asked, "What day is it?"

Poor baby. Zelda had told me that Julie was studying hard and was getting pretty stressed out about her grades, but I didn't think it would look like this. I brushed aside some trash and sat next to Julie on the couch. I took both my arms under hers and hugged her for a while.

"Need anything? Anything I can do for you?" I asked.

"Hungry," she said, and scrunched her nose.

I stood up. "Don't worry, I'll take care of it! And maybe even do some tidying up around here," I said, and went straight for the kitchen. However, once I got in there and started scrounging, I couldn't really find anything fast and easy to make. No ramen, no bread, no cans of anything. *What kind of college dorm was this?* They were stocked enough, but their pantry was all bulk rice and noodles and jars of Asian stuff I had never used before. The fridge was all unwashed vegetables. I started to become flustered and looked around again.

I couldn't ask Julie for help; she had just asked me. I'm sure she could make something super tasty in ten minutes, but then my presence here would have no value and it would take away from her studying besides. But I couldn't mess up her food either. Cooking something that came out badly was the worst-case scenario. I could imagine Julie trying a bite of some slop I came up with, smiling through the disgust, and making herself something else anyway. That wouldn't do.

It seemed like the only move was the desperate one: I'd ask Zelda. I knocked on her room door and entered. I found her inside feeding her goldfish.

"Say hello, Ishmael!" said Zelda in a syrupy voice. "He's so big now, isn't he?" She pointed at him through the glass. I couldn't really tell a difference from last time I saw him; he might have been bigger but it might have just been the bend of the glass. He looked at me too, mutually uninterested, and went back to eating his flakes.

"Hey, could you help me with something?" I asked. "I want to make Julie food but don't really know what to do. Can you help me?"

"Say no more, we're on it."

Zelda changed again, this time into a frilly pink apron, and insisted I wear Julie's brown one. Once we looked the part, we were ready to cook.

"What are we making?" I asked.

"*Jajangmyeon*," said Zelda. "Since Julie showed me how, I've been obsessed. I had to stop eating it every meal because I thought it would turn my teeth black," she said laughing. "But I went to the store and got all the stuff for it again anyway."

Zelda was no master chef, but at least she knew what she was trying to make. I wanted to be helpful, but I hardly knew one end of the knife from the other and got relegated to all the easy jobs. Boil the water. Wash the vegetables. Do some dishes. Take out the trash. Not that I had a problem with it. The whole experience just made me want to do better. Adults should be able to cook their own food. Finally, sauce and steam bubbled around us and coaxed Julie's nose out of her textbook.

"Smells good guys," she said, sitting up. I served up the food in bowls and took extra time to present as neatly as possible. Zelda joined Julie on the couch, and I pulled up a barstool between the couch and TV and sat with my back to the bedrooms.

We slurped and chewed without talking for a while. The food wasn't as good as Julie's: the noodles were a bit soft, the sauce was too thick, and the veggies were cut in irregular shapes, but we'd done it. Julie was eating it and started to look revitalized.

"So how did your midterms go this week?" I asked her.

Julie sighed before she answered, making me uneasy. "Fucking failed them."

"But you've been working so hard."

"I know!" she said. "And that's what makes it so frustrating. It'd be one thing if I never went to class and blew off all the homework, but I never do that. I do every assignment and go to office hours every week and do all the homework and study for hours every day and I'm still failing the tests. It just makes me feel, I don't know."

"Makes you feel like what?" Zelda asked.

"Like… I don't belong here," Julie finished, and started to cry.

Julie didn't cry like Zelda, or for that matter like anyone else I knew. I had seen Zelda cry almost too often for my liking now, complete with swoons, monologuing, and even a limerick once. Julie just sat there, not making any noise. Even her breathing sounded normal. She just sat there like she was stunned, sitting very still. The only motion that gave her away was her blinking. Her eyes welled with vials of tears, and when she blinked I watched them roll down her cheeks, her chin, her neck, and down her chest and out of sight. No sooner had they rolled away than she would refill her eyes and blink again.

Though she couldn't match my angstiness or Zelda's performance art, Julie's wellspring eyes threatened to wash the rest of us out of the picture as she sat there, still as a water feature.

"Oh hey, it's ok, of course you belong here," said Zelda, scooting in. I moved over to Julie's other flank and sandwiched her into a group hug. "You're in the freaking College of Chemistry!" she continued. "Of course it's hard, but I know you got this. You're smart enough to be here, and you're smart enough to make it through. We believe in you."

"Zelda's right," I added. "This is right where you should be. Has Carolyn been helpful?"

"Yeah, I mean as much as she can be," said Julie, wiping her eyes. "We study together all the time. She even lets me copy her notes. I just feel like I do so much until I'm finally ready, but when it comes time to do it my brain just feels empty. I don't know what to do."

"Well, what's your next test, and when?"

"Linear algebra. Monday," she said.

"How much have you studied already?" I asked.

"About four hours today, four hours yesterday."

"Sounds like you need a break. You get diminishing returns after a while anyway," I said. "You smoke this week?"

"Of course not."

"You want to?"

Zelda questioned my idea, but I knew that Julie needed to relax. I could hear Julie's heart beat unevenly when I hugged her. She needed to decompress. We had a nice little smoke on the balcony, shared a laugh when I told her what happened with

Zelda in our class, and settled back into the couch for some *CSI: Miami*. Zelda said she wasn't interested, but ended up getting sucked in anyway.

"I think the motel owner did it," guessed Zelda.

"No way," I said. "Why would it be him?"

"Well, they found the body in the woods, but they said the cause of death was from a fall."

"So what does that mean?"

"Where would you fall in the woods?"

"I don't know, from a tree or something."

"Or, he fell from the motel balcony where we know he stayed the night before and his body was moved."

"Final answer?" asked Julie.

"Yeah," said Zelda, drawing herself up confidently. "Oh also, we saw Dean today."

"Oh yeah?" asked Julie, and turned to me. I nodded and tried to put on a neutral face.

Zelda continued, "Yeah, he invited all of us to his Halloween party! I thought that was nice of him."

"Oh, and what did you say?" asked Julie, looking more at me than at Zelda.

"I said thanks and we'd love to, if you're not too busy," I said.

"Well, okay! Could be fun then," she said, brightening. Then she snuggled in with me and we soon found out that Zelda was right.

Soon, the weed and the cuddles blended into a comfortable fog that blanketed me in place. I looked around. Julie was next to me, decompressed, fed, and happy, and Zelda was at the end, fully converted to our lowbrow trash despite her best efforts. Life was good, and I wanted to chatter.

"Oh, also, I've been meaning to talk to you about something," I said. "Has Zelda talked to you about what's going on with Jian and Carolyn?"

Julie touched the fourth finger of her hand to show she understood.

"Okay cool," I continued. "So what do you think is going to happen with them?"

"Honestly, I couldn't say," said Julie. She didn't take her eyes off the show as she answered. "I think they like each other a lot. Beyond that, I dunno."

"Zelda thinks she'll say yes," I said, raising an eyebrow and looking over.

"And you think she should say no?" Zelda chimed in. She was taking the bait; I felt her eager for another little back and forth.

The topic got my brain spinning and my blood flowing, so I got up to pace as I talked. I stepped in front of the TV as I spoke; the next episode was barely starting anyway.

"All I'm saying is they're pretty young. They seem really happy and a good match, and I'm happy for them. But they haven't even been together long, right? At least not as long as we have." I saw Julie wince a little at the comparison; we still hadn't talked about our official status.

"Jian said it was a pretty normal thing for him to do based on his cultural standards, so I'm sure he'll go through with it," Zelda said.

"Well, even if he does propose soon," I said, "Will Carolyn say yes? Knowing Carolyn—"

"—Knowing Carolyn, what?" said a voice from behind me that chilled my blood in an instant. I whirled and saw Carolyn looking like she might kill me. She was home.

"Uh, hey Carolyn, I'm sor—"

"–No. No. No. No. NO," she said as she walked over to the kitchen. "Knowing Carolyn what?"

"Oh, well, I wasn't going to say any—"

Carolyn picked up a steak knife and walked toward me, brandishing it, "No. No. No. Knowing Carolyn, what?"

Julie stood up, "Hey no, it's ok—"

"—IT'S NOT OKAY," she interrupted, turning to me. She was crying now, still holding the knife. "Why would you ruin it? Why would you ruin it for me? You're rude, you're brainless, you can't think of your girlfriend to save your life, and you don't deserve her." She pointed briefly to Julie with the knife before turning it back on me. "Knowing. Carolyn. What?" Though her voice was breaking now, she punctuated each word with the point of its own blade without raising her voice above its normal level. As she spoke, Zelda edged her way off the couch and inched the long way around the kitchen counter, trying to get behind Carolyn without making any sudden movements. Julie was standing too, trying to get between me and the knife.

"Knowing Carolyn," I said slowly, trying to get her to calm down, "she'll probably want to wait before she's more established before committing to marriage."

Carolyn wailed a cry of bloody murder, and I fell backwards thinking she'd kill me, but she collapsed to her knees and dropped the knife. She kept crying, quieter now, leaving the knife where it fell. "My surprise," I could hear her say in her faintest voice.

"Get out of here. Go now," said Julie. I agreed and didn't waste a second, but it still hurt hearing Julie say it like that. She held Carolyn, who was sobbing quietly on the floor, while Zelda came around and picked up the knife. "He doesn't know me... all I ever wanted..." was the last thing I heard through Carolyn's sobs as I strapped on my backpack and closed the door to the apartment.

I couldn't bring myself to walk back right away, so I just sat on the floor in the hallway and put my head in my hands. I was worthless. Carolyn freely gave me the idea for the best time I've ever had with Julie, and I turned around and spoiled the biggest, happiest surprise she'd ever get in her life. What a joke. I kept thinking about what had just happened. When she pulled out that knife, I was sure she'd use it. I saw it in her eyes; each eye was like a knife of its own. 'He doesn't know me,' 'my surprise,' and 'all I ever wanted' kept running through my head. Maybe she never would have done it, and I didn't know her at all just like she said. Maybe she would say yes to Jian. *She had no idea.*

All these thoughts closed around me like a coffin, and even as I closed my eyes and covered my ears I couldn't stop seeing

Carolyn's eyes, couldn't stop hearing her crying. I grabbed my chest and felt it tighten. I couldn't breathe. I gasped for air and I felt like I couldn't breathe in. I opened my eyes and everything was still black. I tried to scream but no noise came out. I felt like I was dying.

I tried to stand and walk down the hall back to Julie's apartment. It was just about the last place in the world I wanted to be right now, but it felt preferable to dying in the hallway. I tried to stand; I still couldn't breathe. I barely got to my feet, but just one step in and I lost it again and sank to the floor. I was alone in the dark, unable to breathe, for what felt like a few minutes. At one point I was sure I would die. You're supposed to see things before you die. Memories, loved ones, your life before your eyes. I didn't see anything, just red and black. Finally, the East Wind rolled out of the elevator and came down to meet me. I felt hands on my face before I could see them.

"Julie?" I wheezed.

"You wish," said a familiar voice. "Come on, asshole, as much as I'd love to leave you here, you're not dying today." And with that, Rosa put my arm on her shoulder and helped me stagger down the hall to her room. I didn't know it at the time, but she had just aced another midterm.

CHAPTER 26

Rosa's room was warm and dark. At first I thought it was just my eyes, but as my panic attack subsided and my breathing came back to normal, it was still dim inside. Rosa clicked on the only light in the place, a functional-looking desk lamp that threw the wall behind her into high relief. I let my eyes take the place in for half a minute. One bed, one desk, one dresser, one window, no bathroom. The place was smaller than mine.

"You don't have roommates?" I asked. "I thought all freshmen had roommates."

"No," she said. "Regents' Scholars get first choice housing. The others I talked to wanted to live in the fancy new dorms, but I just wanted a room of my own."

"Wait, you got the Regents' Scholarship? You never told me." The Regents' and Chancellor's Honors Scholarship was the last carrot public school had to convince bright young people to come here instead of the Ivies. Free tuition, priority everything, and a nice little chip on your shoulder to boot.

"Yeah, sorry I never told you. You know how you get, though."

I didn't respond; I didn't know what to say. I looked around her room again. On the bright wall behind her desk hung a mosaic of her achievements: debate medals, a 'Most Likely to Succeed' superlative, and a group photo of the time our Model UN club won the conference in Huntington Beach. I looked closer at the photo. I couldn't find myself in it.

I thought for a minute and remembered the day. We were the delegates from Namibia, and Rosa and I had cosponsored a resolution in the Environmental Assembly for the protection of cheetahs and other endangered wildlife. Her prize that day was 'best delegate;' mine was third base on the bus ride home. Why wasn't I in the photo? *That's right... I was stealing the—*

Then I saw it. There on the opposite wall, still in semidarkness, the sight of it brought a smile to my face. I wasn't in the photo because I had snuck away to steal a life-size cardboard cutout of Rosa's favorite U.S. President, Ulysses S. Grant, from an open classroom in an adjoining building. That was a fun day.

"Hey, you want some tea or something?" she asked.

"Yeah, sure." Just as I said so, the electric kettle in the corner started boiling. In all the years we were together, neither of us had ever passed up an opportunity to get caffeinated. I sipped the chai that Rosa always drank instead of coffee and felt for a minute like I'd gone back in time.

"So, how's your history class going?" I asked.

"Oh, alright. We had the second midterm today. I felt fine about it." I smiled. 'I felt fine' was always what she said when she thought she set the curve. "What about you?" she continued. "Did you find another class to take?"

"Umm, yeah," I said. "A friend put me onto Intro to Classics. There weren't any history vacancies before the drop deadline, but there's always next semester."

We were quiet for a while. The silence started to make me nervous. I drank my tea faster; Rosa hadn't touched hers. She just kept looking at me. She wanted me to talk.

Finally, I spoke. "Thanks for helping me back there. I would've been in a lot of trouble if not for you."

"You're welcome." She kept looking at me and kept waiting.

"Alright. Okay. Here's what I really want to say." I shifted in my seat and drew myself up for what we'd never said. It was time. "I'm sorry for being an ass. I wasn't good to you, and that went on for a while before you ended things between us. I felt like I chose to come here to this school so we could be together, and once things started to go bad I felt like I made a big mistake. Whatever the choice, right or wrong, it was mine, and I was wrong to put that blame on you. I'm sorry."

Finally, Rosa sipped her chai. "So that's what you think happened?"

"Yeah, I guess."

"So why do you think I ended things?"

I thought something snarky in my head but took it down a couple notches. "Aren't you supposed to tell me?"

Rosa didn't respond; she just kept looking at me. She could be a stone wall when she wanted to, and that always drove me mad. I thought about getting up and walking out. But no. *I guess that would be wrong.*

"What I think happened," I continued, "was a combination of things. I was unhappy, so I acted in ways that made you unhappy, and once we got here you had… options."

"Options?"

"I'm trying to say it nicely."

"So to hear you say it, your biggest problem in the relationship was that you were unhappy with me?"

I put my cup down. I was getting tired of this. "Well it sure as hell didn't help anything, did it? What is it you want from me?"

"I want you to own how you hurt me!" she snapped, just momentarily, before smoothing her hair back and taking a slow breath. "It's always so hard to talk to you about what you're doing wrong, because it's somehow never your fault. Fine, let's try something else. Let's talk about me."

"Okay, let's."

"I loved you, you know that?"

I was taken aback for a moment. I did know. I was always the sap, I was always the one who said 'love' all the time, and she never did. But I knew she felt it. Every other good memory I had of her came with this look in her eyes, a look like she would fall down into me. More than anything we ever said, that look made me feel like she was mine, body and soul. I loved the power it gave me as much as I loved the person.

"I did," she continued, "since we were fifteen. I thought I'd found the one. It makes me feel so stupid now, but I always thought we'd go to law school together, become the next Bill and Hillary. That's how I always treated you. Was that how you treated me?"

I didn't know what to say, so I looked for the answer in the black liquid in my mug. I didn't find it.

"I didn't think so," she said. "You treated me like competition."

"Well, I wouldn't go that far."

"Oh really? Do you remember what you said to me when I got debate team captain over you?"

I did remember, but I didn't repeat the words. *More of a political choice than anything. I would've been too busy anyway.* I frowned but kept quiet.

Rosa continued, "and I always wrote it off. I told myself we were both chasing excellence, we made each other better, all that crap. Then you got that damned acceptance letter."

"I was excited about it," I grumbled.

"You were insufferable!" said Rosa, throwing up her hands. Cardboard President Grant frowned at me from behind her. "It was all you talked about for weeks, even after I asked you to stop. You *always* thought you were better than me, better than everybody, and after that letter you had receipts to wave around."

"I'm sorry about that, that was wrong of me. I'm not better than anybody, and though it took me a while to settle in, I've really started to find my place here."

"Fuck you," she said, throwing up a hand and spilling some tea in the process. "You said I'd trapped you. You said you'd thrown away your future for me. You said that I'd better make it worth it for you." Rosa's debater's composure was slipping now. As she spoke, her mouth twitched down into a frown, fighting to stay level.

"I–I shouldn't have treated you like that, I'm sorry," I said. "You didn't owe me anything, and I was wrong to think you did. I'm sorry I made you do... things you didn't want to do." My throat hurt as I said it. Most of the time I tried not to think of summer, but I had to now.

"You know that weaponizing guilt to extract sexual favors from your partner is abuse, right?" Her eyes were full of tears now, but she wouldn't look away. She held my gaze, defiant.

I grabbed my stomach and felt the truth of her words. I remembered the summer. *It sucks here... I did this for you... You don't want me to be happy?*

"I'm so sorry. That was... despicable," I said, grasping at the appropriate word. "You didn't deserve that, nor does anyone deserve that treatment from their partner. It was abuse."

I felt my eyes watering now, but I wiped them quickly. My feelings weren't the point. I'd hurt my partner, the person that I had loved, and she might always have the scars I'd given her.

"Also," she continued, putting her cup down, "I wanted to talk about how you were at the end."

"Okay," I said, wiping my face and sitting up straight.

"Threatening to kill yourself if I left you was also abuse."

I couldn't hold back the tears anymore. I sobbed into my mug, loud and ugly, confronted with the truth of my actions.

What kind of monster could have done these things? But I knew what kind.

Why had I done it? What did I want back then? Three years together, three mostly happy years, just to end like it did. We hadn't drifted away all at once. Even when things were hard, I was her companion. When things got hard for me, she was my possession. That couldn't last.

"I'm so sorry," I said, hugging the warm mug. "Being together was so special to me, and I fucked it all up. We had a chance and I threw it away. And I knew it too. I would never have killed myself, I didn't mean it, and it was wrong of me to say. I wanted to hurt you and I did. I don't ever want to be that person ever again."

Rosa sipped her chai again. "You're right about that. And it was emotional abuse."

"Yes it was."

Rosa let herself exhale. "Okay then, thank you for saying so. I've been wanting to have this conversation with you for a long time. At one point I thought of bringing it to the Office of Student Conduct. But I'm glad to hear you say these things to me and I'm glad we agree." Rosa was crying too, but she wiped her eyes and collected herself.

"Also, for my part, I guess I should apologize for getting with Dean when we were technically still together. I had my reasons, and after you said what you said I felt scared and trapped, but I'm still sorry."

"That's okay," I said, wiping my eyes again and clearing my throat to keep my voice from cracking, "like you said, you had your reasons. I'm sorry for my antics since the breakup too. I'm embarrassed of myself."

"I'll forgive you for that, even if I won't forget it," said Rosa. "I just have one more thing to ask. That girl you're with now, Jamie? Jackie?"

"Julie," I said. *She knew her name.*

"Yes, that's it. Are you being good to her?"

"I believe I am." And I did. "I'm educating myself, trying every day, and acting like the partner I know she deserves." My voice wasn't cracking anymore. I spoke it with my chest.

"Good," she said, looking at me over her mug. "Because if I ever hear otherwise, Dean isn't the only one who's going to kill you. Understand?"

I nodded, finished my chai, and put the cup down. "So what does this mean now?" I asked. "Are we… friends?"

Rosa threw her head back and laughed, the exact same laugh as when I told her she looked like a sexy disco ball at prom. *Her real laugh.* "I wouldn't go that far," she said. "Let's just say next time you're having a panic attack in the hallway, I won't wait so long before stepping in." I nodded, stood up, and began to gather my things.

"And Carlos," she said as I opened the door to leave. "Did Dean invite you to the Halloween party?"

"Yeah."

"Don't go."

I was taken aback, and didn't know how to respond, so I just ducked my head a little and closed the door behind me. I thought about texting Julie once I got in the hallway, but decided not to.

I took the long walk down the foothill, not caring if I got hit by a bus or not. Julie, Charles, Carolyn, Rosa. It seemed like I was a cancer on almost everyone in my life. I had to do better. I stepped into traffic, drawing an angry honk from a campus shuttle driver. I didn't care.

I was emotionally depleted all the way down to zero. Reckoning with the two worst things I've ever done back-to-back left me feeling like the lowest scum on Earth. And maybe I was. I just had to get back to my bed now. No more adventures.

I was able to successfully dissociate, just enough, for the rest of the walk back. No sights, no sounds, no thoughts. Thankfully, when the elevator reached the eighth floor and I peeked out expecting some disaster, I found all was quiet. No mattress jousting, no alcohol poisoning, not even any open doors. No Charles. I turned the key, relieved to be home at last.

I came in to find Eddie at his desk playing some video game. He was sitting there shirtless. From his collarbone to his bellybutton, his dark skin purpled like it had been beaten with 2x4's. Bruises and welts covered his whole t-shirt zone, and the moment he saw me he scrambled into an old hoodie lying behind him on the bed. *I'm sorry man, I can't today.*

I didn't even look at him again as I walked straight to my bed and collapsed into it. He seemed just as relieved as I was that we wouldn't talk about today. He finished his round in the game and then looked over at me. I hadn't fallen asleep yet. The voices were still with me.

"Hey man, you need to smoke or something?" he asked.

"You got anything stronger?" I asked. "I need something that will take me out of this life for a bit."

"Actually, yeah, I've got just the thing. Hold on." He got up from his chair and rummaged through his closet until he found a clear bag of pills. He tossed them onto the bed next to me. "Take half of one and you should go right to sleep."

"What is it?" I asked, looking closer at the bag. Inside was a handful of rectangular white pills, each imprinted with letters and numbers on one side.

"Xanax," said Eddie. "Or similar."

"What do you mean, 'Or similar?'"

"Well you know," he said, shrugging, "name brands are expensive. They're kind of from everywhere, but sometimes you get a different dose or cut with something for cheaper."

"Oh, hell no," I said, and turned away. I lay there for about an hour unable to sleep, thinking of the day I had, the pain I'd caused. The crying. *Fuck it.*

"How much for the whole bag?" I asked.

Eddie looked up. "Uh, I don't know. Thirty bucks." I checked my bank account. Thirty bucks was just about all the money I had left. I took it as a sign.

"Deal, just charge me later," I said, and reached into the bag and snapped a pill in half. "See you tomorrow," I said, and swallowed.

"By the way, you talk to Charles lately?" asked Eddie. "I've been trying to talk all week since the hospital. I think he's avoiding us."

"No, sorry." I closed my eyes.

When it took me, the bottom fell out of the world. No dreams, no flashbacks, no faces. Just black. I felt happy about it. Well, to be exact, I didn't feel anything, and I was happy about *that. Next.*

CHAPTER 27

Whatever my anxieties, specific or general, the pills flipped my stress to easy mode, and I wondered why it hadn't always been this way. I'd started off the first night just taking half before bed like Eddie said, but soon the pressures of being awake prompted me to self-medicate.

Monday was our Classics midterm. Three in-class essays, two hours, 30% of our final grade. Zelda had nearly spun my head off in her frenzy to prepare. She'd even offered me Adderall, which she always took when she felt herself under pressure to perform. I'd seen her on it before, and my heart beat faster when I remembered how her usually diffuse radiance focused into a beam that blasted away whatever she put in front of her. Though it could have helped, I declined. I wondered if I'd do better settled down than wired up. I decided to try a Xan, and we clinked our different pills together in my room before we left for class. By the time I sat down in the classroom, I started to feel the effects.

When I'd taken it at night, half a bar made me instantly drowsy. Now, with the help of my coffee, I pushed through the initial drowsiness to come to a headspace I'd never known before. There in the classroom, I closed my eyes and felt a wave of calm come over me. The test started, but I kept them closed for half a minute and took stock of my feelings. I felt, not good exactly, but right. I felt as if there was a piece of my mind, the piece that gave me fear, anxiety, and worry, that I detached from the rest like a Lego brick and set off to the side. The feelings were still there, but instead of controlling me, my anxieties stepped away and watched my life from a nearby rooftop while the rest of me stayed in my seat. My brain felt quiet. I liked that.

The meds didn't make me do better on the test. Instead, I thought I'd lost my edge, and for every essay I felt my practiced quote, paraphrase, or example just out of reach. Maybe it was on the rooftop with the others. But I didn't mind it. I looked over at Zelda: the whole two hours, she looked like she might spontaneously combust. She was relentless the whole period; she attacked her essays and only stopped moving her pen to speedread. I was happy for her, but that wasn't what I wanted. I wanted peace and quiet.

I barely finished in time, but I did. From what I gathered, my essays were about half the length of Zelda's, but they'd do. I'd pass the class, and now I'd do it worry-free. As usual, Zelda wanted to stay after to talk to Alix, so I stayed in my seat when everyone filed out. As they talked, I felt like I was sitting on the sand, watching two ships at sea.

"Thanks so much for all your help at office hours," said Zelda, handing Alix her test booklet and mine.

"Don't thank me," they said, "You did most of the talking. When I agreed to help Professor Garvin this semester, I never thought I'd be learning the finer points of Roman literature from an undergrad." Zelda smiled and kicked the floor.

"Have you given more thought to that other thing we talked about?" she asked, turning her eyes upward.

They looked around and leaned forward so I could barely hear. "Yeah, I'm in. I've been meaning to cut my hair anyway." Zelda nearly squealed. "Shhh," said Alix. "Nobody can know."

"Sounds good. We'll discuss it at your next office hours." I looked on, almost the only person left in the room at this point, and almost forgot I was there. Everything felt somehow farther away than it was, though it all looked just the same. Zelda nearly forgot me too in her happiness, but turned around at the last moment to grab me on the way out.

"What was that about?" I asked as we walked.

"It's a secret," said Zelda, almost skipping as she went. "Don't worry about it."

"Don't worry?" *The magic words.* "Alright then."

Not until our walk started inclining uphill did I realize where Zelda was going. "Oh, wait, are you going back to your place?"

She stopped in her tracks. "Oh, yeah, wait... I think Carolyn—"

"—It's alright. I totally get it. I still feel horrible about before."

"It could have been any of us. It happens."

"Is she doing alright?" I asked.

Zelda frowned. "That night was pretty rough. Julie stayed up with her until the morning to help her feel better."

"The morning? I thought Julie had to study for her midterm." *Shoot, that was today.*

"Yeah. Do you need company? We could get boba or something."

"No," I said, "I'll probably just go home and nap."

"Okay." We stopped in the middle of the walkway, and Zelda stepped off to the side. "Oh, I don't know if you heard. Jian's doing the proposal this week."

"Oh really?" The news almost brought my anxiety back despite the meds. "Does Carolyn know?"

"Well, I'm not going to tell her," said Zelda, and laughed for a moment before she saw that I didn't. "Sorry. It'll be this Friday after her last midterm."

"It's okay, I assume I'm not invited," I said. *I'll sleep it off.*

"Should I ask for you?"

"No, that's alright."

I felt my forehead with my hand. I needed another half Xan. "I'll catch up with you some other time," I said. We said goodbye and went our separate ways.

As I walked home alone, I texted Julie.

Hey! How was the midterm?

I looked down at my phone for the rest of the walk back. No response. I finally pocketed it as I stepped into the lobby of my dorm building. I looked up just in time to catch the eye of whoever was in the elevator, the door closing between us.

"Hey, hold the door! Wait!" I said, striding across the atrium and waving. The person inside clicked away at their button, but I couldn't tell if they were pressing 'door open' or 'door close.' It kept closing.

"Hey, asshole, I said wait," I said as I stuck my whole arm into the gap. The door clamped my forearm for an instant before lurching back open. "Oh, hey man."

Charles took his eyes off the button console. He looked everywhere but right at me, then fixated on the wall like he was trying to match its color and disappear. He made a short sound that I took for a greeting.

"How've you been, man?" I asked him. "Eddie and I haven't seen you at all this past week. Everything good with you?"

Instead of responding, Charles pressed the 8 button again and waited. It didn't light up this time; the elevator just made a grinding sound and stopped. The doors flung open and went still.

"Shoot, I think it broke," I said. "Sorry about the stairs. Looks like we're walking."

Soon, our hollow steps and labored breathing filled the stairwell. Though I was taking it slow, still barred-out and half-present, Charles went slower still. I waited at the top of each new floor and watched him. He looked at every step like it was trying to trick him.

"So, I hope you didn't have to pay too much for that hospital visit. How's your head feeling?" I asked.

He still wasn't looking at me. "Fine. Insurance covered. Deductible whatever."

"Your car came up pretty big. Pretty cool that we didn't end up paying for an ambulance, right?"

I shouldn't have said it. He started climbing the stairs faster, and soon caught up to me. "My car..." he said. "It has a weird smell now."

I'd practiced the lie in the mirror a few times, and with my chemically-lowered heart rate it came easily now. "Yeah, I noticed that too. I'd actually been meaning to ask you about it but I haven't seen you. It was like that when we got it, I'm not really sure."

I braced myself for his follow-up question, but it never came. We just kept ascending stairs until we reached the top floor.

I tried talking again when we reached the top. "Hey, are you doing okay? Eddie and I have been worried about you since your trip last week."

Charles didn't respond, but held his room key straight in front of him and walked towards his own door. I thought about how he'd always been so welcoming into his space, so sociable, if only to trade in rumors and information. He felt like a completely different person now.

"Hey man," I continued, following him towards the door. "If you want to be alone, that's fine, but we're trying to help you here." He never looked back at me, but put his key into his door and walked through, leaving it to swing closed behind him.

A little concerned and a little annoyed, I walked up and stuck my foot in the door to stop it closing, then walked in after him.

"What the hell is this?" I asked.

I had never seen his room like this before. It was unnaturally clean, almost concerning. I looked around and couldn't find a crumb or speck of dust in the place. He had never before been accused of keeping the space too clean, and now it seemed so sterile that I felt like I contaminated it with my presence. I breathed in the air. Before, it had been earthy, oily with the smell of three young men and their laundry. Now, despite a two-inch-open window letting in the October chill, the place smelled strongly of household chemicals. Charles didn't say anything, but sat down and started spraying his laptop with canned keyboard cleaner. I watched his hands as he did so; they were bandaged and scabby.

"Charles, you gotta tell me what's going on, man. You're acting really differently now, and I don't know if it was the trip or smashing your head or what, but I need to know what's going on with you."

Instead of answering me, he put on his headphones and retreated into the blue glow of his screen. I was growing tired of him, and now that my coffee was wearing off, the anxiety meds started inviting me back to my bed for a nice nap.

I didn't have any patience for getting stonewalled, so I resolved to turn and leave. I had only taken a step when the sight of a great green bed sheet arrested me. It covered floor to ceiling behind the door, exactly where the full–length mirror had been. So unlike the sights and smells of the rest of the room, it drew me in like a window to a strange place. As I advanced toward it, my eyes caught some glittering grounds on the carpet which I took for flecks of mirror glass. The great green sheet caught the draft from the open window and waved at me for a moment before going still. Automatically, I raised my hand to the fabric and tugged until it came free.

"Don't touch that!" Charles cried, knocking off his headphones. But it was too late. With one final tug, the top of the sheet fluttered to the ground, revealing Charles's craft project from Hell.

Charles caught his own eye in the reflection of a shard for only a second before letting out a scream, diving to the floor, and going still. I registered what he did, but I barely looked over because the sight in front of me consumed all of my attention.

The mirror was still broken. Some pieces remained where they were, some gathered in a tidy pile on the floor, and some looked as if they had been glued back on in places where they weren't supposed to be. In the plywood gaps where the mirror had fallen away were the runes. Some looked familiar to me: a pentagram, a hexagram, a cross. Others looked vaguely familiar but I couldn't quite place. Maybe Egyptian, maybe Celtic, maybe some kind of Asiatic. Some I had no idea, and just looked like infernal drawings or even letters in a language I couldn't guess. Everything was painted on in some dark red paint that smeared all over, a messy job. I looked closer at the drawings, then at Charles on the floor. It wasn't paint. It was blood.

The discovery set my heart beating, and soon it outpaced the upper limit set by the medication and broke me through. I didn't know whether to scream, run for help, or start interrogating Charles right then and there. The whole thing looked so infernal that it mesmerized me. I caught my own reflection in a shard. I remembered Charles's demonic facial expressions that night, the way his features gnarled into that evil grin. I don't know why or how, but there in my reflection I tried to mimic what I'd seen, twisting my brow and gnashing my teeth until I scared myself with the sight of it and had to stop.

Charles went completely catatonic. I covered up the mirror again, closed the windows, covered him in a blanket, and made some tea for us before he moved or spoke again. Finally, after a long while of us both deciding we had nowhere else to be, he finally sat up on the floor and began to drink his tea.

"Do you still see them?" I asked. "The scary stuff you saw when you were tripping?"

"Yeah. Every day."

I raised my eyebrows. "When was the last time?"

"When you lowered that curtain."

"Shit, I'm sorry man," I said. "I just wanted to see if I could help you with anything. I didn't mean to scare you."

"That's okay."

I took another look at Charles. I hadn't really seen him since the hospital. His forehead, still crossed with stitches, showed the dun color of partial healing. His forearms were red with fresh scratches, which I guessed he'd done to himself. Above all, his usually wry shiftiness manifested differently now. As he stole glances at me when he thought I wasn't looking, he looked more furtive, even hunted, than I'd ever seen him. I moved closer to him.

"If you don't mind my asking," I began, "that's to say, if you can tell me without getting too upset... What was it that you saw?"

Charles frowned and set his mug on the ground next to him. For a moment, seeing him wrapped in his blanket up to this head, I didn't think he would tell me. "Well, I guess I saw me," he began. "It looked like me but it wasn't. Sometime after taking the second tab that day, Eddie left the room to smoke on the fire escape and I stayed here. I always liked my own company alright, so I sat up in front of that mirror and started looking at myself and making faces. That's when I saw him."

Despite the fact that I'd closed the window already, a cold chill ran through me as I listened to his words. *That's when I saw him.* "Who was it?"

"He never said his name, but he has my face," Charles said. "He looks exactly like me, and he lives just there, inside the mirror." He pointed as he spoke. "He told me he wanted to be my friend, and he spoke it with my voice when I was alone. He smiled, and I felt myself smiling with him. He's evil, I can tell. And he's from the place where all evil things are from."

"What does he want?"

"He says it's crowded where he is. He says he's been searching for someone to swap with for a long time, but up until now nobody could see him. The acid trip brought us together."

322

"But you've sobered up now, right?" I asked. "Shouldn't it have worn off?"

"That's what I thought too," he said, "but on my first day back from the hospital he started talking to me again, right in that mirror. Any reflection anywhere I go might be me, but might be him instead."

"So that night when you ran into that mirror?"

"He was trying to take me, and I was trying to stop him." I shivered and looked back at the great green sheet. I wouldn't touch it again.

I gathered myself for more questions. As strange as this all seemed to me, Charles said it with such conviction that it compelled me to believe him. Julie and I hadn't experienced anything like this on our own acid trip, though Charles took the same stuff. Was it the second tab that did it? If I'd taken a second, would I have been hunted by my own personal demon that followed me into the next week? I couldn't say, but I didn't think so. I remembered what Julie had said when we first took our tabs in the hot tub. *Your attitude determines your altitude.* I'd felt like I was being watched too, but I wasn't scared of the redwoods. Maybe there was more to it.

"Your cousin, the one that had the bad trip. What did he see?"

Charles leaned forward and made his voice lower in a play for theatricality. I smiled at the nice bit of old Charles I'd brought out. "Well, he watched a nature documentary on ants, and after he got too high he said he could feel them crawling all over his body, biting him even when he slept. He ran the bathtub all night and nearly drowned himself trying to get the feeling to go away but it wouldn't. Even afterwards, even now, he still feels them sometimes."

"Oh my God."

"Yeah, I guess I'll finally have some relatable conversation with him at Thanksgiving this year." He tried to laugh, but I couldn't.

"What about all those symbols under there? Is it really blood? Was that… him too?"

"Yeah, it's blood," said Charles, holding up two bandaged hands. "But it was me that did it. I never believed in God, astrology, or any of that fortune cookie stuff before, but an experience like I'm having has a way of changing my perspective. I spent a lot of time this week researching demons, summoning, and the paranormal. It's the best protection I could find. I know how it looks, but it helps me sleep."

I looked again from Charles to his bandaged hands. "Hey man, I don't mean any offense or anything, but I think you need some professional help."

Charles looked back at me and made eye contact for the first time today. He smiled and I drew back, mistaking it for his evil smile. But soon he softened, and I sighed with relief. "I know, man. You think I don't know what this sounds like? But what can I do? Withdraw from school and give up my future? Start paying my student loans with nothing to show for it? I already saw it with my cousin and his whole thing. If anybody remotely 'professional' takes me seriously, I could spend the next years paying to live in a padded cell instead of getting this degree."

"You could talk to one of our university health counselors."

"Have you talked to one of our university health counselors?" asked Charles.

"No."

"Well, they'll probably just tell me to start meditating and cut out caffeine. Why bother?"

"I have some anti-anxiety meds here, why don't you take one and see how you feel?"

Charles turned away from me. "I know you're trying to help, and I know I was the one who asked, but trying the shit you gave me is the whole reason I'm like this, so I think I'll pass. I don't think I'll be doing any drugs anymore. Clearly, it doesn't agree with me."

I had reached into my pocket to offer him a bar, but drew my hand out empty at his refusal. "I'm just concerned about you, man," I said. "God forbid something happens to you, we just want to know—"

"—that it wasn't your fault?" Charles interrupted. "Sorry man, I can't make you feel better. There's blame to go around. I'm just going to deal with it my way. You don't know a lot about me, but I've been fighting for my life for a long time and it's worked so far, so I'll just keep doing that."

I finished my tea and stood up. "Have you told Eddie about any of this?"

"Why would I?" he asked. "I'll be fine, and we're not together."

"Well, you might be fine, but I'm worried about him," I said, walking towards the door.

"What do you mean?"

I made a show of opening the door to go and then closing it again. "The other night," I began in a low voice, "I came back pretty late. I saw Eddie at his desk with no shirt, all black and blue, looking like he'd been beaten within an inch of his life."

"What the hell?" he asked, and through his spark I caught a glimpse of the old Charles flickering back.

"Yeah. I don't know for sure, but I suspect it's the guys at Theta Chi hazing him. It's getting worse."

"Those bastards," Charles said to himself.

"I don't really know what's going on between you two or how you left off, but it's brutal out there. Days are getting shorter and colder, and real ones need to stick together."

"Cuffing season," said Charles, and laughed his old laugh that felt like it was from a hundred years ago.

"Yeah. Take care man, and keep each other safe please." At last, I opened the door and ducked out of it, heading back into the very next door to take a long day's nap.

Thanks to the zombie-like fugue state I discovered on two bars, the rest of the week passed quickly enough. As long as I didn't care what happened outside of my bed, I had my own personal fast-forward button through life. After waking up from a 9-hour sleep, I reupped with another bar and some water and went down for 12 more. I only had the one midterm on Monday, so I was alright for skipping the rest of my classes this week. I might have carried on like this indefinitely if not for two problems that I became more aware of every time I awoke. First, my supply was limited to the dozen-or-so pills I got from

Eddie, so living like this wouldn't last me through the week. Second, after the third time in a row I emerged from the formless dark, I felt so hungry and weak that I feared I couldn't leave the bed even if I wanted to. Thankfully, Eddie was in the room.

After I paid Eddie for the Xan, I really was completely out of funds. I considered asking Mom for help, but decided it wasn't worth it. Even if she did send me something, it would probably come with a closer look at my bank statements and hell to pay when I came back for winter break. I'd already put in for another loan from the school's financial aid office, but they told me there was some kind of administrative backup and relief was slow in coming. Earlier in the semester, I'd applied to work at the donut shop, a boba place, and the campus bookstore, but I ended up getting beat out by people that could work either nights or full-time. Now, on the second day of starvation, fearing Eddie would find me dead in bed one of these days, I asked him to help me steal food from the school. It wasn't my first choice, but more pills and a healthy dose of moral relativism kept me from getting too down about it.

"Even going to this school is so expensive, how can they expect us to live?"

"My college should care if I'm food insecure and step in, right? And since they're not, I can just show myself in?"

"It's just food. It's not really stealing if I'm not taking it from someone who needs it."

"Peace, land, and bread."

Eddie was supportive of me, and a couple times that week, he let me into the campus dining hall through the emergency exit in the back and we had some meals together. He wasn't always around, though. When I was by myself, I walked into the little self-serve grab-and-go cafeteria on campus and put something under my shirt before walking out. Only once that week did an employee see me. She looked like a student and thankfully didn't say anything. I was careful to make sure she didn't see me again.

I passed the rest of the week with a full belly and empty head until I reached the bottom of my bag on Friday. It was the day of Jian's proposal.

As I suspected, I wasn't invited. That was okay with me, I'd be happy for them but I was glad I wouldn't be taking more air out of their special moment. Still, I was happy when Jian messaged me with his location and time and told me he'd be okay with me watching from a distance out of sight. So there I was.

I saw their long shadows crowd and clump in the last light of that autumn evening. I could make out Abhas and Priyanka, Julie and Zelda, from my perch under a nearby breezeway overlooking the bell tower esplanade. Despite the distance and the trick light of sunset, I could make out Jian by his perfect posture, and soon Carolyn, to whom everyone else turned. I wondered if her nails were done.

The tower bells started playing. I'm sure Carolyn could have played it better, but Jian had one of her carillon classmates up there playing their song. It sounded through the quiet of the evening, asking on its ring that question only Carolyn could answer. I watched the clump of shadows, hugged myself, and felt the last pill in my pocket. I took it out, palmed it, and swallowed it.

From where I stood, I watched two shadows merge into one in the fading light. I heard clapping and cheering and knew it was my time to turn and leave. Though my body floated home below my empty head, I could still hear the bells ring out all evening, not sure if they were real or imagined. *Happy trails, friends.*

CHAPTER 28

It seemed like I only blinked once and it was Halloween Saturday. All day, I felt my heart race and I couldn't calm it down, either from nervousness about Dean's party or from the Xan withdrawals. About midday, I drank a coffee and considered throwing it up after it nearly gave me another panic attack.

One hour fashionably late, Eddie, Zelda, and I made the walk from our dorm to Theta Chi. I thought about the first time we three made this walk together and how much had changed.

"Where's Julie? Meeting us there?" asked Zelda.

"She told me she was going early to help Dean set up," I said.

"Oh nice. Do you know what she's going to be for Halloween? Did you guys do a couple's costume?"

"No, I actually don't know what she's going to be, she just told me she does the same thing every year."

Since I'd spent the entirety of this week barred-out, I only had today to put together a low-effort costume. I took my old Clayton Kershaw Dodgers jersey out of the back of my closet, borrowed some beat-up baseball pants from Charles, threw on the hat, and called it good. *Maybe I'll go all-out next year.*

I looked back at Zelda to admire her costume again. When she first walked up to my door earlier this evening and asked me to guess who, I almost mistook her for someone else. She wore sensibly heeled dancing shoes, a champagne-colored sequin fringe dress, costume pearls, and a jeweled headband with a feather. And she'd cut her hair.

Her hair was the boldest change. Her blonde ringlets were all gone, and now she wore it short like a boy's. Despite this, she still smiled and tossed it around as she walked like it was still back-length, and in her costume, she could have passed for Carey Mulligan from the movie.

"And Alix dressed even better, you want to see a photo?" she asked.

"So, if you're Daisy, that makes Alix... Gatsby?"

Zelda threw her head back and laughed like she was in character. "As if! Can you imagine?"

"So, Tom then?"

"No, of course not! Alix is Nick, they're such a Nick!" Zelda pulled out her phone and showed me a picture of the two of them in costume. Alix had gotten a haircut too. They looked good together.

Next to us, Eddie was quiet the whole walk up. He looked anxious and generally in a bad mood, fiddling with his utility belt. He'd dressed as Robin.

"So, who's Batman?" I asked him.

"I don't want to talk about it."

After the long walk up frat row, we made it to the front door of Theta Chi and encountered another familiar face.

"Who do you kn–hey, look who it is!" said Bobby, chewing on the end of his vape as he recognized us. "Very nice, very nice," he said to Zelda, drinking her with his eyes before turning to me. "Well now, this won't do, will it?" At first I didn't understand him, but once I took the moment to register what he was wearing, I shrunk back in horror.

Bobby was wearing the exact same costume as I was with exactly one distinction: he was a Giants fan. "I don't know if I can let you in here wearing this kind of trash," he said.

I started to get angry and considered going home. "We were a great team and we're going to be even better next year."

"Chill, I'm just messing with you, man, you can come in. But one thing first. What's the difference between a Dodger dog and a Giants hotdog?"

I sighed. "I don't know, Dodger dogs are all beef?"

"You can buy a Giants dog in October! Eyo!" he said, waiting for an answer. I shook my head, happy he was letting me in at least.

Bobby stopped Eddie with one arm as he tried to follow us in.

"Not you. They need you for rush stuff downstairs."

"Even tonight? Come on, man, I've been taking this stuff every day, I just want—"

"—I don't care what you want, recruit, now get your ass down there if you know what's good for you." Eddie shrank down like a little kid, shuffled in after us, and disappeared into the house. I tried to catch Eddie's eye for a check-in, but he wouldn't look at me as he left from my sight.

"I wonder what that was about," I said to Zelda as we walked in.

"Oh, I was wondering if you could tell me," she said. "I'm not really a football person."

"Not—nevermind. I need a drink."

Inside was exactly how I'd always remembered it, though thankfully it wasn't hot these days. Zelda and I snaked our way around beer pong tables thronged with players and spectators. Zelda looked interested in taking the ball from a sexy Peter Pan who wasn't playing well, but I only wanted to find Julie, so we kept moving. After peaking our heads into the bar, the patio, the deck, the kitchen, the beer game area, and Dean's room without finding her, we made our way to the dancefloor as a last resort. There, at a little corner booth next to the dancefloor, sat Dean and Rosa. Though I'd have preferred going the whole night without speaking to them, they surely knew where Julie was. We saw each other at the same time.

"Hello," said Zelda, walking up first.

"My friends!" said Dean, standing up and greeting Zelda with a hug and me with a handshake. I didn't like it. He seemed elated, expansive. *Suspicious.* Rosa smiled at Zelda but didn't even look at me, which was fine. She looked like she'd been crying earlier.

"Have you guys seen Julie?" I asked. "She told me she was here, but I haven't seen her yet."

Dean smiled. "She went to get drinks. She'll be back in a minute. Why don't you guys sit with us?" They moved over and we squeezed snugly into the seats with them. As I did so, I accidentally brushed against Rosa's leg with the back of my hand. We both felt the awkwardness for a moment before turning away from each other.

I couldn't tell what Rosa was for Halloween, and I couldn't ask. She was wearing a short satin dress that reminded me of sexy pajamas, along with pointy ears and the tail of an animal I couldn't quite place. Cat? Dog, maybe? She turned to Zelda.

"I love your costume!" said Rosa.

"Aww thanks," Zelda said, brushing the boyish bangs from her forehead. "I was worried people wouldn't be able to tell who I was."

"Are you kidding? Daisy Buchanan! You look exactly like I always imagined her! Can you do an impression?"

Zelda beamed like a starlet. She paused for only a moment to feign bashfulness before touching her forehead with the back of her hand and launching into her performance. "I hope she'll be a fool! That's the best thing a girl can be in this world, a beautiful little fool."

Rosa clapped wholeheartedly, and even Dean nodded in approval. "Amazing," said Rosa.

"You look so good, yourself!" said Zelda. "This fox thing! Very sexy." Rosa shrugged her shoulders and smiled in return. Just then, the song that was playing ended, and everyone on the dance floor stopped to applaud.

"What's going on?" I asked.

"Probably the next singer up," said Dean. I looked to the far corner of the room and saw Bobby waving a microphone and thanking the crowd. He had done so well that I didn't even realize it wasn't just a recording. "Anybody want to sing next? I bet you do, huh," Dean said to Zelda. I knew she wouldn't miss a chance to cover herself in glory. She followed him to the other side of the room, already radiating.

"I thought I told you not to come here," Rosa said when we were alone.

I frowned. "Well, I was invited, thanks. And as soon as Julie shows up, we'll be out of your hair anyway."

"You're gonna find that harder than you think." I followed her gaze and saw Dean come back to us arm-in-arm with an inflatable T-Rex. The T-Rex walked up to me and laid its long tail in my lap. "Julie?" I asked.

"Surprise!" she said, and popped her head out of the top of the costume. I smiled at her entrance, and for that moment everything felt perfect.

"How was the midterm on Monday? I haven't seen you all week!"

"Oh, I don't want to talk about that now," she said, and laid her head on my neck. Fine by me.

"Julie told me what a fun time you two had tripping in the Redwoods," said Dean. "Sounds like a great time, I've always wanted to see them." I didn't know what to say, so I just nodded and said nothing. I looked at Dean intently for the first time tonight. He made a convincing Ziggy Stardust. He had the wig, the full-face glam makeup, and a tight-fitting zap suit complete with shoulder pads just like Bowie's. But something about how Dean was acting didn't sit right with me.

I looked back at Julie, who was sitting in my lap now. Her smile was as big as I'd ever seen it, and when she opened her eyes and swayed to the music, her pupils looked the size of small coins. She raised her hands and cheered for Zelda, who for all her enthusiasm wasn't very good. Zelda stuttered, forgot some words, and came in at the wrong time on some 2000's pop song I thought I'd forgotten years ago. Despite this, Julie swayed and raised her arms like Adele was up there.

"Hey, are you okay?" I asked Julie. I had to raise my voice over Zelda's din. "Did you take anything earlier tonight?"

"Yeah, I'm feeling great! No, we just smoked earlier and then I had a couple drinks."

Dean stepped forward, almost coming between us. "Yeah, man, I think she's just trying to have a good time, and you should too." He took a full cup of something and put it in my hands. "Here, Julie got these earlier and looks like there's one extra." I took the cup without thinking and drank a long gulp of some bitter-tasting beer, not being able to shake the suspicion that something felt wrong with them. Before long, Zelda finished her song and sauntered back to us. She flitted easily by most of her admirers, but she stopped by Bobby and they got to talking. Dean stood up as the next song began.

"Is this what I think it is?" gushed Julie, standing up as well. I strained to listen to the opening chords and bouncing 80's instrumental over the frat house speakers.

Smooth as anything, Dean pulled a second microphone from his back pocket and beckoned her to join him at the flipped crate people had been using as a stage. "Ready to get your redemption from choir banquet?"

"I thought you'd never ask," she said, and took his hand to follow him away. I hardly had any time to feel what was happening when all of a sudden Rosa and I were alone again, watching our partners duet a love song from their shared past.

I felt trapped where I sat, captivated by what I was seeing and hearing. First of all, they made beautiful music together. I'd only ever heard Julie sing a few times when she was messing around, and it made me sad that I'd never fully seen such a beautiful piece of her that she had hidden away. Dean was amazing too, and with his rocksteady baritone voice and David Bowie stage presence, they almost sounded better than the original song.

As they sang, they laughed and played like I'd never seen either of them before. He spun her, he dipped her, he broke out choreography that she inexplicably knew. I hugged myself as I watched them, feeling cold on a cold night.

Finally, sad sounds around me broke the spell and I turned to see Rosa. She whimpered like an animal as she watched them from her seat, and in that instant she noticed me and we watched together. She looked away from me and stifled her sadness back into silence. I wanted to ask her what was wrong, but I was afraid of the answer. The next moment, Zelda reappeared.

"Hey, guys," she said, "aren't those two amazing? Hey, what's wrong?" Rosa didn't answer, but wiped the wetness from her face, got up, and walked away.

"I'll take care of it," I said to Zelda, and followed Rosa out.

"Hey, are you sure th…" she said, but I couldn't hear the rest as I receded out of earshot.

I found Rosa at the back deck, leaning against the railing and looking out into darkness. She stood with her back to me, so in the dim light of the evening I knew her by the curve of her body first and by the fox tail second, though I tried not to let myself think about that now. Other than a sleepy-eyed trio of boys out there to shotgun beers, we were alone.

"Hey, are you ok?" I asked as I walked up to the railing.

"Oh, it's you."

"Are you surprised?"

"Maybe I shouldn't be, it looked to me like you don't have anywhere better to be anymore."

"If you're talking about in there, it's just a song. They're having fun and they're friends from way back."

"Can I ask you a question?"

"Sure," I said.

"Why are you so stupid?"

I didn't know how to respond.

She continued, "If you thought that was just a song, there's nothing else I can say to you."

The way she said it made me uneasy. I leaned on the railing and nudged her shoulder with mine. "Do you know something I don't?" I asked.

She nudged me back with her shoulder, and for a moment I felt like we were back in high school. "Yes, as usual. Dean talked to me earlier this evening."

I felt my heart drop when she said it, and I felt scared of what it might mean. She looked at me like someone died. I wanted to shrink away from her and forget all about it so I could feel safe again. I looked down and saw that she was touching my hand; I didn't know when it started or how long it had been. I instinctively pulled away.

"He told me earlier this evening, when it was just the two of us," she continued, "that though we'd had nice times together and I didn't do anything wrong, our relationship was over. He said his heart belonged to someone else."

Her words shot me through with terror, and my first instinct was to drop everything and run instantly to Julie to get her out of there. So this was what his smugness and good mood was all about tonight. He had some scheme going.

I turned to make my way back, but one last look at Rosa made walking away feel like wading through mud. I hadn't taken five steps before turning around again.

She looked deflated now, exhausted. I didn't think Julie was in danger or anything for hanging around Dean. Despite my fears, despite my past with Rosa, or maybe because of it, I couldn't leave her now. I walked back to the railing and came up next to her on the other side.

"So, if he said this to you at the beginning of the night, why were you still sitting with him when we saw you?" I asked.

"I don't know. I guess I just didn't know what to do. I thought about telling him off, storming out, making a scene, all of it, and I even saw myself do it in my imagination all night.

But then she showed up, and they seemed so happy that I felt like I got trapped in glue."

"What were they doing? How did they look together?"

She made a face that I understood as pity, which I took as a bad sign. "They were just there together, you saw it. She was sad about failing some midterm at first, but he made her feel better. They had a drink, a smoke, and she lightened up."

"Did he confess his love to her?"

"If he did, I never heard it, but we've been gone a while." I started to panic again and turned back to look at the door. Rosa grabbed my wrist.

"Why won't anyone be good to me?" she asked. She was tearing up again. "Not him, not you, I don't know what to do. I'm fun to be around, right? I'm smart as fuck. I'm going places. I'm pretty too. We had fun, we hardly ever fought, I don't understand. I just want someone to take care of me, but in every relationship I just feel so alone. What's wrong with me?" She started to turn away. Before she could, I spun her back to squarely face me and hugged her with my whole body.

"It's okay, it's okay," I said, and patted her gently between the shoulder blades. I wanted to reach up and touch her hair, but I didn't, not wanting to give either of us the wrong idea. I kept hugging her as I spoke. "Look, I wasn't good to you when we were together, and I'm so sorry for that. I'll never be able to give you that time back. It was my fault. As for Dean, I always thought that guy was shady. But his feelings aren't your fault, okay? There's nothing wrong with you. You're a delightful person that anyone would be lucky to be with and you deserve better than him anyway. Fuck that guy."

She trembled as I spoke, and before long I felt the last emotional barriers fall away. She sobbed aloud now, clutching me with both arms like someone might tear us apart by force. She buried her face in my chest, and I watched tear and makeup stains start to form on the white of my jersey. Between sobs, I felt her breathe me in as deeply as she dared, and I couldn't help but do the same. I don't know how or what she used, but Rosa always smelled like apples in the fall.

Finally, she raised her head. "If... if they end up together after tonight, do you ever think you and I might... might give it another try?"

We were still hugging, so I stepped back to arm's length before I could say it. Her tears were still there and her eye makeup had smudged us both, but she smiled so sweetly when she asked that her face reminded me of a window that had caught the sunset. For that moment, it made me want to say yes.

"Rosa. You deserve to have everything you want. You know I believe that. But I also feel like our time has passed. I'm sorry." Her face fell, and I felt like I'd shouted down the sun.

"Do you love her?" she asked.

"I haven't told her yet, but I do."

She smiled sadly. "Okay, I wish you both the best then."

She hugged me once more, and from the way she held me I knew it would be the last time. I thought about everything we'd been through, and everything we'd been to each other for years.

This was our end. I felt my cheek, thinking that Rosa had wiped her crying face on mine, but the tears were mine.

"What the hell is going on here?" said a voice from behind us. I wheeled around and stepped back from Rosa. Dean and Julie were standing behind us.

"Carlos, what's happening?" asked Julie, who looked anxiously between me and Dean.

"They were talking about getting back together, I heard the whole thing," he said.

"Is that true?" Julie asked, looking right at me.

I looked between everyone for a moment. I had no idea how long they'd been standing there. There was nothing I could do but be honest. "Well, yes, we talked about it, but—"

"—See! He admits it!" Dean interrupted, reflecting a gleam in his eyes like a cat's. "And you saw them holding each other! Who knows what would've happened if we didn't catch them when we did!"

Rosa stood by in silence, holding her arms in a way that only made her look more guilty.

"No, you don't understand, it wasn't like that!" I said. "Dean's a bad guy, and Rosa was telling me about it, and—"

"—And so you thought you could make a move on her?" asked Dean. "Stop embarrassing yourself, we saw everything. Why don't you get out of here?"

I turned to Rosa for help, pleading with my eyes for her to explain the situation. It was like she couldn't even see me. She was only looking at Dean, who had her in his petrifying gaze. It was like he had some kind of power over her, but she didn't move, didn't speak, and just stood there frozen.

"Julie, please!" I said, turning to her now. "I only love you! I swear, I always have!"

"Oh really?" asked Dean. "Because Rosa told me last week that after you finished seeing Julie, you went straight down the hall to Rosa's to tell her how sorry you were for everything wrong you ever did. Isn't that right?"

Without breaking from his domination, Rosa only nodded.

"Is that why you've been avoiding me all week?" Julie asked. "I thought I was just being too much after my midterm, but were you trying to get back with her?"

"No, I haven't been avoiding you! It was just the Xanax, it made me—"

"—Xanax?" she interrupted. "How long have you been taking that? Carlos, it's like I don't know who you are. Has this really been going on all this time?"

I clenched both my fists and wanted to scream. I had no idea how any of this happened. I looked from face to face. Rosa still looked spellbound, unable to break from Dean. Julie's face stabbed me as I watched her feelings for me change. She looked crushed, disappointed, angry, even disgusted. Then I turned to Dean. His eyes shone with an intensity that was almost bloodlust, and he wore a shit-eating grin I couldn't resist knocking off his stupid face.

As it happened, I felt like I was watching myself do it from outside my body. I took one of my balled-up fists, raised it above my head, and ran headlong as fast as my legs would take me and punched him as hard as I could squarely in the jaw. I felt my wrist bend unnaturally, and I quickly grabbed it and held it to my chest. Dean reeled for a moment but didn't fall. He didn't even raise a hand to stop me, though I ran at him from across the deck. He rubbed his jaw with his hand for a moment and then turned his cheek so I might punch the other side if I liked. As he turned his face out of Julie's sightline, I saw him wink at me before smiling bigger than ever.

I dropped to my knees. I felt beaten, like I had nothing because he'd taken everything and I had no way to stop him. On top of everything else, I felt ten times as drunk as I should have because my legs gave out from wobbling despite having only a few sips of that gross-tasting beer. *Wait a minute.*

"Julie, please, taste this but don't swallow," I said, handing her my solo cup.

"I don't want any."

"Please," I begged, still on my knees, "everything will make sense in a minute, just taste."

Julie took a small sip and swished it around her mouth for a moment before spitting it back out onto the deck. "That's vile," she said.

"Dean gave me that, I think he put something in it."

That wiped the stupid smile off his face. "How dare you!" he said, blowing up almost instantly. "Do you have any idea of what you're accusing me of?"

"I do," I said, getting up. "And Julie, go to a mirror or your phone and check your pupils. You said you just had a smoke and a drink. If you take a drug test tomorrow, you'll probably find that wasn't the case. Yours was probably E or Molly."

Dean started to look back and forth between us, growing flustered. It seemed like he was caught off guard. "There's nothing wrong with this one, see? I'll prove it." Though he looked afraid, he grabbed the cup from Julie and drank the whole thing in one draught.

"Way to get rid of the evidence," I said. "Julie, don't be surprised if he gets drowsy pretty early tonight. He set me up. He set us all up."

Julie looked between me and Dean over and over, and for a minute we all stood there, not knowing who she would believe.

"Rosa," she said finally. Rosa had fully dissociated since Dean's entrance, but Julie's pleading voice and entreating eyes brought her back. She continued, "All night you seemed really sad, but I felt too shy to ask you what was wrong. Did something happen between you and Dean before I arrived?"

Rosa nodded and slowly raised her eyes to Julie like she was resurfacing from underwater. "Before you came, Dean said we were over because he was in love with someone else."

Dean grew angry now and stepped in front of Rosa. "She's lying! It wasn't like that!"

"Oh, she's lying? How dare you," Julie said. Though she was small, Julie raised herself up with the ferocity of the Tyrannosaurus Rex. "I know you. I've known you for years. You planned all of this. I know you're manipulative, conniving, and always trying to make people do what you want. But I tried to look past that because I thought you were a good person at

345

heart and because we always had each other's backs. I was wrong. I don't want to see you anymore."

I smiled and walked toward Julie as I saw Dean at a loss for words.

"And what are you smiling about?" Julie snapped at me. "You're a liar too. Why are you visiting your ex in secret? Why are you doing Xanax in secret? I needed you all week, where were you?" She turned to face both of us. "I'm leaving. Alone. And you better believe I'm taking that drug test first thing in the morning."

"Julie, wait!" said Dean, grabbing her arm.

"Get your hands off me!" she yelled, and wrenched herself free. Then she bolted and ran back inside. Dean followed her, running just behind. I felt Julie was in danger, so I ran after them too.

She ran as fast as she could through the party, not caring whose shoes she stepped on or whose drink she knocked over. Dean was more careful, trying not to draw attention to them, but his long strides kept pace with her short ones. I thought she would head for the door, and so did Dean, who got there first to cut her off, but to our surprise, she made a hard left and ran up the stairs. As Dean and I reached the foot of the stairs at the same time, we watched her lose her footing and slip, twisting her ankle before getting back up. Dean shoved me hard out of the way and ascended two steps at a time.

We found her in his room. She had his desk open and was holding a fistful of Ziploc bags in each hand. "Was this the one you used on me, huh, asshole? What about this one?"

"Those are mine, step away from those," he said, trying to modulate his voice to sound calm.

"Or what, you're gonna drug me again?" She moved to the far corner of the room and opened the sliding glass door to the balcony. To call it a balcony was generous: it was more like a big window with standing room for one over a waist-high railing.

"Get away from there!" said Dean.

I had to speak up then. "Hey, Julie. I agree with Dean. You may not feel it, but you're really high right now, it's dangerous."

"Well, that's nice," she said, and held the bags over the balcony railing. Among them was the Dantesque sheet of acid paper we bought from Dean before the trip. She was holding it in her bare hand, letting it flutter in the wind.

"Alright, Julie, I'm sorry," said Dean. "You're right, I did put something in your drink. And his too. I love you, I always have, and I'm way better for you than this asshole. I wasn't trying to hurt you, or anybody. I just wanted you to see that things would be better with me."

I was stunned at his admission, and for a moment so was Julie. She let her hand drop down to the safe side of the railing and looked at Dean with agony in her eyes. One second was all it took for him to bound across the room and get on top of her. Before I knew what was happening, he grabbed both her wrists hard and twisted them until the Ziploc bags fell from her hands. The only thing she held onto was the acid paper, which crumpled in the tightness of her grip. Dean held her wrists hard, but Julie kicked him with both feet there on the edge of the balcony. She kicked him hard in his knee, and for a moment looked as though she was climbing up the side of his body. Then his grip loosened, and she was gone.

I never saw her fall. I never heard her either until she hit the ground. She never screamed or made a sound. She might not have even realized she went over. As I ran across the room to the balcony, she just disappeared for an instant and reappeared a moment later as a bone crunching crash down on the sidewalk at the front of the house. As I looked out from the balcony, the half-deflated T-rex costume hid the fact that her legs were bent the wrong way around. After the crash, she didn't move again.

Dean and I looked at each other. For a moment, I thought he might go over the side and join her. He snapped out of it though, and sprang into action, running out of the room yelling, "Emergency! Emergency! Out of the way! Someone fell out the window! Call an ambulance!"

For a moment, I grabbed my chest, thinking another panic attack would start. It didn't yet, because nothing felt real. I felt sleepy, maybe from the drugs, or maybe from the long semester that was only half over. I reached for my phone to call an ambulance, but my phone was gone. I floated down the stairs, putting all my strength into steadying myself and not falling headfirst. I was greeted at the bottom by Zelda hysterically crying and shaking me, but for some reason I couldn't hear her. I couldn't hear anything after Julie didn't scream.

Independent of my thoughts, my feet took me down more stairs to a basement I'd never seen. I opened the door, and despite still being in shock, the strong stench of blood and shit anchored me to the moment. I looked around the dim basement. Five guys, freshmen recruits, lay there bound, gagged, wearing diapers, half stripped out of their Halloween costumes, bruised to a pulp, and covered in some kind of animal blood. As my eyes adjusted to the dimness, I saw they were evenly spaced in a circle, five points of a pentagram. I knew Eddie by his Robin costume and dark skin, but otherwise he was unrecognizable. He was breathing, but motionless.

I dropped to my knees, ready to fold. *This can't be real.* It had to all be a dream. I hit myself on the head and poked my eyes, but everything stayed as it was. My legs failed me then, my breathing grew heavy, and I unwillingly joined them on the floor. Moments later, the basement door burst open and a dark figure stormed in with a heavy step. He went straight for the bound victims and started untying them, taking photos the whole time and bringing them water to drink. Then he noticed me.

"Batman?" I asked. "What the hell is happening? Is this real?"

"It's real," said Charles. "Come on, let's get out of here. I brought my car, I'm taking you all to the hospital."

By the time I helped those guys out of the basement and into Charles's car, Julie was gone. An ambulance had come, and all that was left was a bloody spot on the sidewalk. That was the last thing I remembered before I lost consciousness in the car.

CHAPTER 29

I woke up in the hospital in the early hours of the morning. It took me a few seconds and a look around to be able to tell where I was. Everything washed out in the sterile, fluorescent light of the room. I saw an IV drip of saline solution with a hose running down into my arm. I was wearing a hospital gown now instead of my normal clothes. Below my ankles were scratchy cotton socks, more like sacks, that fit loosely on my feet like bags of chips. And my right wrist was in a splint.

"Oh, look, he's awake," said a voice by my feet. "How are you feeling?"

I reached over to the bed table next to me and found my glasses, and as I put them on, Zelda and Rosa came into view. They were smiling at me and wearing normal clothes again.

"I feel... not bad," I said. I sat up in bed and took stock of my body. I felt rehydrated to the max thanks to that saline solution. I even had to pee. My wrist felt tender but fine as long as I didn't move it. "What happened?"

"A lot happened," said Rosa. "What's the last thing you remember?"

"I remember Batman… some kind of Satanic ritual. Was that a dream?"

"It was real."

"It was?" I thought for a moment, trying to remember more details. "Julie! Is she—"

"—She's resting," said Zelda. "She's in another room. We visited her earlier, but nurses said only two at a time so Jian and Carolyn are with her now."

I was on the verge of jumping out of bed, but Zelda's reassurances let me lie back down.

"How is she?"

"Not great, but she'll recover. The doctor said she broke both tibias and was concussed. She's not sure what she's going to do next."

I felt stupid for wanting to ask, but I couldn't help myself. "Has she mentioned me at all?"

Zelda and Rosa shared a look for a moment before turning back to me. "She said she doesn't want to see you."

My heart fell at Zelda's words. I thought about the nightmare that had just occurred, and I thought about what I wanted. I wanted to hug Julie and never let her go again, but I couldn't do anything that would disrespect her wishes. I would try to check in on her soon and try to be whatever she needed. In the meantime, I had enough to do here.

"What about Eddie?" I asked. "When I found him, he looked like he'd been through Hell."

"They dropped you and the other frat recruits off here at the hospital, but as soon as we showed up, Charles drove Eddie back home," said Zelda. "He said it was just body blows and psychological torture. He said he didn't have hospital money anyway."

Just body blows and psychological torture. I thought back to last night. When I found Eddie, I thought I'd discovered a crime scene. And he couldn't even go to the hospital for it. I could hardly afford it either, but I didn't get a choice when I lost consciousness. It made me so mad, but I didn't know who to blame. The American healthcare system in general, I guess. At least I didn't have to pay for an ambulance.

"And what about Dean?" I asked.

"Dean is here too," said Rosa, and for a second I bolted up in bed thinking he might have been in the room. But he wasn't. "Pretty much right after we got here, he showed up, declared he'd been poisoned and needed his stomach pumped, and collapsed right in the waiting room. I saw him earlier, but he was still unconscious."

I shivered at the thought. Was that from the drink he tried to feed me? Did he try to kill himself after Julie's fall and then change his mind? Was it just another scheme to get him out of trouble? I hoped he'd end up in jail, and I was scared he wouldn't.

I checked out of the hospital within an hour of waking up. I considered myself lucky: the doctor said the only things wrong with me were a fractured wrist and an iron deficiency, both of which I could work on. They let me borrow the hospital phone to call Mom so I could tell her to expect the bill. I said I was sorry, that I'd also lost my phone, and that I'd pick up a job to help support myself. She told me that it was okay, she was glad I was safe, and we'd talk more soon. I was surprised. We don't usually speak to each other like that.

The hospital gave me back my clothes. They'd cut open my jersey with shears, so it was ruined, but I put it on anyway because it was the only shirt I had. They couldn't find my shoes, so I felt as bad as I looked when I walked the mile back to my dorm with just the hospital socks on my feet. Back at my own dorm door, as tired as I'd ever been, I saw the sock drawing on my dorm room white board. I just laughed to myself and slept through the morning in Charles's empty room, which he was nice enough to leave propped open for me.

Around noon, I finally got a change of clothes and returned to the hospital to see Julie. When I arrived, I found that Carolyn was still there. She looked like she hadn't left since last night. She was still cold toward me, but fourteen hours in the hospital seemed to have softened her a little.

"Hi, Carolyn, is Julie awake?"

"Yes. She doesn't want to see you."

"Zelda told me. Would it be alright if you asked her again?"

Carolyn looked up from the work she was trying to do and gave me a look of disbelief that shone through her tiredness. "And why the hell would I do that?"

I took a deep breath. "Because I was spiraling last week, I wasn't there for her when she needed me. I didn't know how bad Dean really was, but if I was more vigilant, I could have been there for her yesterday and prevented all this from happening. Everything bad that ever happened between us came from me staying away when I should have tried to help. I'm trying to help now."

"And what are you going to say if she wants to get back together?"

"Well, that's what I want, and I'll respect her wishes no matter what."

"You'll respect her wishes like showing up here when she says she doesn't want to see you?"

I squirmed under her scrutiny, but I couldn't just let Julie go. "Ask her. Please. If she says no again, neither of you have to see me ever again if you don't want to. Dean and I are not the same. Please."

Carolyn closed her laptop and gripped it hard in her hands. As usual, I couldn't hold out against her intense gaze, and my eye wandered until it found the engagement ring on her left hand. She saw me notice it and stood up, moving it out of sight.

"Fine, I will. But only because never seeing you again sounds nice. I'll hold you to that if she sends you away this time." Without looking at me again, Carolyn walked off to find an employee that would let her in to see Julie. I waited a few minutes, growing more anxious as the time seemed to slow. Finally, Carolyn reappeared.

"Go, before she changes her mind," she said, and sat back down with her laptop.

Julie's room was almost identical to the one I woke up in this morning. Cold, bright, and sterile. She sat up in bed when I came in.

I'd heard the extent of her injuries earlier, but she looked worse than I'd imagined. Both her legs were splinted from ankles to hips, and she winced in pain as she tried to sit up. She would probably get fitted for casts soon.

"Hey."

"Hey."

"I just wanted to check in," I began, "and tell you that I'm sorry for everything that happened."

"Oh good," she said, and reclined back into a laying down position to look up at the ceiling.

"I guess starting with the most recent stuff, I'm sorry about last night. I never liked Dean, but I didn't know he was like that."

"That's okay, I didn't really know either," she said without looking at me.

"Also, I wanted to clear up some things that we had said before that. I wasn't trying to get back together with Rosa. She was just sad because Dean broke up with her, and I felt responsible for helping her because of unresolved trauma I'd caused her in the past. I don't have any feelings for her, I only want you."

"Well, that's nice at least." She still wouldn't look at me.

"And also about last week. I wasn't there for you when you needed support. I bought some Xanax from Eddie because I was feeling overwhelmed, and I fell into a spiral until I ran out of pills. It's not an excuse, I should have been there for you, but I just wanted to tell you the whole truth and that nothing else is going on."

"Hm. Okay. Anything else?"

"Yeah. I know your feelings about me are probably… mixed right now, but I just want you to know that I'm here for you, whatever you need, in whatever way I can be helpful to you. I want to be together, and I want to deserve a place by your side. I love you."

Julie's eyes flitted up at me for a moment before sliding away again. "Alright. Is that all?"

I looked at her confusedly, unsure of what else to say. "Well, uh, I actually lost my phone last night so I may be without one for a while in case you need to contact me."

Julie sat up in bed and finally looked me in my eyes. "Listen to yourself. What is this? Why did you come here? Apologies? What's an apology good for?"

"Umm, it's good for clearing up misunderstandings between us, letting you know the seriousness of my commitment, and rebuilding some of the trust that was lost between us."

Julie let out a dry half-laugh that hurt my feelings. "Trust lost between us? That's a nice way to put it. Here's what apologies are good for. An apology is better than no apology, but everyone knows that. I knew what you were gonna say, and that's why I let you in here today. I'm sure your ex loved your apology. Maybe I'll feel the same one day. But does an apology unbreak my tibias?" She winced as she tried to sit up again. "Does it pay for my casts or my ambulance? Does an apology keep me from failing out of school at the end of the semester? Does it put the tears back in my eyes that I cried all last week because I thought you were cheating? Does it give me the week back that I missed you after you said you'd be there for me during an acid trip? No, it doesn't give me any of that, so thanks for noth..."

She broke off into quiet sobs, unable to finish.

"You're right," I said. "An apology doesn't do much. I had to say it first, but that's not why I'm here. You've got tough times ahead, and I'm here to show you I'm committed and here for you." As I spoke, I walked around to her other side. I leaned over the hospital bed, careful of her splints and mine, and hugged her gingerly, placing my forehead on hers and breathing slowly until she stopped crying. I wiped my tears before they could fall on her.

"Moving around, cooking, getting work done, getting class notes, emailing professors, all of that is going to be way harder now and I want to be everything that helps make it happen," I continued. "I wanted to be official since our acid trip, but I feel like an idiot because I never asked you. I know what the road ahead looks like. I know you belong here, and I want you to lean on me as you succeed. Together, we can have everything we want and make ourselves happy here. I love you, and I have for a while. Would you like to officially be my partner, my girlfriend?"

Julie paused and looked at me hard. She was really considering it. "And what would you get in return for being boyfriend of the year? Sounds like a hard time."

"I would get to see the person I care about most thrive and succeed. I also feel like I'll continue to learn and grow from being in a relationship with you. I've learned so much already, and I believe we have something special if we keep working at it."

Julie sighed and let me hug her again. We stayed there for a few minutes before she spoke again. "I want to believe you. It sounds so nice. Dean always sounded nice too."

"I'm not him," I said, standing back straight.

"I know you're not. I know you, and I know all the things you might do and might not do if we're together. But I knew him for years. He was my friend. I trusted him. And now I feel scared to trust anyone who has feelings for me like this."

"I understand. You went through a lot. But we can work on it. I can prove to you over time that I'm dependable. I know I can."

She looked at me then like a pet she had to put down. "If it were just me and the support of my friends," she said, "I know I can get through this. I always have. But if I were counting on you to be there for me and you let me down, I don't know if I could survive something like that again. I need to be okay, and I can do that with the support I have. I'm sorry."

At that moment, I felt my stomach turn to brick. "Okay, I understand. Your well-being is the most important thing right now, so you deserve to have everything you want. Would you accept any help from me as a friend, or would you like to not see me anymore?" My heart hurt as I said it, and I hoped it wouldn't be goodbye forever.

Julie smiled at me then, her old mischievous smile like she was planning a new adventure. "Text me when you get a new phone. Then we'll see if we can start doing things that friends do."

I hugged her and said I would. I didn't want to let go, because when I did our relationship would be over. But Julie patted me three times on the back and I finally stood up. Even though I was losing the relationship, I hoped that I wouldn't have to lose the person. For the first time that day, I thought things were going to be okay.

Carolyn slammed her laptop closed and ran to me when she saw me smiling on the way out. "She didn't take you back, did she?" she asked.

"No."

"Then she doesn't want to see you anymore?"

"Not exactly."

"Then what are you smiling about?"

"We're going to be friends."

Carolyn smoothed her hair back in a self-soothing gesture, then in an instant shot her hand out and grabbed me by the collar. She looked me dead in the face with an intensity that I remembered well.

"You want to be friends? *Then be one.*" She let me go, and I took the bus back this time.

EPILOGUE: SIX WEEKS LATER

For better or worse, the semester was finally over. I had technically finished back on Wednesday, when I submitted my final paper for Intro to Classics. I gave Alix my best take on Augustine's *Confessions*, and Alix gave me a B in the class. I wasn't worried about it. Not like today.

I ascended the walk to east campus for what would be the last time this semester. It was Friday of Finals Week, and anyone who hadn't finished their finals already was now sitting for their last one. Just in the last few days, the whole energy of the place had changed. The air had buzzed with nervous energy back on Monday, but every day since it unwound bit by bit toward the sleepy stop about to set in for the winter. As I walked past the bell tower, I stepped around a chattery group of friends about to shotgun celebration beers. They all had red noses and chapped lips from the cold, and though no one had a drop to drink yet, I almost got a little buzz when I lingered a moment too long to admire their holiday faces. The spell broke only when they noticed me, and they took a long look at my grocery store flower bouquet as they let me pass.

Other than the squirrels, I didn't see another soul the rest of the way up. The chill wind rustled my flower bundle, and I had to stop myself from fidgeting with the cellophane in my nervousness. I spent the final 15 minutes of Finals Week on a stone bench in the College of Chemistry courtyard. Some forlorn-looking girl sniffled away on the next bench over. I felt like I knew her from somewhere, but I couldn't remember. I guessed she had given up and left her test early, as she wasn't dressed for the outdoors and didn't look like she had anywhere to be. As usual, I was too obvious and she caught me staring. I only managed a weak smile before she broke eye contact and put her head back down. *Seasons change.*

I stood up and pulled one of the flowers from my bouquet, one of the edge ones so it wouldn't mess up the arrangement. I walked over and gave it to the bench girl. She seemed surprised but took it anyway. All I could manage was, "careful, the thorns," and the briefest eye contact before turning away.

Finally, the bell tower sounded 6pm, and the rest of the College of Chemistry filed out into the courtyard wearing the sum of their semesters on their faces.

I craned my neck to scan the ambling crowd. *She would be one of the last ones.* I saw the wheelchair before I saw her. I saw the two bright-orange boot casts covered in Sharpie get-wells from toes to knees. I took a deep breath, ready to read the final verdict for the semester etched on her face. *Whatever happened in there, I hope she smiles back.* She did me one better.

When she saw me standing there, Julie pulled forward just enough to get out of the crowd and spun her wheels hard in a wheelchair 360, letting her hair (it was now back to its natural darkest-brown since she cut it and let it grow out again) stream along behind her until she tipped back and almost fell over. I lunged forward and caught the back of her chair just in time for her to smile up at me from the flat of her back.

"Jeez, that bad huh?" I asked, tipping her back upright.

"Grades don't come out until later today. Still, I put an answer for every question this time! I just hope it was enough to pass."

"I'm sure it was. I'm proud of you." We shared a look that lasted a moment too long and collapsed into awkwardness. We did that a lot these days.

"I got these for you," I continued, handing her the flowers. "Congrats on everything you overcame and accomplished this semester."

"Thanks," she said, and looked at them without looking at me. "And thanks for everything you've done to support me. I couldn't have done it without you."

"Yeah, you could've, you're amazing." Another silence. I looked down at the roses I had placed in her lap. I had wanted to get red ones, but Carolyn told me I couldn't because red was for lovers. Zelda had suggested I get yellow roses for friendship, but I couldn't do that either because it wasn't where my heart was. I settled on white roses. I didn't know what they were supposed to mean, and that somehow seemed right.

"Are you excited to be out of this thing soon?" I asked, rattling the wheelchair as I took it from behind and started to push her out of there.

"Yeah, the doctor says if there aren't any other complications, I get to transition to a walker first thing Monday."

"And that's why you have to fly back home tonight?"

"My parents need help at the restaurant. You know, family business?"

"How are you going to help them with two leg casts?"

"They'll probably set me up with a stool at the register or in the kitchen making sides. I'm sorry."

I gripped the wheelchair handles and took a moment to breathe. Just like that, our time was gone. "No, I'm sorry," I said. "I'm sure you miss home and they miss you. I just thought we'd have more time to celebrate what we've accomplished here."

"We still have the party. And you can still drive me to the airport, right?"

"Yeah, of course."

It wasn't really the end. It had been hard, but we'd made sure it wasn't the end. At first, even Julie thought she would fail out and have to start over at Florida State next year, but all us friends really came together. Carolyn was relentless in filling out all the paperwork Julie needed to get Disabled Students Program accommodations, and without the flexible homework due dates and the extra testing time, she might really have failed out. Zelda cooked for her four times a week, and Jian took her to physical therapy on days that I couldn't. Even Charles started lending us his car again as soon as I earned enough money at my new job to fix the roof and the smell, though I suspect Eddie worked hard to convince him.

When I wasn't in class or with Julie in her classes, I was working the cash register at our local noodle shop a few blocks from my dorm building. The owner, an older, friendly-faced Korean man, started letting me have a second shift meal to bring home after I wheeled Julie into work once and she made a good impression on him. "For your girlfriend," he would always say when he boxed up the meal, though I'd always correct him.

I rolled Julie's chair down Telegraph Avenue until we reached the local burger joint where Jian and Carolyn were having their engagement party. The place had a small event space in the basement, and though Carolyn nearly had a conniption when she found out it wasn't wheelchair accessible, I had told her not to worry. Carolyn met us at the top of the basement stairs and took the wheelchair while I scooped Julie under the knees and carried her down. As we crossed the threshold at the bottom of the stairs, she grabbed my neck and joked that she felt more like a bride than Carolyn. I laughed and felt thankful for all the time I'd spent at the gym with Julie while she was in physical therapy.

As Carolyn wheeled Julie to the seat next to hers, she asked me with only her eyes how the Chem finals went. I felt her finally relax when I gave her two thumbs up, and she offered me the chair on Julie's other side in a sign of approval.

"So, now that we're all here," said Charles, looking around the room before stopping on Jian and Carolyn, "Tell us. When's the Big Day?"

Carolyn got suddenly bashful, as she only ever did with Jian, and he squeezed her hand as he fielded the question for both of them. "We decided to do a long engagement," he said. "We have lots of school left, and we only finished the first semester after all. But as soon as we have a date, you guys will be the first to know."

Charles nodded and poured himself more beer from the pitcher he was sharing with Eddie. Sitting next to them, Abhas watched the glass fill but stayed with his sparkling water. In the next seat, Priyanka chewed her nicotine gum and, for today, stayed with Abhas.

"Surely you guys are at least moving in together next semester?" Priyanka asked. "Actually, the second bedroom in my apartment just opened up! Wouldn't it be fun if we were all roommates again?"

Abhas looked at Jian and sipped his soda water, but this time Carolyn answered for them both. "Like we said, we're going to have to let you know."

Zelda listened without saying anything, instead taking down notables and quotables in a leather-bound quadrille-lined notebook. It had been her new fixation this past month or so, when she'd decided that our lives were 'just too exciting' and that she'd have to start writing us into her novel immediately. I told her to count me out because I didn't want anyone to know my business, but I secretly always thought I'd make a good story. Once the chatter started up again, Zelda leaned over and asked low enough so Julie didn't hear, "How'd the hearing go this week?"

"Put that thing away and maybe I'll tell you."

She clicked her pen and closed the notebook in her lap. "That doesn't sound good."

Dean's student conduct investigation had been a blot on an otherwise clean end to the semester. Since that night in the hospital, there were endless reports, statements, depositions, and interviews that taped up the path between us and our sense of justice. Despite our hourly struggle to keep Julie from failing out, we kept having to make time for another callback and rehashing with someone new until talking about that night started to feel more real than actually living it. The hazing stuff was pretty open and shut, so thankfully Theta Chi's frat activities were suspended for the semester, but Julie's inpatient hospital stay stopped her from getting that drug test that would have been evidence, so after all of Dean's drugs mysteriously disappeared, everything else was just hearsay.

The hearing had been Monday of Finals week, just about the worst timing they could have thought of. Julie dressed up for it and looked sympathetic enough in her wheelchair, but under questioning she had to admit that she didn't think Dean pushed her out the window and that it was just an accident. For his part, Dean showed up looking like a Heisman winner on Draft Day. He cried right on cue and armed himself with a carousel of character witnesses who pleaded for his 'bright future.' Though I didn't say anything to Julie, I felt we were lost. The only bright spot of the hearing was Rosa's testimony. With legalistic precision, commanding stage presence, and surprising pathos, Rosa marshaled her slash-and-burn debate skills to paint a scathing picture of Dean's behavior that night and of his general character. Afterwards, she gave me a handshake and Julie a hug out on the wheelchair ramp and told us she would be at every hearing until we had our justice. She ended up keeping her word. In the next semesters and years, I saw her around campus, but by and by she didn't really see me anymore until we became strangers again.

Thankfully, the Desi Student Association fared better in their own investigation. They found the poisoner: some sicko with hate in his heart, and thankfully they threw the book at him. It was a grim reminder that hate is real and we all have a role in snuffing it out.

I drove Julie to the airport in Charles's car. Carolyn had offered hers as well, but that deal came with Carolyn driving and me sitting in the back. As I turned to Julie in the gray-black twilight of West Oakland, I blinked into an acid flashback more real than the real life in front of me. I saw her as she was, curled up in the seat, sleeping in sunbeams. I felt the hot wind again surging through the open cartop. I smelled the weed and the weird car smell and found the cumulonimbus Ankylosaurus in the sky. It took running a red light for me to snap out of it.

"Sorry, I spaced for a second."

"It's okay," she said, and unclenched her grip from the overhead roof handle. "What were you thinking about?"

As she asked me, I noticed the distant lights of Oakland airport grow brighter. I tapped the brakes, going slower than the flow of traffic. I was out of time.

"I was thinking about... us."

"Hey I don't—"

"—Please," I interrupted. "I'm not trying to be weird, but I need to tell you something before we don't see each other for the rest of the break."

"Alright then."

"I committed to being friends back in the hospital, and I haven't talked about that since then, right? Is it okay if, now that we've taken care of everything else, we talk about us again?"

Julie shifted in her seat, and I wasn't sure if she was trying to face me or scoot away. "Okay," she said, "But one thing first. Final grades just came out."

This answer induced as much anxiety as any she could have given. If she left now without anything to show for it, there was no reason for her to come back in January. She'd live at home and commute to Florida State like she always said, and nothing she or I did this year would have been enough to stop that. There would be no point in talking about us. There's no us if there's no Julie. I pulled into the terminal loading zone and felt an anvil press my chest. I forgot to breathe as I watched her phone's blue glow scroll across her face.

"I... passed. I passed. I did it!" she whispered, then said, then yipped with excitement. I felt the weight melt away, then dropped my face into my hands with relief. In a moment, I felt her hand touch my neck, then I turned and we were forehead-to-forehead, crying together.

"Well, I mostly passed," she said finally. "I still failed linear algebra, but I can retake one class next semester. In everything else I got C's."

"Hell yeah! C's get degrees."

"C for Chemistry!"

"C for College graduation!"

"C for... Carlos?" *Stupid, why'd I say that?*

Airport security didn't let us linger in the loading zone, so we circled again.

"Really though, I couldn't have done it without you."

"Yeah you could've."

"Carlos, I know you want to talk about us. Let's talk about us. I have to ask you, and I need you to be honest with me, okay?"

"Okay."

"Back in the hospital, you said you were okay with being just friends. Were you really? Or were you playing a long game so you could prove yourself and we would eventually get back together? I know you and Dean aren't the same, I get that, but I've been reflecting a lot on that relationship and I see now that's what he was doing. I'm scared. I need you to tell me the truth."

It took me a minute to get my words right. Not because I was lying or because I was trying to match what she wanted to hear, but because I knew our ending deserved both the factual truth and the feeling truth of the soul, and saying both together was hard. We almost passed two more terminals before I had it.

"At first, there at the hospital, I really meant that we only ever had to be friends. I wanted to be in your life so badly that I would have taken any role, and there was almost no better one than someone who would support you through a hard time and help you achieve all your dreams. If you could be alright, then

I would be alright too, regardless of 'us.' Then it got hard. It got hard because going to your classes with you was hard, working and bringing you food was hard, helping you prepare for the hearings and police reports was hard."

I paused for a moment to try and read her face. I had her attention, and in the expectant silence, I found the feeling in her eyes that gave me the courage to go on. "These things weren't hard in themselves. Yeah, they were challenging, but I spent my whole life in a pressure cooker, so what's a few more tasks? After all this time we spent together as friends, what was hard was this feeling I got every time you smiled at me. Every time we were there for each other, supported each other, made each other laugh, talked about the future and our dreams, we would look at each other just like this, and in that moment I knew I loved you and you loved me back but we weren't together. From that point on, I waited. You coming back next semester was more important than anything else, so I didn't want this to be a distraction. But now, here we are."

"Dean thought I secretly still liked him too. What makes you know better?"

I smiled to myself. I did know better. "You have a tell. I told you back on our acid trip."

"I don't remember that."

"Sometimes when I make you feel alone or sad, you do this thing with your eyes where you look at me but somehow feel like you're getting farther away. I called it 'telescoping.' Well, there's a flipside too, and that's how I know you love me back. Sometimes, when I bring you food you didn't ask for, or find something important you lost, or joke back and forth with you until we degenerate into nonsense, you look at me like you're zooming in, like you want to close all the distance between us until we're one and the same. I call it 'microscoping.' Since that night at the hospital, I've done everything to see that look again, and I've been keeping track. It's been working."

Julie crossed her boot casts over each other and thought for a moment. We were back at her terminal again, and I saw airport security recognize our car from the last loop around.

"You think you're so smart, don't you? Well, for the record, I believe you. I can always tell when you lie to me. So you have your ways of knowing me, huh?" she asked, poking me in the ribs. "Well, lucky for me that I have my ways as well. Kiss me."

I was in disbelief for a moment. "Yeah of course," I said, and began to lean forward, but something in her look made me stop. "I feel like I'm insane to stop and ask you, but why?"

She smiled mischievously and rubbed her hands together in that way that never failed to make me smile. "One kiss and I'll know everything. Everything about you, sure. That's easy. But everything about how I feel too. It's been a while, and it's possible that this is your last chance ever, so make it count."

I closed my eyes as I leaned forward to kiss her, but in my nervousness, I peeked at the last second. Julie was leaning too, eyes wide open. *Man, I wish I chewed some gum or something.* It didn't matter. Our lips touched, and everything fell away. Six weeks of pent-up-something washed over both of us all at once. I tasted like engagement burgers, and she tasted like that phlegmatic throat coating one gets from crying, but I wouldn't have had it any other way. I touched her hair and she touched mine and our hands wandered until we were on each other. We chafed at our buckled seat belts, and if the security guard didn't tap on our window right then, we might have gone right on like we were in our bed at home. We snapped out of it, and I helped her unload her wheelchair and luggage.

"Damn you, Carlos Vasquez, I think I love you too." We checked her bag at the gate.

"So can we make it official?"

"Maybe ask me when I get back?"

"Oh come on, you even said you love me! That's what girlfriends say to boyfriends."

"Alright, let's call ourselves... more than friends."

"Julie."

"Okay, more than friends and I'll call you when I'm home safe! Final offer! I'm gonna miss my flight."

"Alright, get going. Love you."

"Ugh, you just want me to say it again. Alright love you too, there. See you soon!" she said as she rolled away. *Sooner than you think*.

I drove around to the cell phone lot and parked so I could finalize my plans. I couldn't pull the trigger unless things went well with Julie, so I was happy that they went better than I could have imagined. I found the flight I had bookmarked, Julie's return flight in January, and bought the seat next to hers so I could surprise her at the Tallahassee airport. Carolyn had helped me with the details, but the idea was mine. I drove back home, looking forward to a restful winter break.

ABOUT THE AUTHOR

Chris Elisondo is the author of Higher Education. He loves classic literature, the LA Dodgers, and traveling to national parks in his van. Chris lives in the Bay Area, California, with his partner, Joyce. This is his first novel.